PRIME IMPACT

BOOK 2 IN THE TYLER BANNISTER FBI SERIES

C.W. SAARI

BQB

Virginia

Prime Impact: Book Two in the Tyler Bannister FBI Series
© 2020 C.W. Saari. All rights reserved.

No part of this book may be reproduced in any form or by any means, electronic, mechanical, digital, photocopying, or recording, except for the inclusion in a review, without permission in writing from the publisher.

This is a work of fiction. All of the characters, names, incidents, organizations, and dialogue in this novel are either the products of the author's imagination or are used fictitiously.

Published in the United States by BQB Publishing
(an imprint of Boutique of Quality Books Publishing, Inc.)
www.bqbpublishing.com

Printed in the United States of America

978-1-945448-63-8 (p)
978-1-945448-65-2 (e)

Library of Congress Control Number: 2020932093

Book design by Robin Krauss, www.bookformatters.com
Cover design by Rebecca Lown, www.rebeccalowndesign.com

First editor: Caleb Guard
Second editor: Olivia Swenson

"Be true to yourself, help others, make each day your masterpiece, make friendships a fine art, drink deeply from good books—especially the Bible, build a shelter against a rainy day, give thanks for your blessings and pray for guidance every day."

— Coach John Wooden

OTHER BOOKS BY C.W. SAARI

The Mile Marker Murders, Book 1 in the Tyler Bannister FBI series

CHAPTER 1

ATLANTA - 2004

"Paper targets don't shoot back," Special Agent Tyler Bannister muttered to no one in particular as he reloaded his remaining rounds. This was his first visit to the FBI range since being wounded and killing a man earlier this year. Bannister's mind flashed back to a face-to-face standoff with the serial killer who had murdered his best friend. The killer had fired once as Bannister's two return rounds proved fatal.

The firearms instructor's voice crackled through the loudspeaker from the range's tower. "Ready on the left? Ready on the right? All ready on the firing line? Shooters, watch your targets."

At the first sound of the horn, Bannister and fourteen other FBI agents took two steps forward to the five-yard line, drew their automatics, and fired twelve rounds, including one magazine change, in ten seconds.

When the horn sounded a second time, firing stopped and the instructor bellowed, "Any alibis?" No hands went up for a jammed bullet or other malfunction. "Holster a safe and empty weapon. Pick up your empty magazines and go forward to score your targets. Agent Bannister, you've got a call up here."

Bannister secured his Sig Sauer nine-millimeter before turning around and giving a thumbs-up signal. He went forward and pulled his target from its stand before walking sixty yards down a concrete path back to the firing range's tower at Sweetwater State Park outside Atlanta. After climbing ten steel stairs, he pushed open the door and was welcomed by a blast of cold air. The instructor swiveled his chair around and handed him the phone.

"Bannister here," he said.

He was answered by the monotone voice of the Assistant Special Agent in Charge (ASAC) of the Atlanta field office. "This is Gary Witt. Assistant US Attorney Kendall Briggs has been murdered. His body was found early this morning by a foreman for a marble company in Dahlonega."

Bannister became rigid. This was the second time in a year when one of his friends was murdered. Briggs was one of the few public officials Bannister respected. He was thorough in his case preparation and tough in court. He was just as sharp a competitor on the racquetball court where the two faced off regularly.

"How'd it happen?"

Witt did not answer Bannister's question.

"I'm assigning the case to you. Derek Barnes will assist." Bannister was next in rotation for major case assignment. He groaned, not because of the assignment, but because Witt knew Barnes was scheduled to leave for Lima, Peru, next month to help the Peruvians with their counterterrorism program. If the decision had been up to Bannister, he would have tasked someone else to assist with the case, but the Atlanta agents had all grown accustomed to Witt, who frequently used the "Ready, Fire, Aim" approach to problems.

"Who's handling the crime scene and where's the body now?" Bannister asked.

"The medical examiner transported the body from the quarry to the Lumpkin County morgue where he's going to perform the autopsy. The GBI was first on the scene and they have an inspector there now. I don't have to tell you this is our jurisdiction. Coordinate with them but don't leave any doubt we're the lead dog." By GBI, Witt referred to the Georgia Bureau of Investigation.

"Sure. Do you have any other details?"

"Only that the murder scene is isolated," Witt said.

"Do we know how Briggs was killed?"

"It looks like someone cut his throat."

"Well, that someone must have incapacitated him. Briggs was big, strong, and extremely quick. What do you want me to do first?"

"Grab Barnes and head out to Dahlonega. I want one of you to witness the autopsy and both of you to report downtown and search Briggs's office. Mercedes Ramirez is on standby. She'll meet you with an evidence kit at the federal building. How long before you and Barnes can get to the crime scene?"

"Barnes is here at the range with me. We just finished shooting. We'll clean up and get there as fast as we can."

"Good. I dispatched the ERT to search his condo. The GBI has agents there now. They got the condo management to open the locked door. They did a quick check to ensure no one else was in the unit before sealing it. Any questions?" Witt asked. ERT meant the Evidence Recovery Team.

"Yes. Where is Briggs's condo?"

"It's one of those fancy lofts." Witt gave Bannister an address on Marietta Street.

"One request, Gary. I'd like the Rapid Start Team to be activated. Ask them to begin loading data on everything we know about Briggs."

"I'll do that. I plan on being with US Attorney Winston Prescott, who's scheduled a press conference for five o'clock."

Neither Bannister nor Barnes had their coats and ties today, but at least they were wearing FBI polo shirts with collars. Bannister appreciated that Barnes was a no-nonsense agent. He worked as hard as anyone on the task force and rarely smiled. His piercing gray eyes along with his deep gravelly voice usually let anyone he was interviewing know right away he wasn't a person to mess with.

Bannister briefed Barnes after they turned in their scores.

"Witt named me as case agent," Bannister said as the two agents walked to their cars.

"I want you to go to the ME's office to witness Briggs's autopsy.

He was my friend. I just don't want to have to deal with that." ME was short for medical examiner.

"I understand." Barnes's response was automatic. As a former police officer in Phoenix, he'd dealt with death many times and knew enough to leave Bannister alone with his thoughts for now.

"Thanks. While you're at the examiner's, I'll meet with the GBI Inspector at the crime scene. When we're both finished in Dahlonega, we'll head to the Federal Building and search Briggs's office. The last thing Witt ordered us to do was meet our crime scene techs at Briggs's downtown condo."

"This is going to be a helluva long day," Barnes said. "You don't suppose we could swing by a drive thru on the way there do you?"

Bannister shook his head. He knew his partner had already fast-forwarded through their investigative priorities of the day and those priorities did not include meal breaks.

"Yeah, I figured as much. I'll have a couple of breath mints for lunch."

The two agents stopped as they arrived at their cars. "How far back do you and Briggs go?" Barnes asked.

"I've known him three years." Bannister lifted up his left pant leg and pointed out an ugly round bruise in the middle of his calf. "That's from one of Briggs's attempted kill shots when we played racquetball last week."

"How well did you know him outside of the courthouse?"

"Just as a racquetball partner. We played hard and really enjoyed the competition. He usually took three out of five games. Good player." Bannister paused for a few seconds. "I can't believe he's dead." The two were silent for a minute.

"Two years ago, he prosecuted a racketeering case of mine and convicted the ringleaders of an alien smuggling operation. The government took possession of four Atlanta restaurants they owned," Bannister remarked.

"Yeah, I remember that," Barnes said.

"Last year he was the lead prosecutor on the Global Waters extortion case," Bannister said.

"Do you think there's a connection?" Barnes replied.

"That's something we'll have to figure out."

Before they left the range, Bannister called Inspector Glenn Yates of the GBI to let him know he was coming to the murder scene.

Fifty minutes later, after driving north on the 400 Parkway with blue lights for seventy miles, Bannister and Barnes pulled their government cars onto an exit which led to the Memorial Marble Company quarry where Briggs's body had been found. Bannister drove down a gravel road marked with "Private Property, No Trespassing" signs. They stopped their vehicles once they reached the yellow crime scene tape. Barnes stayed in his car as Bannister got out.

Bannister motioned for Barnes to roll down his window. "I'm assuming the autopsy will be completed before we're finished at the quarry. Meet me back here when you're done."

Barnes nodded. "I'll call you with the preliminaries and let you know if the ME finds anything unusual. You can phone the results to Witt."

Yates had walked up to their cars and now shook Bannister's hand. Yates had been with the GBI for twenty-five years and worked his way up to his current position. Although Bannister was eight inches taller, each man weighed two hundred pounds. Yates was built like a bouncer and had an iron grip. He spoke in a syrupy drawl, had a reputation for working long hours without complaining, and drove like a NASCAR racer.

"What can you tell me, Glenn?" Bannister asked.

"As you probably know, the victim's body is now with the Lumpkin County Coroner."

"Right. Agent Derek Barnes is leaving now to witness the autopsy."

"Well, we haven't got much. No suspects. No witnesses. Just a dead government attorney and the burned carcass of his new Jaguar. That's it sitting on the flatbed." Yates pointed toward two GBI technicians who were strapping down the charred remains of the victim's car.

"What was he doing in Dahlonega? In the middle of nowhere?" Bannister asked.

"That's what we'll need to find out. His office said he was the guest speaker at a dinner last night in Atlanta for a conference of insurance fraud investigators. One of the lawyers from Briggs's office was also there and saw him drive away from the hotel's parking lot shortly before ten p.m. It's twelve miles from the conference location to the downtown exit for Marietta Street, all interstate."

"You have a team at his condo now?" Bannister asked.

"Yes, and after my boss talked with your Special Agent in Charge, their orders were to babysit the unit until the feds arrived. My men reported no one was inside the condo and that there were no obvious signs of a struggle. There were no signs of forcible entry, and they observed what appeared to be Briggs's briefcase on an entryway chair."

"If his briefcase was inside his condo, we can assume he made it home before the fateful trip to the quarry," Bannister said.

"Looks that way," Yates said as he typed something into his iPhone. "One way or another, he and his car traveled up the one road leading into this quarry. The road isn't fenced. At the rear of the quarry are two dirt roads leading out. One goes to a hunting lodge and the other ends up near a back entrance to the Amicalola Falls State Park, exactly seven miles from the start of the Appalachian Trail. Here, look at this Google map showing the gravel road and hiking trails." Yates showed Bannister a map on his phone's screen.

"What's your opinion?" Bannister asked.

"I'm just guessing, but someone had a real ax to grind. Whoever it was, and I'm assuming there were at least two people, wanted to destroy the man."

"How so?"

"His car wasn't stripped, but was burned to a crisp. I think whoever killed Briggs also intended for him to be consumed by the fire. His body was discovered fifty yards from the car, face down, hands tied behind his back with flex cuffs, and throat slashed. He had on the same business clothes he wore to the speaking engagement. He reeked of gasoline, but for some reason they didn't torch him."

"Can you show me where you found his body?" Bannister asked.

"Sure. Follow me." The two investigators walked a distance half the length of a football field to a section of the gravel path stained a deep garnet.

For a minute they both stared at the three-foot section where Briggs bled out.

"I wonder why they didn't light him up," Yates said.

"That's something we'll have to ask the killer," Bannister replied. He was glad his friend had not been burned. "Who found him?"

"The foreman of the marble company spotted the body and didn't touch a thing. Just walked up to where Briggs was lying on the path and after seeing all the blood, figured he was dead. He was the one who called Lumpkin County 9-1-1."

"What about possible witnesses in the area?"

"No luck. The quarry's manager made all eight of their employees available. We questioned them but no one saw anything unusual yesterday or earlier this morning. An hour ago he cut them all loose for the day." Yates continued, "I had a couple agents canvass the neighborhood. As you could tell driving up here, it's pretty damn rural. The nearest home is one mile from the quarry road."

Just as the GBI finished searching and processing the crime scene, the crunch of gravel announced the arrival of a vehicle. Bannister turned to see Barnes pull up and get out. The two FBI agents and Yates watched the flatbed pull out of the quarry with the hulk of Briggs's car.

"What'd you find out at the ME's office?" Bannister asked.

"Briggs's autopsy results confirmed, from stomach contents, that he'd eaten the banquet food from the hotel where he gave his speech. He had a fracture to the back of his skull, apparently from being struck with a blunt object. He died as a result of having his throat cut. The examiner's opinion, from the direction and depth of the knife slash, is the killer is left-handed."

"At least that gives us something to work with. I'll meet you guys at the US Attorney's Office," Yates said before he turned and left.

Barnes looked at Bannister. "Ty, do you remember the coffee cup you got from that CSI tech with the LA County Coroner's Office? It had a chalked outline of a body on it, but I forgot what it said."

"It said, 'Our day begins when yours ends.'"

"Right. Well, our day's still going so let's head downtown and see if we can find some leads to the coward who killed your friend," Barnes said.

CHAPTER 2

At 4:00 p.m., Bannister and Barnes arrived at the Russell Federal Building, a twenty-six-story monolith on the edge of downtown Atlanta. As they rode the elevator to the fourth floor, Barnes asked, "How come you smell so good and I still smell like gunpowder?"

"'Cause I took a Harlem shower before getting in the car."

"What's that?"

"Washed my face at the range and threw on a heavy splash of aftershave." Bannister grinned.

Inspector Glenn Yates had beat them there and was talking with Sherrill Newsome, the US Attorney's secretary. As Bannister approached, he overheard Newsome say "—just shocking; we're all stunned." Newsome was an attractive, thin brunette. With the sling back heels she was wearing, she was the same height as Yates. Her eyes were puffy, and it was obvious she'd been crying. Newsome glanced at the two agents and said, "I have to get back to the reception desk."

As soon as she was out of earshot, Bannister asked Yates, "Do you think someone followed him from the dinner or had staked out his condo?"

"Don't know. My guess is he drove directly home and something happened soon after he arrived back at Marietta Street," Yates said.

"And because his briefcase was inside his condo, we're assuming he made it through the door before the trip to the quarry," Bannister said.

"Right."

Just then, Mercedes Ramirez, escorted by Newsome, came down the hallway to the outside of Briggs's office where Yates, Barnes, and Bannister were talking. Ramirez had been a Special Agent for three years. She and Bannister's girlfriend Robin were both thirty-three. Physically, although Ramirez was only five foot three and 115 pounds, she was exceptionally strong. The guys in the weight room joked that pound for pound she was probably the strongest agent in the office.

Ramirez set her evidence kit on the floor. "I was helping on another case but got here as fast as I could."

Newsome said, "I pulled Mr. Briggs's schedule of appointments for the past thirty days. Mr. Prescott instructed me to give that to you as well as access to Mr. Briggs's office and computer. If you're here after the press conference, Mr. Prescott would like to meet with all of you."

"Thanks, Sherrill," Yates said.

"Mr. Prescott also asked me to print out summaries of Mr. Briggs's pending cases and all the people he prosecuted over the last two years. You'll have to talk with the US Attorney himself for access to the actual files." Newsome admitted the four investigators to Briggs's office.

As soon as they stepped inside, Yates asked, "Do you want to call the shots here?"

Bannister replied, "I'm sure you know Washington will instruct us to take over the investigation, and Prescott might want to cut the GBI out of looking at pending cases. Why don't you start reviewing all the printouts while you have the chance? Mercedes will keep the evidence log and process the computer. Derek, how about checking out the bookcase and its contents? I'll examine Briggs's desk."

Inspector Yates had asked Newsome to make an extra copy of the memoranda. It listed a dozen men, all of whom, through the prosecutorial efforts of Kendall Briggs, now received their mail at the same post office box—the Atlanta Penitentiary.

"We'll have to check out everybody. In eighty percent of the cases, the killer is either a family member or someone with whom the victim had a personal relationship," Yates said.

Barnes nodded. "We also need to keep our eyes open for any dirty laundry."

Yates added, "By the way, Briggs had his wallet with $350 in cash and cell phone on him. We'll get you an inventory of his credit cards and wallet stuffers. One of our techs is doing a printout of his phone numbers, contacts, and recent activity. He was also wearing a nice Omega watch. You wonder why they didn't take the stuff of value. If they had, we would have considered robbery a motive."

"That's something else we'll have to figure out," Bannister said, picking up a small gold-framed photograph from the right side of Briggs's desk. "What do you make of this?" he asked, turning to show the team a picture of a smiling, scantily clad female.

"Looks like one of those glamour shot photos women give to their boyfriends or lovers," Barnes said. He paused before leaning in for a closer look. "She looks hot."

Bannister handed the photo to Mercedes to tag.

"This office is unusually neat. There's no dust anywhere and everything seems to have been put away. Do you know anything about Briggs's personal life?" Bannister asked Yates who had sat down in Briggs's office chair to read the file summaries.

Yates shrugged. "Only the basics. Win Prescott gave me the official bio when I got here. Newsome filled in some blanks. He was thirty-eight. Got his law degree from Stanford where he was on law review. Been a prosecutor in Atlanta for seven years. Three years ago, he divorced his wife. No kids. The ex still lives here in Atlanta, and his mother lives somewhere in Maine. Scuttlebutt is he hasn't spoken with his wife or relatives since the divorce. Don't know why. He lives, correction, lived alone in a swank loft condominium on Marietta Street. We need to get over there, by the way. No significant other according to Newsome but we'll have to check that out."

"Any chance Newsome had something going on with Briggs?" Bannister asked.

"Possibly. She mentioned Briggs was the only man in the office who was sensitive and understanding when she went through her own divorce last year," Yates said.

"We'll have to ask her if she knows who the bimbette in the picture is and see if she can tell us anything about Briggs's former wife. We'll definitely have to interview the ex," Bannister said.

"I'll volunteer to interview the blonde in the photo," Barnes said, smiling, catching a finger waggle from Mercedes.

Yates said, "You guys should have a complete file on Briggs since the FBI did his background investigation. That'd be a good starter."

"We'll check it out when we get back to our office."

They finished their search and decided not to stick around to hear Winston Prescott express outrage at the death of one of the finest of his seventy-five lawyers, or how every effort would be made to bring his killer or killers to justice as soon as possible. As the group left to go search Briggs's apartment, they were all hoping they didn't run into Gary Witt.

CHAPTER 3

Artists Square Apartments was one of those new "green" buildings that use recycled products for everything. Carpeting, furniture, and even paint were made from reusable plastics, wood, and trash. Kendall Briggs supported the Sierra Club. His living in an environmentally friendly habitat made sense. His condo was one of six lofts located on the second floor. The lower level was occupied by five art and design studios, anchored on the corner by a wine bar restaurant. A large blue awning marked the front entrance to a small lobby for use by tenants and guests.

Two GBI agents were standing outside Briggs's unit. Yates relieved them from guard duty and had them join the FBI agents outside checking the neighborhood for leads. The FBI's evidence recovery team was inside the living space taking photographs and processing for latent prints and trace evidence.

The ERT supervisor, Carrie Howell, met the investigators at the door and had them sign in before turning the evidence log over to Mercedes.

"What'd you find so far?" Bannister asked Howell.

"Nothing. No signs that his place had been searched. No indication of a struggle or even the presence of another person. We used the ultraviolet light and blood scanner and didn't detect anything. There was nothing unusual in the drains. The trash cans were empty. We printed all logical surfaces and came up with a dozen latents we'll check from the lab."

"Any other observations?"

"Outside and inside. Inside there was an empty gun box in his closet. Outside we found a small blood smear, which appeared to be recent, near the victim's assigned parking space directly in back of these units. A few feet from the smear were some blood droplets and black scuff marks. Inspector Yates said the deceased was wearing the same clothes he wore to the office and the dinner speech, so the marks might be from the heels of Briggs's shoes if he was abducted from here. We took samples and will compare them with his shoes."

"Good work."

"Thanks. Also, inside, you'll notice he has a collection of five bronze sculptures, each on its own thick glass shelf. There's one shelf with nothing on it. Maybe a piece is missing. You know, for a guy's apartment, this place is super organized and extremely clean. His walk-in closet could be used in an advertisement."

"How so?" Bannister asked.

"Your victim folded his underwear and arranged his rolled socks and handkerchiefs by color," Howell said. "All his shirts are arranged from light colored to darks. The bathroom has all the toiletries displayed in small wooden containers. There was one bottle of lithium pills, brand name Eskalith, prescribed by Dr. Jeffrey Fisk. No other meds. By the way, we photographed and printed but didn't look into the brown leather briefcase that was on the entryway chair when we arrived. Thought we'd leave that to you."

"Thanks. We know Briggs had his briefcase when he left the US Attorney's office for his speaking engagement. Since his briefcase is here, we have to assume he came home and shortly thereafter either voluntarily left his condo or was abducted from it."

"You're the investigators," Howell said. She handed Bannister the key to the condo and requested he lock up and have Mercedes bring the evidence log back to the office.

As Howell and her team left, Bannister walked into the center of the living room and stopped. An old Cleveland homicide detective once told him, "Don't be in a rush. Let the crime scene talk to you. You'd be surprised at what you hear."

Bannister was more surprised at what he saw. He had not been in

Briggs's place before and wanted to get a better feel for how his friend lived. Howell had left all the lights on. Except for one lamp by a reading chair, every light was recessed, even in the kitchen. The place was painted in complementary earth tones. The only light-colored items were a white Flokati area rug on the living room floor and two large paintings identified with brass plaques as being by Itzchak Tarkay. One was of a reclining nude female; the other was of a seated woman in brightly colored clothes and hat. Briggs probably enjoyed looking at women. Both paintings were illuminated by small spotlights. The atmosphere was relaxing and in stark contrast to the violence that shattered Briggs's calm world.

Yates took a phone call and relayed information. "That was my guy in charge of the crime scene at Dahlonega. Not much to report. Plaster casts and photos were taken of some boot prints near a trailhead. The only tire tracks were from Briggs's Jaguar. Signage at the quarry indicates a North Carolina stone company owns the land where his body was found. The adjacent land is leased to a hunting club in Atlanta. We'll do follow-up tomorrow. His wallet had a concealed weapon permit as well as membership cards for the Ravinia Health Club and the High Museum of Art."

"Did you find a gun in the car?" Bannister asked.

"No, and Briggs didn't have a gun on his body. We didn't find one at his office and it isn't here."

Bannister's phone buzzed and he took the call from Sherrill Newsome, who told him the beneficiary on Briggs's two insurance policies was Theresa Andrews. Bannister reported this to Yates and Barnes.

"Who's Andrews?" Yates asked.

"Don't know. Maybe she's the blonde in the glamour shot from his office."

An hour later, the search was finished. Bannister and Barnes had gone through Briggs's unlocked briefcase: three index cards with talking points for his speech, two newspapers, one file folder, a compact umbrella, and some miscellaneous stuff. No gun. They would inventory the contents back at the office.

Mercedes came out of the den with Briggs's laptop computer and a plastic envelope. The Bureau's computer team would examine the laptop in the morning. As Mercedes walked toward them, she held up a clear envelope containing a four by six photograph.

"Found this in a book on his shelf. Thought you'd be interested in it."

They all stared at the photo. Five people stood near some trees on a bluff with a river in the background. Briggs was in the center flanked by two women and two men. All were smiling at the camera. One man on the end was wearing an oversized pair of sunglasses. The five people had their arms around each other. They were all completely nude.

CHAPTER 4

On Bannister's desk were three folders. The first contained a copy of the FBI's background investigation of Briggs prior to his being sworn in as an Assistant United States Attorney. The second had current information on Briggs—everything he owned, motor vehicle information, credit reports, recent charge card purchases, and travel itineraries. The last file covered personnel. It listed his relatives and associates and had results of a records check on Briggs's ex-wife, Amber Gallagher. A copy of her driver's license photo was clipped to the front. The license indicated she was thirty-five, five foot nine and 125 pounds, with red hair. She wasn't one of the women in the pictures Briggs kept.

Bannister called Gallagher's home number. When he explained the FBI needed to talk to her about Briggs, she said she heard about the murder on the evening news and was expecting to be called. She agreed to see Bannister and Ramirez even though the hour was late.

While Barnes stayed at the office to do paperwork, Mercedes and Bannister drove five miles to Gallagher's Morningside area bungalow. The front porch light was on.

"We're sorry about Kendall's death," Bannister said, extending his hand to the woman who answered the door.

"So am I," she said, introducing herself as Amber Gallagher. She wore white slacks, a mint green sweater, and black flats. She had on makeup and her auburn hair was in a ponytail with a tortoise shell clip. "It's shocking. Please come in." Her voice had a slight quiver. She directed the agents to a small den to the right of the foyer. Mercedes and Bannister sat on a love seat opposite a winged back chair.

"I know it's late so I put on a pot of decaf coffee. I also have hot tea if you want."

Bannister went for the coffee. Mercedes and Gallagher each had a cup of some orange-scented tea. Gallagher crossed her legs and folded her hands in her lap. She certainly appeared relaxed for someone being questioned about her ex-husband's murder.

"Interviewing anyone under these circumstances is difficult. I hope you understand," Bannister said.

"I know you have a job to do and I'll help any way I can."

"When was the last time you saw Kendall?"

She put her finger alongside her left cheek and looked toward the ceiling. "Let's see. Earlier this year at a charity fundraiser for the High Museum of Art. I was with a date. Neither Kendall nor I knew the other would be there."

"And?" Bannister said, nodding for Gallagher to continue.

"He walked up to us. To my date and me. And introduced himself. The three of us chatted for a minute or two and then went our own way. I told my date Kendall and I used to be married."

"That must have been awkward."

"It was." Gallagher scrunched her nose as if reliving the incident.

"Why did the two of you get divorced?"

"Logical question." Gallagher paused. "I'll give you the simple answer. I wanted children right away. Kendall wanted to wait a few years. He said we ought to travel and do some of the different things couples enjoy doing before they get tied down with kids."

"What changed?" Bannister asked.

"He did. After three years he said he didn't want children at all. He wouldn't talk about it and was totally inflexible. We got divorced. Funny thing is we never did travel even though we saved up for it."

"You got married again, right?" Mercedes asked.

Gallagher sighed and leaned back in her chair. "Yes, six months after Kendall and I divorced I married Roger Gallagher."

"Are you still married?" Mercedes asked. The agents had already noticed she wasn't wearing a wedding ring.

"No. Let's just say things didn't work out. We were only married five months."

"How long were you and Kendall married?"

"Four years."

"Was there anyone else in his life?"

For a second, Gallagher stared at Bannister. "What are you getting at?" she said calmly.

Bannister just opened his hands outwardly.

"You mean, like was he having an affair or something like that?" Her voice this time was firm and she spoke in a louder tone. Mercedes and Bannister continued to look at her.

"I believe he was faithful to me. We loved each other, at least the first three years. The last year we grew estranged but neither of us looked to others for emotional support. Let me save you some time. The Kendall Briggs I knew didn't cheat, use drugs, or have a drinking problem. There weren't any health issues. And he wasn't into any crazy activities like he was last year."

"What do you mean?" Bannister asked.

"When we chatted at the art museum he mentioned he'd been skydiving and found it, in his words, 'a life-altering experience.'" She paused. Bannister jotted down a few notes. "Just seemed out of character for him. Before we parted I remember him saying, 'You need to step out of the box, Amber. Try some new things this year. You might discover a new you.' I don't even know why he'd say something like that." Gallagher shook her head side to side and her mouth turned up as if in disgust.

Bannister switched topics. "Did he ever mention being threatened?"

"No."

"What about finances? Any problems with investments or outside ventures?"

"Not that I knew about. You agents must know what his job pays. I've worked for five years as a marketing rep for a company that refurbishes hotels. We weren't rolling in dough but we were comfortable."

"Was he under any stress or pressure?"

Gallagher was quiet for a few seconds and took a sip of her tea. "He started seeing a therapist about six months before our divorce was final." She said it softly with her lips drawn tight. She started massaging her hands.

"For what reason?"

"I don't know. At first, I thought it was about having kids. I asked him if he thought it would help if we saw the therapist together. He said no, that it was something else. I thought it might be about his relationship with his parents."

"Why?"

"Almost as soon as he started seeing the therapist he just up and announced, 'I know Christmas is around the corner and that's a time to think about being with family. For a while I'm going to limit my contact with my parents and sister to cards, and I'm not going to invite them to Georgia. I've got my reasons and when the time is right I'll try and explain.'"

"And?"

"He never did explain. You know, the first three years we were married we were happy. We were in love and building our future together. But then—I guess it was the decision about children—we drifted apart. Two months after he started seeing his therapist, I got a phone call from his mother. His parents live in Maine. She thought I had something to do with his ignoring her calls or cutting them short. I asked her if she knew her son and I were getting divorced and she was surprised about that. She hadn't known. I tried to explain that I never said or did anything to drive a wedge between them. She seemed to think Kendall wasn't acting rationally and maybe some kind of stress was getting to him."

"When was the last time he saw his parents?"

"Three years ago when he went home to see his stepfather, who was dying."

"But the family stayed in touch?"

"Yes, until the last couple of months we were married. There were occasional phone calls and birthday cards back and forth. But that was about it. They didn't talk on the phone very long and Kendall never told me what they talked about. I know they never asked about me. I'm positive his mother didn't know he was seeing a therapist. Do you want more coffee?"

"No thanks. Do you know the name of his therapist?"

"Andrews. Dr. David Andrews. His wife's a therapist also. I think they work together. I have his card. I'll get it for you." Gallagher got up and stepped over to a desk at the side of the room.

"Could the wife's name be Theresa Andrews?" Mercedes whispered.

"Possibly. We'll check that later," Bannister said.

He turned back to Gallagher. "Is there a chance Kendall was a patient of Andrews's wife?"

"Maybe. That's something you'll have to ask Dr. David Andrews."

"Did Kendall have any close friends?"

"None in Atlanta. He did things with people at the office and worked out regularly with some guys at the athletic club. But, no, I don't think he was close to anyone."

"While you're looking for that card, would you write down contact information for his mother and any siblings?"

"Sure. He only has the one sister who also lives in Maine. Has his family been notified?"

"Authorities were supposed to contact them earlier today since they're next of kin. They'll be interviewed."

"I still can't believe Kendall was murdered," she said. "I did love him at one time. I wanted him to be the father of my children. I guess when I pulled the plug on our marriage I pulled the plug on my emotions. I hope you don't think I'm insensitive."

Bannister did, but kept a straight face. "We'll probably need to talk to you again. We may need your help in identifying people in some photographs Kendall had." Bannister stood up. "We appreciate your cooperation."

Gallagher gave them Dr. Andrews's address and phone number along with a list of names and numbers for Kendall's family members. Mercedes and Bannister left their cards with her.

As they walked down the brick sidewalk to the car, Mercedes said, "Seeing a shrink puts a whole new light on things, doesn't it?"

"It can complicate things for public figures, particularly if they might be interested in running for public office someday. I think Dr. Andrews and Dr. Mrs. Andrews just went to the top of our list of interviews for tomorrow."

CHAPTER 5

S pecial Agent in Charge Leon Brennan stood to address the investigators assembled in the conference room. "As you're probably aware, United States Attorney Winston Prescott has pledged the complete cooperation of his office. He promised not to interfere with or steer our investigation in any direction." Bannister glanced at Mercedes whose face had that "yeah, right" look. "FBI Headquarters has made this a priority matter and assigned the name KABMUR to the investigation."

Taking off his gold wire-rimmed glasses and using them to point toward his ASAC at the opposite end of the table, Brennan continued. "Gary will give me daily updates on your progress. Make sure any contact with the media goes through this office. Anybody have heartburn with that?" Brennan looked around at the members of the team. All heads nodded in unison.

"Good, I know you have a lot to do and I'll let you get on with it." He turned and left.

Besides Bannister, others seated around the table in the Counterterrorism Task Force's conference room were ASAC Gary Witt; Inspector Glenn Yates of the GBI; Lou Spina, the Dahlonega Chief of Police; and Special Agents Derek Barnes and Mercedes Ramirez.

"Why don't you go first, Chief," Witt said. "By the way, the name KABMUR comes from Briggs's three initials and the word murder. His middle name was Anthony."

"Thanks, but I already figured that out," the chief said.

Spina, dressed in his uniform of light gray trousers and long-sleeved shirt, had burgundy colored epaulets with gold stripes. He'd been Dahlonega's chief of police for sixteen years. The city was known for being the site of the first gold rush in the United States. Now it would draw attention because of a murder.

He placed both of his hands, palms down, on the glass-covered table. "I'm not here to flap my gums. This is only the second murder case we've had in our city of four thousand in three years. The other was a murder-suicide with a note written by a disabled farmer who shot his wife before turning the gun on himself. That case was a no-brainer.

"The GBI processed the crime scene so I'll defer to Inspector Yates on that. We worked with his agents up there who checked the neighborhood this morning. The only thing we came up with was a teenager driving home at 2:30 a.m. He called our office after hearing the news. He had to take a road that snakes behind the outlet mall. When he went around a curve, he saw a car off to the side. All the kid remembers is the car, maybe a white Taurus or Focus, was running with the light on inside. As he approached, the light went off. He saw the silhouette of one person on the driver's side, but couldn't tell if it was male or female."

Yates spoke next. "We trailered the remains of the victim's car to our lab where it's being processed. Don't hold your breath for any CSI-type revelation. It's basically a charred hulk, but the techs are sifting through the ashes. On the ground opposite the driver's door was a thin burn trail as if from some type of fuse. On the front floorboard was a metal statue mounted on a stone base. Behind the driver's seat was a glob of melted plastic, possibly what's left of a small gas container." Yates glanced over at Derek Barnes.

"Since you witnessed the autopsy, could you share any significant findings?" Yates asked.

Barnes leaned forward. "The medical examiner cut the flex cuffs on Briggs before beginning his examination. The official cause of death was exsanguination. Toxicology tests are still being completed. The ME said there was a one-inch fracture at the back of the skull and hemorrhaging in the area. Other signs of violence were scrapes on the deceased's left knee and the right side of his face, and a cut throat. There was some slight discoloration on the victim's wrists where the cuffs had tightened. Whatever the weapon, it had an extremely sharp blade. The carotid, windpipe and all soft tissue were severed. Death was rapid. Time of death was approximately 1:00 a.m."

"What have you come up with, Mercedes?" Witt asked.

Mercedes flipped open her notebook and pushed her hair back to the side as she looked at her notes. "We know five of the six mounted shelves at Briggs's condo held small bronze statues. One shelf was empty and I'm guessing it held a missing statue, which might be the one recovered from Briggs's car. Some latent prints were found in the condo, mostly on the edges of the countertop separating the living room from the kitchen. On the underside of the toilet seat in the powder room was a thumbprint from someone's left hand. We're running all prints through the system now."

"Has his gun been found?" Yates asked.

"No. A gun cleaning kit and a box for a Kahr nine-millimeter semi-automatic were found in his closet. The gun box had a serial number and address for KAI in Worcester, Massachusetts." Mercedes turned to her left and looked at Barnes.

"KAI is the manufacturer. I'm contacting them to find out where and when the gun was sold. The gun's been entered into NCIC. We also reviewed the security tapes covering the parking lot of the hotel where Briggs was last seen alive. They show another prosecutor walking to his own car as Briggs entered his Jaguar and drove away. That attorney was interviewed. He waved at Briggs, who was alone in his car when he pulled out. The time was 9:57 p.m. A bank down the street has a CCTV camera, which we've arranged to check out to see if a vehicle might have followed him.

"I sent a lead for our Charlotte division to interview the owner of the Memorial Marble Quarry property where Briggs's body was found," Barnes said. "We also dumped the calls from his cell phone, which was on his body. We're going through the numbers now. Agents interviewed Briggs's neighbors. None of them knew him by name. A young couple who live next door to Briggs arrived home at 8:30 p.m. and didn't see or hear anything. Atlanta PD says there have been no crime reports from Artists Square since it opened last year. It's your show, Ty." He waved his hand at Bannister.

Before speaking, Bannister looked down the table at Gary Witt who was rocking backward in his chair with his hands interlaced behind his head.

"We're trying to focus on a motive. Once that's identified it might point us in the direction of his killer. There's a ton of stuff on Briggs's office computer, which will take time to analyze. Twelve people he prosecuted are currently serving sentences in the Atlanta Penitentiary. Two are incarcerated at Allentown, Pennsylvania, which many of us refer to as Club Fed. One inmate in Atlanta who directly threatened Briggs is doing a mandatory twenty-five years on a habitual criminal rap. That doesn't mean he didn't hire someone on the outside. Although this doesn't have the appearance of a contract hit, we're checking all of them out. Another person of interest is a federal fugitive—Terry Hines."

As he said the name, Bannister's mind flashed back to the threatening letter Hines had sent and his words in the courtroom that he'd get even with Bannister. He looked at Chief Spina, whose frown and narrowed eyes showed confusion.

"Chief, nine months ago Hines was being prosecuted for the extortion of five million dollars from Global Waters here in Atlanta. We recovered all of the money except for $50,000. Hines's mother and father fronted his million-dollar bail, which was forfeited when he fled. They lost their home and his father died of a stroke a few weeks later. Hines blamed everyone except himself and threatened to get even with all those responsible for his arrest, including me. His case was being prosecuted by Briggs, who argued against bail since Hines had sent a biological poison to Global Waters."

"Any indication Hines is in Atlanta?" the chief asked.

"No," Witt answered. "The investigation went cold in London three months ago."

"Briggs's ex-wife was interviewed last night and was cooperative," Bannister added. "No animosity toward him or apparent reason for her to be involved. She gave us some background on his family and put us on to a therapist Briggs was seeing."

"Why was he seeing a therapist?" Yates asked.

"We don't know," Bannister said. "We've set up an interview with the doctor after this meeting. His name is Dr. David Andrews. Supposedly he has a practice with his wife who's also a therapist. Her name just happens to be Theresa Andrews."

"Could she be the Theresa Andrews listed as the beneficiary on Briggs's insurance policies?" Yates asked.

"Yes," Mercedes said, "but our analyst, Germaine White, said there are six Theresa Andrews just in Atlanta."

Bannister added, "We don't know if the doctor is the beneficiary. Assuming she is, we have to figure out the connection. The change in beneficiary was made two months ago. Before that it was Briggs's sister and mother. Why did Briggs name Theresa Andrews as beneficiary? Was she having an affair with Briggs? By naming her as beneficiary, and if he confided that fact to her, did he hope that would convince her how serious his feelings were? Did David Andrews know about it? Could either of them be involved in Briggs's death? These are questions we need to answer."

"Can the US Attorney hold off notifying the insurance company until we rule out Andrews?" Mercedes asked.

"His office is under no obligation to make any notifications other than next of kin, which it did. I relayed our request to his office and they agreed they wouldn't contact Metropolitan Life until they heard from us," Bannister said.

"Could Theresa Andrews be the mystery blonde in the photo on Briggs's desk?" Barnes asked.

"Possibly. Right now, there's a lot of smoke," Bannister said.

During the next hour, the team mapped out its strategy and made assignments to try and clear the air.

CHAPTER 6

A t the same time the meeting was being held at the FBI, another one was taking place a few miles away. Kevin Middleton arrived at Caribou Coffee on Ponce de Leon Avenue fifteen minutes early. He looked forward to his first cup of coffee. The stress and extra hours he'd been working at the Centers for Disease Control had changed his appearance.

Two months ago, a couple of the CDC's female microbiologists told him they considered him dark and mysterious. The compliment caused him to smile, showing off a perfect set of straight white teeth. Lately however, he had a haggard appearance, not swarthy but sinister. Although he had just turned thirty-seven, he looked sixty. The bags under his eyes coordinated with his black mustache and perpetual five o'clock shadow.

Middleton was a regular at this coffee shop near the heart of Emory University. The coffee was good and the place was located a mile from his job. While sitting outside on the patio waiting for his coffee to cool, he opened the Atlanta newspaper and stared at the lead story. Assistant United States Attorney Kendall Briggs had been murdered. Middleton had mentioned to his new partners two weeks ago he and Briggs were acquainted, but he couldn't risk telling them how they'd met.

"See you got here first," Hassan Fadi said as he walked up behind Middleton, patting him on the back as Americans often did. He pulled out one of the wrought iron chairs and sat down. Fadi, tall for a Palestinian at over six feet, held a ceramic coffee cup which seemed small in his large hands. "Espresso. I like the way it heightens my senses."

"I know what you mean." Middleton took the Metro section of the newspaper and slid it to cover up the front-page article.

"Have you completed your arrangements?" Fadi asked.

"Everything's been handled."

Fadi looked directly into Middleton's eyes as he laid a thick manila envelope on top of the newspaper. "Half of the $20,000 down payment is in that envelope. Any questions?"

"What about the other half and the balance you promised?"

"As agreed, the deposit was also made this morning. You can verify any time you want. The balance will be wired after you complete your part. We control what we can but some things depend on God. You assured us you would be able to hand over the item in a week. We must not have any delay."

"I understand," Middleton said.

Fadi leaned forward and said in a quiet voice, "I don't need to remind you to be careful. I wouldn't take that envelope into work." Fadi grinned, showing his yellow teeth. He put a small red box on the table in front of him and tapped out a Dunhill cigarette.

"I don't recognize the brand," Middleton remarked.

"It's English. Your friend in London gave me a carton. Anyway, American cigarettes are weak."

After Fadi finished his espresso and left, Middleton waited five minutes as agreed upon before getting up, carrying the newspaper and envelope in his left hand.

Neither Middleton nor Fadi had looked in the direction of the man sitting at a corner table. The man's appearance had been altered since he had last seen Fadi and Middleton. He had met with Fadi and one of his men in London and provided Middleton's name and information to them. In London, the man had been clean shaven. Now he had a beard and mustache. He wore a gray Emory University tee shirt, a blue baseball cap with Emory spelled out in yellow, and wraparound sunglasses. No one paid him any attention but as Middleton left, Terry Hines got up from his corner table, walked to the front of the patio where he could observe the side street. His eyes followed his former fraternity brother until he got into his car. Hines returned to the corner table and finished his coffee.

Middleton avoided saying anything to those in the parking lot or walking on the sidewalk. He didn't use his cell phone. He started his car and bent over to open the envelope on his lap. Inside a zip-locked plastic bag were two stacks of new hundreds along with a card. Presumably the entire $10,000 was there. He popped open the trunk of his car, walked to the rear, and placed the envelope and newspaper in a briefcase before getting back behind the wheel and pulling into traffic.

Three cars behind him was another car with two occupants. While one man drove, keeping a discreet distance behind Middleton's Toyota Camry, his partner scanned the roads in all directions. Fadi's orders were to follow Kevin Middleton and try to determine if Middleton was being surveilled by anyone else.

Middleton fought to contain his excitement and focused on acting naturally when driving up to the guards at the CDC. He didn't smile or greet them when he showed his access badge. For the past month he had worked long hours documenting his research. He had been careful not to do anything that would attract attention. All required reports were submitted ahead of schedule. Middleton knew that in two weeks all of his problems would be solved and the CDC would just be a part of his past.

CHAPTER 7

Bannister drove to The Andrews Group located in a commercial building off Peachtree Street behind the Ritz Carlton Hotel. Sitting behind the reception desk in the center of the room was a secretary who pushed a button on her console announcing their arrival to Dr. David Andrews. The walls in the reception area were hung with reproduction French landscape paintings.

"I wonder what clients would think if they had abstract paintings on the wall," Ramirez said, smiling.

"Probably that they were at the right office," Bannister replied.

The two were directed through French doors on the right to another waiting room—this one for Dr. David Andrews. They didn't even have a chance to pick up one of the magazines on the table before Dr. Andrews came out. After introductions and showing of credentials, Ramirez and Bannister were escorted to a private office which had two areas. The back wall was lined with bookcases. A computer sat on a desk situated within arm's length of the books. The larger front section had a couch and heavy chairs similar to those in an upscale hotel lobby. On one wall was a large painting of a sunrise in the desert. On the wall directly opposite was another painting. This one appeared to be a sunset in desert mountains. Ramirez and Bannister sat on the couch and turned to examine the paintings.

"I like them," Ramirez said.

"Thank you. I bought both on a trip to Santa Fe. The sunrise is a mesa in New Mexico; the sunset shows the Superstition Mountains in Arizona." With his arms outstretched pointing in each direction, Dr. Andrews said, "I occasionally use both pictures in my therapy. You know, a new day, a new beginning," as he gazed on the sunrise, "or," turning to point at the sunset, "putting a problem to rest."

"Well, we have a problem that we'd like to put to rest and that's the murder of Kendall Briggs," said Bannister. "Was he a patient of yours?"

Andrews had taken a seat in his large armchair, crossing his legs and interlacing his hands around one of his knees. He was dressed casually, light blue denim shirt, tan corduroy slacks, and brown tassel loafers. His tortoise shell glasses gave him a professorial look.

"To begin with, I'm a counseling psychologist; Theresa, my wife, is a clinical psychologist. I primarily work with patients having family or marital problems, stress management, loss or grief issues, physical or sexual abuse and eating disorders, to name a few. Issues run in cycles. Eating disorders seem to be back 'in.' Theresa's patients typically have more severe problems such as bipolar disorder, phobias, and schizophrenia. In any event, Kendall Briggs thought he needed help and came to see me. You must know the doctor-patient privilege doesn't automatically end when the patient dies."

Ramirez was busy taking notes.

"We know that," said Bannister. "But since the patient is the victim of a murder, I don't think there will be any issues with that. Do you agree?"

Dr. Andrews rested his chin in his left hand. "If the FBI says so. Anyway, a year and a half ago, Briggs came to see me. He said he'd begun feeling depressed about two years earlier but didn't know why. To cope he decided to work extra hard while on the job and, when he was off the job, try different things."

"Apparently his self-prescribed regimen didn't work," Bannister said.

"Correct. It helped manage his stress but not his inner feelings. After taking his personal history and talking with him about his family, his divorce, and general health, I came to the conclusion he had a more serious problem and might be bipolar."

"Could you explain that?" Bannister asked.

"I could, but Terri—my wife—would be in a better position. I referred Mr. Briggs to her, and he was a patient of hers since that time."

"We'll need to talk to your wife."

"I'll call her. Terri's first appointment won't be here for thirty minutes." David made the call and she agreed to see them.

As they walked past the receptionist and this time through the white French doors on the left, Ramirez asked, "Are you going to bring up the insurance beneficiary issue?"

"Why don't we see where her answers lead? It's possible she doesn't know about it."

As they entered her office, Bannister observed Dr. Theresa Andrews closing a two-drawer safe. Ramirez looked at Bannister with the recognition that the doctor was not the mystery blonde in the photo on Briggs's desk.

"I'm Terri Andrews. I was just pulling Kendall Briggs's file," she said, with a quick forced smile as she walked from behind her desk. She looked to be in her early thirties, maybe five foot five, one twenty. She had dark auburn hair, worn in a bob, and light brown eyes. She wore a white sleeveless sweater and a flowing beige pleated skirt with a large gold metal belt. Bannister was surprised by the unusual strength of her handshake. He noticed she wasn't wearing any rings. She motioned for the two agents to sit in high-backed leather office chairs surrounding a low coffee table.

The décor of Dr. Terri Andrews's office was different from that of her husband's. The ergonomic chairs had soft curves and swiveled. The office walls were painted in shades of muted green. On each wall were framed black-and-white photographs, which appeared to be taken in national parks. Bannister pointed to one on the left side.

"That looks like Cathedral Ledge in New Hampshire," Bannister said.

"It is," Andrews responded with a surprised look. "Have you been there?"

"A long time ago I tortured myself on the Thin Air Climb."

Ramirez turned to stare at Bannister with a squint.

"I took that photograph after descending the summit," Andrews said. "Photography and rock climbing are hobbies of mine."

"They sort of complement each other. I'd like to compare notes, but we're here about Kendall Briggs."

"It's hard to believe he was murdered," Andrews said with no signs of emotion.

"How long did you know Mr. Briggs?"

"Three years."

"Has he been your patient that long?" Bannister asked.

"No, he's been my patient for a year. If you'll ask me specific questions, I'll give you direct answers." Bannister liked her response; she was a person used to being in control. Her eyes were penetrating. She leaned back crossing her legs and folded her hands in her lap.

"Do you know Dr. Jeffrey Fisk?" he asked.

"Yes. Mr. Briggs saw him briefly as part of his treatment. Dr. Fisk prescribed lithium for him. I think the analogy of 'the cart before the horse' is appropriate here. Normally, a psychiatrist examines a patient and then, if the condition is one for which counseling is more suitable, will recommend an appropriate psychologist for treatment. In Briggs's case, he happened to see me first and I believed his situation could be aided with medication, if my preliminary diagnosis was accurate. Dr. Fisk has recommended patients to me in the past. So, after I initially saw Briggs, he went to Dr. Fisk for two sessions and then was referred back to me for treatment. Dr. Fisk confirmed my suspicion that Briggs was bipolar and that's why he prescribed lithium."

"How did you first meet Mr. Briggs?"

"We both worked out at the Ravinia Club and played racquetball. He also worked out on the Nautilus equipment. I tried to talk him into trying the rock climbing wall, but he took a pass on that. In any event, we occasionally had a fruit smoothie in the club restaurant before heading off to work."

"Did he know what you did for a living?"

"Not really. I usually tell people I'm an adjunct professor at Georgia Tech, which I am, by the way. When my husband sent him to my office, Kendall was surprised."

Bannister noted she switched to the familiar first name. "How so?"

"He'd never made the connection between me the club member and me the psychologist. I asked him if having a professional relationship would make him uncomfortable when we worked out."

"And?"

"He said no, that he would restrict personal topics to our regular appointments."

"How often did you see him?"

"I saw him at least once a month, sometimes twice, usually for forty-five minutes."

"When was the last time you saw him?"

"A week ago."

"Did you still concur with Dr. Fisk's earlier diagnosis?"

"Yes. There are numerous degrees of bipolar disorder. It was my opinion that Mr. Briggs had a mild mood disorder termed hypomania."

"Could you explain that for us?" Bannister asked.

"Kendall fit a clinical definition." Bannister noted she again slipped back to the familiar first name. "He felt optimistic and didn't believe he needed much sleep. While some people demonstrate poor judgment and irritability, others are full of energy and desire to channel that karma into creative tasks. That was Kendall. Some will experience hyper sexuality."

"So far, that doesn't sound too bad," Bannister said.

"If certain triggers occur, the patient's condition can deteriorate. A person can have simultaneous episodes of mania and depression or a serious episode of either state, which can jeopardize one's well-being. In any event, with the minimal medication Kendall was prescribed, he was living a perfectly normal life."

"Other than at your office or the Ravinia Club, did you see Mr. Briggs?"

"We had dinner twice this year, once at the Atlanta Seafood Company and once at Bacchanalia. They were my suggestions. I didn't bill him and he picked up the tabs. My husband knows about it." Again, she looked at Bannister and Ramirez with penetrating eyes and then turned over a couple of pages in Briggs's file. Ramirez shot a glance at Bannister, twisting her lip.

"Isn't that a little unusual? Dating a patient," Ramirez asked.

"I didn't view those as dates. I do consider myself unorthodox. Unusual? Yes. Effective? Definitely. You see, I wanted to evaluate Kendall in a social setting where he could loosen up. I could catch him off guard with some subtle questions and get a better handle on his problems," Andrews said.

"Like his family situation?" Bannister asked.

"You know about that?"

"Only that he had broken off personal contact with his mother and sister. Did he tell you why?"

"Yes. When he was a child, his stepfather molested him." Andrews's eye muscles tightened as she said that. "Apparently he confessed this sin to Kendall while he was dying in the hospital. I was trying to determine if that might have been a causative factor in Kendall's hypomania or a tripwire for some of his subsequent activities after it was revealed to him."

"Did Briggs say if anyone else in his family was abused or knew about his abuse?" Bannister asked.

"If there was someone else, Kendall didn't bring it up. I asked him if he wanted to talk about what happened and he did. He told me his stepfather, Orville, fondled him on two occasions when he was nine years old. Both incidents took place in the family's barn. The first time Orville stopped when there was a loud noise outside the barn. On the second occasion, about a week later, Kendall just firmly said to his stepdad, 'Stop it! Don't ever touch me again!' He then ran out of the barn and went to the house."

"Do you think those were the only occasions?" Bannister asked.

"I don't know. I explained to Kendall that an abuser will try and gradually manipulate his victim with attention, affection, and maybe gifts. They'll often try to maintain secrecy and may even attempt to convince the child that they encouraged the conduct and liked it. Kendall said there wasn't any mention of keeping a secret, but that he was confused by his thoughts since he didn't understand what was happening. He didn't believe he suffered any psychological harm and this conclusion was reinforced years later when he was writing a law review article at Stanford. He had to research victims' rights and potential damages from sexual abuse by members of the clergy."

Bannister made a mental note to explore this family drama and possible motives when they interviewed Briggs's sister, JoAnn Crawford, who was coming to Atlanta to make funeral arrangements for her brother. He decided to switch gears with Dr. Andrews. "Did Kendall bring up his former marriage to Amber Gallagher?"

"Yes. We talked about it during an early session."

"Did he ever mention having serious issues with anyone?" Bannister asked.

"You mean like with someone who might have a motive for killing him?"

Bannister took note of Andrews's mannerisms and tone of voice and appreciated her continued directness. "Yes."

"Well, he thought some of the men he sent to prison hated him for prosecuting them, but he didn't feel his personal safety was at risk. His ex-wife certainly didn't hate him. Part of my ongoing treatment of Kendall was to help him work through any relationships he believed contributed to his stress. I don't think any of the people he mentioned would have a reason to kill him."

"Did he discuss his sexual interests? You did mention hyper sexuality."

For a split second, Andrews's lips hinted of a smile, but then just as quickly tensed. "I think I know where you're headed. He was heterosexual with no unusual fetishes. He said he was seeing a woman.

I didn't ask for particulars. He denied ever having had any homosexual encounters. He said he never visited prostitutes and absolutely was opposed to any kind of drug experimentation. He said he'd lose his job if he ever used an illegal drug. To be frank with you, I can't think of anyone who would want to harm him. I think he must have been a victim of some kind of crime that went horribly wrong."

"That's what we're going to try and find out," Ramirez said.

"I'm sure there's more information I could furnish, but right now my light's flashing. My patient is here. If I can be of further help, please call me. You can go out this door." She threw a quick smile at Bannister and pointed to her right. "It's unmarked and opens to the corridor. Turn left and go around the corner to the elevator."

Waiting for the elevator, Ramirez said, "I often wondered about patients bumping into someone they knew coming out of the office."

Bannister nodded absently, distracted by the interview with Andrews. "What's your read on her?"

"To begin with, I was disappointed she wasn't the mystery blonde in the photograph. This doctor's tough. Her responses are like those teasers advertising soap operas. I question the whole propriety of her dining with a patient. I think she's holding back and may have been having an affair with Briggs. Did you notice she kept referring to him by his first name? *Kendall*? Also, telling her husband about dining with Briggs would protect her if someone spotted them together."

"That's good. Anything else?"

"I don't think she's been climbing any rock walls recently. The rock climbing thing might explain her not wearing any rings, but it doesn't answer why she'd waste money on a French manicure. What are your thoughts?"

"They're in sync with yours. We've just touched the surface with her. We're going to have to do some digging. By the way, you can't have dinner at the Bacchanalia restaurant without making reservations a month in advance. She definitely gave some thought to dining at one of the best restaurants in the South."

"Incidentally, were you bullshitting her about climbing that mountain in the photo?" Ramirez asked.

"No. I did a fair amount of hiking and climbing when I went to Dartmouth. I guess you could say it was a legitimate way of looking for thrills." Bannister smiled at Ramirez, who didn't smile back but stuck her nose in the air.

CHAPTER 8

Five minutes of blowing morning rain showered Clifton Road with slick, wet leaves. Kevin Middleton stopped his car at the entrance to the CDC and handed his badge to a guard, who swiped it and waved him through. He parked outside Building G-2, which housed the Biosafety Level-4 laboratory where he did vaccine research. After punching in a PIN number and inserting his right hand into a biometric hand scanner, he entered the facility.

The men's outer cabinet room was empty when he put his clothes, wallet, cell phone, and keys into one of the eight tall wooden lockers. He glanced in the mirror. The face staring back at him looked like a sad drunk. When his wife served him with divorce papers three months ago, he swore to himself he'd get back in shape. The mirror showed he'd broken another New Year's resolution. The Forum Fitness Club's membership expired last year and now his stomach reminded him of the joke about a Budweiser tumor.

Concealed in Middleton's left hand was a three-inch strip of double-sided mounting tape. In his right hand was his identification card, which he inserted into a radio frequency card reader that scanned it and would retain it until he was ready to exit the facility.

Middleton then walked nude into the decontamination shower room and was subjected to a variety of sprays designed to eliminate bacteria and any possible insect life. The fingers of his left hand remained curled. After spending a minute under a hot air dryer, he pressed a saucer-sized button for access to the interaction and changing room. This final door opened after the interlocking doors communicated electronically with each other and signaled that the outer chamber was sealed.

Middleton put on a set of disposable undergarments before pulling on a set of large green scrubs. Next, he stepped into a one-piece positive pressure suit weighing ten pounds and then sat on a white plastic bench. After putting on synthetic socks and blue pull-on shoes, Middleton placed the strip of tape concealed in his hand underneath his left shoe between the heel area and the sole. This would be removed later and attached to the bottom of his bare foot before entering the showers. He then taped his pant cuffs to the socks, folding over the last inch, a trick he'd learned that saved at least five minutes when trying to free himself from the clothes at the end of the day. The last item was a pair of plastic gloves that Middleton folded over the same way as his socks before taping them to the sleeves.

Finally, he adjusted the flexible clear plastic hood and zipped it shut. He then attached an air valve that inflated the suit so he could check for leaks. A pressure gauge mounted on the suit's sleeve indicated everything was airtight. Satisfied with the containment suit's fit, Middleton activated the auxiliary oxygen pack and walked over to the next door. He entered his PIN number into its reader, looked into an iris scanner, and pressed a six-inch flat "Enter Chamber" button. With his identity reconfirmed, he stepped into the man-trap chamber. The steel door, with its special air bladder, sealed itself shut. Middleton reached over and pressed a different "Enter Chamber" button. Once the light came on indicating this door was sealed, the final door into the BSL-4 Lab slid open. Middleton immediately connected his suit to one of numerous yellow oxygen hoses suspended from the ceiling. Unlike the air in a commercial jet, the lab's purified air was completely exchanged twenty times a day.

Each time he entered the lab, Middleton repeated this same half hour procedure. Leaving the lab took about the same amount of time but the procedures included a second separate chemical decontamination shower with twenty different sprays while wearing the CDC work suit. The last shower in his birthday suit always made Middleton feel like his problems were being washed down the drain. Lately, the only thing he knew for sure that had gone down the drain was his marriage.

Middleton wished his wife could be here to see everything in the lab and appreciate him and how important his work was. Their divorce would be final in a week, and he still smarted that she claimed he was emotionally abusive, neglectful of his family, financially irresponsible, and addicted to gambling. A divorce is tough enough on everyone involved. He just hoped his wife's accusations didn't screw up his security clearance and jeopardize his job at the CDC.

As he always did at the beginning of his shift, Middleton looked up and waved at the pan-tilt camera on the ceiling above him. This camera system was in place for after-action documentation in case of an accident. Middleton knew all the procedures and when the time came, was positive the camera wouldn't detect anything out of the ordinary.

For a second he didn't see there was another person already in the lab until she stood up. The similarly suited but shorter figure turned to him and said, "Hi, Kevin."

He knew the face. "G-L-O-R-I-A. Glow-ree-ahh! Hey, you're looking good today. I like your outfit."

Gloria Sanchez wasn't amused. "C'mon, Kevin, knock it off. That's getting old." She made a note on a clipboard then replaced it on its hook along with the magnetic pen.

"What are you doing here today? I thought you were off," Middleton said.

"I'd planned on going shopping. You know, some girl stuff, but my friend called last night with laryngitis. She was embarrassed about sounding like a frog, so I gave her a rain check and decided to come in. Why waste vacation hours?"

Sanchez, who was thirty-two, six years younger than Middleton, had been with the CDC a year longer than he. For the past four months, the two had been assigned to the same vaccine research project. Middleton, however, was listed as the primary and enjoyed pissing off

Sanchez during the staff's technical briefings by referring to her as his assistant. He looked for opportunities to flaunt his knowledge.

As if on cue, Middleton said, "You know there's no cure for laryngitis."

"Are you going to tell me you also researched that at the private lab before joining the CDC?" Sanchez asked.

"As a matter of fact, I did."

"I knew you were doing cutting edge research on Alzheimer's but you never did tell me exactly why they let you go."

If Sanchez had peered through Middleton's face shield she would have seen him glaring. "The FDA issued an adverse ruling on one of the company's drugs that caused the company's stock to fall. The bottom line was they cut back on research—my research. They're all a bunch of assholes. I'd just made some connections between Cruetzfeldt-Jakob disease and Alzheimer's. I tried to convince management they were wrong to cut back on the R&D program, but it was no use."

"Is that when you started believing some of the anomalies of Cruetzfeldt-Jakob were connected to mad cow disease?" Sanchez asked.

"Exactly. Everyone in the field assumed both diseases were caused by an unconventionally slow virus similar to those that cause several cancers. But we found that the cause of CJD and mad cow was not a virus or any known infectious agent. We couldn't destroy the CJD agent. We used every known disinfection technique against it, plus boiling, ultraviolet irradiation, and even heating it in an autoclave. Nothing worked. Its survivability was downright scary. We had samples that were buried in the earth for three years. When we took them out, they were still infectious."

"And that's when you came to the conclusion that what you were dealing with had absolutely no genetic material, right?" Sanchez moved forward toward a refrigerator while still looking at Middleton.

"Right. We discovered we were dealing with an abnormal protein

—a prion. Something that was not only infectious, but could be inherited." Middleton was smiling smugly behind his Plexiglas face plate.

Sanchez stopped what she was doing. "A prion is the culprit behind mad cow disease. So, if we can identify how an abnormal protein converts a normal protein into a diseased form, like in mad cow, then we're on track to finding a cure for Alzheimer's. Is that what you're saying?"

"Bingo! Let's just say for now you and I have a giant lead on the private labs, like the one that cut my research."

"Wow, Kevin. I just thought you were weird. But now I can see maybe I was too quick to judge you. You're actually brilliant weird."

Middleton turned toward Sanchez. She was smiling.

"Well, would you think it weird if I asked you out to dinner?"

"Yeah, you're married."

"Well, technically, only for another week."

"I don't think that's a good idea," Sanchez said as she leaned over and opened an incubator.

"Well, would you go out with me if I told you I'd won the lottery?"

"You can tell me anything you want. Talk is cheap. I like dealing with facts, remember? Check back with me when you can show me a winning ticket."

"Don't be surprised if I do that," he said.

Sanchez twisted her head toward Middleton. Staring into her mask, he saw the arching of her eyebrows and furrowing of her brow.

CHAPTER 9

I t was 6:40 a.m. when Bannister stopped by Barnes's workstation, where he sat hunched over his keyboard typing like crazy. Barnes typed with just two fingers but was as fast as many secretaries.

Bannister noticed he was dressed in a blue sweat suit with white stripes. "What's with the casual attire this morning?"

"Sorry about that," said Barnes. "I was down in the gym when I got paged I had an important call upstairs."

Members of the Terrorist Task Force dressed differently than agents assigned to work fugitives or drugs. Same mission—catching the bad guys—but different style. Commander Stu Peterson required everyone to wear suits or sport coats. Ties were optional; coats were not. Warm-ups were not on the list of approved wear. Seven agencies were represented and all their agents had to abide by Stu's dictates. He wanted the task force to look at least semi-professional. In his words, "No blue jeans, tee shirts, or shirts with cute sayings or pictures. This ain't reality TV."

To help pinpoint where the Kendall Briggs nude photo was taken, Barnes had sent a copy of the photo, minus the five people, to a certified arborist for study.

"The call I got was from the arborist," Barnes said. "He was able to identify the trees—a sycamore, a sweet bay, a couple of laurel oaks, and, get this, one of the rarest trees in the US. He said it's a Torreya conifer which only grows in central California, Japan, China, and a ten-mile area in northwest Florida. He's actually seen those rare pines at Torreya State Park, which is on the Apalachicola River. I've got another guy trying to help us identify nudist camps near that river."

"Well, keep at it. Mercedes and I are heading out. Call me if anything breaks."

"We should have more by close of business. By the way, I confirmed Briggs had a concealed weapon permit for a Klar nine-millimeter, which he'd purchased eighteen months ago. It hasn't shown up yet."

"Be sure to check out the pawn shops just in case."

"I'm on it," Barnes said.

Bannister nodded to Ramirez through the glass wall of her cubicle and the two left the office. Bannister suggested grabbing some breakfast to jump-start their day.

"You said you were taking me to an upscale place for breakfast," Ramirez commented as they walked through the back lot of the FBI building to where her government issued car was parked. "How do you define upscale?"

"The menu doesn't have pictures of the food." Bannister grinned and she laughed.

"Why don't you drive, since you know where we're going." Ramirez tossed him the keys. Bannister unlocked the car and groaned as he promptly smacked his right knee into the bottom of the dashboard.

"Did you loan this car to a midget?" he asked, rubbing his throbbing knee.

"Don't be a smart ass. You should have figured someone a foot shorter than you would have the seat moved up."

"Right. Hey! That reminds me of something. Do you know what the headlines read the morning after a midget fortune-teller escaped from custody?"

"No," she said. "Do I want to?"

"Small Medium at Large!" Bannister was still smiling as he hit the brakes for a delivery truck that pulled in front of them.

"By the way, speaking of fugitives, did you read the e-mail I sent you this morning?" Ramirez asked.

"Didn't have time."

"Last night I met with Gloria Sanchez from the CDC. She and I worked together at the CDC before I joined the FBI. She and a co-worker, Kevin Middleton, are doing bioterrorism research with anthrax, botulism, and other infectious agents. She told me Middleton's been acting really strange lately and we might want to check him out discreetly without jeopardizing his job. She also mentioned that when Terry Hines was arrested last year, Middleton told her he wouldn't be surprised if he were contacted since the two had once roomed together at a frat house at Georgia Tech. If we have enough to open a preliminary inquiry on Middleton, we can use that connection to set up an interview. What do you think?"

"We might just interview him anyway."

They reviewed their schedule for the day before Bannister found a parking spot on McLendon Avenue opposite the entrance to the Flying Biscuit Cafe.

After they each consumed a plate of oatmeal pancakes topped with warm peaches, Bannister drove the three miles from the out-of-the-way restaurant to the Russell Federal Building. He cut up Highland Avenue past rows of refurbished 1930s bungalows and steered around a curve where they both shot a glance at the Jimmy Carter Presidential Library. After exiting off Spring Street, Bannister pulled into the last Law Enforcement Only space in the basement of the federal building. They grabbed their coats and badged their way past security guards before catching an elevator to the fourth floor.

The morning would be busy. They'd arranged to meet with Glenn Yates so they could agree on what they would tell the US Attorney and what they would conveniently omit. After meeting with Yates, they would see Winston Prescott and then interview JoAnn Crawford, Briggs's sister, who had flown in from Portland, Maine, to claim her brother's effects and make arrangements for his burial. After talking with her, the two agents would drive seventy-five miles to Dahlonega, meet with Sheriff Spina, and visit the murder scene before returning to the office.

The receptionist ushered the two of them into a small conference room.

"Coffee's good. It's fresh and it's free," Yates said, greeting them. The three took seats at the conference table and opened their notebooks.

"What has your lab come up with, Glenn?" Bannister asked.

"The preliminary work is done. Nothing worthwhile from the exam of the charred vehicle. The accelerant used was gasoline."

"Has the medical examiner gotten back with you?" Bannister asked.

"I know Agent Barnes was a witness to the autopsy, but the written results and tests weren't done until after Barnes had left. The doc's completed report was waiting for me when I got in this morning.

"What about toxicology?" Bannister asked.

"Two findings. One was the presence of lithium in his blood. That's a no-brainer since he had a prescription for Eskalith. The other finding came up with traces of carbon tetrachloride."

"What's that?"

"The most common use today is in the semi-conductor industry where it's used to recover tin from tin waste products. Carbon tet is a clear liquid that was sometimes used in fire extinguishers. Its most widespread use, however, was as a dry cleaning solvent and spot remover until it was discovered to be extremely harmful to your liver and kidneys. Its commercial use declined after 1986 when it was banned from pesticides and cleaners."

"Why would that chemical show up in his blood?"

"Don't have a clue. We'll have to do some digging on that one," Yates said.

"Any more on the property where the body was found?"

"Here's a printout showing who owns it." Yates handed each of them a copy. "The company's in Raleigh. The second page lists their officers."

"Got it," said Bannister. "This matches the tax info our analyst pulled. Derek Barnes asked our office up there to contact them. We should have some answers by the end of the day."

"Incidentally," said Yates, "the owner of the hunting lodge next to the quarry said they were in between hunting seasons and the lodge was locked up. No members or guests had visited there for the past month. We photographed some partial footprints from a trail that intersected with the roadway where Briggs was lying." He passed a photo to Bannister. "The footprints were recent and look like they were made by new hiking boots—you know, the kind with Vibram soles and a waffle pattern. We should be able to determine the brand. Shoe size was average. Could have been worn by either a man or a woman. The unusual thing was someone, probably the killer, used a pine bough and brushed out the tracks from where Briggs's body was found all the way back to the hiking trail."

"Are you saying the killer brushed out most of the footprints but missed some?" Bannister asked.

"Looks that way," Yates said. "There aren't any lights out there. Also, there were no tire tracks other than from Briggs's Jaguar."

"So, do you think the killer walked out of the area?"

"At least to where a vehicle might have been pre-positioned, or to where an accomplice picked him up."

"How about his residence?" Bannister asked.

"Nothing unusual there. The condo didn't have an alarm system, which surprises me, but there was a decent deadbolt and the door was locked. Place was tastefully furnished but he didn't have a lot of expensive props. Just a medium-sized flat screen TV, laptop, and compact bookcase stereo speakers. Doesn't look like he owned a digital camera or other electronics."

Yates finished his cup of coffee and put his pen down before continuing. "This morning our techs reviewed the footage from CCTV cameras from the bank down the street and a musical instrument store directly across the street from Artists Square. Nothing of help to us. So, what's hot on your plate?"

"Barnes is trying to track down the nudist camp where the photo was taken. Maybe we can ID the others in the picture and determine their relationship to Briggs. We also need to know when the photo was taken. Mercedes will interview people at the Ravinia Health Club and the High Museum. We'll probably have dozens of additional leads after going through his work computer, personal laptop, and appointment book."

Ramirez looked at both men and asked, "What bothers you guys the most about this case?" There was a pause before Yates nodded for Bannister to go first.

"Motive and determining how many people were involved." Bannister took his last gulp of coffee and tossed the Styrofoam cup into the waste basket. "If Briggs was abducted at the condo or rendered unconscious there, how and why was he moved from his residence to Dahlonega? And, if you're going to kill him, why not just do it at his place? Why go through all the trouble and risk of taking him out to Dahlonega? And why Dahlonega? Where did the killer or killers go after the murder? How did they leave the quarry area? The condo scene bothers me, too."

"How so?" asked Yates.

"His briefcase wasn't taken and was on a chair in the entryway. Briggs had on the same clothes he wore to the speaking engagement earlier that night. And where's his gun? Did he have time to retrieve it but got disarmed by the killer? If someone held him at gunpoint and then drove him all the way to Dahlonega, why kill him with a knife?"

Ramirez said, "I think whoever did this was familiar with the Dahlonega area and was comfortable with using it as the kill site. I assume they knew how to get in and out of that property."

"Maybe when you two go for a look-see this afternoon something will click," Yates said. "Ask Chief Spina for his opinion. He's a good guy and really knows the area. Let's keep him in the loop."

"So, what's our approach going to be with Prescott?" Yates asked.

"Why don't I handle that," Bannister said. "We'll tell him our theory is that the murder was premeditated and carried out by someone who knew Briggs and his schedule. The killer wasn't just interested in murdering Briggs, but wanted to destroy the man. The killer was comfortable with the outdoors, knew how to handle a knife, was left-handed, and was someone filled with rage. That'll let Prescott know we at least have a working theory. Sound good enough to you two?" Yates and Mercedes nodded in unison.

As if on cue, Prescott walked in, an apologetic smile on his face. "Something's come up and I'm sorry to have to cancel your briefing. If you find out anything important, let Leon Brennan know. He'll keep me up to date. For your info, I talked with Briggs before he went to that speaking engagement last night. I told him I considered him to be our best prosecutor and the person I would recommend to replace me when that day arrived. He thanked me and then mentioned he had a family situation that was causing him some concern."

Yates asked, "Did he say what it was?"

"No. I asked Kendall if he wanted to talk about it, and all he said was 'maybe later.' That's the last thing he said to me. His sister is here and I know you plan on talking to her. See if she knows what was bothering him." With that, Prescott turned and walked out of the conference room.

Yates stood up. "If there's no briefing, I'm going back to my headquarters."

Bannister looked at Ramirez. "Well, let's see what the sister has to say."

CHAPTER 10

Sherrill Newsome escorted JoAnn Crawford into the conference room. Bannister pulled out a chair for her, thinking she looked like an Amish housewife, complete with long black skirt, white blouse with simple ruffle, and hair in a topknot bun. No lipstick or makeup.

"We're so sorry about your brother and appreciate your meeting with us," Bannister said.

"Thank you," she replied, placing her folded hands in her lap. She had piercing eyes that looked slightly bloodshot. The thought that she may have been crying was dispelled when she spoke.

"I'll save you some time. My brother and I weren't close. We didn't love each other, but we didn't hate each other either. We were just distant. I haven't seen him in two years. We exchanged birthday and Christmas cards."

"Where did you last see him?" Bannister asked.

"He came back to Lewiston when our stepfather was dying."

"Was he close to him?"

"No, that's what's strange," said Crawford. "Our parents divorced when Kendall was eight and I was six. Mother married Orville a year later. Kendall never liked him and missed his real dad. When Orville realized he was dying, he asked Mother to call Kendall. Said he had to see him. The night Kendall arrived, he went to the hospital and saw our stepfather alone. The next morning my brother just up and announced he was returning to Atlanta. No explanation. He didn't say anything about his conversation with Orville and refused a ride from anyone. He went through the hassle of calling a cab to cover the thirty miles from

Lewiston to Portland where he caught his flight. I think he deliberately wanted to avoid the family."

"Does anyone know what he and your stepfather talked about?"

"No. Said it was personal. Orville died in his sleep the day Kendall left. My brother hasn't seen any of us since then. My husband Frank agreed to call Kendall and try and find out what was wrong. My husband teaches psychology at Bates College. During their telephone call Kendall was cordial to him, said he was fine, but there wasn't anything he wanted to discuss."

"So, what happened?"

"Nothing. Frank tried to draw my brother out, but Kendall said he didn't have anything to say and that he had an engagement. He hung up on Frank. That may have been the last time anyone in the family spoke to Kendall."

Bannister assumed Briggs hadn't confided in any members of his family that he'd been molested. If the stepfather molested Kendall, it was logical to conjecture he may also have molested Crawford. If that was true and she had never mentioned it to Kendall, she may have a guilt complex for her silence over the years.

While Bannister mulled over those thoughts, Ramirez pointed to a cardboard box on the table and said to Crawford, "This is your brother's property from his office. We have a couple of things we're processing for investigative leads. That includes his laptop computer and appointment book. When we're finished we'll call you and make arrangements for their delivery to you."

Mercedes slid a spread of photos in front of Crawford. "Do you recognize anyone in these pictures?" The pictures included cropped portraits of the people from the nudist camp shot, the mystery blond, Dr. Theresa Andrews and her husband Dr. David Andrews.

"I've never seen any of them," said Crawford, looking at the array of photos on the table. "Do you think one of them is involved in my brother's death?"

"We're just trying to identify your brother's contacts right now," Bannister said.

Crawford spent the next half hour furnishing background information on Briggs's upbringing and his relationships with other family members. After she was finished and escorted out, Ramirez and Bannister proceeded back to the parking garage.

"Not a lot of emotion in that woman," Ramirez said, easing herself into the passenger seat.

"Perhaps those Maine winters have something to do with it," Bannister mused.

"Well, maybe her husband can help her make sense of it all. It looks like the stepfather's secret died with him. Do you think she told us everything she knew, Ty?"

"I always trust my hunches, and my gut tells me she may have known more about her stepfather than she wanted to admit."

Before driving to Dahlonega, Bannister told Ramirez they needed to stop at a trophy store on the other side of the Georgia Tech campus. He'd agreed to pick up a plaque with an engraved glass peach for Stu Peterson's retirement dinner. The dashboard clock showed 11:18 a.m.

"Sun's out. Nice day for a drive," Bannister commented.

"I'm going to sit back, relax, and go over my notes. Let me know if you see anything interesting," Ramirez said.

As they passed the Georgia Tech campus Bannister turned off Hemphill onto Northside Drive. He and Ramirez both saw the same thing.

"What the hell is that?" Ramirez said, unsnapping the holster of her .40 caliber Glock pistol.

"Something's going down," Bannister said, bringing the car to a quick stop and slamming the transmission into park.

As if in slow motion, they watched a black male exit from the driver's side of a double parked cream-colored Lincoln with silver mag spinners. He held a chrome-plated gun and began chasing another man around two parked cars. Ramirez jumped out of their car and started running down the sidewalk on the right. A couple seconds later Bannister ran down the right lane of the road. Both of them had drawn their weapons.

The man with the chrome-plated gun caught the second male and in a split second shoved him backwards across the hood of a parked car and pumped two rounds into the man's head. The sound of the gunshots reverberated off the buildings. As the shooter's gun hand came down to his side, Ramirez yelled, "FBI. Drop the gun! Drop the gun!"

The shooter looked at her, dropped his weapon, and slowly raised his hands above his head.

Bannister shouted for the man to keep his hands up and get down on his knees.

"It was him or me, man. Check Furious out. He always be packing a piece or a blade."

Mercedes ran over to the victim, who had slid off the car's hood and was now lying on the street face up near the front left fender. She checked for a pulse then looked at Bannister and shook her head. The young man's eyes stared upward as a large volume of blood pooled on the asphalt.

"Call it in, Mercedes."

Bannister ordered the shooter to lie on his stomach with his arms to the side. He then stepped to his left, grabbed the suspect's wrist and cuffed him. The man was well dressed. Brown leather jacket, designer jeans, and Bruno Magli loafers. A search revealed no other weapons. His wallet contained a driver's license identifying him as Rashone Green.

"Metro's sending two units right now," Ramirez said, returning from their car and pulling on a pair of latex gloves. She began a careful search of the victim. In the inside left pocket of his jacket was a steak knife with a five-inch blade. In the lower right pocket of the victim's jacket were eight two-inch packets with a white powder. The victim's wallet was in his left jacket pocket. A driver's license, depicting a smiling man with an inlaid gold star in one of his front teeth, was issued to Fury Webber, age twenty-seven. Ramirez's search was interrupted by the arrival of marked Atlanta cruisers. As two officers secured the scene, two others who'd arrived switched out Bannister's handcuffs on the subject, patted him down again and put him in the back of their car.

Ramirez and Bannister spent twenty more minutes at the scene, exchanging information with the uniformed officers and giving them their statements. One of the officers told them a detective would call that afternoon and arrange for a detailed interview.

From the time the shots were fired to the time they were cut loose was one hour. Statistically, Bannister knew two murders were committed somewhere in the United States every hour. Somewhere else in this country there was another. Every hour of every day, a family would have to try and come to grips with a violent death. He and Ramirez walked past a news team that had been at the intersection for fifteen minutes. Bannister doubted whether the cameraman and reporter would give a second thought to some family having to make funeral arrangements.

"You did well," Bannister said. "Do you want to go back to the office? Feel like you need to talk with anyone?"

"No, I'm okay. I've just never seen anyone die like that."

Bannister looked at Ramirez. She had distinguished herself at the FBI Academy when she became a member of the Possible Club, a recognition reserved for those new agents who fired a perfect score during pistol qualification. He had seen her name on the board outside the FBI's armory the last time he was at Quantico.

"I can read your mind, Ty. You're wondering, could she have pulled the trigger? If that guy hadn't dropped his gun when he did, I would have double tapped him in a heartbeat."

"That's what I figured. I'd just lined him up in my sights when the gun fell to the ground. You know, I think your voice scared the shit out of him." Bannister grinned at Ramirez. She smiled back.

"I wouldn't mind if we stopped at a gas station on the way. I want to wash my hands."

"No problem, partner."

CHAPTER 11

When Bannister got home from work, he found a notice from FedEx taped to his mailbox. They had a package requiring a signature and would hold it for three days. He hadn't been expecting any special deliveries so was curious what it was. He went to the FedEx office, which was open for another hour.

Once there, the clerk handed him an overnight envelope. He looked at the return address: Jennifer Van Otten, Kairos Kare, Thousand Oaks, California. There was a name that was a blast from the past—twenty years ago. The envelope was marked "Priority Overnight." He thought about opening it while still in the parking lot but decided to wait until he got home.

Once inside his house, he put two bags of groceries on the kitchen counter and stepped into the great room. He put on some blues by Mississippi John Hurt and tore open the envelope.

Inside were a letter and a four-by-six photograph of a blond female in blue UCLA workout gear. He set the picture aside and started reading the typed letter.

Dear Tyler,

I've lived with secrets and lies that I need to set straight. I'm currently in hospice. I have an inoperable brain tumor and the doctors have given me only weeks to live. The young lady in the picture is your daughter, Madison.

He stopped reading, stunned. Was this for real? Was it possible? He did the math—it could be. He looked at the sentence again to make sure he had read it correctly, and then continued.

By the time you read this, I will have told Madison you are her father. It's so complicated, but I will do my best. When I met you at Malibu Beach that beautiful afternoon, I knew you were special. You told me you were working for Mobil Oil in Virginia and were spending ten days with your parents before starting some new job that you never told me about. I guess it must have been the FBI since that was in the report the private investigator gave me.

When we met, neither of us was looking for a relationship, but in the week we had together, I fell in love with you. I wasn't honest with you then, but I will be now. I told you I was on birth control. I wanted you so badly that first time that I lied. The night and days we had together were so very special. I thought I had found my soul mate, and then you were gone. I hoped you would call me, tell me you loved me, and then send for me. You know—like in the movies. But that was just the dream of a romantic young woman. When I found out I was pregnant, friends urged me to get an abortion. For a while I thought I would. I remembered you telling me how you believed you'd get married someday and have a houseful of kids. I cried and agonized about my decision. Forgive me for not involving you with that choice. Several times I picked up the phone to call your parents to ask for your number but just couldn't dial. I felt it was my decision and eventually, I chose to keep our child.

On Madison's birth certificate I listed the father as unknown. Maybe I should have put your name down but I didn't. My mother was her babysitter while I worked as a nurse. About the same time I was promoted to nurse administrator and Madison turned eleven, Mom died. We were both heartbroken. Not long after that, Madison started asking me if there wasn't some way to find her real father. I told her there might be a way we could find out, but I procrastinated.

Two weeks ago, I hired an investigator to locate you. I didn't think it would be too hard since I knew your full name and date of birth. Do you remember on our first day together we joked about neither of us knowing anyone else who was born on the Fourth of July? Anyway, his report indicated you started with the FBI at the end of that summer and are still with them, in Atlanta. He also said your wife died in an accident five years ago. I am sorry about that. He didn't know if you had any children but said he thought you didn't.

I know all of this is a shock to you. I'm not writing to cause any trouble or for any other reason except to let you know. I don't know what you will do with this information. I do not know what Madison will do, but I think when the time is right she will try and call you. You should know she will be nineteen in three months and just finished her freshman year at UCLA. You'd be proud of her. Madison's been a great daughter and never been in trouble. She continues to be a bright student. She received academic honors and is attending UCLA on a volleyball scholarship.

My life insurance isn't going to be a lot, but there will be enough to pay for her undergraduate college and a little left over. After that, she'll be on her own. I'm including the telephone number for my room if you want to talk to me.

Sincerely,
Jennifer

Bannister went into the kitchen and picked up a wine glass. His hand was shaking and he needed something stronger. After pouring a glass of Michael Collins single malt whiskey, Bannister returned to his chair and picked up the photo of Madison again. He just kept staring at her.

He spoke aloud to the empty room. "I have a daughter. This is my daughter." She was certainly attractive and had his green eyes. She could even pass for a younger sister of Robin.

Bannister had only known Jennifer for a week. She'd never bothered to call him to tell him she was pregnant. Was she worried he would be angry or resentful because she lied about being on birth control? Did she wonder if he would even consider marrying her? Of one thing Bannister was certain. Regardless of the questions Jennifer had back then, if she had at least told him about her situation, he never would have forced her to make such an important decision alone. And even if they never got married and Jennifer resigned herself to living as a single parent, Bannister would have at least known he was a father and not missed out on nineteen years of his child's life.

CHAPTER 12

While Bannister and Ramirez were witnessing a murder, an FBI agent from Tampa, Florida, had driven to the Spa at Egret Bay to show a photograph to its manager. The Spa at Egret Bay was the closest nudist colony to Torreya State Park, which had the rare tree that was in the background of the photograph showing five nude people standing on a river bluff.

The Spa's manager declined to furnish a guest list without a subpoena but was willing to look at the photo. Luck was on the FBI's side. The manager identified one person other than Briggs. Hannah Michaels had given the manager her business card before she left, telling him she wouldn't mind getting referrals from the Spa, even though her business was in Atlanta.

The day after she'd been identified, Michaels agreed to meet with the FBI at The Natural Way, her interior decorating business located at the edge of Virginia Highlands in Atlanta. All she was told was that it involved a federal investigation and that the agents would explain when they got there.

Bannister drove to Michaels's studio. Ramirez was unusually quiet.

"Did you sleep all right last night?" Bannister asked.

"I did. I thought maybe I'd have that shooting scene replay over and over in my mind. But I didn't think about it. Am I okay?"

"Sure. You're okay. I just wanted to ask."

Ramirez rubbed her eyes. "You know yesterday, when you pulled into that gas station so I could wash my hands, I just stared at the water as it ran over my fingers. I looked in the mirror and thought about choices people make—like that guy who pulled the gun. I also thought about Paco and the choices he has made. I wondered if some day he might end up like that victim. Just another dead body lying in the street." Talking about her family always made Ramirez seem vulnerable, but especially when she talked about her youngest brother Paco. She'd do anything to reverse the direction he was headed.

"Do you think your family needs you back in LA?" Bannister asked as he pulled onto Piedmont Drive.

"I don't think they need me as much as they miss me. They hate that I live so far away, and they're always begging me to come home. Maybe this Christmas."

Ramirez was the oldest of seven children and the only one to have gone to college. Her parents and four of her brothers and sisters still lived in a three bedroom, sixty-year-old bungalow in a barrio in Pico Rivera, a tough suburb of Los Angeles. She'd been notified yesterday that Paco had been arrested for armed robbery. Although Paco was a juvenile and a first offender, Ramirez worried about the outcome and his future. She was also hoping the office never heard about it. She'd shared the information with Bannister, the only agent in whom she confided. None of her brothers and sisters knew, but he did, that each month for the past two years she had been making half the family's mortgage payment. That way she hoped her siblings might have a chance to further their education.

As Bannister turned onto Morningside Lane, Ramirez switched the subject back to work. "You ever interviewed a nudist before?"

"I don't think so," Bannister said. "How about going over what we know from the records checks about Miss Michaels."

Ramirez flipped open her notebook and pulled down the car's visor to block the sun. "Her driver's license says she's twenty-six, five foot eight, 135 pounds, with brunette hair and brown eyes. She has a master's in interior design from the Savannah College of Art and Design and has owned her own decorating business for three years. She drives a three-year old BMW Z-4 convertible. She's single, has a good credit rating and no criminal record. She was a larceny victim three years ago when someone broke into her car and stole her laptop.

There's one press release indicating she was Miss Hooters, Savannah, four years ago. I'll let you explore that fact if you want. That's it. If you take the lead, I'll take notes."

The two arrived at The Natural Way thirty minutes before the store opened and Bannister rang the bell.

Hannah Michaels unlocked the door as they held their credentials up to the glass. "You two are fashionably punctual," she said as she let them in and relocked the front door. They followed Michaels across a wood floor, zigzagging past three tall glass display cases, to her office in the back. Michaels's features and style of hair, although a bit longer, matched the nudist camp photo. Today she was wearing clothes—a white blouse and beige linen jacket with black slacks. She wore large gold circular earrings.

"Make yourselves comfortable," she said, pointing to matching white side chairs flanking a burgundy sofa opposite her desk. "Coffee's in the pot behind you."

As Bannister took her up on the offer and poured coffee into a china cup, Michaels removed her beige jacket, revealing her blouse to be sleeveless.

"The air conditioning hasn't fully kicked in yet," Michaels said, aware that Bannister's eyes had been drawn to her right arm, which was tattooed from her wrist to her shoulder. She was probably used to the reaction. In the nudist photo, her right arm had been concealed behind Kendall Briggs.

"During business hours I wear a long-sleeved blouse or leave my jacket on. Not that I have to or anything, but some potential clients might be put off seeing my body art."

The arm-length tattoo in various shades of greens, reds, and browns depicted a woman in the cubist style. "It looks like a Picasso to me," Bannister said.

"You're right. It's his 'Queen Isabel.'" Michaels had a warm smile. "I fell in love with the colors."

"Whoever did it must be very skilled," Bannister said.

"A seventy-something-year-old man named Ernesto who runs a small parlor outside of Puerto Limon, Costa Rica."

"How long have you had it?" Ramirez asked.

"Four years. During one of my summers when I was attending SCAD, I took a trip to Central America and had it done. I have no regrets." She crossed her legs and looked at both of them. "Obviously, you didn't come here to discuss body ink," she said, smiling at Bannister for the third time.

He put his coffee cup down. "We're investigating the murder of Kendall Briggs."

"That was just horrible. Absolutely terrible," Michaels said.

"How is it that you know him?"

"We met at a resort last May."

"Which one?" Bannister asked.

"It's called the Spa at Egret Bay. It's in Florida."

"Isn't that a retreat for naturalists?"

"You know it?" She sounded puzzled.

"Please, tell us more," Bannister continued.

"It's well run, pricey, discreet, and totally nude. It's not one of those clothing optional places. There's no alcohol, cigarettes, or children. Really serene."

"What's its draw?" Mercedes asked.

"It emphasizes a naturalist lifestyle. People who go there don't have a sexual agenda, and it's not one of those family-oriented places like the Quaker and Christian fellowship camps. The Spa offers seven-day retreats twice each month. Kendall was there the same week I was."

"Did you have any interaction with him?" Bannister asked.

"I did. He was a really nice guy. That was my first visit and Kendall's also. The Spa does a criminal records check of guests before accepting their payment. It has a policy that all guests are referred to only by their first name or initials. They can choose an alias if they wish. If guests wish to exchange personal contact information, they're encouraged to wait until the sixth day of their stay."

"Did you socialize with Mr. Briggs at the Spa?"

"Only in normal group activities. I didn't know his last name. I only knew he was a lawyer from Atlanta. I remember we both attended a guest lecture on Twentieth Century American art. He said he supported the High Museum. We had a couple of interesting talks. I remember asking him how he got interested in a nudist resort and he mentioned watching some segment on a TV show like *Dateline* or *60 Minutes* during which they described a lot of nudists as professional people like himself. He said it got him thinking about the idea and here he was. I told him I was an interior designer from Atlanta and gave him my card when I left."

"Could you elaborate on the interesting talks?"

"As I mentioned, that was our first visit to a naturalist resort. We chuckled at the rule that it was considered impolite to stare. He made me laugh the first time we met. He said 'nice towel.' Throughout the grounds, the spa had numerous containers where you could pick up or drop off a small towel. These were for sitting on. There's a significant emphasis on making and keeping eye contact with everyone you talk to. We both agreed our listening skills were really sharpened and we enjoyed our conversations with the other people a lot more. As we got to know one another, he confided he had found out something about his family that was disturbing and that it had turned his life upside down. He said he wanted to gain fresh insights into his own sexuality, morality, and relationships."

"Did he tell you what it was about his family that bothered him?" Bannister asked.

"No, and I didn't push. I told him if he felt like talking about it, I'd listen. He didn't bring it up again."

"Did you see him any time after you left the resort?"

"Yes, he called me the week after our stay and asked if I'd help redecorate his new condo. He gave me his name, phone number, and address. I visited his place at the Artists Square twice after that. The first time was to evaluate his tastes and help him pick out sculptures and wall accessories. As you could tell walking into my store, I specialize in bronze sculptures and large ceramic works. Anyway, the second visit was to suggest to him where his purchases should be placed and what type of lighting would best illuminate each piece. After that I never saw him or talked to him. I have digital photos of the pieces I sold him."

Bannister took out the nudist camp photo and handed it to Michaels. "Do you know who the other people are in this picture with you and Briggs?"

"I'd forgotten about that," she said, picking up the photo and studying it. "A group of us hiked up a path leading to a bluff." Without looking up from the photo she said, "I remember I put my right arm around Kendall. Queen Isabel didn't get into the picture. Anyway, the other woman's name was Camille. She said she was a music teacher who taught voice classes at the university in Columbia, South Carolina. I can't remember anything else about her. The guy next to me was Todd. He said he'd had a mild stroke the year before and said he owns a fishing business in Fort Walton Beach, Florida. I can't remember the name of the guy with the sunglasses. It was Devin or Kevin or something like that. He was a real jerk. He boasted he was a microbiologist with the CDC but couldn't talk about his work." Ramirez and Bannister looked at each other at the same time. "I think it was all bullshit—excuse me."

"I didn't think cameras were permitted," Mercedes said.

"They aren't at any resort if there are people attending under the age of eighteen. Pictures are okay as long as everyone in the photo gives permission."

Ramirez and Bannister spent another fifteen minutes talking about the resort. Michaels then printed out a color copy of the bronzes and ceramic pieces Briggs had purchased. She was visiting relatives out of town the night Briggs was murdered and could offer no information as to any enemies he might have had.

"If you think of anything at all that he said or did that might be helpful, please give me a call," Bannister said, handing Michaels one of his cards.

"You know whom you might want to try and locate?" Michaels said. Ramirez and Bannister looked back at her.

"The woman who took the picture," she said.

"What do you mean?" Ramirez asked. Bannister couldn't respond because he was too busy trying to resist the urge to smack his forehead.

"The woman with the camera and Kendall often took walks together. Maybe he said something to her. All I know is she's a doctor here in Atlanta. She said her name was Terri."

Bannister reached into his notebook and took out an enlarged copy of a driver's license photo and showed it to Michaels.

"That's her. That's Terri."

Ramirez looked at Bannister and neither said anything. The driver's license photograph was of Dr. Theresa Andrews.

CHAPTER 13

Several days later Bannister sat in an empty chair in what would be Stu Peterson's office for only two more hours. A couple of weeks ago Peterson recommended sending Bannister to a counterterrorism conference in Los Angeles since he was the most experienced agent on the Task Force. Bannister, however, suggested Ramirez. That was before Kendall Briggs was murdered. Everyone on the Task Force thought the investigation meant no one would go, until Witt spread the word he was considering going himself. After hearing that, Bannister suggested Stu mention to Witt that Headquarters would frown on his being away during a high-profile case and that Mercedes Ramirez was a more logical choice. The office nominated her.

Bannister knew the best way for an agent to gain experience, in addition to working good cases, was to meet other agents around the country who could offer insights, techniques, and lessons learned. Stu shared his thinking and after assurances Ramirez was current on her assignments and would check in with Bannister twice a day, decided to send her. Bannister hadn't told him about Ramirez's brother Paco but knew she would be able to visit her family and maybe talk some sense into her brother while he was out on bail. Ramirez was returning from LA on a 4:00 p.m. flight and Bannister was picking her up in time to attend Peterson's retirement dinner that evening.

For a couple of minutes Bannister sat quietly looking over the tops of two large cardboard boxes on Stu's mahogany desk. He could see the empty brass picture hook on the wall. Until recently the hook held a photograph of a young Stu Peterson and the other fifty-one US hostages freed on their 444th day of captivity in Teheran, Iran, minutes after Ronald Reagan was sworn in as president.

Bannister's time for reminiscing was interrupted by a call from Ramirez saying she was on the tram to the airport's main terminal. He'd arranged to meet her outside of baggage claim in a parking area reserved for law enforcement vehicles.

She walked out of the terminal carrying a clothing bag over her shoulder and pulling a suitcase. She wore a beige suit jacket over black slacks. Bannister liked that Ramirez always wore her gun under her jacket and didn't carry it in one of the Bureau-designed handbags. She put her right arm around his waist and gave him a quick hug.

"Was the trip worthwhile?" he asked.

"Absolutely. When I called Stu from LA to touch base with him, he told me you gave up the slot and recommended me for this training. You never told me that. I really appreciate what you did."

"You deserved it. How are things at home?"

"Well, I spent all day Sunday with my family before checking in at the hotel for the conference. I had a one-on-one with my brother. He feels absolutely awful about the situation he got himself in and is hoping for the best. We went together to St. Hilary's church and met with Father Rodriguez. He's taken Paco under his wing and got him a good pro bono lawyer."

"How are your parents handling it?"

"As well as can be expected. They're proud people and naturally embarrassed and disappointed. There were a lot of tears and hugs and some great home cooking. They still treat me like I'm a princess." Ramirez was beaming.

"Well, I'm happy for you. Hope you made some good contacts at the conference."

"You bet. The three days were packed with information and literally flew by. I figured if anything significant happened on KABMUR you would have called."

"Absolutely. We haven't had any breakthroughs on the case but have cleared about fifty leads. I can honestly say I'm glad you're back.

"Thanks. And FYI, I learned a lot at the conference and even found out a few things about you I didn't know."

"What do you mean?" Bannister glanced at her as he pulled out of the terminal lot.

"Guess who was in the room next to me?"

"No idea. Angelina Jolie?"

"Another attractive woman—Robin."

"I knew she was one of the two Washington office reps," Bannister said. Although he'd talked with and e-mailed Robin, he hadn't seen her since May when the two of them had taken a vacation together to Antigua the week after her graduation from the FBI Academy. Because of the case, he'd forgotten to tell her Ramirez would be in LA.

"We ate dinner a couple of times. Lots of girl talk." Ramirez smiled as she playfully jabbed Bannister's arm.

Stu Peterson's retirement dinner was scheduled for 6:00 p.m. at the Druid Hills Country Club in Decatur. Even though it was a Thursday, the Atlanta traffic would be bad, as always. Since Ramirez's apartment was an hour north of the office, Bannister had suggested she change at his home, which was ten minutes from the club.

After winding down Valley Road, they arrived at a set of large black iron gates at the bottom of a tree-lined driveway. He activated the signal, and the heavy gates swung open.

"I heard you lived in a big house but had no idea," Ramirez said. "Ty, this is really a mansion!"

Bannister drove the Bureau car around a circular front driveway, past a stone tower anchoring the left side of the home, and then underneath a stone archway before turning into the right bay of his three-car garage.

"What kind of car is that?" Mercedes asked, pointing to a silver convertible next to a Toyota 4Runner.

"It's a 1957 Mercedes 300 SL Gullwing. The doors open up into the air. I always loved that car. My grandfather left it to me." Bannister held Ramirez's clothing bag as she removed her cosmetics kit from her suitcase. Once inside the house, he showed her where the guest room and shower were. He took the time to put on a fresh powder blue shirt and double-breasted navy blazer. As he walked into his great room, he spotted the photo of Madison and Jennifer's letter. He slipped them inside the book next to the lamp. Bannister had made the decision he definitely would fly to LA this weekend, case or no case. Tomorrow after work, he would call Jennifer and tell her, or leave a message, that he would be in Los Angeles this weekend and wanted to see her and possibly meet his daughter.

Twenty minutes later Mercedes emerged from the guest room dressed in a black A-line dress, accented by a black-and-white beaded necklace and matching bracelet.

"What do you think?" she asked with a demure smile.

With his hands in front of his face, Bannister pretended to take her picture as he said, "You look great."

A short time later they arrived at the Druid Hills Country Club about the same time as fifty other people. One thing about FBI agents is they were on time. If there was an open bar, they'd be early. The weather was perfect, parking ample, and inside the dining room were three separate bars. The eighty guests included the Special Agents in Charge of the FBI and Secret Service as well as Winston Prescott. All were expected to use the opportunity to give brief comments.

At least a dozen of the agents brought their wives. A few of the single guys were accompanied by dates. As he handed a glass of Riesling to Ramirez, Bannister glanced toward the back of the room where Stu Peterson was chatting with two couples.

His eyes narrowed. "I propose a toast, Mercedes," he said, clinking his glass of wine to hers.

"To what?" she asked.

"Luck! Be casual, but take a look at the woman standing next to Ted Mims."

Ramirez glanced in Agent Mims's direction and then just as fast looked back into his face. "It's her," she said. "The mystery blonde!"

"Why don't you go introduce yourself to her. And without setting off alarm bells, see what you can find out."

Mercedes returned five minutes later, raising her eyebrows a couple of times while she walked back. "That's Audrey Mims, Ted's wife. Ted is one of the accountants who helped trace funds on one of our terrorist cases. They have two daughters—ages nine and eleven. And Audrey said she works as an assistant manager at Guaranty Bank in Norcross. Why would an Assistant US Attorney have a revealing photo of the wife of a federal agent? And why would Briggs have it right out in plain sight on his desk?" Ramirez turned her head to look back in the direction of the Mims. "What's the answer, Ty?"

"I don't know. Maybe he just took it out once in a while. Maybe he'd called her and looked at it to bring back memories. Hell, I don't know. Guys do stupid things. Do you remember Briggs had several notations in his appointment book of 'A.M. meeting'?" Bannister asked.

"You're right." Ramirez's mouth dropped open as she stared at Bannister. "Those weren't morning meetings. He was seeing Audrey Mims!"

"Well, tomorrow morning you and I are going to have an 'A.M. meeting' of our own at Guaranty Bank."

CHAPTER 14

Bannister got to the office early. He and Ramirez planned to be at Guaranty Bank in Norcross to interview Audrey Mims after the bank opened. The bank's director of security had arranged with the manager to ensure Audrey was available with no mention of the FBI.

While they interviewed his wife, Special Agent Ted Mims would be given a polygraph exam at the office. Witt had told Mims it was part of the Bureau's program to conduct counterintelligence polygraphs of agents who worked national security cases. The examiner would throw in one or two questions concerning knowledge of Briggs's murder. Bannister was counting on Mims cooperating with their examiner and not invoking any legal rights. Two task force members had already checked out his whereabouts the night Kendall Briggs was murdered. His activities were accounted for up to 8:00 p.m.; however, his physical location after that was unknown.

It turned Bannister's stomach every time he heard about an FBI agent accused of a criminal act. Until they proved otherwise, they had to consider Mims a suspect. If he knew about his wife's infidelity, then he had both the motive and the means to kill Briggs. They needed to rule out the opportunity and, although unlikely, also rule out his having hired someone to do it. The polygraph examiner would follow up if any deception was indicated.

Witt insisted that, after the polygraph, Mims be brought to his office before Bannister and Ramirez interviewed him. The ASAC wanted to personally break the news of the wife's relationship with Briggs.

Ramirez met Bannister in the task force conference room promptly at 8:00 a.m. His open notebook and empty coffee cup were in front of him.

"You ready?" Bannister asked, without getting up.

"I guess." Ramirez shrugged then pulled out a high-backed leather chair at the table. She sat down and took a deep sigh. "You know, Ty, this is a first for me. I've never investigated one of our own."

"It's never easy. The way to make it more comfortable is to put your personal thoughts aside and just do everything professionally. Go by the book. You can sort out your thinking later."

"I hope so. I've reviewed everything in the file. I printed a copy of Mrs. Mims's driver's license photo taken three years ago. It shows her with brown hair and highlights. A lot different than the glamour shot."

"At least in the DMV photo she was wearing a turtleneck," Bannister replied.

They spent the next fifteen minutes going over their game plan. Bannister grabbed a refill of coffee on the way out of the office for the ten-mile drive to Norcross.

Once at the bank, he and Ramirez were given use of a small conference room used by customers to sign loan agreements. He'd barely had time to look around when their witness walked in.

"Hi. I'm Audrey Mims. My boss said there were some investigators who wished to speak with me. How can I help you?" Today, Mrs. Mims was dressed in a white dress patterned with lots of blue bubbles. Her navy blue and white heels complemented the ensemble. She had excellent posture and a firm handshake.

"You look familiar," she said as she let go of Bannister's hand.

"We're both agents in the Atlanta office. We work with your husband, Ted." They introduced themselves and mentioned seeing her at Stu Peterson's retirement dinner last night. As Bannister offered her a seat, he stated they were investigating the murder of Kendall Briggs. At the mention of Briggs's name, her smile disappeared, and her face paled. She sat down, crossed her legs, and placed her hands in her lap.

"That was awful, just awful," she said, shaking her head from side to side. They didn't say anything. After about ten seconds of silence, Audrey asked, "What does his murder have to do with me?"

"How well did you know him?" Bannister asked.

"I knew who he was. I met him a couple of times at charity events Ted dragged me to."

"Were you friends?"

"No," she said too quickly. "What are you getting at?" Audrey looked at Bannister and then at Ramirez. Bannister handed her a copy of the glamour shot photo.

"Where'd you get this?"

"It was in a frame next to the phone on Kendall Briggs's desk at his office."

"Oh, my God. I can't believe it," she stammered out. "You know."

"Yes" is all Bannister said as Audrey Mims burst into tears. With a sympathetic look at the woman whose secret world had just crashed in on her, Ramirez reached over and handed Audrey a packet of facial tissues she had brought to the interview, just in case.

"Does my husband know?"

"Before we get into that, why don't you start from the beginning?"

For the next twenty minutes, Audrey Mims bared her soul. At the beginning of June, her husband went to the FBI Academy at Quantico for a white-collar crime training session. At the time, her two girls were spending the first week of summer vacation at their grandparents' home in Alabama. Audrey said she was home alone, had time on her hands, and was bored. She was looking for some excitement.

One night she went out for a drink in Virginia Highlands. She stopped at the Highland Tap, a watering hole popular with lawyers and local politicians. She was on her second cosmopolitan when she met Briggs and was instantly captivated by his good looks and muscular build. She felt reckless and thought she was recreating a scene out of a Nora Roberts novel. She propositioned him and ended up at his condo where they engaged in what she described as torrid sex. She agreed to meet him two nights later. The scene repeated itself. It wasn't until the end of the second rendezvous that she discovered he was a federal prosecutor. She told Briggs she'd been married. What she didn't tell him was that she was still in that marriage. Briggs didn't pursue finding out the truth.

Audrey belonged to an environmental group, Metro Green Space, which met twice a month to discuss how city urban planners and homeowners' associations could work together to add walking paths in the suburbs. She saw Briggs on two occasions after attending the group's meetings. She told her husband the women considered those evenings as a girls' night out and that some of her friends stopped off for a drink afterwards. She failed to tell her husband the meetings were always over by 7:30 p.m.

She didn't know whether she became infatuated with Briggs or was falling in love with him. On impulse, for Briggs's birthday, she gave him a leather notebook embossed with his initials in gold. Inside the notebook she'd included the sexy photo with a card. She recalled writing the phrase, "Like the title of the James Bond movie, this is 'For Your Eyes Only.'"

At the end of June both of them realized the relationship wasn't going any further. Briggs told her he'd been married before and wasn't interested in tying the knot again. Audrey admitted she enjoyed Briggs's companionship, his sensitivity, and his sexual stamina. She said they were both fueled by mutual lust and raw physical passion. One night Briggs simply announced it might be a good idea if they had a cooling off period. He used as an excuse that he had a big case coming up and needed to focus on it.

Audrey had also been wondering how she might end their affair. She found herself saying it was okay. In the back of her mind she felt he might be seeing someone else but never asked him about it. She remembered saying to him, "If we're going to end this thing, let's end it with a bang and not a whimper." She recalled they laughed at her remark and then had sex for the last time. This was a month before his death.

Audrey denied having any contact with Briggs after that last rendezvous. She never dreamed he would put her picture on his desk at work. She said she would never hurt him, had absolutely nothing to do with his death, and couldn't think of anyone who would want to kill him. He always acted upbeat and never mentioned being threatened.

"So, does Ted know?" she asked again.

"I don't know. Do you believe he knew you were seeing Briggs?"

"No way. He wouldn't be able to keep that inside. He would confront me." She twisted the tissues she was holding. "Can you keep him from finding out? Please?" She stared at Bannister, her moist eyes pleading, but he didn't answer her.

"You're going to tell him, aren't you?" she asked.

"Yes," Bannister said.

With that, the composure she'd been trying to regain evaporated. Her upper lip quivered right before she again burst into tears. She held her head down in her hands and sobbed, blew her nose a couple of times, and cried some more.

"I'm sorry," she said, dabbing her eyes with another tissue. "I must look like hell."

She did, but Bannister decided to stay on track with their questions.

"Do you think Ted is capable of killing Kendall?"

"No, he's too kindhearted. Believe me, I know him. If he knew I was having an affair he'd be shocked at first and then feel terribly hurt and betrayed. But he wouldn't kill anyone over this."

"We have to tell your husband. He's going to be interviewed at the office. We need to eliminate him as a suspect. He'll be questioned about his knowledge of your affair with the victim."

Ramirez finished the interview of Audrey Mims and obtained specific dates and places they would later confirm. Ramirez asked about Briggs's mental state, his work, and outside activities. She asked Audrey about her husband's activities the night Briggs was murdered.

Audrey vouched for Ted Mims being at home with her. She remembered that after putting the girls to bed, the two of them watched the movie *Hangover* and had some good laughs.

When the interview was concluded, Audrey left with her head down and slumped shoulders. There'd be no laughing at the Mims' home tonight.

CHAPTER 15

Gary Witt's office had a choice view. Situated on the north corner of the fourth floor, it enjoyed panoramic vistas through two connecting glass walls. Dekalb County and the outskirts of downtown Atlanta stretched out over the treetops. Witt told Bannister to go in and have a seat; he'd be back in a minute. Bannister sat in one of the blue Queen Anne chairs with his back to the view. He wanted to be able to study the expressions and body language of Ted Mims. He set his notebook on Witt's glass table. Witt strutted in and hung up his suit coat on the back of his door and closed it. He no sooner had taken a seat on the couch when there was a light knock and Ted Mims stuck his head in.

"Come in, Ted," Witt said.

Mims gave a quick forced grin and settled into the armchair across from Bannister. Without prompting, he said, "I'd forgotten how stressful a polygraph can be, even if you have nothing to hide. I wasn't deceptive, so why am I here?"

Witt had said he wanted to break the news, but in his typical style, looked at Bannister and said, "Go ahead, Ty. Fill him in."

Bannister opened his notebook to get a couple of seconds to gather his thoughts. "You passed the polygraph. No problems with that. Do you remember the questions about the murder of Kendall Briggs?"

"I thought they might have been control questions."

"They weren't. We needed to make sure you had no involvement with his murder."

"What are you talking about? You're not thinking I'm some kind of a suspect are you?" Mims asked, bracing his hands on the arms of the chair as if to stand up. He glared at both of them.

"No, you're not a suspect. But you do have a connection to him." As Mims frowned, Bannister reached across the table and laid down in front of him a copy of his wife's glamour photograph. Mims picked it up and stared at it for a few seconds.

"I've never seen this. Where'd this come from?" He looked at Bannister and then at Witt.

"There's no easy way to say this, but it was in a frame on Kendall Briggs's desk at the US Attorney's office."

"I don't get it. That doesn't make any sense at all. This picture either has to be someone who looks like Audrey, or it's some kind of perverted joke."

"I'm afraid not. It's her. She gave it to Briggs. I interviewed your wife this morning at the bank. Audrey admitted to having had an affair with Briggs."

"I don't fucking believe this!" Mims shouted and pounded his fist on the edge of a side table, knocking over Witt's fake ivory statue. He got up and walked towards the back window. Witt replaced the statue and was about to stand up when Bannister motioned for him to sit back down. Mims continued staring out the window. No one said anything for a full minute.

Mims turned around and walked back toward his chair. "So . . . you guys think I knew about it and might have killed Briggs? Is that what you're getting at?"

"Sit down, Ted," Bannister said, pointing to his seat. "I don't believe you knew and I don't think you had any involvement in Briggs's murder. But you know how we work. You're a fellow professional. You understand we had to rule you out. And we had to rule out Audrey."

"Jesus. Audrey and Briggs? How long was it going on? What did she say? Where is she now?"

"When we left her, she was still at the bank."

"Was she still seeing him when he was killed?"

"We don't think so. Audrey said they called it off and hadn't seen each other for a few weeks prior to his murder."

"Who else knows about this?" All the color had drained from Mims's face.

Bannister ignored his question. "I'm going to level with you, Ted. This is a shock. I'm not going to sit here and tell you I know what you're going through, because I've never been through it. You're a good agent and a decent man. You're just going to have to take this one step at a time."

"How many people in the office know about this?" he asked again.

"I won't lie to you. Right now, a dozen," Bannister admitted.

"Ah, geez." Mims started rubbing his forehead with his left hand, as if he were trying to slow down the torrent of thoughts pounding in his head.

"I told your supervisor you had a personal situation and might need to take some time off," Witt said.

"Well, that's putting it mildly."

Bannister ignored the sarcasm. "Ted, I'm sure you're going to do the right thing."

"What am I supposed to do now?" was his next plaintive question.

"Go home. I'll drive you in your car. Mercedes Ramirez was with me on the interview. She'll follow us and give me a ride back to the office."

"That'd be okay, I guess." Mims uttered the words in a monotone, slumped in the chair.

"I asked Walt Thompson to talk with you," Witt said. "As our employee assistance coordinator, he might be able to help you. You may not know that when Walt was assigned to Philadelphia, his wife had an affair with one of the guys on his squad. If you decide to talk with him, it will be confidential. It's your call." It was refreshing to hear Witt saying something positive.

The three men stood up. "Can I take this with me?" Mims asked, holding out the photo.

"Leave it on the table, Ted," Bannister said. "We're still conducting a murder investigation."

Witt glanced in Bannister's direction. "What about his gun, Ty?"

Mims turned abruptly, his eyes riveted on them and his nostrils flaring.

With a simple comment, Witt had managed to undermine the feeling of trust and rapport Bannister had built with Mims. It had to be turned back around and fast. "Gary's right, Ted. For tonight, I'd remember to put the lock on your gun." Bannister wanted Mims to think they were concerned about the possibility of Audrey doing something stupid and not that he would.

"I'm going back to my desk to get my stuff," Mims said and left the office.

"Is he going to be okay?" Witt asked.

"He'll survive. On the drive over, I'll talk to him about his girls. They're nine and eleven. They'll pick up really quick that something's rotten in China."

CHAPTER 16

Bannister and Ramirez arrived at the office at the same time.

"I've got a favor to ask you, Mercedes. You're planning to write up the Audrey Mims interview, right?"

"First thing this afternoon. Why?"

"When you're finished, fax it to me in care of the Los Angeles office. I'll give you the number."

"LA?" Ramirez's mouth dropped open.

"I have some personal business out there which I hope to be able to handle in two days. You recall I worked in that division before transferring to Atlanta, right?"

"I forgot about that." She stared at him with a look that said *If you want to tell me about it, okay; if not, then that's okay, too.*

"I called my former supervisor who's still running one of their counter-terrorism squads. He'll have the duty agent fax back any additions or corrections on Saturday."

"Is the rush because Witt's micromanaging again?"

"You got that right."

"Everyone's noticed he's been acting kind of weird lately. Do you think he's looking for an excuse to jump in your shit?"

"Witt doesn't want to be embarrassed by anything. He's a necessary evil in such a high-profile case, so we need to keep him in the loop. Call me if there are any developments this weekend."

Their hope was that Witt would have been promoted to Washington, DC, by now and out of their hair. The boss's secretary, Bannister's main office source, advised him on the QT that Witt's transfer was on hold. Apparently, there'd been an allegation of sexual harassment filed by a female analyst. The resulting internal affairs inquiry, even if it found in Witt's favor, would probably add six months to his departure date.

SAC Brennan called a meeting for 4:00 p.m. for those working KABMUR. Special Agent Natalie Fowler, an FBI profiler, had finished an assignment in Little Rock and agreed to stop in Atlanta to review Briggs's murder before returning to Quantico. Bannister drove to the Doraville subway station to pick her up.

He recognized her as she got off the train. Fowler was lanky, five-ten, trim, and this time had wavy shoulder-length reddish brown hair.

"Good seeing you again, Natalie. Hair looks great."

"Thanks, Ty." Fowler broke into a wide smile. "After each major case success, I do something different about my appearance. My own version of a stress reliever. The Bureau arrested a subject I helped identify in Little Rock last night. I haven't had time to figure out a way to celebrate that case yet. Usually, I buy a new outfit or something. After working your case earlier this year, I decided to change my hair color. I'm pleased you like it. The shrinks could analyze me and come up with a logical explanation for my idiosyncrasy, but what the hell, I'm not a suspect." Fowler laughed.

Bannister grabbed her small carry-on suitcase.

"How long are you staying?" he asked.

"I have a flight back to DC at 9:30 p.m."

Fowler was one of the Bureau's best profilers. She had a doctorate in abnormal psychology from Johns Hopkins and six years' experience working serial offender cases. Last year in Washington, D.C., she helped a task force identify the serial killer who had murdered Bannister's best friend.

"I have the key to Briggs's condo. In your call you said you wanted to go directly there."

"That's right. I reviewed all the notes and photos taken at the murder scene. Although I would like to visit the Dahlonega site, it'll have to wait for the next trip. But I do want to examine his residence and the area in back where he may have been initially attacked."

Bannister drove them to Artists Square. On the way there, he filled her in on the developments from yesterday, particularly the information furnished by Audrey Mims. Once they arrived at the condo, he kept quiet while Fowler examined the rooms and furnishings of the late Kendall Briggs. She had a small digital camera and took photos of the unit and its contents as well as several shots of the parking area and driveway in the rear.

After a half hour, he asked, "Got what you need?"

"I think so. Along with the new information, this will help with my assessment of his lifestyle and personality characteristics."

As Bannister drove them back to the FBI office, he put on a classical music station. While Fowler typed notes on her small iPad, Bannister thought about Madison and his upcoming trip. He'd called SAC Brennan last night and told him he wanted to go to LA because a friend was dying. After the boss said no problem, he made airline and hotel reservations.

He had questions but no answers. *What's best for Madison? What does she want to do? Will Jennifer's insurance cover her college costs? Will she be willing to let me help her financially? I'm sure she'll think it is a part of a guilt trip on my part, but I can live with that.*

"Nice building," Fowler said, snapping him out of his thoughts as he drove to the fenced FBI parking area behind the Century Boulevard office building. "I've never been to this office before."

Five minutes later they were in Brennan's office where Bannister introduced Fowler. The three of them then walked down the hall, joining the others assembled in the conference room. All agents not out covering leads were present.

Fowler addressed the gathering. "As you're aware, the Director has made this case a priority and he's confident you will solve it. SAC Brennan asked me about the unsolved West Coast murder of another Assistant US Attorney. Have any of you worked on that case?" One hand went up.

"Some of you may not remember that exactly one month after 9/11,

Thomas Crane Wales was working in the evening at his home computer in Seattle. An unknown assailant walked into Wales's back yard and fired three rifle shots through a window, killing Wales instantly. It's highly unlikely there's a connection between that case and this one. I mention it because, even though it's been over seventeen years, it's still an active investigation. We haven't quit looking for Wales's killer and we won't quit looking for Briggs's murderer either. The FBI never quits. We're going to work this case until it's solved." Fowler looked down at her notes.

"Keep in mind the profile our unit developed is a preliminary one. I've studied numerous photographs including enlarged ones of the victim's wounds as well as pictures of the entire area around the scene where the victim's body was discovered. I've reviewed photographs of his workspace at the Federal Building. Agent Bannister and I just returned from looking at Briggs's residence and surrounding neighborhood. I've reviewed the medical examiner's report and Atlanta's initial investigative findings, which included what we know about the sequence of events the day Briggs was killed." The hand that went up earlier was raised again. Fowler nodded in his direction.

"Miss Fowler, your colleague who put together a profile of Wales's unknown killer concluded the crime was the work of one person. Do you have enough information to reach the same conclusion in Briggs's murder?"

"It's still too early, but I'm leaning toward calling it the action of one person. Let me continue.

"The financial section of the report is incomplete and maybe we'll all get an update at this meeting. Your teams have done a commendable job thus far on Briggs's background. We have a fairly comprehensive tracking of his life, including his scholastic achievement, work history, lifestyle, personality and demeanor, residences, medical history, and personal habits, such as the use of alcohol and prescriptive drugs. We've reviewed his work relationships and court activity, both personal and professional, covering the past five years. All of this information is analyzed to come up with the 'what' of the crime. My assignment, which I can't fulfill without input from all of you, is to determine the 'why' of the crime—that is, what the motivation was behind his murder. We're all working under the premise that if we can determine the 'what' and the 'why' of Briggs's murder, then we'll be able to identify the 'who.'

You have in front of you a summary of the evidentiary timeline covering the 3-1/2 hours from when Briggs arrived home from his dinner speech to when he was killed at the marble quarry. Some of the known facts are that blood droplets from the driveway behind the condo came from Briggs and, we know he was inside his condo for a brief period. There were no signs of a struggle inside his residence. Although a brass statue that had been in a dispay case was found in his burned out Jaguar, his pistol has not been located. Robbery was not the motive since Briggs had his wallet with credit cards and $350 cash. He also was wearing an expensive watch. His key ring was found in his car's ignition.

"I don't believe this was a random attack. The victim and killer were probably acquainted. I say killer, but it is possible more than one person was involved.

"The ME's report indicated the cause of death was exsanguination by a knifelike instrument cutting the throat. Briggs also had a fracture to his skull which was premortem. There was no postmortem slashing or cutting.

"My analysis of the crime scene shows both organized and disorganized factors. The facts that the victim was initially immobilized at one location and transported to a second location where he was killed shows organization. At some point, the killer had available flex cuffs, which were used to tie Briggs's hands behind his back. In addition to bringing a container of gasoline to the murder site, the killer also had at least one weapon—a knife or cutting instrument. I believe the killer was probably left-handed. Although only ten percent of the population are lefties, more than half of those suffering from autism or schizophrenia are left-handed, so keep that in mind if any suspects have a mental disorder."

"The perpetrator was disorganized in that the victim was killed and left at the same location. Although the quarry area in Dahlonega was isolated, there was no effort to conceal Briggs's body, but there were signs that footprints in the area of the body had been brushed out. Only one set of prints was found. I believe the murder site is one the killer is familiar with and has frequented in the past. It may even be close to the offender's residence or place of employment."

Fowler spent some time answering questions about Briggs being obsessive compulsive and the victim of child abuse, engaging in nudist activities, and being a sexual partner of a married woman who might have brought him into contact with his killer. She took a half hour to help task force members prioritize new areas of investigative interest before they took a break to answer missed calls.

"You've given us a lot with what little we've given you," Bannister said as the two of them stood by the conference room door.

"I received an emergency call from Quantico and need to catch the next available flight back to Washington," said Fowler. "Sorry to cut the meeting short."

"We'll keep you up to date," Bannister said.

He had one message—from Chief Spina in Dahlonega. As Fowler gathered up her materials, he returned the call.

"Agent Bannister, we may have the murder weapon. One of the quarry workers, about as smart as the rocks he cuts, apparently found a ceramic hunting knife."

"And he turned it in to you?" Bannister asked.

"Not exactly. He and some of his buddies were out drinking last night when he showed them a hunting knife he said he found on a quarry road while walking back to his front-end loader two days after Briggs was murdered. I guess the dumb shit didn't hear Briggs died by having his throat slashed, but one of the other guys had. Long story short, during his lunch break he reported his find to his supervisor, who called me."

"Have you got the knife?"

"Ten-four. I just turned it over to Inspector Glenn Yates who's going to have the GBI lab examine it tonight. Even though the quarry guy said he cleaned the knife, Yates and I agreed there might be some trace of blood in the knife's housing. Worth a shot. Thought you'd like to know this right away."

"Thanks, Chief. What kind of knife is it?"

"It's a Boker Ceramic Infinity folding knife. Black with a folding four-inch blade. Supposedly, ceramic knives are harder than steel, don't rust, and don't need to be sharpened. I know you can't detect them with those airport magnetometers."

Bannister wrote down the description and said, "I'll follow up with Yates."

"Yeah, and I'm going to have the quarry guy show us exactly where he found it. Might be able to figure out if it was dropped or thrown there."

"Good thinking. Keep in touch," Bannister said.

He relayed the information to Fowler as she picked up her suitcase to go outside to wait for the cab to the airport.

Fowler nodded thoughtfully. "Some people who purchase ceramic knives get freaked out since they're so lightweight and razor sharp. If this was purchased for hunting, it reinforces the idea the killer is a more intelligent, confident person. The killer might also be familiar with that hunting lodge nearby. Find out how far and in what direction from the body the knife was found. Send me photos of the knife and the quarry area where it was located as soon as you can. You could use a break," she said.

"I agree." Bannister was already thinking about how they might trace the knife to an owner.

CHAPTER 17

B annister arrived at the American Airlines ticket counter an hour before his flight. He received a weapons carriage permit, got a boarding pass, and checked one bag. The only things he carried were a digital camera, which was in his sport coat pocket, and a copy of Michael Connelly's *Two Kinds of Truth*. Madison's photograph and the letter from her mother were inside the book's jacket cover. He still didn't know what he would say to either of them. He hoped his thoughts would come together by the time his flight landed.

He rang the buzzer at the checkpoint door used by law enforcement officers to bypass the TSA screening lines. The officer checked his identification and ticket and logged him in. As he walked around the side, a voice said, "Hey, Bannister." He turned to see a familiar uniformed Atlanta officer.

"Hi, Brian," Bannister said, extending his hand.

"It's been awhile. You still owe me a barbecue lunch at Harold's."

He noticed Brian Duffy was now a major. He was a lieutenant six years ago when he drove out to Bannister's house and broke the news to him that Bannister's wife Erin had been killed in an automobile accident. Duffy came to her funeral and even called Bannister a month later to invite him for a drink, just to see how he was adjusting. He definitely fell into the category of "good people."

"What are you doing at the airport?" Bannister asked.

"Filling in for my boss this week while he's in DC for emergency operations training."

They chatted a few minutes before Duffy's radio announced a call. As Bannister rode the escalator down to the train platform, thoughts of Erin swept through his mind. Lord knew, he'd love for her to be alive, but he didn't know how he'd handle all of her questions about Madison. They'd talked about starting a family and how many kids they wanted to have. They were only married three months. There were a lot of ifs. If she were alive; if they were still married; if they had kids. He didn't know how their marriage would have changed, but he knew that was something they would have had to work through.

Once at the concourse, he headed toward the gate and, with the thought of Harold's Barbecue in his subconscious, stopped for fifteen minutes at Neely's to wolf down a pulled pork sandwich.

Remarkably, his flight lifted off on time. He put in the earbuds for his iPod and selected blues recordings by Big Bill Broonzy and Snooks Eaglin. Closing his eyes, he let his mind bring up memories from twenty years ago. More specifically, the last day in June. The last day he saw Jennifer. The ten-day visit with his parents had blown by like a Santa Ana wind, and the next day they'd be dropping him off at the airport for a morning flight back to Virginia. He hadn't clued them in about his social activities.

He called Jennifer and told her he wanted to see her. It was her day off and she suggested a day at the beach. He picked her up and they drove to Santa Monica. After lunch and a walk on the pier, they headed to Venice Beach to catch some rays. Her idea again. They strolled along the beach, kicking at the sand as they stole glances at each other. Muscle Beach in Venice was in its glory with hard-bodied rollerbladers in bikinis gliding along the serpentine sidewalk, tattooed males and females boasting hair jobs with all the colors of rainbow sherbet, and even a family of dwarfs buying souvenir trinkets from one of the stands. In the background were two muscle-bound guys competing with each other by doing pull-ups from permanent bars set in the sand.

Jennifer squeezed his arm as they both became intrigued by a guy wearing a porkpie hat. What set him apart was not the way he looked but the way he was juggling three growling mini-chain saws.

"Why would anyone think about doing something like that?" she asked.

"I guess because he can" was all Bannister could come up with. They watched him complete his routine, and Bannister dropped a five-dollar bill in an open case by his feet. It was worth it. The two sauntered onto the beach where they spent the rest of the afternoon basking in the sun, swimming, and just talking.

Finally, the tangerine sun sank into the horizon. The wind picked up and became cooler. Families had already left and even the diehards were packing up. Jennifer suggested they get a picnic dinner and drive someplace where they could watch the stars come out. They stopped at a Dean & DeLuca's on Ocean Drive. With their large black-and-white bag of gourmet sandwiches, desserts, and bottle of Zinfandel, they felt like upscale tourists.

Upon reaching Malibu, Bannister turned onto Las Virgenes Canyon Road and followed its winding course to a dirt cutoff he knew about. It formerly was the backroad entrance to an outdoor movie set used for Westerns and old TV shows like Mash.

Even today he could remember where he had parked near the trailhead, as well as the clearing halfway up a hill where he spread their blanket. He could recall the color of the mountains, what they ate and what they were wearing. He had no idea, however, of what they talked about for hours. But one thing he'd never forget was making love to her that last time. They clung to each other for a long time, not saying anything.

Finally, they realized it was time to go. When they got up to leave, it was quiet, still, and dark. Above them stretched a wide bracelet of stars in a black sky. He held Jennifer's hand, then turned to hug her close. She didn't say anything, but cried softly. He wiped her tears with his hand, kissed her gently on the lips, and then drove her home. He called her a week later from Virginia. They both knew that what they had, what they shared, was something they would not be able to sustain over time and distance. Their conversation ended when she said, "Call me if you come out here again," and he said, "You'll be the first person I call." He never talked to her after that.

The passenger next to Bannister tapped his arm. She needed to use the lavatory. As he opened his eyes and unfastened his seatbelt, he heard Leroy Carr singing, "Sometimes I wonder and do not know." Well, tomorrow he'd find out.

CHAPTER 18

Bannister checked out of his motel in Santa Barbara at 10:00 a.m. and climbed into a convertible. The rental agency didn't have the Ford Mustang he'd reserved but gave him keys to a Mitsubishi Eclipse Spyder for the weekend. The weather prediction was for blue skies and a high of ninety. As he drove south through Goleta, he stopped at a florist and picked out a dozen multi-colored roses and a vase. He put the wrapped bouquet on the passenger floor mat. The vase fit securely under the seat. The convertible let him savor the scenery of the ocean to his right and the mountains to his left as he continued down the Pacific Coast Highway toward Thousand Oaks. The hospice was an hour away and after driving thirty miles, he called Jennifer's room.

"Good morning," she said.

"I hope it will be. This is Ty Bannister. Can I stop by and visit with you?"

"Oh my gosh. Ty! You got my letter. Where are you?" He had hoped she'd be pleased. She sounded excited but her voice was soft.

"Let's see. I just passed Mugu Rock near Port Hueneme and I'm heading toward the Ventura Freeway."

"You're here? You're coming now?" Her voice became louder.

"Yes, if that's okay. I'd really like to talk to you before you call Madison."

"Sure. I just can't believe it. Did you come all the way out here just to see me?"

"Yes. And to see our daughter."

At the Kairos Kare facility, he checked in at the main desk. He told them he was a friend and they called Jennifer. An attendant came and escorted him to her room. Jennifer was propped up in her bed and stared at him.

He stopped at the side of her bed. "They told me it was okay to give you flowers." The attendant put the vase down on a cabinet and left the room. He noticed three of the walls were a pastel green; the longer wall with a window was painted a deeper green. Everything else in the room, even the upholstered armchairs, was white. He hadn't rehearsed his comments but had thought about what he wanted to say, as well as what he should say, to a dying woman. Walking over to the right side of Jennifer's bed, he leaned over, squeezed her hand softly, and kissed her on the forehead. Her eyes glistened with tears.

"You cried the last time I saw you," he said. Jennifer gave a quick laugh. Bannister didn't know if it was real or fake. He moved one of the two chairs closer to her bed. On the left side was a rolling metal stand with a couple of clear IV bags hooked up to her arm.

They spent the next half hour catching up with each other, just like any couple who hadn't seen each other in a long time might have done. Their conversation wasn't forced. She talked about her job, where she'd lived, and how her life changed after they found the tumor. Most of all, she wanted to talk about Madison. She told him that since she'd been admitted to hospice, Madison had visited her every night.

"She's an instructor this summer at a volleyball camp at Pepperdine University." Jennifer's voice rang with pride. "She calls me every day during her lunch hour."

"Why don't you call her now?" he urged. "If she's free tomorrow, I'd like to meet her for lunch, if she agrees."

Jennifer called Madison, who picked up right away. They talked for a minute and Jennifer confirmed Madison didn't have any plans yet for Sunday. Jennifer said, "Honey, I have a surprise for you. Your father is here with me right now. He'd like to speak with you." She handed him the phone.

He had thought about what he wanted to say but worried it wouldn't sound right. He also wanted to sound normal even if he didn't know what "normal" was.

"Hello, Madison. It's me. I know this whole thing has been a shock to both of us. But I want you to know this surprise is a wonderful one for me. I really want to meet you. How about lunch tomorrow?"

"That sounds great. I really don't know what to say right now. I can't believe you're here." Her voice was jubilant. "You may not believe this, but I was going to call you. When Mom told me about you and then showed me a copy of the letter she sent, I didn't know what to think."

"That makes two of us. What were your thoughts after you read the letter?" he asked.

"I was happy and then I really got pissed off. Excuse me. I took the letter and walked outside where I read it again slowly. All the time I was thinking, how could she have held this back from me for all these years? And why? I didn't deserve it. After I had my own pity party, I went back into Mom's room. We talked and cried and ended up hugging each other for a long time. Anyway, I'm not going to pick on her right now. Having a chance to see you in person will be a thousand times better than a phone call." She paused for a few seconds. "Where would you like to meet?"

"I'm staying at a hotel in Beverly Hills. What I was thinking is having lunch at noon at The Little Door Restaurant on West Third Street. Do you know where that is?"

"I've been by it but I've never eaten there."

"I could pick you up or meet you there. It's your choice."

"I'll meet you there. How about sending me a text message when you get there and tell me where you're sitting. Is that okay?"

"Sounds like a plan." He gave Madison his cell number and the address for the restaurant. He handed the phone back to Jennifer. The two women talked for a few more minutes then Jennifer ended with, "Like I told you before, honey. I'm so sorry. Try to find it in your heart to forgive me." Jennifer started sobbing and held the phone out to the side. She let Bannister take it from her.

"Madison, your mother's happy and a little bit overwhelmed at the same time. Let me talk to her for a while. You'll be able to talk this out tonight." Here he was having his first conversation with his daughter and already sounding like he was giving her advice.

He told Jennifer to be patient with herself and her daughter. This whole situation was a life changing event for all three of them. Hopefully, they'd find a way to resolve their issues. He needed to go to the Los Angeles office, but let Jennifer know that if things worked out, he and Madison would visit her together tomorrow.

Bannister left the hospice with mixed feelings. He popped a couple of Rolaids he'd picked up at the airport. Jennifer Van Otten was an attractive, strong woman. For someone dying, she looked good. They both knew that if she'd made a certain phone call twenty years ago, their lives might have gone in different directions. He wasn't going to speculate on what he might have done. He drove back to the Pacific Coast Highway and headed for the FBI office.

The interviews Ramirez had written were waiting for him. He visited with a couple of agents in the office with whom he had worked during his prior assignment. They were writing up some investigative reports but took a break to bring Bannister up to speed on LA's priorities before leading him to an empty interview room for his use. He marked some changes on the paperwork and faxed everything back to Ramirez in Atlanta before driving to his hotel in Beverly Hills.

CHAPTER 19

The next morning, Bannister got up at 6:15 a.m. He needed to keep busy and try to sort out his emotions before seeing Madison. He made a cup of coffee. Just one. His corner suite had two large windows that slanted dramatically inward. The sun was just rising and cast a glow across the gray and purple horizon of the San Gabriel Mountains. He drove to Griffith Park to jog. The last time he'd been there was to run in the Stuntmen's 10K race, which, instead of beginning with a starter's pistol, began with a stuntman falling off a thirty-foot tower.

He parked at the Los Feliz entrance and decided on a route to the LA Zoo and back. He jogged slowly for fifteen minutes, ran hard for four miles, then used the last fifteen minutes to cool down and enjoy the clear skies and smell of eucalyptus trees. On the way back, he stopped at Beverly Hills Juice and ordered a Banana Manna Almond shake to go. Best breakfast in a glass he'd had in a while.

After showering, reading the *Los Angeles Times*, and having another cup of coffee, he got dressed and went to the lobby. He went over a couple requests with the concierge. The Little Door Restaurant was a ten-minute walk away and he planned to get there early.

After pushing through two rustic wooden doors, he had a choice of four different themed rooms. He opted for the Garden Patio, a room with lush ferns and greenery as well as bougainvillea blooming with white and magenta flowers. A tiled Mexican fountain overflowed into a pool with koi gliding below the surface. There was one couple seated at the far end of the room. He chose a table opposite them toward the back with a view of the entire room.

Exactly at noon his phone vibrated. A text message from Madison said, "I'm here. Where R U?" He got up without responding and walked around the corner to the hostess stand where Madison was waiting.

She looked prettier than her picture. She was wearing black slacks with a black-and-white striped sweater. Her long blond hair had a bounce to it. She looked radiant.

"Hello . . ." There was a pause. "Mr. Bannister."

"Hello . . . daughter." They both smiled and he held his arms open. They hugged each other for a full minute. His throat closed up and, as they pushed apart, he had to take a long deep breath. The last time he felt this emotional was when he was standing at the grave site of his wife. Madison started crying.

"I'm sorry. I told myself I wouldn't do this," she said as he handed her a handkerchief.

"Let me show you to our table."

"I saw Mom last night. I think she was more excited than I am now. She said you were just like she remembered, tall and handsome. For so many years I wondered who my father was, what he looked like, what he did for a living. Mom would just say, 'Maybe one of these days you'll find the answers.'" Madison dabbed at her eyes and tilted her head.

"You may not find all of the answers, but some of your questions should get resolved."

"I'm happy, sad, and mad all at the same time," she said.

"Well, I'm happy, sad, and confused. I'm so happy we found each other, sad that we've missed out on so much time, and confused because I don't know what I should be saying to you or even what I think you might want to hear. Am I making any sense?"

"I think so," Madison said, looking at his face. "Gee, Mom didn't mention I have your eyes." As he pulled her chair out, he judged her to be maybe an inch taller than his girlfriend Robin, perhaps five foot ten.

"There's so much to talk about! Maybe we won't get to cover it all, but we can sure make a dent in it, right?"

"I hope so." Madison grinned as the waitress arrived with menus.

"Hope you have an appetite," he added.

"I do. I got up early this morning and went for a long run."

"Well, that makes two of us. We can eat without guilt." Madison picked up her napkin and arranged it three or four times on her lap before straightening her knife and fork alongside her plate. She laughed again and made him smile.

"The candle holder on our table is really different." Madison pointed at the three-legged wrought iron holder which stood three feet high with a solitary white candle on top. She gazed upward towards the ceiling. "And the large skylight makes me feel like we're dining outside."

Their waitress returned and asked for their drink order.

"I'd like an ice tea," Madison said. As if reading his thoughts, she added, "If you want a glass of wine or beer, go ahead."

He opted to stick with water.

Madison ordered the pistachio-crusted New Zealand snapper while Bannister chose the potato-crusted northern halibut.

As the waitress left, he reached across the top of the table and patted Madison's hand. "I don't intend to lie to you today. Hearing about you was a shock. But I'm really happy to have a daughter. It's just too bad that I never knew . . . and missed out on so much of your life."

"So, until Mom sent you that letter and picture, you never knew about me?"

"That's right. Flying out here I tried to figure it out, but just couldn't come up with the answers. We were both young back then and had only known each other for a week. We had our entire lives ahead of us. Your mom discovered she was pregnant and made the decision to go it alone. That had to be tough."

"If she had told you, would you have married her?"

"I don't know what I would have done. I told your mother I was in California visiting my parents. That was true. I didn't tell her I was reporting the next week for training at the FBI Academy. But wherever I was, I would never have let her make that decision alone. I guess she just didn't know me well enough."

"If she hadn't found out she was dying, I don't think she would have tried to find you."

"Maybe not. But I wouldn't punish her by demanding an answer to that. Let's go on the assumption your mother would have done this anyway, now that you're a young woman."

Madison studied her hands. "You know, at first when she said she'd found my father, I thought maybe Mom might have kept it a secret all these years because you weren't a nice man. I'm glad that wasn't the case. All I know now is that I don't want to be angry. I've got so many things to ask you—like I even made a list." She laughed.

"What was the first thing on it?"

"I wrote, 'Listen to him more than you talk.'"

"Well, I reminded myself to do that, too. I said, 'Remember, she's your daughter, not a suspect you're interviewing.'" Madison laughed again.

"How long are you staying?"

"I have to go back to Atlanta late tomorrow."

"Can we both go visit Mom tonight?"

"I'd like that."

Just then the manager came over to the table to inquire if their table was all right. When Bannister introduced himself earlier, he had asked the manager to take a couple of pictures.

As Bannister posed with his arm around his daughter, the manager took the first pictures of a father with his daughter.

Bannister told Madison it was "girls first" and she should try and tell him what she'd been up to for the past nineteen years. And she did. She bounced around from topic to topic, periodically apologized for rambling, smiled about a hundred times, and finally said, "Okay, it's your turn."

He told her about his upbringing, going to the private Webb School in Claremont for his high school years, then on a lacrosse scholarship to Dartmouth, the Marine Corps, and finally, the FBI. They found out they had more than a few things in common. She was a Spanish major and business minor. She was surprised he was fluent in Russian. They both were athletic and enjoyed running. He told her he'd been married and that she did not have any step-brothers or -sisters. She asked if he was seeing anyone, and he told her he had a girlfriend named Robin who was an FBI agent assigned to Washington, DC. He told her his mother was still alive and that although she used to live in Calabasas, California, now lived alone in Austin, Texas.

They discovered they both loved Italian food and hoped to visit Tuscany one day. When Madison was a sophomore in high school, her mother had insisted she learn how to cook. She owned a number of cookbooks and together they used to make dozens and dozens of different meals for two.

Their entrees arrived as Madison was talking about some of her favorite dishes. The time went by fast. They skipped dessert but ordered espresso.

"Where are you living?" he asked.

"I share a dorm suite on campus with three girls on the volleyball team."

"How do the four of you get along?"

"Great. Even though we have different majors and class schedules, we are all on the same team and that's really built a camaraderie among us."

He nodded and sipped his espresso. The moment stretched long, and Bannister experienced a rare moment of not knowing what to say next. Madison came to his rescue.

"There are hundreds of kids who have been adopted and spent lots of time trying to find out who their real parents are. I just knew that one day I'd find out who my father was."

"Well, during all that time you knew you had a father. Until last week, I never knew I had a daughter."

"So, do you feel like we're strangers?" Madison asked.

"No. We were strangers before today, but now that I've met you we're not. Am I making sense?"

"Yes. Then it'd be okay if I call you?" Madison asked, with a plaintive smile.

"I'd like that. We could also e-mail each other. You can let me know what classes you're taking or whom your team is playing or anything you feel like writing about."

"E-mail sounds great. I know from watching TV that the FBI is not a nine-to-five job." She chuckled.

"Even so, promise me you'll call anytime you feel like talking."

"Thank you. I will."

They verified each other's cell phone numbers. He wrote hers down as she entered his as an emergency contact. When she finished, she didn't say anything for a few seconds and once again, her expression grew distant.

"I know Mom's going to die soon. I'm really trying to be okay with it, but I don't know. We've talked about it for hours, even though I didn't feel like it. Mom said I have to be prepared. How do I do that? I don't know what I will be thinking. I don't know how I will be acting. I feel a whole lot better knowing there's someone I can call."

"Absolutely. I insist. Your mom told me she's arranged for a brief memorial service at the hospital's chapel. When that happens, I'd like to be there with you."

"Thanks." Madison's eyes welled up again. He handed her his handkerchief again and told her to keep it. Madison thanked him for the wonderful lunch. After he paid the bill, she said her car was parked at the Beverly Center mall. He insisted on walking her there.

"Mom got me my car." When they arrived at the mall's garage, he noted her car was a ten-year old white Volvo. "I really wanted a Jeep or convertible but mom said she wanted me driving something safe. It's definitely safe, but as you can tell, it sure isn't a 'guy magnet.'"

He smiled. "During lunch you mentioned you don't have to be back at your volleyball camp until Tuesday. I was thinking about tomorrow morning. If you don't have plans, I could take you out for coffee and maybe you'd be willing to show me around the campus?" He figured this would be something easy to do, and they'd be able to just talk some more and get to know each other a little better.

"I don't have any plans for tomorrow. That sounds great."

"I'd love for you to come out and visit Atlanta sometime. I have a big house and a great kitchen where you could cook up some of those meals you talked about." He knew she'd be facing a whole series of firsts without her mother. Like Thanksgiving and Christmas and all the other days the two of them shared in the past. "Why don't you think about visiting during one of your school breaks? We can talk about it later."

He opened her car door and she turned and gave him another hug and kiss on the cheek before driving away. On the way back to the hotel, he walked past store fronts for Gucci, Burberry, and Louis Vuitton. Through the distant haze he could make out the large white Hollywood sign on the hill. For many people, this was a city where they could search for glitz, glamour, and the world of make believe. For him, it was a city where he was finding reality.

CHAPTER 20

Madison buzzed Bannister from the hotel's lobby. The valet drove his rental car, top down, to the front of the hotel. Bannister and Madison jumped in and took off. The last time he was with a blonde in a convertible was ten months ago when he took Robin for a spin through his neighborhood in the Mercedes Gullwing. Bannister hadn't yet figured out how he was going to tell Robin he had a daughter.

"I know right now it might seem a little strange to both of us, but you don't mind if I call you 'Dad' do you?" Madison asked.

"No, I don't mind and yes, it's strange hearing it," is all he could think to say.

"I mean, I know people call you Ty, or Mr. Bannister, or Special Agent Bannister. Right? Now somebody—me—gets to call you something that no one else can—Dad. Pretty neat!" Madison smiled and giggled.

He had asked Madison to give him a tour of the campus. A few years ago, when he was in Los Angeles on assignment, he'd been able to see the southern end of the campus from his desk on the seventeenth floor of the federal building. He'd visited UCLA's medical school as well as the track and field complex. He just never found a reason to walk around the college's grounds.

He parked at Canyon Point Residential Suites where Madison and her roommates lived. Since she was the only one in town that weekend, she showed him her living quarters. He wanted to pick up the two white tied trash bags in the kitchen but pretended he didn't see them when they left. They walked across campus, past the track and field stadium and Pauley Pavilion, stopping at the Bruin Bistro. It would have been easy to grab a cup of coffee or brunch at the hotel, but Bannister wanted his daughter to pick a coffee shop where she felt comfortable. Right now, he wanted her to be in surroundings that set her at ease.

Almost nineteen years without knowing about each other. Her entire life. They decided to answer each other's questions over lattes and blueberry scones. He listened as Madison talked about what it was like to have to grow up faster than she wanted, being a latchkey kid at twelve, and learning to do a lot of chores around the home since her mother put in long hours at the hospital. She told him how she discovered she had genuine talent at volleyball and how she had come to major in Spanish and business.

She wanted to know what it was really like to be an FBI agent. Bannister talked about the initial training and answered as many of her questions as he could. He mentioned she'd probably have additional questions after he gave her a personal tour of the Atlanta office when she came to visit. She beamed at that idea.

An hour later he was driving back to the hotel. They decided to meet at 7:00 p.m. that evening at Kairos Kare. His red-eye flight was scheduled to depart at 10:30 p.m. and would bring him into Atlanta at 6:00 a.m.

Waiting at the hotel were three gold-framed pictures of Bannister with Madison. One was for him. That evening at the hospice he gave the other two pictures to Jennifer and Madison. His daughter hugged him. Jennifer clutched hers to her chest, saying, "Oh, Ty, you can't believe how happy you've made me. I will look at this picture every morning and evening. Thank you from the bottom of my heart."

They visited another hour. Madison gave the nurse her cell phone to take photos of the three of them. As Jennifer started nodding off, Bannister kissed her on the forehead and told her he had to leave.

"Stay safe," she said in a soft voice.

"I will."

As he turned away, Bannister knew that was the last time he would see her alive. Madison walked him to the lobby.

"Call me whenever you want to talk. Okay?" he said.

"I will. I know Mom doesn't have much time, and you'll be the first person I call." Madison shuddered slightly, put her head down, and was silent.

He put his arms around her. His heart ached for her and he wanted to say words which would give her comfort, but all of this was new. Jennifer and Madison had a wonderful relationship which was coming to a natural end. Bannister knew that grieving the loss of her mother would be the hardest thing Madison had ever faced. He also knew that facing a hard task was less burdensome when others were there to lend a hand. He wanted Madison to know she could take his hand during her time of grief.

"It's okay. My spirit is with yours. You're not alone, honey. Gain strength from knowing that. We'll get through this together." He took out a new handkerchief and dabbed away a couple of her tears. She smiled and they hugged again before he said goodbye.

While driving to the airport, Bannister pulled out Amy Dixon's business card and called her. Dixon was a Beverly Hills lawyer who specialized in family law. She was an expert on pre-nuptial agreements, property rights of domestic partners, and adoptions. He'd gotten to know her after saving her parents from losing a small fortune in a Bernie Madoff-type Ponzi scheme. The last time he had seen her, she gave him her card and said, "I owe you big time. If I can ever help you, call me."

"This is Ty Bannister." He waited for his name to register. "I apologize for calling you after working hours. I thought I'd go straight through to voicemail."

"I'm glad you called. I needed a break. I'm propped up in my bed reading some legal briefs. Is this FBI business?"

"No, personal."

"Where are you? LA?"

"I'm heading to LAX to catch a flight back to Atlanta. It's a long story. Does your offer to help me still stand?"

"Absolutely."

"Then, I'd like to retain your professional services to assist my daughter." For the next ten minutes he filled Amy in on Madison and Jennifer. She agreed to represent his daughter. He told her he would call Madison tomorrow and let her know Amy had agreed to meet her and handle everything to do with her mother's final medical bills, insurance, funeral expenses and any other legal requirements. All billing would go directly to him.

———*ᴥ*———

Back in Atlanta, Kevin Middleton was pacing in the lobby of the Airport Holiday Inn. Over his shoulder was a small blue and white canvas travel bag.

"You're late. I was getting worried," Middleton said to a man who had walked directly up to him after entering the lobby.

Looking around and noticing they were alone, Hassan Fadi said, "Everything in due course." He motioned to a quiet corner where there was a table with barrel-shaped chairs. "You said everything went smoothly."

"Yes. Here is the spice kit you requested." Middleton put the travel bag on the floor between where the two of them were sitting. "The bottle of Japanese sea salt is what you're interested in." Middleton smiled. He had purchased an eight-pack of assorted spices which came in a wooden case. Seven of the bottles contained what the labels said and had never been opened. The one marked Japanese sea salt had been topped off with what Middleton had removed from the CDC lab on Friday.

"That bottle can be used as it is, or you can dissolve the contents in water, making an injectable saline solution. You know, I never asked you what you were going to do with it." Middleton said.

"That was wise."

"What if I had substituted something else?" Middleton asked.

"It will be checked. We are very thorough. If it is not what you claim, then you are a dead man," Fadi said, showing yellow teeth in a grin.

"Don't worry. I kept my part of our agreement."

"Then you will be much richer." Hassan took the travel bag with the wooden case and exited to the parking lot. Middleton waited five minutes, as instructed, before he left to return to his apartment.

—◦◦◦—

Bannister drove directly home from the airport, showered, and changed clothes before heading to the office. He knew it was early, but there was one call that had to be made.

"Robin, this is Ty. When you're free this evening, call me. Everything's fine, but I need to talk to you."

Last week he sent her a dozen roses commemorating a year since their first date. Robin had called to thank him as soon as she got home from the office. It was great talking to her. The realities of the job hadn't yet diminished her love of the work. They chatted about her counter-terrorism assignments before the conversation returned to their fabulous getaway at the Galley Bay Resort in Antigua. Although it had been months since he'd seen her, his memories of Robin were so vivid it seemed like only yesterday they were together. The vacation they shared convinced both of them they were in love with each other. They agreed to maintain a commuter-type relationship for a year. See what happened. Neither of them knew what the separation would bring. The problem was that neither of them was commuting to see each other. Tonight would be a bombshell. He only hoped it wouldn't destroy what they had.

Robin didn't wait until the evening but called at 7:30 a.m. She said, "I don't think I've ever received a call from you so early in the morning. I was in the shower when you phoned. I've got some news for you too."

"I'm all ears," Bannister replied.

"Well, I'm about fifteen minutes from the office. Why don't you go first? I insist."

"I really don't know where to start. It's been a helluva week. I flew in on a red-eye from LA. I visited with a daughter I never knew I had."

He waited for the news to sink in and for Robin to say something. The line was quiet.

"Just hear me out, then," he said. Bannister spent the next five minutes explaining the week's revelations. "Well, that's why I had to call you." More silence. "Say something!"

"I feel like someone in shock. My mind's a blank. Did you have any inkling of this? Did the mother ever contact you in the past?"

"The answer to both questions is no."

"Are you sure this girl is really your daughter?"

He relaxed a little hearing her business-like tone but felt somewhat stupid since he hadn't even thought about paternity. After nineteen years of silence, why would Jennifer lie about something like that? She wouldn't. He was sure of it. "If the mother is to be believed then it's true. It was a bolt out of the blue. I never had a clue. I never imagined something like this happening to me."

He could hear Robin taking a deep breath. "Is there anything I can do for you?"

"I don't think so. Obviously, there are some issues I have to handle. Right now, I don't see it affecting our relationship, but give me a couple of days to get my thoughts together. You know that sounds like something Dr. Phil on TV would recommend, but it does make sense, doesn't it?"

"Yes. I still can't believe this. It just had to be an absolute surprise to you."

"On the flight back I kept asking myself what I should be thinking. What should I be doing? How am I going to break this news to Robin? How's it going to affect our future? I just had lots and lots of questions."

"Well, I wish I had answers for you. This will take some time to process."

"I agree. We're not going to solve anything right away. You said you had some news."

"I almost forgot. One of my cases has a significant Atlanta connection. My supervisor and I are coming to Atlanta next week to brief your task force. And, I think I can read your mind—he doesn't know about us."

"That's great. I mean about your coming here. I've missed you and can't wait to see you. I really mean that."

"I know you do. I love you, Ty. Call me when you want to talk."

"I will."

CHAPTER 21

Bannister had a list of investigative priorities for his second day back from LA. First was a surprise interview of Kevin Middleton, a microbiologist who worked in the most secure lab at the Centers for Disease Control. David Ash, the CDC's Director of Security, had made arrangements for Bannister and Ramirez.

The FBI agents arrived at the CDC's security center early and were given access to a briefing room. David Ash escorted Middleton to the room and left after introductions were made. Middleton was wearing khaki slacks, a blue polo shirt, and loafers. He had on glasses and an Atlanta Braves baseball cap. To try and put Middleton at ease, Bannister shook hands with him. He had what Bannister called the "fish shake," a soft, loose handshake which to Bannister conveyed someone with a weak personality.

"Have a seat." Bannister pointed to the chair directly opposite him. Ramirez sat to Middleton's right and slightly behind him so she could take notes without his observing her.

"What's this all about?" Middleton asked.

"We believe you know someone we're investigating." The color drained from Middleton's face and beads of sweat started forming on his forehead. Bannister was surprised he was this unsettled.

"Are you aware we are looking for Terry Hines?"

"Yes," he replied. After his answer he leaned over and pulled up both of his socks, a classic sign of nervousness and deception.

"Hines jumped bail and is one of the Marshal Service's most wanted fugitives. How do you know him?" Bannister asked.

"We were both Teeks at Georgia Tech."

"Teeks?"

"Yeah, Tau Kappa Epsilon fraternity. We roomed in the frat house our last two years."

"When was the last time you saw or heard from him?"

"Two years ago, we had a reunion of sorts on campus. Our frat won the overall intramural championship and all local alums were invited to the celebration. I saw Terry at the party and we caught up with each other. We reminisced about some of the kayaking jaunts we use to take to Dahlonega and whined about how job pressures were keeping us from staying in shape. Hines said he had a good job at Global Waters here in Atlanta."

"Did he know where you worked?"

"I told him I did research on dangerous biotoxins like anthrax and Ebola. I did add it was in the most secure lab in the country." Middleton moved his head from side to side, obviously remembering his boast. Bannister moved him back on track.

"Did Hines ever talk about his goals or ambitions?"

"Sure, we all did. He wanted to make a ton of money and eventually buy a beach house. I guess he screwed up big time."

"Did he have any close friends?"

"Nah, he wasn't really close to anyone. He had a lot of one-time dates."

"Why was that?"

"Terry was full of himself. You know, he had a big ego and talked a lot. I think he turned off his dates with the boasting and focus on himself. It's warm in here." Middleton took off his glasses and hat and put them on the table. He wiped his forehead with his left hand and then, with his left index finger, he rubbed his left eye. Another indicator of lying. When he looked up, Bannister thought he knew the reason why.

"You know who Kendall Briggs is, don't you?" Bannister asked. Middleton opened his mouth but didn't say anything. Ramirez looked up from her notes.

"Yes. What's this got to do with Terry Hines?" Middleton crossed his arms in front.

Bannister ignored his question. "How did you know Briggs?"

"His picture was on the front page of the newspaper. I read the story about his murder." Middleton's voice got louder. "I knew about him and am sorry that he's dead."

"Did you ever meet him in person?" Bannister asked.

"No." With his left hand, Middleton covered his mouth. One more indicator of deception.

"You don't intend to lie to me this morning, do you?"

"No, why would I?"

"I don't know. That's what I want to find out."

"As I said earlier, what's this got to do with Terry Hines?"

"Hines threatened Kendall Briggs."

"So, in Briggs's line of work that's not so unusual is it?"

"It is when the person threatened ends up murdered. Let's start over. Have you been to Florida in the past year?"

"I don't think so."

"Let me help your memory. How about the Spa at Egret Bay?"

"Ah, shit." Middleton hung his head down. "You know about that? Look, is that going to affect my security clearance?"

"It could if you continue lying to me."

Middleton looked up and wrung his hands.

"I spent a week there. It was expensive and didn't meet my expectations."

"Which were what?" Bannister asked.

"I thought there'd be a whole lot more people. I was thinking it might be a Club Med type of experience without clothes. They confiscated my bottle of Crown Royal when I checked in. The clients there were all pretty damn smart and well connected. I got my picture taken with one gal who had great tats and better ta-tas."

Middleton laughed. Bannister and Ramirez didn't.

They spent another half hour questioning Middleton about what he could remember of the people at the spa. He confirmed the information Hannah Michaels had already given. He didn't get the last names of any of the guests. He was positive he would never go back or try a naturalist retreat again.

"Do you have to report my going to a nudist camp?"

"No. A person's sexual orientation or behavior is only a security concern if it involves a criminal offense, indicates a personality or emotional disorder, or makes the person vulnerable to coercion, exploitation or duress. None of those apply to you, do they?"

"No."

Bannister believed him this time.

"Well, Kevin, you're free to return to the lab. Agent Ramirez will stop by tomorrow morning to show you some pictures of people you may be able to identify."

———

During his lunch break, Middleton called the emergency telephone number he was given. It was answered immediately by a voice on the other end that he recognized as Fadi.

"We need to talk. The FBI was here at my job. They interviewed me about our friend in London. I didn't tell them anything, but I'm worried," Middleton said.

"Call this number back at five o'clock. Finish your shift in a normal manner," Fadi said, ending the call.

Fadi then issued new orders to members of his cell. One of his men, who would be flying to Egypt tomorrow, met with a prostitute. He dropped her off at the designated hotel along the strip frequented by women of the night. He gave her $400 to rent a hotel room for the evening. She agreed to do three things. First, use the name of one of her street associates when registering. Second, tell the desk clerk she needed a room for the night because her husband was looking for her and she was afraid. She would pay cash since her husband had the ability to track her credit card usage. She would tip the desk clerk $100 since she did not want any trouble. The last thing she did to earn a quick $250 was hand over the room key to Fadi's associate. The associate watched her as she sauntered from the front of the hotel and entered a Denny's restaurant across the street.

Before leaving work, Middleton called Fadi as arranged. He was instructed to show up at the Roundtable Motel just south of the Atlanta airport, room 103, 9:00 p.m. sharp.

CHAPTER 22

"Ty, it's me, Mercedes."

"Where are you?"

"At the CDC. Middleton was a no-show this morning. I cooled my heels for an hour with Dave Ash before he called Middleton's cell phone. He also texted and e-mailed Middleton an urgent message. No response. Ash is waiting till noon before he sends security officers to Middleton's apartment. What do you want me to do?"

"Have Ash call me immediately if he hears from Middleton or finds out where he is. You may as well return to the office."

"Okay," said Ramirez.

Bannister spotted Derek Barnes and waved him over to his desk. Barnes then briefed him on the latest reports about Kendall Briggs.

"The computer evidence team made mirror images of the drives on both his personal and business laptops. They printed out all messages, which I finished reviewing. From a professional viewpoint, not much to pursue. His e-mails to the US Attorney and staff as well as outsiders were all routine. No evidence showing any problems. No out of office contacts with Sherrill Newsome. As far as we can tell, except for the nudist camp episode, his sexual activities seemed normal. No porn or kinky behavior."

"What about his appointment calendars?" Bannister asked.

"The guy was meticulous about listing all appointments. He stayed busy, worked out a lot at the Ravinia Health Club, and had a lot of recent interaction with board members of the High Museum of Art. We've interviewed the staff at both places and he got along well with everyone. No one recalls any arguments or indication of any kind of trouble. His participation in the Sierra Club was purely via financial contributions. Supposedly, when he was at Stanford he did a lot of hiking, but no one we interviewed here can recall him hitting any of the Georgia trails. We interviewed two jump masters at the Atlanta Skydiving Center where Briggs completed three static line parachute jumps last summer. They recall he came alone, was an excellent student, handled the jumps well, but never returned. We're busy interviewing all people listed in his Day-Timer for the last three months."

"Good. Any developments from physical evidence?"

Barnes turned over a couple of pages until he found what he was looking for.

"Trace evidence collected four hairs from the front and back of Briggs's blazer. Microscopic examination determined several things. The hairs are human, Caucasian, and from the head. The approximate ages of the persons from whom they originated are between thirty and forty. He could have picked them up anywhere he wore that coat. They're trying to see if there's enough for DNA analysis."

Barnes continued reading from the lab's summary. "The GBI techs used acid to raise a stamped number on the melted metal object found in his car. It matched up with a statue sold to him by Hannah Michaels. The killers may have struck him with it. The lab also got a hit on a thumb print from the underside of the toilet seat in the bathroom of Briggs's bedroom. It belongs to Dr. Theresa Andrews." Barnes shot Bannister a smirk.

"Well, I'll have to add that tidbit to my list of things to ask the doctor the next time we interview her."

Bannister reviewed paperwork for a couple of hours before taking a quick break to go downstairs to the building's deli where he grabbed a sandwich to go. Waiting to ride the elevator up was Agent Ted Mims. Bannister sensed his awkwardness.

"Are you managing okay?" he asked him, trying to sound sincere.

Mims looked Bannister in the eyes. "We're seeing a marriage counselor and hoping to work things out. Thanks for your concern." When the elevator reached his floor, Mims gave a quick nod of his head and stepped out. Bannister thought about how tough it must be for Mims when his cell phone rang. He didn't recognize the number.

"Agent Bannister. This is Detective Roy Miller, Atlanta PD."

"How can I help you?"

"Do you know a Kevin Middleton?"

"Yes, why?" he answered as he walked back to his desk. He had a bad feeling about how this conversation was going to go.

"He had your business card with him."

His curiosity peaked, Bannister asked, "Has he been arrested?"

"No, he's been murdered."

"Holy shit! How'd it happen? I just interviewed him yesterday."

"Two hours ago, the manager at the Roundtable Motel on Riverdale Road called. One of their maids came screaming to the office that a man was dead in Room 103. He had a wallet identifying him as Kevin Middleton."

Bannister considered Middleton to be the linchpin to what might be a terrorist plot. His death would definitely be a setback to their investigation. "How was he killed?"

"He was lying on his back on the hotel bed with a switchblade knife sticking out of his heart. The ME just released his body. I sent a team to Middleton's apartment off Boulevard Drive in Decatur and I'm calling his boss at the CDC to obtain the next of kin. I know you can't tell me if he was a source of yours, but was he a witness or subject in one of your cases? We're trying to figure out who killed him."

"My partner and I interviewed him yesterday morning at his workplace. He had a past connection to Terry Hines, on the US Marshal's Fifteen Most Wanted Fugitives List."

"Hines was that domestic terrorist perp, right?" Miller asked.

"Correct. Are you still at the motel?"

"Yeah, I'm out in the parking lot. Probably be here for another hour."

"I'd like to bring my partner out there and take a look-see, if you don't mind." Middleton's death could not be a coincidence.

"No problem," Miller said.

"Quick question. Did Middleton rent the room?"

"No. We'll talk when you get here."

On the way over, Bannister briefed Ramirez on what the detective had told him.

"Is this coincidental or what?" Ramirez asked.

"Don't know for sure. Middleton's divorce was supposed to be final this week. Maybe he decided to jump start his return to the single life."

"Well, sounds like someone jumped him instead."

As Bannister pulled into the motel's parking lot, Dave Ash called from the CDC.

"Atlanta PD just notified me Middleton's been murdered. Man, I can't believe this has happened." Ash said. He was quiet for a few seconds. "They wanted his emergency contact information. I gave them the name of his wife. They're sending an officer and detective to her house to break the news."

"I just arrived at the crime scene and am going to talk with the lead detective. When I finish I'll come to your office," Bannister said.

"I'd appreciate that. Anything you want me doing on this end?" Ash asked.

"Since we don't know who's responsible for his death, I'd hold off notifying co-workers for a while. The homicide squad will sort things out. I suggest securing his work area and deactivating his facility badges and computer access."

"I'll handle that right now. I still can't believe this has happened."

I can't either, Bannister thought as he and Ramirez stepped out of the Bureau car. They were approached by one of the uniformed officers who pointed out Detective Miller leaning against a black Dodge Charger. After introductions, Bannister and Ramirez accompanied Miller to the outside of Room 103.

"The techs have finished photographing and processing the scene. The body's been removed to the morgue." Miller said.

"Can you give us a summary of what you know?" Bannister asked.

Miller flipped open a small green field notebook and put on a pair of silver reading glasses. He also put a toothpick in his mouth to complete the look of an experienced detective.

"Yesterday afternoon the clerk working the motel's four-to-midnight shift had just clocked in when a black female approached the desk. She requested a room for the night. The clerk thought she might be a hooker by the way she was dressed. Anyway, he listened to her story and bought it."

"What story?"

"She was afraid of her husband and was scheduled to testify against him tomorrow in court downtown. The clerk normally gets a credit card impression even if the customer pays cash, but the woman said she didn't want to take a chance of her husband tracking her card. The clerk pointed out he wasn't charging the credit card but got tired of arguing with the woman and finally overlooked the motel's policy when she tipped him $50. She paid cash for one night, took the key to Room 103 and left."

"What name did she use?" Bannister asked.

"Tamika Johnson."

"What about a car?"

"The clerk didn't see a vehicle and didn't ask."

"Did Johnson's name check out?"

"Yeah. Three priors for prostitution. We pulled her mug shots and showed a photo spread to the clerk. He said Johnson may have been the woman but he wasn't sure. There's a bulletin out on her now. We'll compare latents we lifted in the room to her known prints."

"What about Middleton's vehicle?"

"That's the vic's Camry over there." Miller pointed to a light blue car parked directly in front of room 105. "We processed the car for trace evidence in case this Johnson rode with him to the hotel."

Miller opened the door to room 103. The three of them stepped inside the doorway of the stuffy room and looked at the layout.

"Can you describe the scene as you found it?" Bannister asked.

"The victim was lying on his back on the bed. The comforter and sheets, which had been pulled halfway down, were underneath him. His socks and shoes were on the floor at the bottom of the nightstand. The table lamp was on. The vic's belt was unhitched and his zipper was pulled down. There were no signs of sexual activity.

"His arms were out at a forty-five-degree angle, palms down. A four-and-a-half-inch switchblade knife was buried to the hilt in his chest. The knife had been plunged in from the victim's left side at a slight angle. It missed the sternum and went directly into the heart. The ME said death would have been almost instant. By the way, in case anyone second guessed me, I ruled out suicide since there were no prints on the knife handle." Miller grinned for effect.

Bannister thought the stabbing might be the work of a pro. "Do you have a time of death?" he asked as Ramirez took notes.

"Best guess, based on body temperature and lividity, was between nine and eleven last night."

Ramirez and Bannister moved closer to the nightstand. A pint bottle of Jim Beam bourbon and two glasses sat on top.

"Both glasses were half full when we got here. I sent the contents to toxicology in case the victim was drugged. Only the bottle and glass on the right had fingerprints on them. I'm guessing the vic's."

"What else did you find in the room?" Bannister asked.

"Nothing except his wallet, which was tossed on the floor near his shoes. No cash but his credit cards and other wallet stuffers were inside. He was wearing an Omega watch on his left wrist. His car keys and the room key were on the nightstand next to the bottle. There was no clothing, toiletries or toothbrush, et cetera in the bathroom. No prophylactics or wrappers. The trash can was empty."

"So, how do you think this went down?"

"Well, there's a murder here every three days. I've either worked the cases or read the reports on every one of Atlanta's for the past fifteen years. And this one smells strange. It also looks staged."

"How so?"

"It's meant to look like some hooker killed her john, but some things don't click. Nine out of ten times the victim rents the room, not the hooker or her pimp. They don't want to leave a paper trail in case something turns to shit. And why complicate things with some song and dance about a husband stalking her? We know this Tamika Johnson picked up the room key at 4:00 p.m. Most of the action in that area is not the afternoon delight variety. Why so early?" Miller glanced at his notebook. "Who was using the room and what was happening between 4:00 p.m. and 9:00 p.m.? Who got to the room first, or did Johnson and the victim arrive together? When I called the security office at the CDC, their director came on the line and said Middleton left work at 4:55 p.m."

"So, you'll need to account for his activities for four hours," Bannister said.

"Right."

"What's your opinion about the inside of this room?" Bannister waved his arm from left to right.

"If the woman was working alone, you'd expect her to at least sit on the bed with the victim while either he or she opened his pants. No indication of any foreplay. There was no sign anyone used the toilet or bathroom sink. No signs of a struggle in the room with the exception of the knife sticking out of Middleton's chest. If the hooker and her pimp planned to roll the victim and the pimp put a choke hold on him, he'd be unconscious in eight seconds. They could have taken his money and left. Quick and easy. When he came to he might not even report the crime. Makes no sense to kill him." Detective Miller put his notebook back in his coat pocket.

"So, what's next?" Bannister asked.

"I have a team of officers checking the neighborhood to see if anyone saw anything. No one stayed in room 105. The couple in 107 arrived at 10:30 p.m. and didn't hear any sounds from 103. My officers are checking nearby liquor stores for any purchases last night of Jim Beam. Either the victim or the killer brought it to the motel room. I know it's just a hunch, but if we can identify a sale, they all have cameras that might give us a photo of our victim or perp."

"Good thinking."

"Now it's your turn. As I said earlier, I called the number on the CDC employee badge in Middleton's wallet. It went to their security office and I broke the news to their security director. You mentioned interviewing Middleton yesterday about Terry Hines. Any chance our victim's involved with Hines or is knee-deep in some kind of terrorist conspiracy?" Miller twisted the toothpick hanging from the corner of his mouth.

"Never say never, but right now I don't think so. But as I've told my partner many times, I'm not a big believer in coincidences."

"It's a long shot, but maybe Hines is the one who arranged to meet this Middleton for some reason. But that's assuming he's back in the country. No indication of that, is there?" Miller asked.

"No," Bannister said. "This whole thing stinks to high heaven. See what you come up with. I'll call you tomorrow."

———✿✿✿———

As they approached the guardhouse at the CDC, Bannister got a call on his cell.

"It's me, Roy Miller. I think we need to meet sooner rather than later. Middleton's definitely knee-deep in something."

"What makes you say that?" Bannister asked.

"The detective I sent to check out his apartment found an envelope on Middleton's desk. It had ten grand in it."

CHAPTER 23

A fter parking at the CDC, Bannister called Witt, who was managing the Counterterrorism Task Force until the new supervisor arrived from Washington.

"I was just leaving the office," Witt said. "I've got tickets tonight for *Les Miserables* at the Fox Theater. So, what have you found out about this Middleton murder?"

Bannister felt like saying Inspector Javert was leading the investigation. About once a week, Witt managed to name drop or say something snobbish. Bannister took a breath, and then said, "Atlanta PD is trying to figure out who killed him. Detective Miller, their top homicide investigator, has the ticket on the case and has agreed to meet us at the office tomorrow. We have a lot of unconnected dots. Mercedes Ramirez and I are at the CDC where we're meeting with their security director in a few minutes."

"Brief me first thing in the morning," Witt said.

"Will do. Enjoy the show." Putting Witt off, at least for the night, might give them a chance to find some answers.

He and Ramirez were ushered into Dave Ash's office. Ash was lanky with dark hair around the ears, bald on top. Today Ash was wearing a charcoal gray suit. His appearance contrasted with that of the frowning man standing next to him. The fellow was a solid, square-shouldered, gray-haired man in a white lab coat. Ash introduced him.

"This is Dr. Klaus Wulfsberg. He's our top epidemiologist and our man in charge of the outbreak team. He's the national point of contact for the four hundred laboratories and 14,000 scientists in the country having access to deadly germs and viruses."

After the introductions, Ash went on, "We may have a serious problem."

Bannister asked, "With Middleton's death?"

"No. With what might be missing."

Ash had a big office. Opposite his desk was a large oval glass coffee table. He gestured to two square upholstered chairs opposite a couch. Bannister and Ramirez took the cue. Ash rolled his desk chair out to one side, and Wulfsberg took a seat on the couch. Ash's face was expressionless and pale as he leaned forward.

"I say 'might.' After your call, we followed protocol and sealed off Middleton's work area and secured his locker. I asked Gloria Sanchez, Middleton's partner, to assist one of Klaus's team members with conducting an inventory of all viruses, pathogens, and cultures he had signed out or was working on."

"And something was missing?" Bannister asked.

"I'll answer that," Wulfsberg said. "Two crystal cards of BSE molecular base are unaccounted for."

"Maybe you should translate that for them," Ash said, nodding in their direction.

"At least for me," Bannister said. "Ramirez was a microbiologist who worked here before becoming an agent." Ramirez gave a quick smile.

"BSE stands for bovine spongiform encephalitis. It's commonly referred to as mad cow disease. Middleton and Sanchez were doing research on the transmissibility and prevention of BSE prions from spreading in infected hosts," Wulfsberg said.

"When I worked here we used plug-based protein crystallization for specimens we studied. I'm not familiar with crystal cards," Ramirez said.

"A year ago, we developed flexible crystal cards for storing pathogens. They're still in the experimental stage and not available to the private sector. Think of the cards as the new 'iPad' for microbiologists," Wulfsberg said.

"What's the amount of the pathogen we're talking about?" Ramirez asked.

"Volume wise, the two cards would have a culture area about the width of your thumb nail," Wulfsberg answered.

"How many cattle could that infect?" Ramirez asked.

Ash put his hands up in the air.

"Time out. I don't think we should start speculating on worst case scenarios. Right now, all we know is one of our employees has been murdered and maybe, just maybe, some of the pathogen base he was using in his research is missing. It might have been misplaced or possibly destroyed."

"I don't think so," Wulfsberg said, earning a glare from Ash.

"Then go ahead," Ash said. "If you've got an answer, I'd like to hear it." His voice rose and his face flushed.

"We store the world's most deadly viruses in freezers four stories beneath BSL-4. There are different temperatures for different diseases. And some, like smallpox which is stored at -255 degrees, are so dangerous they have to be reconstituted above ground."

"What do you mean, reconstituted?" Bannister asked.

"Think recombined. Different researchers might be cleared for only one-third of the virus and would require the presence of the other two cleared personnel to obtain a real sample. In any event, I had three people review the video coverage of Middleton's lab for the past thirty days. Only four employees besides Middleton and Sanchez accessed the lab. They were there to observe and discuss a promising study on which Sanchez was the primary. Their total actual time in the lab was ninety minutes each. No suspicious behavior was detected. We've double-checked all inventories, current experiments, as well as all written logs and computer printouts. The only anomaly concerns the BSE prion stockpile. It should total a hundred grams, a little under a quarter pound. That was the amount verified two weeks ago. Today ten grams, or the amount that would fit on two crystal cards, is missing."

"Do you have an opinion about what may have happened?" Bannister asked.

"Yes. Someone walked out with it."

"Come on, Klaus. You're jumping to conclusions!" Ash said.

"That's part of my job!" Wulfsberg paused and looked at the two FBI agents. "I'm in charge of several first responder teams, which are activated in case of a biological outbreak or premeditated attack. Some of the team members refer to me as Dr. Doom because I'm constantly involved with planning responses to the worst cases. Some people call it 'sick think.' This situation may fall into that category. We're pretty sure Sanchez and the other employees didn't remove anything. Middleton was putting in some long days and working irregular hours. He may have deliberately taken BSE prions out of the CDC."

"With the surveillance coverage you have and decontamination procedures, how could he have managed that?" Bannister asked.

"It's speculative, but where there's a will, there's usually a way," Wulfsberg answered.

Looking at Ash, Bannister asked, "Is there anything about Middleton that might lead someone to think he would do something like that?"

"He was undergoing a five-year reinvestigation for his top-secret security clearance. He'd completed the paperwork and turned it in to me. I flagged two suitability issues that needed to be resolved during an interview. He was in debt, and it didn't look good down range for him."

"How much debt?"

"He owed $200,000 on his mortgage. That wasn't an issue, but he owed $25,000 to American Express and had $19,000 charged to other credit accounts." Bannister twisted his mouth and slowly shook his head. Ash went on. "His divorce is final today. It orders him to pay his wife $1,800 a month in alimony and child support."

"How much does he earn each year?" Bannister asked.

"He's at $88,500, excluding overtime," Ash responded.

"You said there was a second issue."

"His wife saw me six weeks ago and mentioned she was going

through with their divorce. But the reason she wanted to talk to me was to let me know her husband had turned into a compulsive gambler and had racked up the $25,000 in debt on their American Express account without her knowledge. He resisted getting help and declined to see a marriage counselor. That's why she filed. She came to my office to see if I could get him some help. She knew if he lost his job they'd lose everything, meaning the house, the kids' education, and the whole ball of wax."

"Well, he found money somewhere," Bannister said.

"What do you mean?" Ash asked.

"Detective Miller's team went to Middleton's apartment an hour ago. They called me after they found an envelope sitting on his desk with $10,000 in it."

The room grew quiet. Ash stood up, interlacing his fingers on top of his head. He turned and faced the others. "Maybe he won a gambling jackpot."

"Or maybe the money is connected to the BSE prions," Wulfsberg inferred.

Ash threw his hands out to the side, then plunked back down in his chair.

Bannister looked at Dr. Wulfsberg. "None of us knows, but everyone in this room is aware the only logical buyer of highly infectious pathogens would be terrorists. So, tell us, doctor, if this turns into a worst case, what are we facing?"

"BSE is just one type of several neurological disorders called transmissible spongiform encephalopathies, TSE. One, which is fatal to humans and which Middleton and Sanchez were researching, is Creutzfeldt-Jakob disease, CJD. We know there are similarities between CJD and BSE. Each disorder involves abnormal proteins and can be spread in animals if they consume feed or supplements derived from rendered animal protein."

"Are you saying someone could poison our country's meat supply?" Bannister asked.

"Exactly. Our country's food supply is now considered part of our nation's critical infrastructure. A successful attack against our beef industry would be absolutely catastrophic. Last year the US sold thirty-six million head of cattle for $42 billion. BSE is a highly infectious and fatal disease in cattle. It can be transmitted to offspring. The incubation period, after a steer or cow eats contaminated food, is generally three to eight years. There is no cure and it has a one hundred percent fatality rate."

"Is BSE restricted to cattle?" Bannister asked.

"No. It's transmissible to other animals and humans if they eat rendered parts of the steer containing the infectious protein."

Ramirez said, "I thought the Food and Drug Administration banned the sale of any feed or food supplement given to cattle or sheep that contained the meat, bone, or fat of any mammal except pigs and horses."

"You're correct. But enforcement is difficult. The animal feed and rendering business in the US involves over 14,000 companies. Guess how many inspectors there are."

"I don't know," she said.

"Just seventeen FDA inspectors check out those plants. About ninety-five percent of the plants aren't inspected. Let me put the potential scope of this thing into perspective. Do you remember what happened last year?"

"No," they all answered in unison.

"In December, Canada discovered four cows that tested positive for BSE. One of them was located in the state of Washington. After Canada made that announcement, Japan, Korea, and most Asian markets immediately banned the importation of all beef from the United States. The US economy was slammed and had to absorb an additional twenty-three million pounds of beef production a week to make up for the closure of those markets. Our country couldn't handle it and the price of cattle immediately plummeted one hundred twenty-five dollars a head. For a while it looked bad, but the one infected cow was identified and euthanized."

"In layman's terms, doctor, how difficult would it be to introduce mad cow into the cattle population?" Bannister asked.

"As simple as mixing some of the prion base into the feed or supplements fed to a herd of cattle or milk cows. By the way, I didn't mention the impact on our milk industry. We have nine million dairy cows in the US."

"You mentioned the incubation period was at least two years, right?" Bannister asked.

"That's true. But consider this scenario. What if CNN announced that unknown terrorists infected cattle in selected stockyards ninety days ago with a disease that would be fatal to humans? Would you order a steak or hamburger in a restaurant after hearing that?" Wulfsberg asked.

None of them answered him. Bannister asked, "What immediate steps are you going to take? We have to look at Middleton's murder as possibly connected to a terrorist plot."

"We have to verify that BSE prion material is in fact missing. If that is the case, numerous notifications have to be made, including to the White House," Wulfsberg said.

"With all the personnel in the notification chain, the possibility of a news leak rises exponentially, said Bannister. "If Middleton took the prions, he may still have them. If we assume he took them and passed them on to people who may turn out to be terrorists, they may be in their possession. And if terrorists are involved, we know nothing of their capabilities, intentions, or timetable. If they hear we're on to them, they might activate their plan if they haven't already done so and flee before we have a chance to do anything."

"What's the FBI going to do?" Ash asked.

Bannister said, "Right now, we have enough to open a terrorism investigation and get warrants to search Middleton's apartment and home. I'm going to notify our Special Agent in Charge and get FBI Headquarters to inform our bioterrorism response experts of a potential bioterrorism event. Some are still around who worked the anthrax case in Washington, DC, the week before September 11, 2001."

"I was on that anthrax task force," Wulfsberg said. "I'll help any way I can. If Middleton stole the BSE prions, they're probably concealed in a common medium. The prions are ten times smaller than any known virus, but we can still test any substance you seize."

"Tell me, Dr. Wulfsberg, how soon after an animal is infected does it begin showing signs of the disease?" Bannister asked.

"As I said, anywhere from thirty months to eight years. There's no cure and it has a one hundred percent fatality rate."

Bannister and Ramirez spent another half hour getting specific information they'd need for affidavits for search warrants. Before leaving, they agreed to meet back at Ash's office at 9:00 a.m. the next day.

Back at the FBI office, Ramirez started drafting the paperwork and Bannister called the United States Attorney on duty and gave her a heads up they'd need search warrants immediately. He left a message on Witt's cell phone and then called SAC Brennan at home.

Ramirez looked up from her computer. "I've got a really bad feeling about this, Ty."

"So do I. The boss called the Evidence Response Team supervisor and told her to have her team here in three hours. If everything goes well, we should know by midnight if this is a case of the 'for reals.'"

CHAPTER 24

I t was late and the Publix supermarket was closed when the search teams gathered in its parking lot on Peachtree Road. Assigned to process Middleton's apartment were Bannister, Ramirez, Frank Jantzen, who was the office's technical supervisor and also a locksmith, and a computer evidence team. The Evidence Response Team had responsibility for the family's residence. Before driving to Middleton's apartment, Bannister called Germaine White, Atlanta's top intelligence analyst. It was 11:30 p.m.

"Did I wake you?" Bannister asked.

"No, I usually talk in my sleep."

"We're going to need your expertise on a special. You don't have to come in tonight, but would you be willing to start your shift tomorrow at 5:00 a.m.?"

"I'll be there," she said without hesitation.

"Good. I'll have instructions on what database searches we need, and if I'm not in the office when you get there, I'll fill you in around 7:30 a.m."

"If you're out and about before that time, would you mind bringing me a chestnut praline latte from Starbucks?"

"I'm at your beck and call, Germaine. Go back to bed."

Some employees go the extra mile, not because they're under orders or deadlines, but because the work is in their blood and they are driven by pride. White was in that club. If it hadn't been for her dedication and intuitive intelligence analysis earlier this year, one or more FBI agents, including Bannister, might have been murdered by a serial killer in Virginia.

"What do you think we'll find?" Ramirez asked as they walked to the car.

"I don't think the biotoxin will be there, but I'm hoping we can identify where the ten grand came from and work backwards. Always follow the money."

Middleton's apartment was on the second floor of an eight-unit building that looked identical to fourteen other buildings in a sprawling apartment complex. His was a one bedroom, one bath unit. An evidence team member was the first into the apartment and photographed each room and all items in plain view. It looked like a typical bachelor's pad. The bedroom was cramped. Along one wall was a desk consisting of a flat wooden door which had been laid atop two filing cabinets. Next to a computer monitor on the left side of the desk was an open shoebox filled with receipts. An inflatable mattress took up most of the floor. The room's one closet with bi-fold doors contained Middleton's clothes, shoes, and three boxes of books. The bathroom had the basic grooming aids. No prescription medicines. In the kitchen the only thing on the counter was a coffee maker. The small living room had a couch, coffee table, and a TV on a black metal stand. Two green canvas camp chairs were on the side of the room near the picture window.

According to Detective Roy Miller, the only item seized by the Atlanta Police Department that afternoon was an envelope containing $10,000. The envelope and bills were undergoing fingerprint analysis by APD after they searched the serial numbers. One of the police officers had left a receipt for the money.

The computer team booted up Middleton's hard drive and made a copy of it before letting Bannister touch the keyboard. Before they boxed it up to take it to the office, Bannister looked at Middleton's home page and clicked on an icon of a chess figure. It brought up a password protected account for Chessboard Contrarian Investments. A quick Google search revealed the company, which advertised it did business in eleven countries, was an Internet offshore banking firm based in New Zealand. Hopefully, the FBI's computer team would break the password for that account as well as others when it did its diagnostics exam back at the office.

However, on the side of the monitor was a Post-It note with three lines of what were possibly passwords. Bannister took a chance and typed in "kmiddleton" for the username and got lucky when the third word from the Post-It opened up the account.

"Mercedes, look at this entry," he said. They both stared at the screen. Middleton had opened an account in Montenegro ten days ago. There was only one transaction listed.

"Oh my God!" Ramirez said. "This is bad."

"You're right. We need to find out who wired him $100,000."

"And figure out how he got connected to Montenegro."

Bannister then scanned through other applications on Middleton's PC as well as his word processing files without seeing any red flags. He'd have to wait for the computer team to access his e-mail accounts.

Bannister turned off the computer and began looking through Middleton's file cabinets. Ramirez took the box of receipts to a kitchen table and began going through them. Fifteen minutes later she said, "One of these receipts is for a gift box of spices he ordered off the Internet a month ago."

"Except for salt and pepper, this place doesn't have any spices. The trash can in the kitchen had TV dinner containers and take out wrappers. This guy's not into cooking. Are you thinking what I'm thinking?" Bannister asked.

"I'm trying not to," Ramirez said.

As the search at the apartment concluded, the team leader assigned to Middleton's house called.

The team leader told Bannister, "We struck out here. Middleton's wife and her sister let us into the house. His kids are staying with the sister at her home. The wife wants to talk with you as soon as possible. I told her you'd call her tomorrow and set up a time. Are you good with that?"

"I'll call her. Go ahead and secure and we'll see you back at the office."

Bannister had promised Roy Miller he'd let him know when they finished their searches. On the way back to the office he called him.

"We have a problem," Bannister said when Miller picked up. "I believe there's more than one person involved with Middleton's murder."

"I agree with you. We identified the female who rented the motel room. When we questioned Tamika Johnson, she had a solid alibi. Someone else used her name. After running the woman's description past Johnson, she said it matched another hooker with whom she had a recent beef. We pulled that woman's booking photo and showed it to the hotel desk clerk. Bingo. He positively identified Krystal Gwynn as the person who paid for the room, using Johnson's name."

"Any luck on Gwynn?"

"Yeah. We tracked her down. Gwynn initially tried to stonewall us, but after I told her she'd be charged as an accessory to murder, she suddenly became cooperative."

"Did she say who she gave the room key to?" Bannister asked.

"She never got a name. After getting paid, she split. We sat her down with one of our police artists and when she was shown the sketch, Gwynn said, 'That picture's spot on.'"

"How soon can you get us a copy?"

"I faxed it to your command center a half hour ago. The artist's sketch matches a video of an unknown male who purchased a bottle of Jim Beam from Sammy's Liquor at 5:35 p.m. yesterday. Only two other purchases of Jim Beam were made earlier that evening, both by black males. I'm having the tape duped and will bring a copy with me to our meeting. The toxicology tests on the drinks in Middleton's motel room verified alcohol but nothing else. Now it's your turn. What have you got?"

"As I said, we believe there's more than one person involved in the murder. We're trying to sort it out right now, but it will take us a few hours to verify some leads. How about we have a show-and-tell tomorrow when you come to the office?"

"Fine. I'll see you then."

Ramirez yawned. "It's 1:30 a.m., Ty. We're the last two in the office. How much longer are you going to push it?"

"About another half hour should do." He glanced down at his cell phone which had been set on vibrate. He'd missed a call an hour ago from Amy Dixon in Beverly Hills.

He looked at Ramirez. "You never asked me anything about my trip to Los Angeles. I was going to tell you a couple days ago, but it felt awkward so I just put it off."

"I know that. I told you when you felt like talking, I'd listen."

"I appreciate that. I've got a call I need to return, and I think I know what it's about." With that, he broke the news to Ramirez about Madison—the teenage daughter he never knew about. When he finished she got up and gave him a hug.

"Let me know if there's anything I can do," she said. "Make your call. I'll see you in the morning. I mean later." Ramirez left.

Bannister needed a few minutes to figure out what to say to Madison if the call from Amy Dixon was what he thought it would be.

"I'm sorry I missed your call," he said to Dixon.

"Madison's mother passed away an hour ago," said Dixon. "I'm at Madison's apartment right now."

"Is she all right?" he asked.

"She'll be fine. Can you talk to her right now? I'll come back on when you're finished."

Madison got on the line, her voice quivering. "Hello, Dad. Mom was fine when I left her three hours ago. I should have stayed with her longer."

"Your mom knew it was time. I'll bet she smiled, squeezed your hand, and told you she loved you when you left. Right?"

"Yeah, she always does."

"Your mom loved you very much. That's why she told you about me. She believed you were a strong young lady who would make the right choices. She knew you were ready to make it on your own."

"I know. But I feel terrible . . . kept hoping she wouldn't die, like maybe some miracle would happen. It didn't." Bannister could hear Madison crying. The next moment Dixon was back on the phone.

"She'll be fine, Ty. Her roommates are all here and they know the situation. They cried together. Let me step into the kitchen." A few seconds went by before Dixon resumed. "There will be a memorial service at the hospital's chapel Sunday afternoon. I prearranged everything. Miss Van Otten gave me a list of people she wanted notified. It was short. I'll call you as soon as I have the final details. Here's Madison again."

"I couldn't keep myself from crying," Madison said softly.

"That's okay," said Bannister gently.

"Will you be able to come out? I mean I don't want you to feel like you have to come, but I want you to be here with me."

"Of course I have to come. You're my daughter and you need me. I'll be there late tomorrow. End of discussion."

"That'd be great, Dad. I love you."

"I love you, too." He said that without thinking, but it felt like it was true. "Would you put Miss Dixon back on the phone?" It took a couple of minutes to coordinate a few more details with Dixon before he ended the call.

Last weekend he was flying to Los Angeles hoping he'd be able to say the right things. This weekend he'd be flying back, hoping he wouldn't say the wrong things.

CHAPTER 25

T erry Hines visited the Old Crom, his favorite Irish pub. Some of the millions spent on it went to creating an old cottage and a museum room that offered a history of Irish pub culture. Since he had last visited this Atlanta pub, it had been remodeled slightly and the outdoor fireplace seating expanded. Hines took a seat inside the cottage room at one of five stools along a dark oak bar. He turned sideways to glance at two yuppie couples sitting at low tables near the stacked stone fireplace in the corner. It was early and the house band, The Charms, wasn't due to start playing for another hour.

It had been a year since he'd sat there contemplating his plan to extort millions from his former employer. He almost got away with it, too. This time he wouldn't make any mistakes. Being an international fugitive had only bolstered his confidence. He knew his plan would succeed.

The FBI had unraveled Hines's false identity in the name of Sean O'Brien. They also discovered all the details of his fictitious company, U.S. Euro Trans-Consultants. But what really hurt was the FBI seizing most of the five million dollars he'd stolen. The Bureau, however, had underestimated him. Sure, they'd indicted him while he was still on a cruise finishing the final details of his plan. They'd also arrested him when he got off the plane in Atlanta. But they never got the satisfaction of hearing a jury verdict. He never talked. He never confessed.

The stupid Bureau never thought he had arranged an escape package. When he created the false identification for Sean O'Brien, he'd also obtained a second set of phony papers. Using the same technique, he printed up a dummy questionnaire with the US seal and Census Bureau address on it. He had "For Official Use Only" stamped at the bottom of the page. It was easy to find homeless Caucasian men approximately thirty to forty years old. The form asked questions like their full name, date of birth, Social Security account number, and mother's maiden name. He paid each of the guys twenty-five dollars for their information for this special research project. Hines then hired an investigative company to do criminal background checks on four of the names. He told the company he was hiring employees for U.S. Euro Trans-Consultants. Three of the names came back negative with no arrests. One guy had served time in two states. The identity he selected to pilfer belonged to an Irishman named Nathan Shane Quinn. Quinn's passport, and $40,000 of the extortion money that the FBI believed Hines had gambled away on the cruise ship, was his ticket to London.

A bartender, who had spiked brunette hair with blond tips, stopped in front of Hines.

"What'll it be?" she asked with a curt smile.

"I'll have a Beamish Stout, twenty ounce, please," Hines said. It was a perfect beer for slow sipping. A beer to enjoy while he went over details of his new plan.

Hines had used the same technique to get his current ID as he did for Sean O'Brien. He'd put down his real address for the Quinn paperwork. It was simple to scan into a Kinko's computer his actual apartment contract and utility bills and then change his name to Quinn. From the Internet he'd ordered a professional theatrical makeup kit along with a beard and mustache the same color as his natural hair. After leaving the Cumming, Georgia, DMV office with his new look and new driver's license, Hines then went to a local drug store where he obtained passport photos.

It was easy for Hines to open a checking account and safe deposit box in the name of Nathan Quinn. He used his real address at the bank but had the bill sent to a separate mail drop location for which he'd pre-paid one year in advance. He used another identity when opening the Pak Mail account. He had successfully tested that mail drop. Two knives ordered in the names of women living in Atlanta had been received last month.

Hines knew his mother was relocating to an apartment in Oyster Bay, NY. He had sent a long letter to his mother's last known address in Long Island, NY, knowing it would be forwarded. He knew the safest way to communicate with his mother was by letter. The FBI could not trace the letter if it didn't have a return address and, even if it was postmarked from England, they could never get a court order to open a letter from an unknown sender. Knowing this, he counted on the love and forgiveness of his mother to send him some of the half-million dollars in life insurance proceeds she received upon the death of his father. Hines requested his mother wire transfer him a loan of $80,000, which he promised to repay within six months. He told her to destroy the letter after following specific instructions for sending the transfer to a friend, Nathan Quinn, in Woking, a suburb of London.

Hines's mother had transferred the money that he was now using. He wasn't a totally ungrateful son. He sent a nice thank you card to her, repeating his request for her to destroy it after reading it. Looking at his reflection in the bar's mirror, Hines smiled at how his actual beard and mustache matched the photograph in his fraudulent passport.

The next afternoon Hines peered through his windshield at the Pinnacle Building on Peachtree Road. Its twenty-one stories of green translucent glass were topped by a restaurant and sky garden. These were covered by a six-story curving structure, which from a distance resembled a giant sail. He could have parked in one of the building's underground levels but opted to pull into the outdoor parking area of the Lenox Square shopping center a block away. The sun was out and the sky filled with puffy white clouds. The offices of McPeak Futures and Options were on the tenth floor. Because he didn't want his broker to be distracted during active trading hours for soybeans, corn, and other grain futures, Hines set the appointment for 3:00 p.m.

He glanced at his list one last time. Every Sunday evening Hines took his old notes from the week before, jotted down tasks he'd failed to achieve, and compiled them into a new one. Ever since his sophomore year at Georgia Tech, he'd always kept lists. Kevin Middleton used to razz him all the time. "Why don't you go to culinary school and be a chef?" Middleton asked. "They love lists. They have lists of recipes with lists of ingredients. You'd feel right at home." Even though Middleton was a dork, he was very smart. Last week Hines crossed Middleton's name off his personal list when it appeared on another one—Atlanta's obituaries.

Waiting for the elevator, Hines rehearsed what he intended to say to the commodities broker. He had all his documentation in order.

Right on time, Joseph Marshall came out to meet him.

"Come on back to my office," Marshall said, extending his hand and shaking firmly. Hines noted Marshall sported a paisley bow tie and his French-cuffed shirt had large silver bull and bear cufflinks. "Call me Joe. Care for some water or a soft drink?"

"No thanks. And call me Nathan," Hines said, taking in the office's Danish modern design with a blend of chrome, glass, and teak.

Marshall leaned his head forward and smiled broadly. "From your initial call, I understand you want to open an account with us. Can I fill you in on how we're different from other trading firms or answer any questions you might have about commodity trading?" Marshall spoke rapidly but with an air of confidence.

Hines slid the office chair closer to Marshall's desk.

"Here's what I'd like you to do for me; I may have a few questions as we go along. I'd like you to buy futures contracts for me for the first of next month. The amounts should be evenly divided among soy-beans, corn, and wheat."

"Do you have a specific margin deposit you're thinking about?" Marshall asked.

"Let's start with $100,000. I have a cashier's check for $120,000 to open my account." Hines slid a Wells Fargo Bank cashier's check across the desk and Marshall picked it up.

"You realize the risks, don't you? You stand to make substantial profits if the contracts move up even slightly, but you face significant losses if they move downward."

Hines had done his homework but wanted to test Marshall.

"Give me an example," he asked.

Marshall spent ten minutes crunching the numbers on a hypothetical investment of the entire $100,000 in soybean futures. If the index gained 5%, Hines would realize a profit of $150,000. However, if the index fell 5%, Hines would lose $50,000.

Marshall asked Hines, "Is the money you want to invest money you can stand to lose?"

"Yes. It's found money. I was the beneficiary of my uncle's life insurance policy. He was a soybean farmer in Iowa. That's why I want to put the money into grain futures."

"That sounds like you'd be honoring his memory," Marshall said.

"That's how I look at it. Uncle Ted was very conservative, but I'm willing to risk it all." Hines had done the math in his head. He knew the index would increase at least 100% and, when it did, he'd earn a quick $3,000,000. The Nebraska State Fair concluded the week before the anniversary of September 11th. Fadi's team would have infected selected 4-H clubs' steers and breeding heifers before the fair ended. At least some of the steers would have been sold and on their way to the slaughterhouses. Once the newspapers were alerted to the attack, all hell would break loose.

For his second appointment that afternoon, Hines, using his alias Nathan Quinn, went back to the office of Bunkie Black of Black Gold Investigations. Last month Hines had done some surveillance work of his own. He'd tracked the federal prosecutor, Kendall Briggs, for three evenings. On the last evening he followed Briggs to the Bacchanalia restaurant where Briggs's dinner partner turned out to be an attractive woman. Hines took her picture and wrote down the license plate of the white Lexus the valet delivered to her. Later, after paying a DMV fee, Hines discovered Theresa Andrews was the registered owner of the Lexus.

Hines had hired Bunkie Black to tail Andrews the following Wednesday and Friday evenings and prepare a background report. He'd told Black that Andrews was his current girlfriend and he wanted to know if she was seeing any other men. Hines recalled the exchange he had with Black when he went to pick up the results.

"Mr. Quinn, before I hand you this report I need to ask if you're aware of her status," Black asked.

"What do you mean by status?"

"You know, single, married, divorced, or just living with someone," Black said.

"You tell me. That's one of the reasons I hired you." Hines had a slight smirk.

Black returned the smile before speaking. As he gave the folder to Hines, he said, "She's married, but I guess you knew that."

"Right. You're good." Hines smiled again and Bunkie Black let out a belly laugh.

"I generally don't make judgments or offer advice. But I'm sure you remember the advice when you were a kid that if you play with fire . . ."

"Yeah, I remember how that goes. Stop, drop, and roll." Both men laughed again.

This week, Hines returned to hire Black's services to investigate the driver of a Toyota 4Runner. Hines said he believed the driver was having an affair with his girlfriend, Dr. Terri Andrews.

He liked that Black Gold's office was just two blocks from the center of Virginia Highlands. He could walk to the bars and restaurants from

Black's office, unwind with a cold beer, and review his plans for the week.

Black was alone in his office when Hines entered.

"Afternoon Bunkie," Hines said. "In your phone call you said all the preliminary work was completed and you had some 'good news/bad news' for me."

"That's right, Nathan," Black said, extending his hand. Black wore a black polo shirt with his company's logo embroidered on the left chest. Hines stared at the embroidered magnifying glass with the gold handle as well as Black's company name and telephone number enlarged in the glass.

As Hines made himself comfortable in the large armchair in front of Black's desk, the investigator said, "Unlike the last case for you, this one's more complicated. My preliminary report is in there. There's a separate copy in the manila envelope, which you can take with you. Take a minute to look at this." Black pushed a brown file toward Hines.

On the left was the contract Nathan Quinn had signed nine days ago. On the right was an enlarged copy of a Georgia driver's license for Tyler Stetson Bannister. Underneath it was a credit report extract as well as an investigative summary, which Black had prepared.

"The good news is the $1,000 retainer covered most of your bill. You only owe me $200. Here's the rest of the good news. Your target's forty-five, educated at a private school in California, and graduated from Dartmouth College. Bannister's a former Marine with a black belt in karate. He was awarded the nation's second highest medal, the Navy Cross, for action in Operation Just Cause. He's currently single but is a widower whose wife was killed in an Atlanta auto accident six years ago. He currently has two cars—the 4Runner you saw and a classic 1959 Mercedes Benz SL Gullwing worth at least a quarter million. No kids. Rich. Net worth is estimated at $5.5 million. He owns a gated home in Buckhead, which sits on four acres. That's the good news."

"So, what's the bad news?" Hines asked.

"He's been an FBI agent for eighteen years."

"Damn."

"Right. That really throws a monkey wrench into the spokes. I took a chance putting an external GPS tracker on his SUV. The printout of all the data streamed to my computer is right in front of you. One of my teams set up in a van on Valley Road for four hours before Bannister left in his vehicle. We made the installation with no problem. Friday evening the tracker indicated his SUV was parked in long-term parking at the airport. It was still there early Sunday morning when we retrieved our device. You'd told us you were suspicious about Wednesday and Friday nights, right?"

"That's correct. My girlfriend said she had to go out of town because her uncle was dying. Do you suppose the two of them flew somewhere to be together?"

"Maybe yes. Maybe no. She might not be meeting anyone. Could just be a coincidence. Or she might be spending time with her husband. One of the last cases I handled involved a minister. I had my doubts until we filmed him and his mistress kissing in a South Carolina hotel parking lot."

"So, where do we go from here?" Hines asked.

"It's your call. I'd suggest you first go through the logs showing all locations where Bannister's SUV has been for the past week and see if any of the places match up where your girlfriend happened to be. If you believe they're having a relationship, I can find out. I'm not going to sugarcoat this for you. It's going to be expensive if you want to move forward with personal visual surveillance. I'll have to use at least two teams, 6:00 a.m. to 10:00 p.m. That alone will run you $2,000 a day."

"That's steep."

"It is. But this guy's a fed. He may be working on surveillance himself or using his personal vehicle to meet with an informant. He'll be super cautious and suspicious as hell. I don't want to get into a pissing contest with the FBI if one of my teams screws up and gets badged by one of their surveillance folks." Black leaned forward, his thick hairy forearms resting on each side of the file. "Comprende?"

"Gotcha. I think what you've put together may give me what I need. If I decide to talk to anyone, it'll be my girlfriend. I'll get back to you in a week with my decision."

"Deal. Be smart." Black pointed his finger at Hines. "I certainly wouldn't confront an FBI guy who's trained in the martial arts and for sure is carrying a gun."

"Thanks for the advice," Hines said, nodding.

"No problem," Black said. "Like last time, leave your check on my secretary's desk on your way out."

CHAPTER 26

The street was quiet at 1:30 a.m. when Bannister pulled into his garage. Despite the unusual hour, his home gym was beckoning. Too much pent-up energy. His fourth-degree black belt demanded consistent practice on his katas. His regular routine was twenty predetermined defenses and attacks against four imaginary opponents who could approach from any direction. He finished the workout by doing ten straight minutes of striking and kicking the heavy bag. The stress melted away as his muscles burned.

A long hot shower was followed with a cold glass of ice water. Before calling it a day, Bannister poured two fingers of single malt whisky from a bottle of eighteen-year-old Talisker and set the glass down next to the computer. Online he purchased a round-trip ticket from Atlanta to Los Angeles and booked a room at the same Sofitel Hotel in Beverly Hills where he stayed the previous weekend. After listing his leads to be covered tomorrow, he savored the final sip of the warm sweetness of smoky peat whiskey as it went down his throat. He picked up the framed picture of his daughter and just stared at her. Although the circumstances were regrettable, he was really looking forward to seeing Madison for the second week in a row.

———⁂———

He drove to the office and parked in the visitor's lot since he'd be leaving for the airport in three hours. Once at his desk, he was scrolling through the office calls when his cell phone vibrated.

"Agent Bannister. This is Hannah Michaels. Remember me?"

"The lady with the Picasso. How could I forget?" he said.

"You're sweet. Thanks. I thought I'd get your voicemail this early.

The morning news had a picture of the guy murdered near the airport. I recognized him. That was Kevin Middleton who posed in that photograph with me at The Spa at Egret Bay."

"I know. I should have called you earlier. The spa's manager identified Middleton on Tuesday. We interviewed him Wednesday and yesterday he was murdered. Agent Ramirez was going to call you this morning to show you his photo. I didn't know it made the local news."

"That's two people I had my picture taken with who have been murdered in a week. I'm kind of creeped out. Am I in danger?" Michaels asked.

That was a good question.

"We don't think so," said Bannister. "Are you at home?"

"Yes, I'm leaving for work in half an hour. You know that three of us in that picture as well as the woman taking the photo are all from Atlanta, don't you?"

"Yes."

"Well, maybe someone in Atlanta is afraid Mr. Briggs said something he shouldn't have to the rest of us and we're being hunted down. Am I being paranoid?"

"Just concerned. I promise you we'll thoroughly check it out. If there's anything, absolutely anything at all, that remotely suggests you might be in danger, I'll get in touch with you immediately. I promise."

"Thanks. I guess I've watched too many of those *Criminal Minds*–type shows on TV. I appreciate your talking to me."

"No problem. Have a good day at your shop."

Bannister pondered what Michaels had told him before calling Ramirez and White and asking them to meet him in Stu's still empty office.

Ramirez showed up first and he informed her he was flying to LA that afternoon and that the memorial service for Madison's mother was Sunday.

"I'm sorry, Ty. Do you want to go through the same drill we did last weekend?" Mercedes asked.

"That'd be great. I'll check in with you periodically, but call me immediately if there are developments."

"You bet," she said.

White arrived and the three of them grabbed chairs around the desk. White put her square gold-rimmed glasses on and snapped open her notebook. Bannister waited for her to look up.

"Germaine, today I want you to concentrate on the Kevin Middleton murder. Mercedes will tell you what we've got, but we believe he may be involved in a possible bioterrorism plot."

He turned to Ramirez. "Can you interview Middleton's wife this morning? She's going to be involved with her kids and may be wrapped up with handling funeral details, but press her for everything you can about Middleton's finances, associates, travel—you know, the whole nine yards."

"I'll handle it. I have an appointment with one of the CDC's inspectors at David Ash's office at noon. They're probably getting ready to sound alarm bells."

"We both know that's premature. Call me when you know what their game plan is. I may be at my gate waiting to take off."

"Anything specific on the Middleton case you want me to be doing?" White asked, tilting her head to the side as she often did when asking a question.

"No. I trust your judgment. I'm going over to Atlanta PD to meet with Detective Miller. He has a photo of someone who may be implicated in the murder. It came from a surveillance tape from a liquor store near the murder scene. The night clerk at the store identified the person as the only customer to purchase a bottle of Jim Beam. A similar bottle was found in Middleton's hotel room. It's a stretch, but you never know."

"Why did he remember the customer?" White asked.

"In his words, the guy looked like a raghead, and they never come into his store. So, he watched him carefully in case he was a robber. He gave Detective Miller some additional descriptive information.

I'm picking up a copy of the photo as well as a dupe of the store's surveillance tape."

"You think the guy in the picture is part of a cell?" White asked.

"Yes, so see what you can do with the picture and the artist's sketch," Bannister said.

White nodded. "The CIA has a new identification program called Omega One that uses facial recognition software. The Bureau's Next Generation Intelligence system is great but we're still working out some of the kinks. Right now, the Agency's system has integrated the foreign subjects and terrorists, and my contact said it's even better than any of the stuff the Brits have. I'll have them run the photo through their program and also query databases at both State Department and Homeland Security. Maybe we'll get lucky."

Bannister met Detective Miller, picked up the tape and photo of the unknown subject, and briefed him about leads the FBI was pursuing. He omitted any mention of the biotoxin. He then spent an hour going over the Briggs investigation with Derek Barnes and told him he had to leave town to attend a funeral of a friend, but that he'd be back in the office Monday morning.

Gary Witt spotted him as he was leaving the office to go to the airport.

"The boss told me a family friend of yours died and you felt it necessary to go to the funeral."

"That's correct."

"With the importance of everything going on here in Atlanta, didn't you think maybe a floral arrangement or fruit basket might have been sufficient?" Witt asked.

There were several responses Bannister considered, but he took a deep breath before saying anything. "Everyone has their assignments and will keep me posted. If they have to discuss anything classified, I'll stop at our LA office and use one of their secure phones."

"All right. By the way, a Washington Field Supervisor and one of his agents are flying in on Monday to meet with our Task Force to discuss an operation which involves us. I expect you to be in the conference room at 1:00 p.m. for that meeting. I will not accept any excuses."

"I'll be there."

CHAPTER 27

Bannister's flight from Atlanta to Los Angeles lifted off at 1:35 p.m. Scheduled arrival was 3:00 p.m. Pacific time.

Bannister wished he knew what Madison was thinking right now. Her mother was all she had. Madison was aware it was only a matter of time, but that time had come. Bannister guessed it would be normal to feel sorry for oneself. Sorry that your mother would not see you graduate, would not be there to help you plan your wedding, would never see her grandchildren, and would never pick up the phone again to answer a simple question.

Maybe they had time to talk about some of that stuff. He'd try and get a sense of where Madison's head was when he saw her later. He'd suggest picking her up at her apartment, driving over to Santa Monica, and then walking along the beach. He hoped Madison would find it as relaxing and conducive to thinking as he used to, to see and hear the ocean. He was counting on them being able to trace together some of the steps he and her mother had taken the summer they met.

The flight was uneventful and for a change, the seat next to him was unoccupied. He went over some case notes, read a few chapters of the book he'd brought, and even managed to catch a thirty-minute nap.

The first stop was baggage claim; the second was the rental car agency where he'd reserved the same model Buick as the government vehicle he drove in Atlanta. He opted not to familiarize himself with a different car's controls while navigating Friday afternoon traffic on LA freeways.

While waiting for the courtesy van to the rental parking lot, Bannister noticed he had two messages. One was from White; the other from Ramirez. He called White, who picked up right away.

"So, Germaine, what've you got?"

"Is there any chance you can call me back on a secure phone?" she asked.

"Good timing. I just left the airport. I'll stop at the LA office and phone you from there. Give me forty minutes, okay?"

"I'll be here. You know you're making me work overtime and forcing me to stand up a date?"

"Well, I know you wouldn't have called if it wasn't important. I'll make it up to you. What if I send you a gift card from Beverly Hills?" He smiled to himself, waiting for her response.

"I'll settle for another Starbucks vente when you return. Call me when you get to the office." He heard her laugh. White hadn't had a date in at least three years, but it was always fun to play along with her.

He returned Ramirez's call, and she went straight to her report.

"Middleton's wife had to postpone our interview until this afternoon. One of her kids got sick. She wasn't much help but gave me a load of financial information on Middleton, which we can follow up on. She had no clue about him visiting a spa in Florida or any other travel. She didn't know anything about his having investments."

"Any indication she may have been complicit in his murder?"

"No, but I think she was doing a little acting. You know, trying to strike a balance between the ex-wife who should be celebrating the finality of her divorce and the grieving mother of Middleton's children who would never get to play with their dad again. She came across as a typical housewife. No tears, but she was puzzled about some of the things her husband had kept from her and clearly disturbed about the violent way he died."

"Did you get to Dave Ash's office?" Bannister asked.

"Dr. Wulfsberg was there with him," said Ramirez. "They're really nervous and don't want to get caught with their pants down. They're positive the item we're concerned about is definitely missing and that Middleton was the last one to have had access to it. I told Ash if we obtain any conclusive evidence that it fell into the bad guys' hands, then both you and the boss would meet with him. At least for now they're okay with that. Did I do all right?"

"You bet. Keep your fingers crossed we don't have a four-alarm fire. By the way, Germaine is still at work. She has something she needs to discuss on a secure line. I'm going to call her from our LA office."

"I'm on my way back to the office to write up interviews. I'll stay there in case I need to come on the line. Everything okay in LA?"

"The main thing is I got here. I'm seeing my daughter later."

"Oh, one other thing, Ty. You know about the Washington supervisor and agent coming to the office Monday, right? You might want to give the agent a call. It's Robin."

He had overlooked telling Ramirez that he knew. He paused for a second. "Thanks for the heads up. I'll handle it."

A half hour later of driving under a smog-less blue sky, he exited the San Diego Freeway and a couple minutes after that pulled into the public parking area in front of the eighteen-story federal building. After checking in with the same supervisor who let him use his office last week, he called White on a secure line.

"Okay, what've you got?" he asked.

"I think the flit's hit the shan. We got an ID on the guy in that liquor store surveillance tape. The Agency's Omega One software made a positive match to Bashir Rahman al-Ahmad."

"Who's he?" Bannister asked, letting White play it out as she wanted.

"Rahman al-Ahmad is a member of Gamaa al-Islamiya, one of the two radical Islamic fundamentalist groups that serves as a feeder organization for al-Qaeda in Egypt. Al-Ahmad is Egyptian. His father allegedly was tied to the Egyptian Islamic Jihad responsible for President Anwar Sadat's assassination in 1981. The father was one of the nine hundred militants later freed by the Egyptian government."

"Okay, so where's this al-Ahmad now?"

"Somewhere in Cairo. He was confirmed yesterday on an Iberian one-way ticket from Atlanta to Cairo, via stops in Chicago and Madrid. He cleared customs in Cairo."

"Can we get the Bureau's legal attaché in Cairo on this?"

"Definitely. But there are three interesting developments. My CIA contact, who didn't have any specifics, did say they had unverified information that the Egyptian Mukhabarat al-Aama detained him at the airport and then he disappeared."

"Isn't the Mukhabarat their intelligence service?" Bannister asked.

"Exactly,"

"What else did your source say?" Bannister asked.

"Only that the Egyptians might be interrogating him for something that happened in Egypt. I don't have to tell you that in Cairo interrogate is synonymous with torture."

"I seem to remember that, Germaine. You mentioned some other developments."

"Right. I checked our terrorist databases and we got a hit. Rahman al-Ahmad is referenced in one of our Washington office's terrorist investigations. They determined the terrorist organization Hamas is sponsoring a group based in Detroit, which has taken over some of the fundraising for the Holy Land Foundation, which we successfully shut down.

"But what our Washington agents found out is that this new Detroit group is raising hundreds of thousands of dollars through cigarette smuggling and then channeling that money to both Hamas and al-Qaeda. Washington believes the cigarettes are purchased in or smuggled out of South Carolina, transported to Atlanta where they're repackaged with fraudulent tax stamps, and then trucked to the Detroit area where they are sold. Supposedly, that's the case the Washington supervisor and agent are coming to Atlanta on Monday to brief us about."

"That's quick work, Germaine."

"Do you want to know what the third development is?"

Bannister patiently played along with her. "Yes."

"One of the two prosecutors, the one who was handling the Atlanta investigation, was Mr. Briggs!"

He thought about that connection. US Attorney Prescott had mentioned Briggs was handling the Atlanta angle of a DC case. Maybe Robin could shed some light on that Monday. White spent another ten minutes updating him on the KABMUR investigation. After he told her he'd be back in the office first thing Monday morning, she reminded him about the Starbucks coffee.

He texted Madison with suggested plans, checked in early at the hotel, showered, and changed into beach clothes. Twenty minutes later he arrived at Amy Dixon's law firm. The outside of her one-story office building looked more like an aquarium than an office. The entrance had white Ionic columns on each side. The firm's two large doors were made entirely of thick dark blue glass. The inside was designed in a tasteful Italianate style that would make her Beverly Hills clients feel quite comfortable. The receptionist took one glance at Bannister as he walked in wearing a robin's egg blue-and-yellow Hawaiian shirt and Teva sandals. She looked anything but comfortable, only relaxing after he told her Miss Dixon was expecting him.

Dixon came out and shook his hand. "Ty, you look like you've come from the beach, not the airport."

"As a matter of fact, that's where I'm heading after picking up Madison." He followed her to her office.

"I wish I could go with you," she said. "I think I've handled everything you wanted done. Jennifer Van Otten signed the trust agreement on Monday, naming me trustee. The amount of the trust is approximately $105,000, which should pay for Madison's last two years of college. Anything left over will be distributed to her when she reaches twenty-three."

"Good. What about the arrangements for Madison's living expenses?" he asked.

"Covered. The billing for her portion of the apartment rent will be sent to me. Her Visa bill will also be forwarded to my office. Naturally, I'll send them to you for payment. She'll also have $1,000 for living expenses directly deposited into her checking account each month. The $25,000 you wired should cover her food, clothing, and miscellaneous purchases until she graduates. Remember, you're responsible for not forgetting special days like her birthday, Valentine's Day, etc. I'll help you out by sending you e-mail reminders, okay?" Dixon smiled and winked at the same time.

"Thanks. I knew I could count on you."

"You know I would have done all this work pro bono, right?" Dixon asked.

"I know. But I feel better knowing I'm one of your paying clients. You'll earn your money. By the way, what about the mother's apartment?"

"I gave management a notice last week and paid the final bill. I went with Madison to the apartment after she and her mother talked about the mom's possessions. Madison took a couple of photo albums, two UCLA sweatshirts she had given to her mother, a black evening shawl, some jewelry, and a new KitchenAid mixer. Not a lot of stuff, but that's all Madison wanted. Her mother desired that the rest of her possessions be donated to the Salvation Army. I've retained the Kleen Sweep Company, which I've used in the past for estate cleanouts. They'll go in, box everything up, and then clean the apartment. Madison should get the security deposit back."

"I appreciate your thoroughness."

Dixon nodded and smiled. "When we last talked you mentioned something about buying her a car and paying for the insurance, taxes, and maintenance. Has she picked one out?"

"Not yet. Madison doesn't know about that. It's a little premature right now. I'm just getting to know her."

"I understand. By the way, the mother's cremation is tomorrow. When Jennifer signed the trust agreement, I went over the cremation options concerning her ashes. She could arrange to have her ashes buried, inurned in a columbarium, kept at home, or scattered at sea. Ultimately, she elected to spare Madison any unnecessary decisions and chose to have the crematorium destroy them."

"That's probably best for everyone," Bannister said.

"The memorial service will be at Saint John's Health Center in Santa Monica where Jennifer worked. It's scheduled for 3:00 p.m. Sunday to coincide with a shift change at the hospital. My secretary put all the information, including directions, in an envelope for you. The only thing I need before you leave is your signature on a power of attorney. Are you still planning on flying back to Atlanta after the memorial service?"

"Yes. I have a pile of work waiting for me."

As if on cue, his cell phone vibrated and he looked down at the number. It was Gary Witt.

"Do you need to make a call?"

"It's one of my bosses who can wait." He'd return his call in the morning. If it was something urgent, Witt would reach out to Ramirez. If she called, he'd answer. Before leaving Dixon's office, Bannister signed the papers she'd prepared and thanked her for everything she was doing.

CHAPTER 28

It was a fifteen-minute drive from Beverly Hills to Madison's apartment. Bannister collected his thoughts and called Madison when he pulled up to her address. She walked down the four steps to the sidewalk out front.

"Oh, Dad." Her quivering smile disappeared as she rushed up to him. The two hugged and held each other for a minute without speaking. He could feel her chest heaving as she fought to regain her composure. The sobs subsided.

"I thought I'd used up all my tears," Madison said, accepting a handkerchief to dab at her eyes. She reached into her shoulder bag. "Here's your clean handkerchief from last week."

"Why don't you keep it," he said. "What can I do to help?"

"I'm just glad you came. It means so much."

"It means a lot to me, too. I know your mother would be happy."

"I know, too." Madison stared at him for a couple of seconds. She was wearing white cuffed crop pants, some fancy blue colored tee, and had a long-sleeved sun gold sweater tied around her waist. She looked like a normal happy coed, but he knew her insides must be churning.

"Where did you want to go?" she asked.

"I was thinking maybe we could walk along Santa Monica Beach and talk. If there's someplace else where you'd feel more comfortable, we could go there."

"No, the beach is fine."

"Do you need help with any of the arrangements for tomorrow?"

"I don't think so. Ms. Dixon and one of mom's friends at the hospital, Janice, have taken care of everything. Janice called me and said she'd be there an hour early."

"What about you?" he asked.

"I think I should be there early, too, so I can talk with mom's friends and thank them for everything. You don't think I'll have some type of emotional melt down while driving there, do you?"

"I don't think so, but just to make sure, how about I pick you up and handle the driving?"

"That'd be great."

They got into his rental car and drove ten minutes to the beach. He was lucky and found a parking spot near the Santa Monica Pier. They got out and headed toward the water.

"Can we walk along the edge of the water?" Madison asked, taking off her gold-colored sandals.

"Sure." They crossed over a bike path as two young guys on skateboards whizzed by.

"You know, I've jogged along this path a few times. I don't make it a habit though. Mom said the pounding on the concrete isn't good for your knees." When she said the word "Mom," her eyes welled up again. He took hold of Madison's hand as she slowed her pace and then stopped, her head dropping. Neither of them spoke. They just listened to the waves methodically rolling in and the distant chatter of people having fun.

"It's okay to cry," he said.

"Have you cried? Have you really cried about anyone?" Madison said, letting go of his hand and glaring at him with wet eyes. Her accusing manner caught him by surprise. He just looked into her face. She was about to say something, then stopped. A solitary barefoot male jogger ran along the water's edge, smiling as he turned his head toward Madison, and then continued his pace toward the pier.

It was a cloudless day with just a whiff of a breeze. A small boy had thrown some popcorn in the sand and was running in circles, laughing and shouting as a dozen seagulls materialized out of nowhere, dive bombing the unexpected treats.

Bannister looked down in the sand for a moment to collect his thoughts, then as Madison turned to face him, smiled and looked into her eyes. "We've only known each other for a week. We can't even begin to understand what makes each other tick. You asked me if I cried. I have. I cried the day my wife Erin was killed in an auto accident." Bannister put his hands gently on Madison's shoulders and let his head drop for a few seconds. "Sometimes, I take out my favorite picture of her and just stare at it. In a minute I can go from smiling and feeling warm inside to feeling empty and alone." He let his hands drop down to his side as they resumed walking down the beach.

A minute later Bannister broke the silence. "I don't like to cry. When I was your age I thought men who cried were weak. But sometimes it just happens. It means you're human. I told you I was in the Marine Corps but didn't mention I was in combat. I was in charge of a platoon of young Marines who had to rescue some American school teachers being held at a foreign university. On the approach to the building where they were held, two of my men were shot and killed. When I knelt down beside their bodies my eyes filled with tears. They were both nineteen and made the greatest sacrifice they could. A week later I choked up again when I wrote letters to their parents."

"I don't think I could do something like that," Madison said, bending over to pick up an intact sand dollar.

"What I'm trying to say is that grieving takes time. Healing is gradual and we all go through it differently."

"I don't even know what I should be doing," she said. "What should I be thinking?"

Bannister had no simple responses to these complex feelings. He couldn't begin to fathom what might be going through a teenage girl's mind at a time like this. What did come out was "I wish I had answers for you, but I don't. I do know you're going to experience a rollercoaster of emotions. One minute you might feel sad, and the next minute panic and helplessness. That doesn't mean there's anything wrong with you. Just go with the flow. If it means stopping what you're doing and having a good cry, then go ahead."

"I don't know what acting normal is. None of my roommates has lost a parent or had a brother or sister die."

"Maybe we can work on some things. Last week you mentioned you're involved with the Christian athletes on campus, right? Do any of them know what happened?"

"The group leader, Dave, called me about a meeting and I told him Mom passed away. He said he'd let the others know."

"That's good. Reach out to them. If they call you, talk to them. They'll help you get through the next couple of weeks. When I worked in our LA office, I met one of the UCLA counselors in the student clinic. He helps students cope with death, whether it's a classmate or a family member." Bannister pulled out his wallet and handed Madison the card on which he'd written the counselor's name and phone number. "If he's still at the health clinic you might consider giving him a call. It certainly wouldn't hurt."

"So, how did you meet him?"

"The college daughter of one of the agents I worked with killed herself."

"That's awful."

"It was terrible. It happened on Thanksgiving Day and she used her father's gun. We all pitched in to do what we could to help him and his wife deal with the situation. He ended up coming back to work but was a changed man. He'll never be able to forget what happened, but at least he was able to return to be a productive agent again. He volunteers with the Suicide Hotline team."

Madison must have felt the need to change the topic, because she said, "My roommates will be there tomorrow. I'd like to introduce you to them, okay?"

"Sure, I'd like to meet them. You did say none of your roommates mentioned suffering a personal loss, correct?"

"Right, but maybe they just never brought it up."

"Well, don't feel isolated if they ignore you for a spell or act embarrassed. They might not know what to say, sort of like your saying you don't know how you should be feeling. They might think if they bring up the topic of your mother it will upset you and just make you cry again."

"One of my roommates already made a stupid remark to me. She said, 'Let's don't talk about that now.'"

"That's what I was getting at. You might have a roommate or team member who tries to be over-protective or tries to comfort you so much that it seems like it's smothering you. They probably mean well, but if it really bothers you, simply ask them to stop."

"I guess I'll recognize it when it happens. You know, Mom sort of smothered me. I used to ask her for advice about all kinds of stuff. Sometimes I already knew the answers and had made up my mind, but I always felt better once I ran it by her. It also gave us something to talk about each night. I'm really going to miss that."

"Do you keep a diary?"

"No."

"You might want to consider that. It doesn't have to be a book diary. You could keep a daily journal on your computer. You'd have a way to record your thoughts and you could think about what Jennifer might say or the advice she might give you. It'd sort of be like you and she were having a conversation."

"I like that." Madison finally smiled.

"Getting back to your life and normal activities doesn't mean forgetting about your mother."

"I'm going to try and take things one day at a time. Come on, let's walk in the water."

The cool water washing over their feet felt refreshing. As Bannister felt the wet sand underneath, his mind flashed back years ago to that evening when he and her mother walked along this same beach. Her mother was just about Madison's age at the time.

"Do you have a boyfriend?" he asked.

"No. Oh, I've gone out with a few of the guys on the men's volleyball team, but nothing serious. We just sort of hang out together. Last week you said you had a girlfriend named Robin in Washington. Have you told her about me?"

"I have. She and her boss are coming to Atlanta next week on a case so I'll get a chance to see her and show her some pictures of you. You'll definitely be a topic of conversation," he said with a tender smile that hid a feeling of awkwardness. His relationships with Robin and Madison were still evolving. He hated not being in control of his emotions or not knowing what to say. He hoped that next week he would correctly read the verbal clues before responding to either woman.

His cell phone vibrated for the second time in an hour. Again, it was Witt, and again he ignored it.

"Isn't it tough having a relationship when you're so far apart?" Madison asked.

"It is. You each have your own jobs and places to live. Your contact with each other is through impersonal means—phone calls, texts, e-mails. You miss the physical connection."

"I guess if it's meant to be, you can work things out, right?"

Bingo. She certainly nailed the major question he had about where he and Robin were headed.

"Like you mentioned earlier, we're taking things day by day," he said.

"I wish you didn't have to go back to Atlanta tomorrow."

"I don't like it either." He paused, then decided to go for it. "Listen, Madison, I had a wild idea on the flight over. We've got so much catching up to do and so little time. There are so many dots we're trying to connect. You have a week free of practice and before classes start, right?"

Madison nodded.

"During your down time, why don't I fly you and a friend out to Atlanta for a few days? I'll pay for a couple of round-trip tickets and you both can stay at my house. I have three extra bedrooms. The two of you can check out Atlanta in my 4Runner. What do you think?"

"Wow! That's fabulous. We'd have a chance to talk and find out more about each other. I could see where you live and work and things like that. That would really be neat. You're willing to do that?"

"Sure, do you have a friend that might be interested?"

"Katie, one of my roommates, and I talked the other day about going to Atlanta to visit you sometime. Neither one of us has traveled further than St. Louis. I don't think we thought it would happen so soon!"

Bannister smiled. "I'm still going to have to work, but I'm sure I can take time off to show the two of you around. Besides, look at it this way. You'd get the answers to a bunch of your questions."

"This is just awesome. I can't wait to tell Katie."

By her glowing smile, Bannister could tell she was all for it. They continued walking northwest along the beach until they could barely make out the Santa Monica Pier. By the time they got back to the car, they had talked for two hours and he believed his daughter was prepared for tomorrow.

CHAPTER 29

Before checking out of the hotel, Bannister changed his return flight to 11:00 p.m. so he could spend more time with Madison. He finally returned Witt's numerous calls. Fortunately, he got his voicemail and left a message he'd be on a red-eye flight and would see him in the morning.

Bannister picked Madison up at the agreed-upon time and let her give him directions to the hospital as he drove. She wanted to review the program for her mother's memorial service. He didn't ask any questions but merely listened. She was calm and had a handle on the details.

The service was brief. The hospital's chaplain gave an uplifting eulogy. He asked everyone to stand while he said a short prayer. After his "amen," the chaplain said, "All of us gathered here do so in a celebration of Jennifer's life. She wanted to leave all of you with these words from William Allen White. 'I am not afraid of tomorrow for I have seen yesterday and I love today.' She tried to live her life by those words."

As he spoke, Bannister reached over and took Madison's hand. Her eyes were moist with tears. When the chaplain finished with the words, "May she rest in peace," Madison shuddered and started crying again. He embraced her until she softly pushed away.

With a tremulous smile on her face, she turned and faced all of those who came to honor her mother. "Thank you from the bottom of my heart. My mother loved all of you."

—⌇∞⌇—

A reception was held in the hospital's training room and Madison introduced Bannister as her father. With grace, she remarked to those whose eyebrows lifted, "I'll explain later."

After the reception, Bannister drove her back to her apartment. Two roommates had gone out for a couple of hours so that he and Madison could visit. Katie, the third roommate, planned to spend the evening in the apartment. When Madison shared the news to her about their visiting Atlanta, they became excited and had a bunch of questions. The three chatted about the city and when they asked about things to do, Bannister told them it would be their trip together and they could plan their own itinerary. Naturally, he would offer suggestions about highlights in town and give them his input about certain areas of the city. He would also assist them if they wanted tickets to particular events.

"I can't believe we'll be going to Atlanta," Katie said excitedly.

"I think you're really going to like the city," Bannister said.

"I'm going to go to my room right now and look up some stuff, while you two visit," Katie said.

He told Madison he'd coordinate details with her later and mentioned he would like to call Katie's parents to answer questions they might have and make sure there weren't any objections.

He and Madison talked for another half hour until Katie came out of her room. The girls had rented several movies and intended to spend the evening trying to unwind and come to grips with Madison's situation. When it was time for Bannister to leave, he felt comfortable about Madison's state of mind.

"I wish you could stay another day or two," Madison said.

"Me too. We'll catch up when you arrive in Atlanta."

He planned to wait until Madison's visit to discuss his financial assistance to her. Finally, it was time to say goodbye. Once again, he embraced the daughter he was trying to get to know. He kissed her on the cheek and then drove directly to Los Angeles Airport.

CHAPTER 30

Bannister finished reading through a stack of recent interviews when White asked him to stop by the vault.

"I came in early today and updated our searches on Bashir Rahman al-Ahmad. Then I called my CIA contact again and she had something new. Six weeks ago, MI5, the British Security Service, asked for a records check on Rahman al-Ahmad. The Agency responded that they didn't have anything current. Thought you'd want to know before the meeting."

"Good work, Germaine. Thanks."

He located Ramirez and requested she send out an urgent request for MI5 to tell them what their interest was in Bashir Rahman al-Ahmad. He told her to volunteer to the Brits that al-Ahmad was a person of interest in an ongoing murder investigation as well as being linked to a terrorist cell in the US.

The counterterrorism briefing was scheduled for 2:00 p.m. Bannister walked into the Task Force space early and spotted Robin immediately. She was chatting with Ramirez, who looked in his direction. As he approached, Robin turned around, a Cheshire-cat smile on her face and a sparkle in her blue eyes. She reached out her hand, which he took in his.

"Hello, Ty."

"Hello, Robin," he replied, matching her hungry look with one of his own.

"Why don't you two use Stu's old office and catch up on things before the meeting starts," Ramirez suggested, giving him a wink.

He opened the door for Robin and, using his back to close it, grabbed her in his arms and hugged her close for a few seconds, enjoying the warmth and scent of her perfume.

"Did everything go okay in LA?" she asked, looking into his eyes.

"It went fine. We'll talk about it later." He held both of her hands. "You smell great. What are you wearing?"

"It's Jo Malone's scent—Lime Basil and Mandarin."

"Well, it's captivating. It makes me want to kiss you right now," he said, staring into her face.

"I'm staying in town tonight, you know."

"I was hoping you'd be able to fit me in."

Robin leaned into him and whispered into his ear, "I'm looking forward to it."

Gary Witt and two guys Bannister didn't recognize walked into the conference room together. He assumed one of them was Robin's supervisor. Witt was wearing a light blue shirt with a white collar and his trademark suspenders which he always referred to as "braces."

Bannister turned and whispered to Ramirez, "Gary must have purchased those for an important presentation."

"I got it," she said, smiling as she stared at suspenders with colored figures of hot air balloons.

"We may as well get started," Witt said, gesturing to the two men.

"I'm Tom Bradley," one of them said, "Washington supervisor of the squad investigating a Hamas terrorist organization operating in several major cities. Special Agent Robin Mikkonen from our office is coordinating the investigation of the Atlanta cell and will follow me with the details you'll need to plan your raid here. Floyd Fox is the Task Force supervisor in Detroit and is directing the operation up there."

Bradley continued. "What we know is that the Detroit organization is currently grossing $2,000,000 a month through the smuggling and sale of cigarettes with counterfeit tax stamps. We estimate $400,000 each month is getting back to Middle East terrorists."

"So how many cartons of cigarettes are we talking about?" Witt asked, with his thumbs inside his suspenders. He leaned back in his chair at the end of the table.

"A tractor trailer load," said Bradley. "Each truck has a load of eight hundred cases or 40,000 cartons,"

"What amount does it take to make it a federal crime?" one of the Task Force agents asked.

"You have to show 60,000 or more cigarettes are purchased with the intent to avoid payment of state taxes to make it a federal violation. For you non-accountants, that's six cases."

"How's Atlanta fit into the picture?" Witt asked.

"The cigarettes are purchased, stolen, or diverted in South Carolina. From there they're trucked to a warehouse in Atlanta, which has counterfeit tax stamping machines and packaging equipment. From Atlanta the re-boxed cigarettes are driven to different storage facilities on the outskirts of Detroit's Metropolitan Wayne County Airport.

"We've had two known cells under surveillance since the beginning of the year. I've been focusing on their representatives in Washington, DC, who handle fundraising and political activity. Many of their money transfers out of the US have been tracked, primarily due to information from a sensitive source inside the World Bank.

"The two cells we've been watching are doing the cigarette smuggling. They're the ones we're hitting in Atlanta and Detroit next week. The third cell, which we believe to be an operational team, just came up on our radar. We don't know who their members are or what their intended target might be but they've been funded out of DC.

"The National Security Agency has stayed on top of chatter and made various analyses. They've concluded with an eighty percent probability that two cell members have been functioning in the Atlanta area. Based on an increase in electronic traffic, NSA is surmising this cell may take action within two weeks."

"A man of interest—Rahman al-Ahmad—has been in the custody

of Egyptian security. Let's just say the Egyptians were successful in getting him to talk," Bradley said.

"I guess they don't have a problem with water boarding," Witt added, displaying a smirk to the agents sitting around the table.

Bradley shot an irritated glance at Witt and continued. "We give Egypt four million dollars a day in foreign aid. Occasionally they give us something back. Rahman al-Ahmad provided the first names of two associates, both operating in the Chamblee area of Atlanta, which, coincidentally, matches up with the location of the cigarette warehouse near the Doraville Metro station. We're pulling out all stops to ID those men."

"What else do you know about al-Ahmad?" Witt asked.

"It's possible he's involved in the murder of a CDC scientist this week and that gives us heartburn. I understand Agent Bannister has been working that case with Atlanta's homicide detectives," Bradley said.

On cue, Witt turned in Bannister's direction. "This would be a good time for you to share what we know."

Bannister handed out a photo sheet with pictures of al-Ahmad, Kevin Middleton, and the prostitute who rented the hotel room. The next fifteen minutes were spent outlining how Middleton, a CDC researcher, had access to biological toxins, was heavily in debt but had an overseas bank account with $100,000 in it, and last week was stabbed to death in a cheap motel. Bannister laid out the facts identifying Rahman al-Ahmad as a person who purchased the same brand of liquor as in a bottle found twelve hours later next to Middleton's body. The morning after Middleton's death, al-Ahmad used a one-way ticket purchased in cash to board a flight to Cairo.

The serious looks on the faces of the agents around the table and the questions they asked left no doubt they believed an attack was planned. Hopefully, the FBI could stop it.

They took a short break before Robin's presentation. Bannister and Robin stood outside the vault in which White was busy finishing a current timeline of Middleton's murder.

"I'm worried," Robin said.

"So am I." Bannister's eyes narrowed and his brow furrowed as he stared at Robin.

"Do you know whether Middleton was connected to one of these cells?" Robin asked.

"No, but my gut's telling me yes."

"Please be careful," Robin said. "I don't know what I'd do if something happened to you." Her blue eyes were wide. Bannister knew she was thinking about January when he was shot.

"Don't frown," he said. "You'll get wrinkles."

She rolled her eyes then grabbed his hand and squeezed it.

In his heart Bannister knew he loved Robin and was certain she loved him. On the final day of their vacation in Antigua last spring, they'd made a promise to take a trip together next New Year's Day. She would have earned six vacation days by then. He already had thirty on the books.

They agreed to spend the week in Paris and explore why it's called the City of Lights. Although it had been nine years since she studied in Paris, Robin was excited about returning and sharing it with him. She knew he'd never been there but gave him responsibility for their daytime activities; she would handle the night. That meant he had to pick some excellent historical sights and museum exhibits and be ready with compliments for the opera or play tickets Robin was certain to buy. In return for his insistence on paying all the bills, she promised to use her command of French to smoothly apologize for any of his faux pas. If everything went the way he hoped, there was an important question he planned to ask her before they flew back.

His thoughts were interrupted when Supervisor Bradley walked around the corner.

"Tom," Bannister said, "I agreed to take Robin to the Silk Restaurant this evening. It's supposed to have the best sushi, and their chef is a Kaiseki master. Do you want to join us?" Robin had already told him Bradley hated sushi or anything to do with fish and that Agent Fox was returning to Detroit.

"No thanks. ASAC Witt said he was going to take me out later for a steak and good cigar," he said. "We're ready to start again."

Robin's presentation went smoothly. Bradley would be in charge of the arrests of the Washington cell's subjects. Fox then discussed how Detroit was going to take down the two storage facilities near their airport. Robin looked at Bannister several times during his presentation. After two hours, plans for next week's raids and arrests had been hashed out. The conference adjourned and White, as she headed out of the office, handed him the murder timeline on which she'd been working. Fox left for the airport; Robin and Tom Bradley left for the Grand Hyatt. Bannister reviewed all the financial data their tech guys pulled off of Middleton's computer and then returned a call from Detective Miller at Atlanta PD.

"This is Ty Bannister. What've you got?"

"We caught a break," Miller said. "We obtained some video you'll want to have enhanced. There was a family from Valdosta, Georgia, who was spending two days at Six Flags Over Georgia. They checked out of the motel the morning we discovered Middleton's body. One of my detectives just tracked them down. The family's son was playing around with their video camera the afternoon before, shooting scenes of his younger sister acting goofy. My detective talked to the father and then drove to Valdosta and picked up the video. We just finished viewing it. In the background there are three guys talking and standing next to a white sedan. Couldn't make out the license plate. But one of the men was definitely Rahman al-Ahmad. A second guy never turned around, but the third one was facing the camera. Can you grease the skids with your photo people?"

"Better than that. If you get the disk to our office by 7:30 a.m., we have two agents who are flying back to Washington on a morning flight. They'll hand deliver it to our lab."

"Great. Consider it done," Miller said.

CHAPTER 31

Bannister had called ahead to Hsu's Gourmet Chinese restaurant and placed an order which he picked up after work. Once home he put the five red Chinese paperboard cartons in the refrigerator. After showering and changing, he drove to the Grand Hyatt to pick up Robin. Thinking about the case's progress, he thought maybe they were getting lucky.

A few minutes later he had no doubt he was the one in luck when Robin exited the elevator and walked directly toward him. Her black heels clicked across the hotel foyer's green marble floor, blond hair swaying in sync with her hips. Robin wore a white denim jacket with some kind of shimmery blouse underneath and black slacks. Finishing off the sophisticated look was a long gold necklace and a red clutch. Bannister knew she gave careful thought to what she wore. He was giving in to thoughts of what was underneath.

"You look great in white or . . ." he started.

"Or?"

"Or nothing at all," he finished, with a devilish smile.

"I love it," she said. "You're not able to read my thoughts, are you?"

"Can I answer that later?"

It only took five minutes to reach his home where he pulled into the third bay of the garage. Once in the house, the two walked into the kitchen where he poured each of them a glass of chilled Pinot Grigio.

"Here's to us," he said. They lightly clinked their wine glasses. "It's been quite a day. There's so much to talk about." He took a few sips of wine before setting his glass down. "You mentioned the Silk Restaurant earlier. Is that where you want me to take you this evening?"

"How about taking me right here?" Robin said, as she put her glass down, leaned into him and gave him a long deep kiss. She pushed away slowly, not saying a word. She deliberately removed her jacket and placed it over the back of one of his kitchen bar stools. When she turned around, the faint points of her nipples showed through her shiny grey blouse.

"Give me your hands," she said. As Bannister obeyed her with the hint of a smile, she said softly into his ear, "I'm glad they're nice and warm." When she gently placed them over her breasts, he instantly got hard.

She whispered, "You're a trained investigator. What do you conclude?"

Excited at her aggression, he murmured, "You're not wearing a bra?" while he applied a string of kisses to her neck.

She framed his face with her hands and kissed him on the mouth as she pressed herself into him.

"Are you going to show me your bedroom?" Robin whispered, her warm tongue teasing his ear with calculated seduction.

Bannister didn't resist the gift she offered as he led her down the hall into the master bedroom where he turned to face her. As he eased off her top, her knowing hands dropped down to his belt.

"You've been on my mind constantly," she said. "I thought of you on the flight; I thought of you during the briefing and I thought of you while I was in the shower." Her fingers caressed his chest, teasing the curly hair. He didn't remember when he'd lost his shirt.

"Well, I hope you're through thinking," he said, his voice almost breathless.

He savored her as he would a fine wine, suckling her breasts and teasing her to new heights of sensation. As they fell onto the bed, he suffered with passion as she stroked his arousal. They started slowly, but the memories of their last time together rushed to the surface. What began as a gradual savoring of each other's body flashed into a hunger for fulfillment. Robin wrapped her legs around him and pulled him to her damp heat. Their rocking motion became faster and faster until Robin's rhythmically arching hips drove him over the edge. He felt her shudder just as he reached that moment of explosive release.

Beneath him, Robin whispered, "Don't let go. Just hold me for a minute. I want to feel us together as one." And then, just as sweetly, she murmured, "I love you, Ty. I can't imagine being with anyone but you."

He confessed, "I love you, too. I really do. You're the only one I want to be with. Ever since I laid eyes on you, I hoped we'd be linked together. I'm really glad you're here and can't believe how much I've missed you." He looked into her blue eyes and stroked her hair.

Gradually their heart beats and breathing returned to normal. Robin turned on her side toward him as he lay there looking at her.

"Why don't you close your eyes and tell me what you enjoyed the most about our vacation in Antiqua," she said. While he thought about what his answer would be, Robin rolled on top of him, her inquisitive hands assuring him she was anxious for more.

They lost track of time but eventually exhausted, they untangled themselves. Robin lowered her head and softly kissed his lips.

"Tonight we had a chance to just enjoy each other and not worry about tomorrow or the next day," she said.

"I wish we didn't live so far apart," Bannister said.

"Well, we've done a good job of getting caught up, don't you think?"

"Absolutely."

"I haven't been away from you so long to forget that after sex you think about food. Well, tonight I've got to admit I'm a little famished. Where are you taking me?" Robin asked.

"I have Chinese food in the refrigerator. I stopped and picked up some tangerine beef, Chinese curry salmon, and vegetable fried rice."

"Oh, my favorites!" She raised an eyebrow. "Hey! You had this planned all along!"

"No, I didn't. I got the idea from you."

"What are you talking about?"

"During your briefing you kept emphasizing the importance of contingency planning," he said.

"And if I hadn't succumbed to your charms, what would we have done?"

"I would have taken you out for dinner some place nice and eaten the Chinese food tomorrow." That earned him a light punch in the ribs.

"Okay, Mr. Planner. Do you want to take a shower together?"

"I think if we did that we'd just end up right back here and you'd probably be too exhausted to return to the hotel."

"What you really mean is you'd be too exhausted to drive me back."

"Ouch. How about I just heat up our dinner?"

"That sounds like a good plan."

—◊◊◊—

It was 11:00 p.m. when Bannister's Toyota 4Runner headed down his driveway toward the iron gates. As it stopped under the streetlight at the end of his driveway, the two occupants looked at each other as their vehicle turned left onto Valley Road. Neither of them paid attention to the seemingly empty blue minivan with tinted windows parked across from Bannister's gates. Concealed comfortably in a beanbag chair in the back of the van, the occupant who was watching was just about to get a view of the female passenger in Bannister's vehicle when she turned her head as it passed. From his vantage point, all that Terry Hines could see was long blond hair and Bannister laughing.

CHAPTER 32

Hassan Fadi had the nightmare again. He'd lost count how many times these past twenty years when the blinding white image woke him from his sleep.

He remembered that morning when the sun had warmed his back as he stood in front of his family's small house in the southern Lebanese town of Sidon. His older brother was laughing as he tried to show his little sister Janna, in her new yellow-and-white striped dress, how to use the side of her foot to kick the soccer ball. The ricochet of the ball off the neighbor's tenement wall was answered by Razak's deft side kick. Although only eleven years old, Razak had shown great promise as a player.

Fadi had been thinking of school that morning at the very moment two arrow shaped shadows streaked over the barren dirt field where his eyes were focused on his siblings. He only had a second to glance skyward at the gray blurs when his entire field of vision turned into a hot silver cloud. The concussion of the bombs threw him backward. The smell of explosives mixed with cement dust and dirt and blood assaulted his nostrils. Lying on the ground, he looked back to where a moment ago his brother and sister were playing. Debris was still falling from the air as his eyes stared at the rubble of what remained of two of his neighbor's homes and an appliance store. It looked like an entire block had been obliterated. His ears were ringing but he still heard faint screams coming from across the field.

The Israeli jets had successfully destroyed a terrorist safe house. Fadi picked up a four-inch piece of yellow-and-white striped cloth with a wet red stain on it. Janna and Razak were blown to pieces. They were considered acceptable collateral damage.

He never had a photograph of his sister or brother. All he had to remember them by was a piece of bloodstained cloth. For him that was enough. And soon he would have his retribution against the Jews and their American ally.

—◦◦◦—

Kasim Musa drove the rental car to the side entrance of the Extended Stay Inn where he and Hassan Fadi had been living in Atlanta. Once inside their room, Musa asked Fadi, "Any word from Rahman?"

"No, and I'm concerned. He has always followed instructions. He called as he was supposed to as soon as he landed in Cairo. He was told to call me at 4:00 p.m. EST every forty-eight hours. He missed the first call and today it is already 4:10."

"Do you think something happened to him?" Musa asked.

"Yes, but we all know the risks," Fadi said.

"The two of us can still carry out the plan, right?"

Fadi closed the lid on his suitcase and locked it. "Yes, Rahman did not know the destination or the time table. We are still safe to go. Any problems getting the car?"

"No, but the Mitsubishi you reserved wasn't there. They upgraded us and I got a Jeep Grand Cherokee for our trip." Musa's face broke into a large smile.

"You idiot. May pus-infested wounds grow in your eyes! You know I hate this country and anything American," Fadi yelled. "How could you rent an American car?"

"I'm sorry, Hassan. I will take it back right away."

Fadi sighed deeply and then calmed down. He should never have agreed to use his wife's youngest brother. But those were his orders. He nodded to Musa. "Take it back, Kasim, and tell them your trip was canceled. Just pay the penalty and don't offer any other information. When you leave there, go to Avis Rent-A-Car and get a foreign sedan.

I don't care if it's a Mitsubishi or Volkswagen. Anything but American. Call me if you have any questions. Okay?"

"I will do as you say. Again, a thousand apologies, Hassan."

CHAPTER 33

I t was Sunday evening and the days were running into each other. Bannister finished paying his household bills and decided to take a stroll through his neighborhood. As he exchanged pleasantries with a woman whose Irish wolfhound was walking her down Valley Boulevard, his phone rang.

"Agent Bannister. This is Terri Andrews. When you gave me your business card you said to call if there was anything I wanted to discuss. Well, this isn't about your investigation but about racquetball."

As soon as she identified herself, Bannister tried to figure out her real purpose in calling.

"Go ahead," he said.

"I'm entered in a tournament next month. My regular partner had some minor surgery and can't practice for a couple weeks. I noticed your name on the men's challenge ladder for A players. I'm listed on the women's AA ladder. I think I could give you a good match if you're interested."

He paused for a second and wondered what Robin would think of this before he heard himself saying, "Sure, do you have a time in mind?"

"I have the first hour on court one for the next two Mondays at 6:00 a.m. I know that's awfully early, but I recall you mentioning you like to work out early. This would certainly give you a chance to jump-start your day."

The last time he played at the Ravinia Club was a month ago. His opponent that day beat him. It was Kendall Briggs.

"I'll see you there tomorrow. How's that sound?"

"Great. I'm looking forward to the competition," she said.

Right now, Dr. Andrews was only a witness in their case. If she was a subject, the only court he'd be able to meet her in would have a judge sitting in front. They still didn't know if she was aware she was the sole beneficiary to Briggs's insurance policies worth $500,000.

When he got back to the house he called Ramirez at home and explained the invitation he'd just received.

"So, what do you think?" he asked.

"The first thought that occurred to me is that she just might want to jump your bones."

"I don't think so."

"Well, maybe she wants to find out how the investigation is going, or maybe she's looking for some competition to help her prepare for her tournament. You know, women are complex," Ramirez said.

"You're telling me."

"Well, tell me tomorrow when you get to work what you found out."

"Will do."

Terri Andrews had a lot going for her. She had a professional practice, was smart, attractive, and athletic. Her dark penetrating eyes exuded sensuality. He tried to figure her out as he retrieved his gym bag, which contained two rackets, shoes, safety goggles, a new glove, and one unopened can of blue racquetballs. He tossed in his faded green Dartmouth hand towel for good luck and zipped up the bag.

His cell rang again. He thought it was Ramirez with an afterthought. He glanced at the number which was from Santa Monica."Hi, Dad. It's me, Madison." She sounded excited. "How are you doing?"

"Good. Can Katie and I come this week? I went to her house after church and her parents are okay with everything. I gave them your address and telephone numbers. We're all jazzed about the trip. I told her mother to go ahead and give you a call. That you didn't bite." She giggled.

"Good. E-mail your flight information to me. I plan on picking the two of you up, but if I'm not there when you get off the plane, don't wait. Take a taxi to the house. My housekeeper, Sophia, has agreed to stay late on whatever day you arrive. Call the house from your phone, or buzz her from the gate, and she'll let the cab in the driveway."

"Ten-four!" Madison laughed.

"You've been watching police shows." He had to smile. "Okay, call me again before you come, all right?"

"You bet. I can't wait to see you. Thanks again, Dad."

He poured himself a glass of red wine and was thinking about tomorrow when his cell phone rang again. This time it was Robin.

"I hope you're glad to hear from me," she said.

"Always."

After a brief conversation in which they ended by wishing each other a positive work week, he remembered Ramirez's comment that a woman is complex. He thought about what he was juggling with Madison, Robin, and Terri Andrews. As he finished the last of his wine, he said out loud, "I surrender."

Bannister walked through the doors of the Ravinia Club at 5:45 a.m. This was the first time he'd been there that early. He grabbed a towel and took two left turns from the men's locker room to the racquetball courts. Each court cubicle was twenty feet wide, twenty feet high and forty feet long. The back wall was thick glass with a small glass entry door with a recessed brass handle.

He and Terri showed up at the court ten minutes early.

"Do you want to practice for a couple minutes?" he asked. Each of them was holding a new can of racquetballs.

"We may as well use mine," he said, listening to the whoosh of air as he opened the vacuum-packed can. They put their bags down outside the door and adjusted their safety glasses and headbands. Terri was decked out all in black—black compression shorts, black warm-up jacket, and black headband. She had a black glove on her left hand. He hadn't played against a southpaw in two years.

They didn't talk at first but practiced some soft high bouncing serves which they hoped would die in the back corner. The temperature inside the court felt like sixty-five degrees.

"So, how often do you play tournaments?" Bannister asked.

"I try to enter at least one each quarter," Terri said. "It forces me to practice harder to stay sharp." With that, she snapped her wrist and hit a rollout, an unreturnable kill shot to the front wall.

Obviously pleased, she said "Ready?" as she walked to the door and took off her jacket. She had on a black sports bra. "I get hot pretty quickly," she said, winking at him. He took in her tightly defined curves and taut muscle tone. This would definitely be interesting.

"Let's do it," he said. They each lagged the ball to see who could get closest to the serving line.

Terri won and as she picked up the ball, he commented, "You have a telltale bruise on the back of your calf. Someone must have got you good."

She turned and looked down at the back of her left calf, which sported a faded red circle where a hard shot must have hit. Bannister had been hit in the same location last month by Kendall Briggs, but he thought better than mentioning that.

"Yeah, I got in the way of one of my opponent's shots. It was match point. We replayed it and she hit another winner. I joked that I was going to be a sore loser."

Their match began.

When he'd first shaken Dr. Andrews's hand at her office, he sensed she had hidden strength. It definitely showed when she struck numerous powerful shots that were difficult to return. He had no intention of letting a woman beat him at racquetball. After twenty minutes, Bannister lost the first game to Terri, fifteen to ten. They took a minute to towel off.

"You're really good," he said.

"And so are you. Ready for another one? Your serve."

He won the second game by two points and Terri beat him in the third and final game.

"I thought we were pretty evenly matched," Terri said. "You really pushed me."

He shook her hand and remarked, "Well, I'm definitely awake now." They left the court and used their towels to dab at the sweat.

"Do you have time to grab a drink at the health bar, say in twenty minutes?" Terri asked.

"Sure. Does that give you enough time?"

"I'm not high maintenance. I'll probably get there before you do."

Terri was correct and had already ordered some kind of cranberry-pomegranate drink when Bannister showed up and settled for an ice-cold chocolate milk. A year ago, Robin had told him that drinking chocolate milk after a hard workout would help replenish his energy faster and also quench his thirst. She was right.

"Here's to a successful tournament for you," he said, raising his glass.

"Thanks. Is it too soon to ask if you're interested in a rematch?"

"Sounds good. Why don't you check with me Sunday evening to confirm." From the itinerary she'd sent, he knew Madison and Katie would be finishing their Atlanta visit that day and would have to get to the airport for their return flight at 5:00 p.m.

He and Terri chatted for another five minutes. When he asked her if she'd thought about doing any mountain climbing, she mentioned being invited to go with a friend to the Patagonia region of Argentina and tackling a couple of peaks there. She said she had to turn down the invitation because right now she didn't think she could justify the cost. That led him to believe she had not been contacted by Briggs's insurance company and was unaware she was the beneficiary of a half million dollars.

As Bannister drove to the office, he tried to figure out where Terri Andrews fit into the picture. Five minutes later his phone buzzed.

"This is Bannister," he said.

"Where are you? This is Derek." Barnes rarely called him unless it was important.

"I'm in the parking lot out back. Be up in a minute."

"Good. I've got some breaking news you need to hear."

Once in the Task Force space, Barnes approached. "I think the spotlight just landed on Dr. Theresa Andrews," he said.

"Don't keep me in suspense."

"Our Denver office contacted the national distributor for Boker ceramic knives. They furnished two years' worth of sales for the type of knife used to kill Briggs. One of the Internet sales came back to a Theresa Andrews and the delivery address was a Pak Mail box in Atlanta, also registered under her name."

"Damn," he said.

"There's more. Chief Spina called from Dahlonega with some information which Germaine confirmed an hour ago. Andrews's husband owns a cabin two miles from the marble quarry where Briggs was murdered. Does this change your priorities?" Barnes asked.

"Yeah. I have to cancel a racquetball match."

CHAPTER 34

Witt called Bannister to his office. He kept a glass jar of Jelly Belly candies on the front of his desk and had the habit of offering some to an agent before giving him an ass chewing. Since he'd been in Atlanta, there had not been an occasion where he'd offered Bannister any candy. Today was different.

"Want some jelly beans, Ty?"

"No thanks. It's too early."

"Well, is it too early in the day to keep me informed of developments? What the hell's going on?" he asked.

At that moment Bannister recalled a response an agent he used to work with in Los Angeles always used when he did something he wasn't supposed to do or had failed to do something he'd been ordered to do. He used to drive his supervisors nuts when he'd lean forward, take off his glasses, and in an innocent voice say, "What prompts your inquiry?" Bannister needed to find out what kind of burr was under Witt's saddle this early in the day.

"Could you be more specific?" he responded.

"I'm briefing US Attorney Prescott after lunch today. What do you know about this shrink Briggs was seeing? Derek Barnes told me the hunting knife that was found had traces of Briggs's blood on it and that it's been traced to the shrink, a Dr. Theresa Andrews."

"First of all, Dr. Andrews is not a psychiatrist but a psychologist and yes, Briggs was apparently seeing her on both a professional and personal level."

"Barnes also told me her prints were found in Briggs's bathroom. Was she having an affair with him? I heard she stands to inherit a half million from Briggs, right? Isn't that enough to arrest her?"

It was obvious Bannister needed to have a chat with Barnes. Agents had a duty to keep superiors informed, but they also had a responsibility not to have them getting information piecemeal from different sources and then running off half-cocked. That's why the case agent or supervisor had the task of briefing the higher ups.

"Based on this morning's developments, you could say Dr. Andrews has gone from being a witness to a person of interest," Bannister said.

"What kind of bullshit are you feeding me?" Witt's face reddened. "How many Theresa Andrews are there in Atlanta, for crying out loud?"

"I wouldn't jump to conclusions, Gary. We're moving fast on this case, but not recklessly. As a matter of fact, there are seven Theresa Andrews in the Atlanta metropolitan area. We need to do more investigation concerning the purchase of the knife used to kill Briggs. Concerning your other questions, it's true a thumbprint of Dr. Andrews was discovered at Briggs's condo, but she's admitted having at least two dinner dates with him. It's possible they stopped by his condo, she used his bathroom, and the print has remained there. Finally, I don't believe Andrews even knows she's the beneficiary of Briggs's life insurance policies."

"How the hell do you know that?"

"I don't. It's conjecture on my part. That's why I want to find out the facts."

Bannister wasn't about to tell Witt he arrived at this opinion after playing racquetball three hours ago with the same woman Witt believed killed their prosecutor. "What you can do is tell Winston Prescott we've identified a person who may have knowledge of Kendall Briggs's murder and that we're going to interview her within twenty-four hours."

"Is she going to lawyer up?" Witt asked, folding his hands and rocking back and forth in his chair.

"She's already talked to us once. I'm optimistic she'll agree to another interview."

"Even after you advise her of her rights?" Witt took the glass lid off his jar and scooped a dozen pieces of candy into his hand.

"I've never found that to be an impediment in the past," Bannister said.

"Well, when is this interview going to be scheduled?" he asked as his jaw worked on the Jelly Bellies.

"As soon as I'm finished with our discussion I can set it up."

"You do that. And remember that until Stu Peterson's replacement arrives, I'm the one running the Task Force."

"We all know that," Bannister said, glad to see Witt's flushed face returning to its normal pallor.

"Are we all set for the raid and arrests tomorrow?" Witt asked.

"I checked with the surveillance supervisor and SWAT team leaders before coming to your office. There have been no status changes and we still have a green light from Washington."

"Good. I'm going to let the Task Force know at this afternoon's briefing that Derek Barnes will assume the role of case agent on KABMUR with you assisting. I want you to concentrate on this Middleton thing. Any questions?"

This caught Bannister by surprise, but was consistent with Witt's reputation of shooting from the hip, even if he didn't know what the target was.

"Can't that change wait until tomorrow? It will certainly raise some questions and might be disruptive," Bannister asked.

"Are you questioning my authority?" Witt asked.

"No." In his mind Bannister questioned his smarts. Barnes was trying to get ready for his temporary assignment to Lima, Peru, next month and was brushing up on both his Spanish and Quechuan languages with State Department tapes. Witt's decision was like changing the quarterback at the start of a football game without letting the team know. Fortunately, Barnes was a solid team player. Bannister would work it out with Barnes despite Witt's micromanaging style.

After leaving Witt's office, Bannister called Ramirez and Barnes and asked them to meet him in the small conference room where they could talk. Once they were there, he broke the news to them of Witt's decision.

"He's turning into a real meddling asshole," Barnes said.

"I heard a couple of Office of Professional Responsibility agents grilled him Friday about some situation," Mercedes added.

"It's about an Equal Employment Opportunity complaint one of the criminal analysts filed against him. He's wired pretty tight since that's been holding up his promotion," Bannister said.

"Yeah, but he shouldn't take it out on his agents. For the record, I'm not interested in grabbing the reins from you," Barnes said.

"I know. Let's just continue like nothing happened, except you'll have to handle regular briefings until the case is solved or you leave for Peru."

"You don't think he'll screw up that assignment for me, do you?"

"No."

"By the way, I didn't brief him on all developments, but I did tell him the particulars about the knife," Barnes said.

"That's okay."

"And for your info, the quarry owners were interviewed in Raleigh. Cooperative but no help. All the neighbors near the quarry have been interviewed and checked out. Nothing there either." Barnes leafed through a folder, then said, "Professor Camille Poston at the University of South Carolina and Todd Watson, the guy that owns a fishing charter in Fort Walton Beach, Florida, were interviewed. They confirmed they were guests at the Spa at Egret Bay the same week as Briggs, but couldn't shed any light on him. They didn't know him before their stay, never knew his last name, and had no contact with him after their vacation ended. Their only socializing with him was on their last day when the six of them hiked to the lookout where that nudie cutie picture was snapped."

The three agents went over their assignments for the remainder of the week. They discussed their roles in the raid tomorrow and were confident they were ready. Satisfied, Barnes excused himself.

Bannister looked at Ramirez. "Witt's seeing the US Attorney in a couple of hours. You're up to speed on Terri Andrews, right?"

"Yes." She tapped her notebook.

"Well, I'd like to be able to tell Witt we have an interview scheduled with her. You know I don't like Witt, but I can't ignore him either."

"Why don't you call Andrews right now?" Ramirez suggested.

Six SWAT agents from Savannah and Augusta were going to be here for the raid and would have rooms at the Embassy Suites. Bannister called one of the guys he'd worked with on a recent case and arranged to use his room for three hours to interview a subject.

"Why aren't we meeting her at our office or hers?" Ramirez asked.

"I prefer not to be interrupted and don't want there to be any question about whether our interview was a custodial interrogation. I want it to be perfectly clear to Andrews she's free to leave at any time."

"Don't we have to get headquarters approval to interview a doctor?" Mercedes asked.

"Only medical doctors," Bannister said. He then called Andrews, who answered right away.

"Hello, Ty. Good timing. I'm between appointments."

"Terri. This is an official call. There have been some developments in our investigation and we need to interview you about Kendall Briggs."

"Sure. How much time do you need?"

"I'm guessing at least an hour, and the sooner the better. Are you free at the end of the day?" he asked.

"I don't have anything after five thirty," she said.

Bannister set the interview up for 6:30 p.m. and gave her directions to the Embassy Suites. He told her he and Ramirez would meet her in the lobby. He called Witt and let him know they were questioning Andrews that night.

"How do you want to conduct the interview?" Ramirez asked.

"Why don't you cover basic background data and a timeline for her appointments and meetings with Briggs. I'll let you handle the interview log and required forms, okay? It's worked well before."

"I've got you covered. I'll bet the good doctor never thought she'd be competing physically with you to start the day and mentally to end it," Ramirez said.

"This is a first for me too. In the meantime, let's get ready for the raid briefing."

CHAPTER 35

Bannister obtained a key to the agent's hotel room they intended to use and arranged the chairs and coffee table in the living room section of the suite. He had a bucket of ice and diet sodas and cold bottles of water. The Savannah agent hadn't dropped his suitcase off yet and had agreed to wait for Bannister's phone call before coming to the room.

Bannister appreciated that Dr. Andrews was punctual and he assumed she'd left work early enough to allow for Atlanta's rush hour. Her stride was purposeful as she made her way across the lobby to where he and Ramirez were waiting.

As they stood near the elevators, Ramirez said, "I like your red briefcase."

Andrews smiled at the compliment. "Thanks. One of my patients commented she'd seen a case just like it on *One Life to Live*. I actually checked that out and discovered she was right. In any event, I just love it. I did bring my file pertaining to the person we came to discuss."

The three went to the fourth-floor suite. Earlier Bannister had laid Ramirez's notebook on one of the guest chairs placed to the left and slightly back of the one where he wanted Andrews to sit. He'd put his notebook on the couch opposite the other chair. The radio was on low tuned to a classical music station. Andrews declined his offer of a soft drink or water.

"Terri, before we begin, I need to advise you of your rights. In these kinds of cases, I frequently do this. I'm going to read you each of your rights and make sure you don't have any questions."

Ramirez handed Andrews an "Advice of Rights" form, and Bannister watched her eyes follow along as he read it aloud. Her pale face contrasted with her bright auburn hair. On the outside she looked serene.

After a minute, she asked, "Do you think I had something to do with Kendall's murder?"

"I don't, but that's what we want to talk to you about," Bannister said.

"Do you think I need a lawyer?"

"You're entitled to have one present before we ask you any questions."

"I've always believed innocent people don't need lawyers. It's always bothered me in those missing or murdered children cases, you know, like that JonBenét Ramsey case or the Caylee Anthony case in Florida, when the grieving mother or father hires an attorney from the beginning." He and Ramirez continued to look at Dr. Andrews.

"I'll sign the waiver," she said.

Ramirez witnessed as Andrews signed with a flourish. Then Ramirez asked preliminary questions such as full name, address and occupation.

In addition to her primary residence in the Dunwoody neighborhood, Andrews revealed she and her husband owned a three-bedroom cabin in Auraria, Georgia, and had a post office box in Dahlonega, five miles away.

She then covered the eighteen-month timeframe during which she treated Kendall Briggs as a patient. Andrews removed two files from her briefcase and periodically referred to documents to make sure she had the correct dates. Finally, Ramirez finished and put her pen down. She nodded to Bannister.

"When we first talked with you at your office, I asked you if you had seen Kendall other than at your office or the athletic club. You said you had dinner with him twice. You led us to believe those were the only occasions," Bannister said.

"I did not intend to mislead you. You did not ask if those were the only occasions. You're the one who drew the conclusion," Andrews said.

"Touché!" She smiled at his response and he continued. "Do you intend to fully answer my questions today?"

"Yes."

"You're not going to lie to me, are you?"

"No."

"Did you see Kendall Briggs other than at your office or the Ravinia Club?"

"And other than at the two dinners I mentioned?"

"That's correct."

"Yes, maybe seven or eight times."

"Did you have a sexual relationship with him?"

She stared at Bannister for a few seconds, leaned back and said, "Yes."

"When did it start?"

"The first time was at the Barnsley Gardens Resort, an hour north of Atlanta."

"When was this?"

"The end of April."

"Whose idea was it?"

"You mean Barnsley Gardens or the sex?"

"Both."

"Both ideas were Kendall's."

"I'm assuming one of you got a room."

"Kendall did. When we had dinner at the Bacchanalia we talked about Georgia resorts and restaurants. I mentioned I had always wanted to visit Barnsley Gardens because of its reputation. One week later he invited me for dinner there on a Friday. It was his suggestion we pack an overnight bag, just in case."

"So, you knew what you were doing?"

"Yes. I was stepping into forbidden waters, breaching the doctor-patient relationship. I didn't know how far it would go." Andrews was wringing her hands.

"Would you like something to drink?" Bannister asked.

"That'd be great. I'll have a soda," she said. Bannister got her a glass of ice and a Diet Coke. After a few swallows, she continued.

"The other two times we had sex was at my cabin near Dahlonega."

"Where was your husband?"

"He was out of town on both of those occasions."

"Did you ever have sex at Kendall's condo?"

"No."

"Did you ever visit his place?"

"Yes. After our dinner at the Bacchanalia, he wanted to show me where he lived."

"Did either of you have something else on your agenda at that time?"

"No. Kendall fixed each of us an Irish decaf coffee. He showed me his condo, we talked for maybe half an hour and then I left."

"Did you use his bathroom?"

"As a matter of fact, I did. That's a weird question."

Bannister ignored her response. "Did your husband know you and Briggs were intimate?"

"No. I only informed my husband when Kendall and I went out for dinner."

"Do you recall where you were the night Kendall was murdered?"

"Yes, I was at my cabin. I remember when I heard about his body being discovered in Dahlonega, I shuddered because I realized I was asleep just a couple miles away when he was being killed."

"Were you there alone?"

"Yes."

"Can anyone verify you stayed there that night?"

"You can ask my husband. I told him that morning at work I intended to go up to the cabin and restock some of our food provisions. I called my husband from the Korner Pantry and asked him if he wanted me to pick up a package of his favorite pipe tobacco, which they stock. I said I'd swing by the house in the morning and change clothes before going to work. You can check with him about that."

"How did you pay for your purchase?"

"I put it on my debit card."

Bannister made a note to pull her card charges and review her phone calls for that day. "Have you ever been to the marble quarry?"

"No."

"Do you know how to get to it?"

"I've driven past the road which says Memorial Marble Quarry. But it's posted 'Company or Official Vehicles Only.' I never had a reason to drive up their road."

"Your cabin is not too far from Amicalola Falls, right?"

"I'd estimate four miles."

"Have you ever hiked in the area of your cabin?"

"No. We've only owned it for two years and use it as an escape. It's wired for cable and satellite but we haven't felt a need to install a TV."

"Other than what you've told us, did you ever have occasion to be out of town at the same location as Kendall Briggs?" Bannister asked.

"Yes." Andrews stared at both Bannister and Mercedes for a few seconds. "I'm assuming you already know."

"Why don't you tell us."

"We spent a week in May at the Spa at Egret Bay with a group," she said.

"Didn't you think that information might have helped us in our investigation?" Bannister asked.

"At the time I believed you were more interested in whether I knew of anyone who might have a reason to kill Kendall. I told you I didn't. Besides, visiting a nudist resort is a topic you just don't normally bring up in an initial interview. If I was wrong, I apologize."

"Okay, whose idea was it to go to the spa?"

"The idea was mine. It was before I ever had a date with Kendall."

"Please continue," Bannister said.

"The year before I went by myself to Hidden Beach, an au natural club, an hour south of Cancun. I wanted to open up my mind and rediscover some things about my inner self. I wanted to experience how people communicated without the normal distractions of designer clothing and jewelry."

"And you thought Kendall might benefit from a similar experience?" Bannister asked.

"Well, yes. I also had a growing attraction to him and thought that by going to a nudist camp it would open up his mind to his own sexuality and help extinguish my growing sexual infatuation with him."

"What happened to your relationship with him in June after you got back?"

"We met one mid-morning at the Nordstrom's coffee bar at Perimeter Mall and had a long talk. We decided to give ourselves a break from each other. I was concerned he was becoming more impulsive. As if on cue, Kendall asked me if I would consider leaving my husband. He asked if there was anything he could do to show how strongly he felt about me. I didn't answer him but suggested we take a few weeks to think about what was important in our lives at that point.

"I thought a separation would help us sort out our feelings. I even suggested to him that he might want to date other women if he had a chance. In the back of my mind I was hoping I wouldn't be the one to determine the direction our relationship appeared to be headed. Kendall said he'd abide by my suggestion but that he was going to be making some important decisions soon."

"Did he say what those were?" Bannister asked.

"No."

"When did you resume seeing him?"

"At the beginning of last month. I told him I couldn't see him professionally anymore because I was falling in love with him." Andrews looked down and rubbed her hands. Bannister waited a few seconds before continuing.

"When were the two of you intimate at your cabin?"

"Over the Fourth of July weekend and again at the end of the month. Just a minute . . ." Andrews picked up her smart phone, scrolled through it, and gave Ramirez the exact dates.

"You told us your husband David was aware of the dinner dates but wasn't aware of your having sex with Briggs, right?"

"Correct. He didn't know we were having sex."

"What would be his reaction if he found out?"

"He'd be shocked. If I asked him to forgive me I'm sure he would."

"Has infidelity ever been an issue between the two of you in the past?"

"You certainly are direct." Andrews took a long sip of soda before continuing. "That issue has not come up before."

"Would your husband be the type to retaliate against Briggs?"

"Do you mean kill him?"

"Exactly."

"No. David is not a violent person. Throughout our marriage I can't recall his ever having raised his voice to me. He goes through life logically talking through problems and issues."

"Do either of you own a gun?"

"No."

"Do either of you own a hunting knife or outdoors knife?"

"David doesn't. I have a knife that I carry when I'm mountain climbing."

"What kind of knife is it?" Bannister asked.

"It's a K.I.S.S. knife. That stands for Keep It Super Simple. I can't remember who makes it, but I've had it for five years. It's extremely sharp and won't accidentally open if it catches on a karabiner."

"Have you ever owned or purchased a ceramic knife as a gift?"

"No."

"Where do you and your husband receive your mail?"

"You mean P.O. boxes?"

"Yes."

"We have a mailbox at our home in Dunwoody. We both share a

P.O. box for office mail and we have a separate P.O. box in Dahlonega for Lumpkin County statements and other local mail."

"Do you have a separate P.O. box anywhere else?"

"No."

Bannister decided to change subjects and carefully gauge her physical reactions. "Are you aware Kendall named you as the beneficiary on a life insurance policy?"

"What? No." Andrews's face paled and for a few seconds her hands visibly shook. "What are you talking about?"

"He had a $250,000 government-issued life insurance policy. In June he filed a change of beneficiary form, naming you. The policy has a double indemnity clause. Upon his death, you are entitled to receive the proceeds. Five hundred thousand dollars tax free." Bannister stared at her.

"Oh my God! Oh my God!" Andrews started shaking and big tears rolled down her cheeks. She sat frozen as if in shock. Ramirez, as was her custom in interviews with Bannister, came prepared and reached over with a packet of facial tissues.

"So, you never knew?" Bannister asked.

"I had no idea. Kendall was impulsive about some things but I didn't have a clue about that. He never said a word." Andrews dabbed at her eyes and blew her nose. "I can't believe it. If he had ever mentioned doing something like that I would have talked him out of it."

"Terri, I have to ask you. Did you kill Kendall Briggs?"

"No."

"Do you know who may have been involved in his death?"

"No."

"Can you think of anyone who might want to frame you for Kendall's death?"

She rubbed her forehead for a few seconds before saying, "No, I can't think of anyone I would consider an enemy or who I may have hurt badly enough for them to do something like that."

"Is there anything else you wish to share with us at this time?"

"No. Are you going to tell my husband about Kendall and me?"

"I don't know, but it might become necessary."

"I understand. Would you let me know before you do?"

"Yes. We appreciate your talking with us. If you think of anything that might help, call me."

"I will. Believe me when I say I had absolutely nothing to do with his murder."

Bannister stared into her eyes and believed her. "I think I can read at least one thought going through your mind. You have some questions about the insurance but feel it would be totally inappropriate to bring it up at this time. So, here's a card with the name and telephone number of the company that issued the policy. I would call them and say a representative of the US Attorney's Office suggested you advise them that one of their policyholders is deceased and had named you as the beneficiary. Let them take it from there. Because their policyholder was murdered, they naturally will do their own due diligence inquiry and, I imagine, a lengthy delay will take place before you receive payment. But if you had nothing to do with Kendall's death, eventually you will receive the money."

"You didn't have to do that," Andrews said.

"You beat me this morning. I owed you something." Bannister saw a sparkle in her eyes as they stood up and shook hands. Andrews moved toward the door.

As she let herself out, Bannister said, "We'll be in touch."

He and Ramirez took a few minutes to finish their notes. When he closed his notebook, he said, "What's your opinion?"

"She's certainly mixed up, but I don't think she's mixed up with murder. You agree?"

"I do. I think someone has gone to great lengths to frame her, either because of a grudge or because they want to shift attention away from themselves. That leaves us with a lot of work left to do."

CHAPTER 36

At 10:00 a.m. in a Travelodge parking lot in Kansas City, Missouri, two men loaded their car with small, tightly packed duffle bags. Kasim Musa closed the trunk of the white Nissan Sentra he had rented two days ago. "Hassan, how far do we have to drive today?" he asked in Arabic.

"We should reach Grand Island, Nebraska, in five hours," Fadi replied. A minute later their car was turning left at the entrance to I-70 West.

"Yesterday it seemed like we were on the road forever," Musa said.

"That's because neither of us had ever driven that route before. Do you remember when we drove from Atlanta to Detroit?" Fadi asked.

"Yes. That trip went fast."

"That's because you had the excitement of seeing people that knew you. From Atlanta to Kansas City is only one hour further."

"Maybe today will go faster because of the excitement of knowing what we are going to do."

"Of that I am certain!" Fadi exclaimed.

———⟨ᴥᴥᴥ⟩———

That same morning, the FBI had also packed supplies for a mission. A convoy of vehicles slowly left a staging area at the Dekalb-Peachtree Airport, two miles from Atlanta's FBI office. The assault team's movement was monitored by an FBI drone circling quietly overhead. Government vehicles headed north on Buford Highway toward a nondescript warehouse near Doraville Plaza.

A dozen SWAT team agents, clad in ballistic armor and helmets and armed with MP-5 machine guns, shotguns, and automatic pistols, had carefully rehearsed what they were going to do. Six of the SWAT agents comprised the entry team; the other six were backup. The blocking vehicles were in place and had cordoned off access to the warehouse and two surrounding roads. Satisfied, Witt signaled the SWAT team commander, Agent Keith Santini, to have his sniper take out the two exterior cameras mounted on the warehouse's roof. Butch Sutton, a former Delta Force commando, aimed two silenced rifle shots, eliminating any video feeds. A second later, Witt gave the order to enter.

An armored FBI vehicle lumbered a hundred feet, crossing a curb and asphalt parking lot. Its hardened steel ram caved in the main warehouse door, the metal framework and support studs crunching under the impact. SWAT team members jumped over the debris shouting "FBI" in unison. Another agent bellowed "police" in Arabic.

Not all of the occupants froze in their tracks. One man in the rear of the warehouse reached for an AK-47 as another man thirty feet to his left began unslinging his machine gun. The man in the rear was lifted off his feet as eleven .40 caliber slugs simultaneously ripped through his body and head. The man to the right was blown apart as four agents unleashed a barrage of rounds at him. A bald-headed man in a glass enclosed office along the right wall had remained motionless for the first few seconds. Ignoring official commands, he bent down and retrieved a pistol from a desk drawer. His motion of raising the pistol was met by the roar of shotgun blasts obliterating the glass wall and slamming his body backwards. The white marker board behind the desk was peppered with blood and body tissue. All three men had died instantly. Seven others in the warehouse had obeyed orders and stood with arms stretched upward, their faces etched with fear. The man closest to the door was holding a clipboard by his side. His eyes glanced downward at the stain spreading across the front of his khaki trousers as his bladder let loose.

Ramirez entered with the evidence search team. Witt and Bannister followed them inside. In ten minutes Witt would be overseeing operations from a tactical command vehicle that had taken up a position outside the complex facing Buford Highway.

Now they assessed the immediate situation. After his men confirmed there was no one hiding on the premises, the SWAT commander corralled the living subjects along the south wall away from the carnage. After being relieved of weapons and cell phones, they were searched and restrained with flex cuffs. They were ordered to remain silent and told to sit on the concrete floor facing the wall. Each would be driven by two agents to an offsite commercial building leased by the FBI. There they would be segregated and interviewed before being taken to the Dekalb County Jail for processing.

Bannister and Witt looked at the body of the first man who had made the fatal mistake of reaching for a weapon.

A SWAT EMT pronounced the man dead, stood up, and nonchalantly remarked, "Looks like a burlap bag of crushed strawberries." Bannister noticed the color draining from Witt's face.

"We've got a lot to do inside here, Gary. I know your phone's going to be going crazy in a minute."

"The boss is with the US Attorney and the Dekalb County Sheriff," Witt said. "I need to call them right away and after things are sorted out here, I'll call the commanders in Detroit and Washington, DC."

"I know headquarters had a shooting incident team on standby to fly here or Detroit if necessary. You might want to let SAC Brennan know everything's under control before calling FBI Headquarters. How about I come out to the command post every twenty minutes and update you?"

Still looking at the body, Witt said, "That's a good plan. You may not believe it, but I've never seen a dead shooting victim before. Look at all this blood."

"We'll process the scene, get the bad guys out of here before the press arrives, and clean this place up."

"Someone should call Inspector Glenn Yates of the GBI," Witt said.

"I just did and asked him to send a medical examiner here for three homicides," Bannister said.

"You mean justifiable killings," Witt said with a smug look on his face.

Bannister forced a smile and nodded. No need to correct him. All murders are homicides but not all homicides are murder. Even though Witt was the senior man on the scene, Bannister didn't want him upchucking on the evidence, embarrassing himself and adding his own aroma to the stench of blood, feces, and the acrid smoke of gunpowder.

The evidence team quietly went about its business. Photographs were taken and markers placed for all shell casings. The office where the alleged manager was shot was sealed off. It would be more thoroughly searched after his body was removed.

An Isuzu twenty-foot box truck was parked in the warehouse bay. It was half loaded with cases of contraband cigarettes. One of the SWAT agents had turned off the packaging machinery located on the left side of the warehouse.

Bannister's responsibility this morning was to get the documentary and electronic evidence to the Rapid Start Team at the office for their analysis. The technical support supervisor gathered up all electronic devices, including cell phones, a laptop, and a desktop PC. SWAT team members cleared seized weapons. Ramirez collected paperwork seized under the warrant and put it into cardboard boxes.

Thirty minutes later Bannister went outside to update the ASAC. While walking to the command vehicle, he sent a text message to Robin: "Nobody hurt. 3 bad guys KIA. Will call tonight." He knew once she heard on CNN about the raid she'd be worried. If their roles were reversed, he'd be concerned, too.

He stepped into the command post and Witt swiveled around in his captain's chair.

"The ME and two ambulances are here. The seven prisoners were just transported to the offsite for questioning," Bannister said.

"Good. The US Attorney is having a press conference at noon. The only people who are going to talk to the press are me, SAC Brennan, and the US Attorney."

"Well, CNN and two of the local stations just arrived," Bannister said.

"We're sticking with the multi-state cigarette smuggling operation story," Witt said.

"What'd you hear from Detroit and DC?" Bannister asked.

"No shots fired in Detroit. It was a clockwork operation: eleven people arrested; a quarter million in cash seized. Two more subjects picked up in DC."

"When's the shooting incident team arriving?" Bannister asked.

"An inspector and his team are flying out and should be here by 3:00 p.m. They want to interview the SWAT guys today and do the rest of their interviews in the morning."

The Counterterrorism Task Force was a hub of frenetic activity the night of the shooting and into late afternoon the following day. The inspector's shooting incident team took over the large conference room. Twenty-two agents and six support employees were interviewed the day of the raid. Evidence Response Team members were interviewed Wednesday morning. Bannister, Witt, and all SWAT agents participating in the raid were separately interviewed by detectives with the Dekalb County Sheriff's Office. Neither law enforcement agency anticipated any public blowback from the killings, which clearly were justifiable. Two of the deceased members of the cigarette smuggling ring were Lebanese nationals here on expired visas. The office manager was a US citizen with a felony record in Michigan. Preliminary indications showed none of the three deceased had relatives in the United States.

Intelligence analysts at FBI Headquarters poured over the data flooding in from Atlanta, Detroit, and Washington, DC. White was in overdrive working her databases and link analysis programs.

At 4:00 p.m. Bannister got a text message from Madison that said she'd call him at 10:00 p.m. Atlanta time. Assuming everything went well, he'd be at the airport in twenty-four hours to pick her and Katie up for their extended weekend.

A half hour later White called and asked Bannister to come to the vault. She said it was important.

After he entered, she closed the door. The silence and air conditioning of the enclosed room were refreshing.

"Ty, Headquarters just relayed a photograph taken this May in London. The photo accompanied a sanitized report from British intelligence. You remember we wanted to know why they were interested in Bashir Rahman al-Ahmad. Their watcher service covered a meeting al-Ahmad had with a Hassan Last Name Unknown and a person the Brits identified as being Nathan Shane Quinn, an American currently living in Woking, a suburb of London." White turned the photo so they could both examine it. "Do you see what I see?"

"I don't believe it."

They both said at the same time, "That's Terry Hines!"

CHAPTER 37

Terry Hines needed to think but he also wanted to relax. Tomorrow the next phase of his plan would take place. It was still early when he arrived at the Old Crom Pub and took a seat at the end of a separate bar in the Cottage Room. The same female bartender that had served Hines during his last visit walked around the corner carrying a wet dishtowel. With one long practiced motion she wiped off the counter in front of him and then smiled.

"Guinness Stout?" she asked, scrunching her nose.

"No, Beamish."

"That's right," she said tilting her head back. She grabbed a mug and took a careful minute of pouring to build him a pint with a solid inch of head.

"Enjoy." She disappeared as quickly as she'd arrived.

Hines's mind retraced the steps that led him here. At his bond hearing last year before the judge came into the courtroom, he overheard Briggs whisper to Agent Bannister, "Hines is a smartass degenerate. I'm not going to be satisfied with anything less than twenty-five years." Hines knew both men were surprised when he was able to post bond, and now he felt a rush reliving his plan to kill Kendall Briggs.

Two months earlier he had followed Briggs for four days. It was a bonus to discover Briggs's condo wasn't alarmed, and the only surveillance cameras covered the street side of the Artists Square development. His patience was rewarded when he followed Briggs to the offices of the Andrews Group near Lenox Mall. He speculated Briggs might be seeing a psychologist. There's a saying that you can be good or lucky. Hines believed you could be both. On Friday of that first week he followed Briggs to the Bacchanalia restaurant. No one dined alone at the Bacchanalia.

A half hour after Briggs had gone in the front door, Hines went into the restaurant and used the men's room. He spotted Briggs dining with an attractive redhead. Ninety minutes later the couple emerged. A valet brought a white Lexus around to the front and held the driver's door as the woman got in. Hines noted the license plate. Another valet brought a Jaguar to the front. It stopped behind the Lexus. Two minutes later Briggs's Jaguar flashed its lights and both vehicles turned into traffic heading south on Howell Mill Road with Hines falling in behind them. A short time later the two cars pulled into parking spaces behind Artists Square. Hines took up a position across the alley. He only had to wait forty minutes before Briggs's date came back out and left in her car. Traffic was light, and Hines stayed far enough behind so the woman wouldn't know she was being followed. After fifteen minutes she pulled into the driveway of a colonial home in the Dunwoody neighborhood. Hines slowed long enough to observe the house number illuminated under the front portico.

The next day, a nominal fee to the Department of Motor Vehicles gave him the registered owner of the Lexus. Public records confirmed her residential address as well as a property owned by David and Theresa Andrews in Lumpkin County, GA. A quick Google search revealed additional background information on Dr. Theresa Andrews including her photograph on the Georgia Tech University's faculty page.

Hines used the information he'd acquired in his surveillance to purchase a six-month Pak Mail post office box rental in the name of Terri Andrews. From the Internet he ordered a twenty-foot length of Visco safety fuse, a Spyder brand handheld blue laser, and a ceramic knife. He paid for these items with a money order in the name of Terri Andrews and sent them to the new mailbox. The weekend after placing his orders, he drove to a gun show at the Jamil Temple in Columbia, SC. He decided to purchase a weapon there because no federal records check was required. He purchased a compact Glock nine-millimeter automatic for $680. He furnished the seller the name of Nathan Quinn, for whom he had both a Georgia driver's license and US passport.

The other items he needed he purchased locally. He needed a substance that would render a person unconscious. He could easily have purchased chloroform from eBay, but the effects from his intended use of the product might take longer than he was willing to risk. Besides, if not used safely, that chemical could result in solvent burns. After doing some research, Hines contacted a cleaning equipment company in south Atlanta where he bought a liter of carbon tetrachloride. He bought a pair of work boots from Walmart. From a security equipment store he obtained a packet of plastic flex cuffs and finally, from a hardware store, he bought a one-gallon gas container.

His game plan was simple, but it wasn't foolproof. Each of the six tenants at Artists Square had their own open carport in the rear. Each carport was separated from the others by concrete panels on each side. Hines intended to confront Briggs after he parked his vehicle. He only needed the right evening. Hines used the name of an officer with the Gwinnett County Chamber of Commerce and made a pretext call to the US Attorney's secretary. He said they wanted to give a surprise award to Kendall Briggs at a speaking engagement. Sherrill Newsome confirmed Briggs would be the guest speaker at the Gwinnett Center in northeast Atlanta Thursday evening.

That particular Thursday afternoon Hines drove his white Taurus rental car to the Smokin Gold Barbecue Restaurant in Dahlonega, two miles from the Memorial Marble Quarry. He called a cab to take him from the restaurant to the North Georgia Outlet Mall in Dawsonville, five miles away. After browsing for an hour, he called a different cab company to drive him to an address two blocks from Briggs's apartment in Atlanta.

Briggs was scheduled to give a half-hour presentation to assembled insurance investigators at 8:30 p.m. Hines assumed that if Briggs came straight home, he would arrive around 10:00 p.m. Hines, carrying a green canvas grocery bag with the items he needed that night, took the Atlanta MARTA train to the stop nearest Artists Square. Earlier he had checked the weather report, which called for overcast skies with a sixty percent chance of rain. Rain would only be an inconvenience. He arrived at Artists Square at 9:30 p.m. and took up a concealed position in the alleyway behind a store that sold rugs during the day.

Briggs pulled into his parking space at 10:20 p.m. and exited his car. He was wearing his blazer and carrying his briefcase. The parking area was empty except for the two men.

The lights on Briggs's Jaguar flicked, and the horn sounded briefly as Briggs hit the lock button on his key ring. He turned around and faced a gun aimed at his chest.

"Mr. Briggs, I'm Terry Hines. I know you remember me. I do not intend to hurt you, but we need to talk. I want to surrender. You need to listen to my conditions, but first, slowly put your briefcase down and turn around." Hines had counted on his offer of surrender to reassure Briggs and guarantee compliance with his request.

Briggs did as he was told and as he turned his back to Hines, said, "If you want to surrender this is not the best way to go about it."

With his left hand, Hines reached into his pocket and from a metallic foil bag removed a cloth soaked in carbon tetrachloride. Hines lunged at Briggs from behind and smashed the cloth over Briggs's nose and mouth. Briggs's hands flew up defensively to pry Hines's hands from his face but it was too late. Briggs gagged and with Hines's hands and arms violently pressing the cloth to his face, Briggs fell sideways to the parking lot, striking his head on the asphalt. Everything was over in thirty seconds. Hines knew from his research that if Briggs had not suffered a heart attack, he most likely would be unconscious for up to half an hour.

Hines grabbed the car keys from Briggs's now limp hand and unlocked the car. He hooked his arms under his victim and dragged the two-hundred-pound body to the side of the Jaguar. He hoisted and shoved Briggs stomach down into a prone position on the back seat.

With the flex cuffs he secured Briggs's hands behind his back. Hines then set the stopwatch function of his watch and returned to the spot near the rug store where he retrieved his shopping bag and placed it on the rear floorboard of the car. He put on a pair of latex gloves, picked up Briggs's keys and briefcase and went upstairs to Briggs's loft unit.

Hines wanted it to appear to police that Briggs opened his door to someone he knew. He put the briefcase down on a chair in the foyer. Hines looked in the case and saw a couple of newspapers and a file folder. The contents didn't interest him. He intended to search the apartment for something that might be used to incriminate Dr. Theresa Andrews. His efforts to find an object that investigators might later link to Andrews proved unsuccessful. However, in Briggs's carefully organized closet he found a gun case on the top shelf and a box of bullets. He removed the nine-millimeter automatic and put it and the bullets in his pocket. From a glass display shelf, he picked up a bronze figure of a female dancer, mounted on a marble base. He looked at his watch. He had been in the apartment for eleven minutes. He locked the front door and walked back to Briggs's carport.

Hines did two things before starting the car. After checking to see if Briggs had a pulse, he picked up the bronze figurine and raised it as high as he could in the back seat of the car and swung down hard, striking the back of Briggs's skull.

Hines drove the speed limit all the way to Dahlonega and, after several turns, exited onto the private road heading into Memorial Marble Quarry. He parked Briggs's Jaguar in a clearing a short distance from the gravel road. Next, Briggs's gun and ammunition were placed in the canvas shopping bag along with his own automatic and a coil of fuse. A half-gallon of the gasoline was poured in the front seat of the car; the remainder was emptied over the motionless body of Kendall Briggs lying on the back seat. Hines placed a foil pouch, containing a cotton handkerchief soaked with extremely inflammable fingernail polish remover, on the front seat of the car. He took one end of the safety fuse and twisted it inside the pouch before carefully unwinding the remainder and stretching it along the ground. Hines then walked to the edge of the clearing and, using the ceramic knife, cut a small pine bough the shape of a fireplace broom.

Turning back toward the Jaguar, Hines heard a noise and, in the shadows, saw Briggs staggering away from the car. There wasn't time to retrieve one of the guns. Briggs started running in the darkness but stumbled and fell to his knees on the gravel road. Hines caught up with him and shoved him face-first to the ground. Briggs was defenseless and with one swoosh of a knife across his throat, the federal prosecutor lay dying in the quarry.

Hines wiped the handle of the knife and flung it down the road where investigators would be able to recover it. After returning to the car, he lit the safety fuse and then began quickly brushing out his footprints for fifty feet. The fuse would burn for seven minutes before reaching the front seat of the car. Hines walked rapidly up an incline to a position about a third of a mile away and waited. He turned around and stared into the blackness until there was a flash of bright orange flames, which danced into the sky. Smiling with his handiwork, he hiked to where he'd parked the rental car earlier that day and drove back to Atlanta.

Hines's thoughts were interrupted when the female bartender returned. "What's the big grin for?" she asked.

Hines opened his eyes in response to her voice. "I was just thinking about a successful venture."

"Well, do you want another Beamish to celebrate?"

"Why not?" he said.

CHAPTER 38

Before departing for Grand Island, Nebraska, Fadi and Musa shopped at a large Goodwill store in Kansas City where they purchased bib overalls, colored tee shirts, work boots, and baseball style hats. Fadi picked out a green-and-yellow John Deere cap; Musa liked his blue Burpee Seeds hat, even though it had an oil stain on the brim.

"I still do not think we need to dress like this, Hassan," Musa stated after they left the Goodwill store with their purchases.

Fadi had a stern look on his face and said nothing until they got near to their car. In a firm voice and looking directly into Musa's face, Fadi said, "Do not question my decisions! I want us to at least look like we could be farm workers. These clothes will make us less conspicuous and we can carry everything we need in the deep pockets."

"Where are you keeping your gun?"

"When we leave the motel, I'll put it in the trunk of the car," Fadi replied.

They had booked a room in Grand Island for two nights at a Red Roof Inn across the street from numerous fast food restaurants and next to the interstate.

Fadi had a plastic thermos, four syringes and two bottles of insulin which he had purchased at a drug store in Atlanta. He knew synthetic human insulin and syringes didn't require a prescription. He didn't anticipate there being a problem at the fair's entrance. If anyone questioned his having needles, he would simply tell them he was a type 1 diabetic and produce the insulin.

That afternoon he preceded Musa through the magnetometer. Fadi set off the alarm and one of the fair's female security guards holding a black wand said, "Step aside, sir."

Fadi said, "I forgot. My needles must have set it off. I am a diabetic and carry these needles for my insulin. Here, let me show you my medicine." He smiled at her.

The guard examined the needles and the two bottles of insulin Fadi produced. After checking the items and then wanding him to make sure he didn't have any other metal objects, she let him proceed. Fadi claimed the rental car keys that he had placed in a round plastic dish. Musa followed him through the magnetometer with no problems. As soon as both men cleared the entrance, they were approached by a woman with a camera.

"How about a photograph to remember your experience?" the young blonde woman smiled at Fadi.

"No thank you," he said, displaying a polite smile of yellow teeth. He knew that tomorrow, *Inshallah* (God willing), would be an experience he would remember for the rest of his life.

Fadi picked up an information brochure and after examining it and orienting himself, lit a cigarette. The two men walked down a midway flanked by vendors selling corn dogs, French fries, something called funnel cakes, and other foods foreign to their tastes. They were surprised at how many young children there were, accompanied by teachers or other escorts. They had to maneuver past many strollers being pushed by fat American women wearing tight clothes. Finally, the two arrived at the Agricultural Arena where an exhibition of Charolais and Red Angus cattle along with various other breeds entered in the 4-H Breeding Beef competition were scheduled to appear tomorrow.

There were eighty exhibitors with booths and information displays inside the huge Agricultural Building. Fadi and Musa meandered through the structure and walked past a large collection of antique tractors and farm machinery near the entrance to the cattle barn. As soon as they stepped into the barn area, their noses filled with the smell of hay and feed and manure. Several young men and women were busy soaping and brushing the coats of the animals, pushing shovels and hosing urine from the cement floors, and otherwise preparing their livestock for tomorrow's competition.

"Do you have specific cows as targets?" Musa asked.

"This entire row of holding pens looks very promising. We will not have a problem and to dose the animals here should only take us a couple minutes" Fadi said.

The two men left the area where the Charolaise and Angus breeds were being held and walked next door to the 4-H building. They repeated the same pattern of slowly walking down the rows among the various pens holding numerous steers and dairy heifers.

"We will also pick out two of the cows in this building," Fadi said.

"There are many to choose from. I've never seen so many different kinds of giant cows," Musa said.

"Neither have I. Supposedly there are over nine hundred different cows in the world. I think all the ones we've seen here must weigh at least six hundred kilos," Fadi said.

Returning to the midway an hour later, both men breathed in the aromas of specialty foods being prepared in trucks lining one side of the median.

"I am hungry, Kasim, and that food stand looks inviting," Fadi said to his partner, pointing to a sign advertising falafels and gyros.

―――∽∾∽―――

After morning prayers, Fadi and Musa repeated their declaration of faith by saying, "*La ilaha illa Allah wa Muhammad rasul Allah.*" (There is no God but God, and Muhammad is the messenger of God).

Fadi, with Musa standing by his side to shield the monitor of the motel's business computer, typed out a letter, a copy of which would be mailed to both the *Wall Street Journal* and the *Washington Post* newspapers. Accompanying each letter would be a thin plastic contact lens case containing samples of the biotoxin obtained from the CDC researcher.

Fadi's letter said: "Dear Editor: Within the last week we infected cattle at three different stockyards in the United States. They have been injected with bovine spongiform encephalitis. You know this as mad cow disease. The enclosed container has the prions causing this disease. This is real and not a hoax. We received the prions from Kevin Middleton who used to work at the Centers for Disease Control. Allahu Akbar!"

Fadi looked it over and then hit "print" for two copies. He used two blank sheets of paper to cover the top and bottom of the printed copies to avoid leaving fingerprints. Satisfied, he placed the letters inside of a People magazine he had purchased and put it in the trunk of their rental car. He and Musa checked out of the Red Roof Inn and drove to the Nebraska State Fairgrounds.

The actual operation went smoothly. Fadi had four prepared syringes with him containing the saline/prion solution. While Musa stood guard to make sure no one walked toward them or looked their way, Fadi injected each animal. Only one of the animals even showed irritation when Fadi stuck the needle into its hindquarter. That one had merely swished his tail when the needle went in.

After each injection, Fadi put the used syringe inside the plastic thermos he had carried into the fair. When he finally exited the 4-H building, he took the thermos and discreetly discarded it in a large trash receptacle near a group of picnic tables.

Fadi and Musa smiled at each other when they passed through the monkey bar exit gate of the fairgrounds. The two then headed back to Atlanta with one planned stop.

At a FedEx office in Kansas City, Fadi sent the two letters he had prepared to the editors of the newspapers. The Wall Street Journal envelope went to their headquarters on the Avenue of the Americas, New York City. The Washington Post package was addressed to their offices on 15th Street NW, Washington, D.C. As the sender, Fadi substituted the name, address, and phone number of the Department of Agriculture, Kansas City, MO. He paid the clerk in cash, took his receipt, and left the office.

As their car eased into traffic for the drive back to Atlanta, Fadi glanced at Musa and, with a devilish smirk exclaimed, "Kasim, what we have done will make a prime impact for our cause. It will be a thousand times more damaging than what our brothers did at the World Trade Center Towers."

Musa whistled and let out a loud ululation. Fadi smiled at him. Musa said in a forceful voice, "They will be proud of us, Hassan."

CHAPTER 39

"Germaine, we need to pull out all the stops to locate Nathan Quinn," Bannister said as he plunked down in a rolling desk chair next to White's workstation. "Before you leave tonight get a priority message out to FBI Headquarters and have them call in any favors they have with MI5. London is five hours ahead of us. It'd be nice to have something current when we come in tomorrow." White swiveled away from her monitor to face Bannister. "Are you going to notify the US Marshals Service? They're going to be super excited since Hines is on their 15 Most Wanted Fugitives List."

"I think SAC Brennan will handle the notification. I'll suggest he let the Marshals know we have unsubstantiated information Hines may be using the alias Nathan Shane Quinn. Hopefully, they'll expedite new traces and coordinate with State Department, Homeland Security, and the airlines to save us time and resources."

White turned back to her computer and pulled up a flow chart. Pointing at the screen she said, "We know Middleton was involved with Bashir Rahman al-Ahman and two unknown subjects in Atlanta. Those three are part of the network stretching to Detroit and Washington. Now we know Terry Hines is connected to al-Ahman, too." She tapped her finger on a photo lying at the side of her keyboard. "Take a close look, Ty, at the man sitting at the far left table behind Hines. Doesn't he resemble the man in the tourist's photo Detective Miller gave us?"

"Sure does," Bannister said after a few seconds. "Again, great work, Germaine." She was smiling as he left.

Before leaving work, Bannister called Brennan and updated him. The boss had found out after the fact that Witt had switched Bannister from primary investigator to being backup to Barnes on the KABMUR case. He assured Bannister he would intervene when necessary. Bannister took him up on his offer by asking to have Agent Ted Mims assigned to their cases. He'd had coffee with Mims the day before to see how he was doing. Mims was appreciative of the way Bannister handled things and expressed optimism he and Audrey would salvage their marriage. He was anxious to prove to the office that personal problems wouldn't affect his work. Bannister told the boss he had confidence in Mims. Brennan said Mims would be ordered to report to the Task Force in the morning.

At home, Bannister ate a salad for dinner and watched a half hour of Fox News before deciding to go out for an easy five-mile jog through his neighborhood. The streetlights came on as Bannister started retracing a favorite route. He and his best friend, Caleb Williamson, used to run this route many times in the early morning hours. It had been a year since Williamson was murdered, and Bannister still missed him.

—⟋⟋⟍—

"Doesn't it seem a little weird to you we're going to spend a weekend at the home of a guy we don't know?" Katie asked Madison as she sat down on the side of Madison's bed.

"He's my father!"

"I know that, but what do you really know about him?"

"You think he's a child molester or something?"

"I didn't mean it that way."

"Well, he's in the FBI!" Madison said in a louder voice.

"I know."

"Look, I'm going to Atlanta. If you don't want to go, that's okay with me."

"No, I'm going. I want to go with you. It should be a lotta fun." Katie stared at Madison and hesitated before speaking again. "Has he shown you a picture of his house?"

"No, why?"

"My mom said not to say anything to you but she looked up your father's address on a website called Zillow."

"And? C'mon, what!"

"It's not like she was snooping—but, you know, she's a mom and just wanted to see where we'd be staying."

"So?"

"The site is a real estate one. It shows aerial shots of neighborhoods and the prices of the houses. It showed the outside of your dad's house and what it was worth."

"So, are you going to keep it a big secret from me?"

"No. But if I tell you, you're not going to be mad at me, are you?"

"No, but I'm starting to get mad because you're not telling me. What does it look like? Tara from *Gone With the Wind*? Spit it out."

"Three million. My mom said a house like that out here would cost at least twice as much."

"Wow! That's a lot. Well, now we all know my father lives in a big house." Madison scrunched her nose and then said, "I'm going to bring it up on my laptop."

"I only mentioned it because you told me you and your mom always lived in an apartment."

"What's that have to do with anything?"

"You don't think we'll be oohing and aahing around your father once we get there, do you?"

"If we do, he'll probably think we're just acting normal. Some of my friends in high school had big houses. And we got along just fine. I didn't have any sleepovers at my mom's because there wasn't any room, but I was still invited to theirs. My mom always told me to be appreciative and say lots of thank you's. I'll just do the same thing in Atlanta."

"You don't suppose your dad's going to want to go out with us, do you?"

"We haven't talked about that, but I don't think so. I know he has to work Friday and, besides, why would he?"

"I don't know. I was just wondering if he might ask us about drinking, fake IDs, whether we've ever smoked pot—stuff like that."

"That's so lame."

"Well, he might."

"I think my father's going to be just as worried about saying the wrong thing as I am." Madison stared at her laptop. "It's ginormous! I can't believe this is his house."

Katie leaned toward Madison to stare at the image. "I told you it was huge. You really want me to go with you, don't you?" she asked.

Madison kept staring at her computer screen. "Yeah, I don't know if I'd go if it was just me. I'm nervous enough as it is. Even though he's my father, I agree he's still almost a stranger."

"I'm sure he's going to want us to be comfortable and have a great time. Let's just see what happens."

—◊◊◊—

Bannister was in his den Thursday evening enjoying a robust glass of Shafer's merlot when Madison called.

"Hi Dad. It's me."

"How are you doing? I can only imagine how tough this week has been."

"It's gone okay. My roommates have all been super. They've done a lot to try and make me keep my mind off Mom. I still cried a couple of times, but I'm okay."

"Are you and Katie ready for tomorrow?"

"You bet. I'm really excited about the trip," Madison said.

"Me too."

"I know you told me that you had not planned anything and that we could schedule some things that interested us, right?"

"Absolutely."

"And you said you had to work tomorrow, right?"

"Right. It sounds like you're already trying to manipulate me," Bannister said, trying to think where she was headed with this.

"Katie's parents wanted to do something special for us so her mom got us two tickets tomorrow night to see *Jersey Boys* at the Fox Theater."

"That was nice of her folks; it's supposed to be a great show."

"That won't interfere with any of your plans, will it?"

"Not at all. Maybe I can meet you two afterward and treat you to dessert."

"That sounds good. I'll let Katie know."

They talked about their day and then went over last-minute details. Bannister enjoyed hearing Madison's voice and still found it hard to believe he'd only known her for a couple of weeks. He was proud of the way Madison reacted to her mother's death. From their conversations the past week he believed she was in control of her feelings and doing her best to get on with her life. Tomorrow marked the start of another unknown chapter. His daughter would be there in person with her roommate. He just hoped she and Katie enjoyed their first visit to Atlanta and that he and Madison would get to know each other a little bit better.

CHAPTER 40

Bannister was surprised at how soundly he'd slept. He had a premonition today would be filled with significant developments. Hopefully, they'd turn out to be favorable.

Frank Jantzen, the office's technical supervisor, stopped Bannister in the parking lot as he got out of the Bureau car.

"I just left you a message. I was wondering if you'd be willing to field test some new equipment," Jantzen said.

"What kind of equipment?"

"Step into my office for a couple of minutes."

Bannister followed him to the back of the fenced parking area where the technical operations offices were located. Once inside, Jantzen handed Bannister two small boxes. "Go ahead. Check them out," he said.

Bannister opened the first box, which contained a man's black Seiko diving watch. He looked in the second box and pulled out what looked like a woman's silver charm bracelet with seven figures of world landmarks.

"I don't get it. What's with the jewelry?" he asked.

Jantzen smiled. "State-of-the-art global positioning locators. Men's and women's models. Both contain a gallium nitride millimeter-wave transceiver."

"How about translating that for me?" Bannister asked.

"In simple terms, you know about LoJack devices that help police track stolen cars, right? Well, their device is about the size of a deck of cards. And GPS devices are vulnerable to the right countermeasures equipment. Our devices work silently and can't be detected. The biggest kicker is the electronics and gallium nitride batteries are so tiny, they can be fitted into a piece of jewelry. That's what you're holding!"

"Sounds great. We certainly could have used one of these last year on the Global Waters extortion case."

"Yeah, I know. I was hoping you and Mercedes wouldn't mind wearing them this weekend and when you come in Monday, I'll show you the results. That's if you two don't object to our knowing where you are over the weekend. It'd certainly help me out."

"Glad to do it." Bannister signed for the two gizmos and put them in his briefcase.

"By the way, don't lose them. Those are prototypes and cost four grand each."

Bannister turned around. "On second thought, maybe this is not such a good idea."

"It's not every weekend, Ty, you get a chance to test cutting-edge technology. It might just put some excitement into your schedule," Jantzen said with a slight laugh.

"Okay, hope you get the chance to do some good tracking. I'll get them back to you Monday."

Once in the office, Bannister booted up his computer. He'd sent Derek Barnes an e-mail the previous night telling him Ted Mims would be reporting to the team first thing in the morning. He suggested Barnes have some meaty financial leads ready for Mims to run with so he felt like he could contribute. On a terrorist case last year Mims really helped them out because of some good contacts at both the Financial Crimes Enforcement Network (FinCEN) run by the Treasury Department, and the Terrorist Financing Operations Section at FBI Headquarters. Bannister was just checking his e-mails when Barnes stopped by his desk.

"Leave your coffee, Ty. Witt wants to see both of us pronto."

"What's up?"

"Never know with him. Maybe he lost a cufflink and needs our help," Barnes said with a knowing, smug look on his face.

"Close the door and grab a seat guys," Witt said leaning forward with his hands interlaced on the top of his desk. "I finished reading

Derek's summary memo last night. Well done, by the way. I've reached a few conclusions."

Bannister waited for the hammer to fall. Derek wanted to update the case to keep Witt from pulling his name from the special assignment to Peru, which started in three weeks. He'd confided in Bannister he would write the summary in such a way that Witt would recognize he screwed up replacing Bannister as the lead and put him back in the driver's seat as soon as Derek departed. But he wasn't ready for Witt's snap judgment.

"We have enough to arrest Dr. Theresa Andrews for the murder of Kendall Briggs. I'd like both of you to meet with the US Attorney today and get a warrant." Witt was smiling as he looked first at Barnes and then at Bannister. "Well? Comments?"

Bannister waited for Barnes to speak first. When he didn't, Bannister had to let Witt know his judgment was flawed and his decision premature.

"This is a high-profile case, Gary. We don't want to arrest the wrong person. That'd give us a black eye and be a disservice to Briggs, who was a painstakingly thorough prosecutor."

"What makes you think she's not good for it? She was fucking the guy. She stood to inherit $500,000. She had the means to kill him and owned the same kind of knife used to cut his throat. She doesn't have anyone to verify her alibi for the night of the murder and Briggs's body was found less than two miles from where she was staying in her cabin in the mountains." Witt started rocking back and forth in his chair. Bannister looked at Barnes. Again, when he remained silent, Bannister spoke up.

"I know it looks bad for her, but the case against Andrews is circumstantial. Personally, I don't think she did it. It would have made more sense for her to kill her husband than to murder Briggs. We're still running down leads and also working to eliminate other possible suspects, like several federal inmates who hated Briggs."

"We need to drive this thing to a conclusion," Witt said.

"And we will. But we don't want to make any mistakes we'll regret. Dr. Andrews is not going anywhere. She thinks she's on good terms with us. Why not give us another week?"

"I'll give you until next Tuesday. If you don't have any breakthroughs by then, get the warrant. That's all."

"Fair enough," Barnes said.

"I can live with that," Bannister said.

CHAPTER 41

Bannister had been at his desk for an hour when he looked up to see a smiling Ted Mims.

"I hope the grin is because of your new assignment," Bannister said.

"You can assume that, but I've got something better. I didn't sleep well last night so I got into the office early and found out the boss transferred me to the Task Force. The change will do me good. I also read my e-mails and saw where Derek Barnes already assigned me some leads involving tracing of funds. You're in luck."

"How so?"

"Last year I helped several European banks. Saved them millions in a cyber-bank fraud case. One of the banks involved was in Podgorica, the capital of Montenegro. An hour ago, I called their general manager, who was familiar with the case and who I knew would remember me. He expressed his thanks to the FBI for helping them avoid international embarrassment. He advised an account in the name of Kevin Middleton of Atlanta, Georgia, was opened with a deposit wired to it by an organization called the Detroit Foundation for Human Rights and Freedom. He could not provide specifics but believed that information would put us on the right track."

"Interesting. Grab a seat, Ted."

Mims pulled up a chair and continued. "My banking contact said if the Bureau can follow up with some official paperwork, they'll be able to furnish us all the details."

"That's great!"

"There's more. The same Detroit organization that wired the deposit is a fundraising front for Hamas and, it's also linked to the lease of the cigarette smuggling warehouse you guys raided. I'm still pouring over some of the documents that were seized and might have more for you Monday."

"I couldn't ask for a better start from our newest member."

"I appreciate what you're doing and your suggestion to talk with Walt Thompson. It has helped Audrey and me. I didn't realize the situation Walt went through was almost identical to mine."

"Well, keep me informed," Bannister said standing up to shake his hand, but Mims remained seated and continued.

"I carried my boxes up to my new cubicle earlier but will probably work from my old space for the next couple of days. Oh, for what it's worth, one other name popped up that may be involved in your investigation. You might want Germaine to check him out. One of the credit cards issued to the Detroit foundation is a Visa card in the name of Kasim Musa. He wasn't one of the men arrested during the raid, but I tracked his account history because he's had a lot of gas purchases in Atlanta. He's moving around. It also shows gas purchases last month in Detroit and this week in both Kansas City and Grand Island, Nebraska." Mims stood. "I'm going back downstairs to settle in. I'll write this stuff up electronically and enter the details into the case file."

Bannister nodded and the two men shook hands. "Thanks again."

Bannister mulled over what Mims had said. Musa might be the third guy in the cell with Bashir al-Rahman and Hassan Last Name Unknown. He left his desk and paid a visit to White.

"Try and work your database magic," Bannister said. "Run the Detroit Foundation for Human Rights and Freedom and Kasim Musa from top to bottom." He handed her a Post-it with the names spelled out.

"I'm on it."

Bannister called Detective Roy Miller and gave him the name of Kasim Musa as a likely accomplice of Bashir al-Rahman. The two investigators agreed to stay in close contact.

—⟨⟨⟩⟩—

Two hours later Bannister finished reviewing the work schedule for the weekend and assigning priority leads. White called and said to come down to discuss a development. On the way, Ramirez also called and asked where he was; she said she had some major news, so Bannister told her to join him and White.

He and Ramirez arrived at White's vault at the same time and sat down opposite her monitors. Bannister looked at White.

"Go ahead. What've you got?" he asked.

"MI5 has a Cairo source that confirmed Bashir al-Rahman is dead. Their source reported that Egypt's Mukhabarat al-Aama, their intelligence service, is claiming al-Rahman committed suicide while in custody."

"Suicide?" Ramirez questioned.

"That wouldn't be the first time something like that happened," Bannister said.

White smiled, tilted her head to the right. "There's more. MI5 said al-Rahman was a member of an al-Qassam Brigade terrorist cell. Al-Qassam is the violent military wing of Hamas. The pieces of the puzzle are coming together."

"I'll say it's coming together," Ramirez said. "The DNA results from the hairs recovered from Kendall Briggs's sport coat came back. You're not going to believe this."

They both stared at her.

"They belong to Terry Hines!"

"Holy shit! That means he's here," Bannister said. "How sure are you?"

"One hundred percent positive. The lab just called me. If Hines is in Atlanta he may have killed Kendall Briggs and maybe even Kevin Middleton."

Just then Derek Barnes popped his head in the door. "One of the guys said you were here at the vault. The Brits located and searched a flat rented by Nathan Shane Quinn. It's on a farm about thirty miles outside of London." Barnes paused for effect.

"Don't keep us in the dark. What'd they find?" Ramirez asked.

"Here's what they came up with. A sheep farm owner rented a small apartment for six months to an American who said his name was Quinn and that he was an oil engineer doing long-term site visits around the North Sea. He hasn't been seen for over six weeks. Left an old Austin Healy he bought in the garage and some clothes in the flat. The landlord said the guy never had any visitors. Paid in cash. Still has two months left on the lease. MI5 said there were no perishables in the refrigerator and no paperwork or documents of any sort in the living space. Other than a small radio, no electronics. They don't know if he was planning on returning or not."

"Anything else?" Bannister asked.

"They're giving it the full Monty right now. They dusted for prints and are running them as we speak. What they did come up with was this: Quinn booked an open return flight from Heathrow to Montreal six weeks ago. Again paid in cash. They're sending the scan of his passport, photo, etc. to our Headquarters. His passport only had one visa in it—when he originally entered the U.K. six months ago."

Bannister nodded and looked at White. "The dots are connecting, Germaine. You're doing a fantastic job but I need you to push even harder. Get everything you can from your contact at the Marshal's Service on Hines, who probably has been using the identity of Nathan Shane Quinn. Hopefully, the Marshals will have pulled all airline and passenger manifest lists for possible hits on both names. We also need everything anybody's got on Kasim Musa. Make him the highest priority and get it out to FBI Headquarters, CIA, MI5, the US Marshals Service, and the Canadian Security Intelligence Service."

"Could you slow down a second?" White said, flipping a page over on her note pad. "I'm fast, but not supersonic."

"Sorry. I know the Canadians are in the dark right now but they'll jump on this, especially if Hines, a.k.a. Quinn, entered the US from their country. Oh, and check Kansas City and Grand Island, Nebraska, for any special events. Questions?"

"Nope. As soon as you guys leave I'll start my bunny hop."

"Good work, everyone. We've all got tons to do now," Bannister said as the three of them left White to work her databases.

As Barnes left, Ramirez asked Bannister, "You're still leaving for that special airport pickup, aren't you?"

"Yes. The timing is bad, but I'm taking three hours off. I cleared it with the boss and will be back in the office later."

"I'm staying late tonight. I have a volume of data to sift through. I'm going out to get a bite to eat so I'll see you in the office in the morning," Ramirez said. She and Bannister walked to the elevator together.

"I have to brief the boss and Witt and then will call Detective Miller at APD from my car," Bannister said.

"I'll contact the other task force agents and ask Derek to update all of them," Ramirez said as she grabbed his hand and squeezed it. "Don't worry about things here. Go pick up your daughter and her friend. At least get them settled. I've got your back and will call immediately if there are any developments or problems."

"I know I can count on you. Thanks."

CHAPTER 42

While driving to the Atlanta airport for the third time in a week, Bannister called Detective Roy Miller.

"Did you hear the latest on that Rashone Green shooting you and Agent Ramirez witnessed?" Miller asked.

"No."

"He entered a not guilty plea at his preliminary and requested a jury trial. Word is he's going to claim self-defense."

"You've got to be kidding. That was a cold-blooded execution."

"You and I know that, but if he gets a twelve-person jury of Atlanta numb nuts, anything can happen. Anyway, what's up?" Miller asked.

"We've got new intelligence on who may have been responsible for the Middleton murder. We think three men were involved. Two of them are in one of your hotel parking lot pictures. One subject is Hassan Last Name Unknown and the other may be Kasim Musa, whose name I gave you earlier. The third subject is dead in Egypt. We need a sit down. You available early Monday at our office?"

"Yeah. I think I can read between the lines."

"I'll leave you a message Sunday night with details."

Madison and Katie's flight landed at 4:10 p.m., a half hour early. Bannister showed his badge and credentials to the Atlanta police officer at the checkpoint, telling him he was meeting an incoming flight. Technically, he had to be on official business to do that. He wasn't, but signed the log anyway and headed to the arrival gate. The last time Bannister met an incoming flight was a year ago when he and Ramirez arrested Terry Hines coming back from the Bahamas.

Bannister still found it hard to grasp he had a grown daughter. After the first-class passengers quickly exited and about fifty of those in coach had waddled through the aircraft's gangway, he spotted Madison and Katie. He hadn't realized just how pretty both of these young ladies were. He observed two college-aged guys, casually dressed, sitting in the boarding area. One jabbed his friend and pointed toward the girls. Oh well. Madison saw Bannister and turned to give the handle of her zebra-striped rolling suitcase to Katie. She ran up to him and wrapped her arms around his waist. He responded with an awkward embrace.

Exuberant, she gushed, "I'm so glad to be here. I didn't think you'd be able to meet us."

Disentangling himself from Madison, he said with a big smile, "You two are my priorities this weekend. How was the flight?"

"It really went by fast. By the way, neither of us has any checked luggage. Surprise, surprise."

Bannister smiled and led the way to the car. Even though traffic was heavy, the three arrived at Bannister's home in thirty minutes. After introducing his housekeeper, Sophia, he asked the girls where they wanted to sleep. They opted to share the guest suite on the opposite side of the house. It had two double beds and a large spa-type bathroom.

"Sophia prepared a tray of fresh fruit and a vegetable platter for you, in case you wanted to have a bite before leaving for *Jersey Boys*."

"That's really thoughtful," Katie said.

"To be honest, we're both a little hungry," Madison added. "All we had were pretzels and drinks on the flight." She sampled a few of the apple slices and carrot sticks.

After devouring a few snacks, Katie said, "I'd like to freshen up before we leave for the theater. I know you probably have some things to discuss with Madison, so I'll leave you two alone for a while." She smiled and turned to go to the guest suite.

"I know during our last call you said you looked forward to driving my SUV to the theater, but I'd feel more comfortable with you taking a cab," Bannister said to Madison.

"I've been driving in and out of LA traffic for three years so I think I can handle yours. What could go wrong? You're not worried about me with your car, are you?"

"No, it's just that you're not familiar with our streets and the crazy drivers we have."

"You know, you're acting just like a dad." Madison smiled, pulling out one of the stools at the kitchen counter and grabbing a large fresh strawberry from the plate.

In a condescending voice, Bannister said, "I thought you might have a stubborn streak like me, so I put a map of Atlanta on the front seat. I know you have your cell phones but I updated my GPS, and Katie can act as your navigator if you insist on driving,"

"I do."

"Okay. I plugged in the address for the Fox. My house is listed as "BC" for Bat Cave."

"That's neat. Have you seen the Batman movies?"

Bannister shrugged. "Yeah, but it's been awhile. Sometimes coming up the driveway at night I picture myself steering the Batmobile into the garage."

"That's real Gucci," Madison said.

"What?" said Bannister.

"It means really cool," Madison explained.

Switching subjects, Bannister asked, "I know you just got here, but what time did you two plan on leaving?"

"The 'will call' window opens at six o'clock. I thought we could pick up our tickets and then explore the area around the theater until show time. Does that sound okay with you?"

"Sure."

"You did tell us we were free to plan some of our own activities, right?"

"Absolutely. I wish I didn't have to meet with my boss at the office at five-thirty, but there's a lot happening on a couple of investigations I'm working on, so I'll be leaving in the FBI car before you two go.

If you want me to meet you downtown after the show, just call me; otherwise, I'll see you girls when you get back."

Madison said, "Don't feel guilty. It's not like you're abandoning a child." She gasped. "I didn't mean to say that."

Bannister stared at her blushing face and broke the awkward moment by winking and handing her the keys to his SUV. He explained that what looked like a garage door opener on the visor was actually the control to the iron gates at the bottom of the driveway. She didn't have to worry about his alarm code since the house would be unlocked because Sophia was staying until either he returned from the office or the girls got back.

Bannister had both Madison and Katie's cell phone numbers, and confirmed they had his cell phone number and the FBI's main number entered into their phones.

"I have two requests," he said. "I'm not trying to act fatherly, but I'd like you to call me as soon as you pick up your tickets. That way I'll know you're at the theater and didn't have any problem with parking." Bannister didn't want to come across as bossy, nor did he want Madison to think he was questioning her intelligence and maturity at handling herself in a strange city.

"Sure thing," Madison said. "What's the other request?"

"How would you like to be a guinea pig for a practical exercise? I promised our technical supervisor I'd assist him with some equipment testing." Bannister reached into his pocket and took out the modified charm bracelet. Its individual pieces were recognizable landmarks such as the Tower of Pisa, the Great Pyramid of Giza, and the Coliseum.

"I was wondering if you would be willing to wear this tonight. It would help us map some signal strengths in the downtown area. My partner was supposed to wear it this evening, but she's going to be working with me at the office tonight and probably all day tomorrow. I'll get it back from you when you return home. And in case you're wondering, I'm wearing the guy's version." He pointed to his wrist.

"You mean that watch?" Madison furrowed her brow.

"Exactly. Both pieces are actual jewelry, but contain special electronics. The Eiffel Tower is particularly special." Bannister was hoping his daughter might jump at the chance to help him and, at the same time, realize that he trusted her.

Madison took the bracelet and after examining the charms, clasped it on her left wrist. "You know I'm going to be sitting in the theater. This isn't going to make some kind of weird noise or something while I'm wearing it, will it?"

"No. If you're uncomfortable doing this, we can skip it."

"No, that's fine with me. It's actually kind of pretty and, if it helps you out, I'm glad to do it. It'll make me feel a little bit like I'm a spy."

As Bannister turned the FBI car left out of his driveway onto Valley Boulevard, he called the office to let both SAC Brennan and ASAC Witt know he was returning. Bannister turned down Habersham. When he got to Roswell Road and exited to the right, he glanced at a white panel truck with an Atlanta Package Services sign on its side pulling into his neighborhood. The company's name didn't register with him and he continued to the office.

At 5:30 p.m. Bannister walked down the hall to his boss's office for their meeting. At the same time, Madison was guiding her father's Toyota 4Runner down the tree-lined, two hundred-yard driveway toward the iron gates at the entrance. Just as the gates swung open, a white panel truck pulled across the driveway, blocking the 4Runner from exiting. The truck's driver, dressed in white coveralls and matching baseball cap, slid the side door to the van open where a medium sized cardboard box could be seen. He waved to the blonde woman driving the SUV to approach the truck.

As the woman exited the SUV and walked toward the driver, he shouted in her direction, "I have a package for Tyler Bannister that someone's got to sign for." He held a clipboard in his right hand.

"Are you his wife?" the truck driver asked the young woman.

"No, I'm his daughter," Madison said, as she stepped toward the side of the van.

When she was six feet away, he pulled his left hand from around his back and pointed a gun at her chest.

CHAPTER 43

T erry Hines raised the gun to Madison's face and grinned when her quivering voice asked, "Who are you? What do you want?"

Hines ignored her. "Tell your friend to come over here to help you."

Madison turned toward the 4Runner and called out "Katie!" As Katie opened the passenger door and stepped out, Madison shouted, "Run, Katie! He's gotta gun!"

Infuriated, Hines slammed the gun butt into the right side of Madison's head, knocking her unconscious. He grabbed her slumping body and shoved her into the opening of the van. He turned and noticed Katie had frozen still. Realizing he was looking at her, the girl heeded her friend's warning and started running up the left side of the driveway.

The tranquility of Bannister's neighborhood was shattered by two gunshots as Hines aimed and fired at the fleeing girl. The second round struck Katie, sending her sprawling into groundcover twenty yards past Bannister's SUV.

Hines lifted the unconscious Madison into the van's rear seat. He reached into a gym bag removing a pair of handcuffs and a roll of duct tape. To prevent her from jumping out of the van, he yanked the seat belt across her body and cuffed one of her hands in front before looping the other cuff under the seat belt and tightening it on her other wrist. He ripped off a strip of tape and stretched it across Madison's mouth, then jumped into the driver's seat.

Hines fingered the gun's trigger as a car drove past the van, its female driver talking on a cell phone. When the driver appeared oblivious to what had just happened, Hines relaxed and drove slowly down Valley Boulevard toward Peachtree Road. He had driven this route before and knew it would take less than twenty minutes to reach Bankhead Avenue and the detached two-car garage he had rented for six months.

Back at Bannister's driveway, Katie pushed herself to her hands and knees. She looked back toward the road. The van and Madison were gone. She glanced down at her right buttock from where the pain was radiating and pressed her fingers on a damp sticky spot on the side of her slacks. When she moved her hand free she saw it covered with blood. She'd been shot!

She struggled up the driveway, ignoring the bolts of pain from her wound. When she reached the front entrance, she rang the bell and started pounding with both fists on the door, shouting, "Sophia! Sophia!"

As the door opened, Katie pushed her way in and yelled, "You've got to call the police and Madison's dad. Madison's been kidnapped!"

"*Madre de Dios!*" Sophia said, bringing both her hands up to her face. She looked at Katie and saw the blood.

"Oh my God! You're bleeding, *conchita!*"

"Call 9-1-1!" Katie demanded, only now remembering she had left her purse and phone in the car.

Sophia used the house phone to call 9-1-1 and, intermingled with Spanish, provided the information requested from the dispatcher who told them an ambulance and police officers would be there in minutes. Sophia grabbed an entire roll of paper towels and wadded up a handful for Katie to press against her wound.

"Call Mr. Bannister," Katie pleaded.

"But you're hurt."

"Call him now! Time is vital and we're wasting it on me."

Sophia called Bannister's number and put Katie on the phone.

—⁓⁓—

Bannister was almost finished providing Leon Brennan and Gary Witt with the latest case developments when his cell phone rang.

"Sorry, boss . . . thought it was on vibrate." He glanced down at the number and recognized his home phone. "Mind if I take this?"

"No, go ahead," Brennan said.

"Yes, Sophia."

"Mr. Bannister. It's me, Katie." Her voice was flushed with controlled panic. "Madison's been kidnapped. You've got to come."

Bannister had seconds to process this stunning news. "What happened?" he asked.

"A delivery man in a van at the end of your driveway blocked us from getting out and then he waved at us and Madison got out to check what he wanted. She shouted for me, but as soon as I stepped out of the car, she yelled, 'Run, Katie. He's got a gun." I turned and started running and then heard gunshots and suddenly got knocked off my feet. I fell down near your driveway and realized I was shot when I tried to get up."

"How badly are you hurt? How long ago did this happen?"

When they heard those questions, the SAC and ASAC looked at each other.

"Just a couple of minutes ago. He shot me in my butt."

"Where are you?"

"I'm in your kitchen with Sophia. We're waiting for the ambulance and police . . . I think I hear sirens now."

Bannister spoke very slowly into the phone. "I need you to listen very carefully to me. Tell me exactly what happened from when you left the house."

Katie related what happened. She didn't see anything once she turned to run after Madison's warning. She gave a description of the white van and the man with the gun. She remembered he had a beard and baseball cap, was wearing sunglasses, and was the same height as Madison.

Bannister wondered if the mystery man could have been Terry Hines. Katie remembered seeing the word "Package" to the right of the van's open side door. The man held the gun in his left hand. She told him what Madison was wearing and said she might recognize the man if she saw him again.

"You're a brave girl, Katie. We'll get Madison back soon. Now, put Sophia back on the phone and don't let her hang up. I'm going to keep this line open. Okay?"

"Okay."

Bannister held the phone out to the side and looked at both Brennan and Witt. "My daughter's been kidnapped at my house and her friend's been shot," Bannister said.

"Daughter? What daughter? You've got a daughter?" Witt asked.

"Shut up, Gary," Brennan said, standing up. "Quick, Ty, give us the down and dirty."

Two minutes later Brennan barked out orders. "Gary, activate our kidnapping plan. Get Jantzen and his equipment out to Bannister's house. Tell Jantzen to put a trap and trace on the home phone. Call Atlanta PD and tell them to keep the responding officers on the scene until we get there and don't let them broadcast there's been an abduction. Find out where they're taking the wounded female." Looking at Bannister, he asked, "What's the girl's name?"

"Katie McDonald."

"Gary, find out where they're taking Katie McDonald. Send two agents, at least one female, to the hospital and have them stay there with the victim. Ramp up the operations center here in the office! I'm going with Bannister to his house. Oh, have Jantzen bring out a couple of extra radios." Brennan looked at Bannister. "Anything I forgot?"

"Mercedes Ramirez is upstairs. I'd like her to come to my house also."

"You got all that, Gary?" Brennan asked and, seeing the affirmative nod, asked Bannister, "Where are you parked?"

"Out back in the cage," he said.

"Me too." Grabbing his suit coat, Brennan said, "I need to hit the head and then I'll follow you to your house. We'll be going lights and sirens." Patting Bannister on the back, Brennan said, "We'll get her back, Ty."

Bannister couldn't believe what was happening. He needed to think fast and stay focused.

"Sophia, are you still there?" he asked as they exited the FBI building.

"Yes, sir. The ambulance people are in the kitchen."

"Can you put one of them on the phone?"

"This is EMT Fann, Unit 18 out of Piedmont Hospital."

"This is FBI Special Agent Tyler Bannister. What's the condition of my house guest, Katie?"

"We're just getting ready to leave. I think she's lucky. We've got a drip going and she's conscious and stabilized. She's been shot once, in the right buttock. It appears to be a perforating wound with no bone, nerve, or major vessel damage. We won't know for sure until she's had a CT scan. There's some blood loss, but her pressure's within normal limits."

"Thanks for your quick response. One of our agents is going to need to interview you later. Tell the ER to treat her clothing as evidence."

"Will do. We're leaving now. Here's your housekeeper."

Bannister let Sophia know there'd be a bunch of agents showing up at the house and he'd be getting there with his boss in fifteen minutes.

He and Brennan pulled out of the office lot in two cars, with Bannister taking the lead.

Bannister had violated one of his guiding principles: trust your hunches and follow through. He second-guessed himself for letting Madison drive to the Fox Theater. His gut had told him that if he couldn't drive the girls there himself, have them call a cab or use Uber. But he caved in to his daughter's sense of maturity and independence. If he'd challenged her, she might have thought he was questioning her judgment and intelligence or that he didn't trust her with his car. Bannister didn't like Monday morning quarterbacking and he hated negative thinkers. Right now he blamed himself for what had happened. It was his fault Madison and Katie were placed in harm's way. He forced himself to refocus on the situation facing them.

CHAPTER 44

As Bannister and his boss turned their cars onto Valley Road, a half mile from the home, they killed the lights and sirens. An ambulance, siren wailing, passed them going in the opposite direction. Bannister assumed it was the vehicle with Katie inside.

At the end of his driveway were two Atlanta black and whites. He and the boss pulled in behind them. Bannister's 4Runner was parked in front of the cruisers facing down Valley Boulevard. The gates to his entrance were open.

He and Brennan approached the uniformed officer closest to them and showed him their identification.

"I live here and that's my vehicle," Bannister said.

"Yes, sir. We got on scene at 5:40. Your SUV, engine running and front passenger door open, was at the end of your driveway."

"Who moved it?" he asked.

"I did, sir. The 9-1-1 operator advised there was a female gunshot victim in the house. The dispatcher said an unknown assailant had fled and kidnapped the friend of the wounded female."

"And?"

"My partner and I called for backup and went to your front entrance. We didn't know if there was more than one assailant. My partner stayed with the injured girl while I went back down to the front gate. You've got a heckuva long driveway. And before you ask, I moved your SUV so the ambulance could enter. I set your remote to 'gate control manual.' The ambulance just left."

"It went by us a minute ago," Bannister said.

"Before moving your vehicle, I took photos inside and out and marked where it was parked."

"Good," Brennan said. "Who we waiting on?"

The young officer continued, "Our crime scene techs should be here in a couple of minutes. Officer O'Hara spotted two cartridges on the road, between our cars. Look like nine mil to me."

"We're staying off the radios," Brennan said to the officer. "We're driving up to the house. There'll probably be another three or four Bureau vehicles arriving within twenty minutes. If you're still here, send them up. Have your senior officer check in with me when he gets here. We're running this as a kidnapping. Okay?"

"Affirmative," the officer said to them. He handed the 4Runner's keys to Bannister.

"Let's get started," Brennan said. "I'll follow you up."

Bannister told him, "Leave your car at the start of the curved driveway in front of the stone tower so you can get out if you have to."

Brennan had just parked his vehicle when Bannister's cell rang.

"Ty, it's me Jantzen. We've got two signals. Yours and another one which is steady and not moving."

"Talk to me, Frank. Where is it?"

"It's at the end of Lewis Street. That's a dead end, north of Bankhead Highway. Hell, it's a half mile from the Fulton County Jail."

"Are you sure the signal's stationary?" Bannister's heart was racing and in a second, he felt the paralyzing fear a parent experienced when they realize their child is missing. *Could Madison be dead? Had the bracelet been tossed? Or is she still wearing it?* Jantzen's voice brought him back to reality.

"Positive. The SWAT commander is still next door loading gear. He called the pilots and ordered the Nighthawk with its thermal imaging equipment to be on standby. I'm going to have him come inside and look at our 3-D map images to see what we're dealing with. Better let the boss know what we've got."

"He's here with me. I'll fill him in. Call me right back."

"I'm on it," Jantzen said.

CHAPTER 45

Madison opened her eyes and was instantly aware something was wrong. She was lying on her left side on a large piece of cardboard on a concrete floor, her face inches from a dark splotch reeking of oil. There was a band of tape across her mouth and the right side of her face throbbed. She smelled adhesive and tasted blood as she ran her tongue around the inside of her mouth, detecting a swelling that hadn't been there before. Her eyes were heavy as she glanced down toward her feet. Her hands were restrained by handcuffs in front with a heavy chain looped through them. The chain went up to a pulley attached to a steel beam. She was in some kind of small warehouse or garage.

Standing with his back to her about fifteen feet away was a man wearing white coveralls. He appeared to be adjusting some type of squawking radio on top of a long work bench. The last thing she remembered about the attack was a man in the van striking her in the head with a gun right after she shouted a warning to Katie. She thought the man at the work bench could be the same guy. No hat, black hair. Questions tumbled inside her head.

How long have I been unconscious? Where am I? What happened to Katie? Who is that man and what does he want with me? Does my father know I've been taken? Of course he does. What does he expect me to do? Think. Think. It's like I'm one of the girls kidnapped in the movie Taken. *That's it! What did Liam Neeson in the movie tell his daughter? "Where are you? Describe exactly what you see. Details are important." Okay, I'm doing that. I've still got the bracelet on. Dad, find me. Please find me!*

Her mom always said if someone with a gun ordered you into a vehicle, don't go. Once you got into the vehicle you were in real danger. Instead, run. That's what she had yelled for Katie to do.

She remembered her mom saying most people can't shoot straight. She also had advice for a potential knifing, too. If a person brandishes a knife, drop to the ground and use your legs to fend them off while screaming for help. Madison remembered telling her mother, "Mom, quit being so melodramatic. The odds of something like that ever happening are a million to one." Well, the *one* had happened. She knew she couldn't panic and would have to resist the urge to struggle.

Other than the blow to her head, she didn't believe she was injured. She was wearing the same clothes as when she left. She knew if she moved, the chains or handcuffs would rattle. *If he turns around I'll close my eyes and pretend I'm still out. Until then I'll try and figure out as much as I can. I can move my lips and mouth but the tape is too tight for me to yell. I feel sick. Oh, please don't let me puke. My feet aren't bound and I can kick him if I need to. He's turning around. Close your eyes.*

"Hey!" The man's voice was loud. "What's your name?"

He was testing her to see if she was conscious. She kept her eyes shut and remained motionless. When she heard radio channels being adjusted, Madison opened her eyes a crack and saw the man with his back to her standing at a workbench. Daylight was coming in through the blinds of a window behind the bench. A shop light was on. *What time is it? Why didn't he tape my eyes shut? Maybe not enough time. Or maybe he's not worried about me seeing him because he intends to kill me. Oh, my God! Got to keep thinking.* Madison slowly turned her head to the left and saw a van—the same one that stopped at her father's driveway.

CHAPTER 46

The boss helped Bannister carry two patio tables into his great room where the tech squad would set up. Before moving extra chairs, Bannister filled him in on his arrangement with Jantzen.

"So, let me get this straight," said Brennan. "Jantzen has some prototype tracking devices concealed in jewelry, and you and Ramirez were going to test their signal strengths this weekend. Right so far?"

"Yes."

"You're wearing the man's watch, and until at least an hour ago, your daughter was wearing the woman's bracelet?"

"Right again," Bannister said. As Brennan shook his head, Bannister continued, "I know I screwed up. Mercedes was supposed to wear the bracelet tonight, but she said she was going to be tied up in the office all evening. I anticipated meeting my daughter at the Fox Theater after a concert and retrieving it from her. I thought Jantzen could map both signals and get some better data."

"Well, you made a bad decision concerning that bracelet, but it may end up saving your daughter." Brennan's cell phone rang. The boss looked at the number and said, "It's Jantzen."

He answered. "Frank, I'm here with Bannister and am putting you on speaker phone. Give me a status report."

"The kidnapping supervisor's in the command center with four agents and Germaine White. Right now, we're running with the theory we have one subject. Germaine thinks it's the fugitive Terry Hines."

"Tell me something I don't know," Brennan said.

"Okay. If the van with the girl in it drove directly to where the signal is coming from, it would have passed two major intersections outside Bannister's neighborhood. At one intersection there's a Bank of America; at the other is the Ritz Carlton Hotel. Both have excellent exterior surveillance cameras covering their parking lots and adjacent roads. I sent tech agents to both places. They'll call if the van pops up in either cameras' coverage. If it does, hopefully we'll be able to tell if there's just one guy in the vehicle and see if the description matches Hines. We might also get a tag number."

"If the driver is Hines, it ices probable cause for warrants and lets us know who we're dealing with."

"Correct."

"Where's SWAT now?" Brennan asked.

"They're mobile. The SWAT commander is in our tactical operations command vehicle parked at the Fulton County Jail compound near where the bracelet's signal is coming from. Our pilots just lifted off in the Nighthawk and activated all sensor systems."

"Good. What else?"

"Germaine identified the owner of the property from where the signal's transmitting. It's a single-family home rented to a couple who both work for Blue Cross. She's running everything on them. She came up with a craigslist ad they placed that indicated that address had a large garage for rent."

"How long before she's able to tie it together?"

"Maybe fifteen minutes. Oh, one other thing. She just received a photo taken at Niagara Falls at the New York border two months ago. The photo is from the Canadian service and shows a white male with dark beard and mustache. The man had a passport identifying himself as Nathan Shane Quinn. Our photo lab is putting that picture into a six-photo spread to show to Katie McDonald. One of the guys will run it over to the hospital to see if she can identify him as the kidnapper."

"Excellent. Keep me posted," the boss said before ending the call. He turned to Bannister.

"Do you want something to drink?" Bannister asked.

"Not right now. I have a feeling things are going to work out.

Incidentally, right before we left the office the Chief Inspector called from Headquarters and said our SWAT personnel were cleared on the DeKalb warehouse shooting. Ty, I need to ask. Are you going to be able to work this and take orders?"

Bannister raised an eyebrow and a corner of his mouth before saying, "I think so."

"Looks like something else is eating you."

"It is. While driving to the house I recalled a case that happened when I was in school. A guy named Singleton picked up a teenage girl in Modesto, California, and raped her. If that wasn't bad enough, he cut off her forearms with an axe and then threw her off a thirty-foot cliff like she was a piece of garbage. Somehow, she survived and managed to crawl to the highway where a motorist rescued her and took her to the hospital. I watched her come out of the courthouse with prosthetic arms. It's a scene I've never forgotten."

"A man like that should be burned alive," Brennan said.

"If Hines or whoever's got Madison hurts her in any way, I just don't know how I'm going to react."

"You'll react the way you're trained to do. I'm going to be making the hard calls, but you'll know what we're doing every step of the way. I've got to level with you, though. I don't believe this is a kidnapping for ransom," Brennan said.

"No. It's personal. If it's Hines, I think he'll be working alone. He would have had to do some legwork to identify my house and scout it out. Maybe I was the target and my daughter and her friend were victims of circumstance."

"Possibly. But you drove out in the Bureau car shortly before they left, correct?"

"Yeah. He might have arrived at my driveway after I left for the office and before Madison departed for the concert."

"That could be true," Brennan mused.

"Only a few people knew my daughter was flying in, and they're with us. My home phone is unpublished so I don't anticipate the abductor calling in on that line. If he tries to make contact it'll be through my cell phone or the office number, and we've got them covered."

Brennan rubbed his forehead for a couple of seconds and said, "I changed my mind, Ty, I'll take that bottle of water." They both looked out the front door and saw the first of four vehicles pull up. Tech guys, kidnapping squad agents, and Ramirez exited the cars.

In ten minutes, seven agents who'd just arrived were at tables with their equipment and laptops running in full mode. Sophia put out a few trays of snacks on the counter.

"What do you want me to do, Mr. Bannister?" she asked.

"You can go home. I know this has been very upsetting to you. Please don't talk to anybody about what happened here today until you talk with me."

"I won't say anything. You will call me, yes, if you want me to come to work tomorrow? I will pray for you and your daughter." Sophia waved, grabbed her purse, and went out the front door.

Brennan turned to Bannister and said, "I just touched base with Witt back in the command center."

Bannister's cell phone chimed once and before he could respond, one of the tech guys said, "Bannister's got an incoming text message; Northern Virginia area code 703; subscriber ID'd as Robin Mikkonen." Bannister had forgotten there was electronic surveillance of all his phone numbers.

"Isn't that the Washington agent . . ." Brennan started to ask.

"Yes, that's her. She's working the smuggling case." Bannister looked at his boss. "She's also a friend and was with me earlier this year when I got shot," he said, realizing Robin had no idea of what was happening. He'd call her later.

"Everyone listen up," Brennan said. "I just got off the phone with Witt and here's what we know. The Nighthawk imaged the house and garage where we believe Bannister's daughter is being held by a kidnapper. Everything's pointing to the guy being Terry Hines, the escaped fugitive responsible last year for ripping off Global Waters for five million. Thermal readouts from Nighthawk indicate two humans are inside the garage along with one vehicle whose engine is still glowing. No other persons or dogs in the immediate area."

"Is the engine signature from the kidnapper's van?" one of the agents asked.

"Yes, it's probably the van, but hold your questions till I'm finished," Brennan said. "Keith Santini and the SWAT team are in the tactical operations vehicle near the site. They've evacuated the neighbors and established a security perimeter. A deliberate rescue plan is in place. It'll be dark in an hour and we need to move fast, but the main focus is rescuing the hostage without anyone getting hurt. Questions?"

One of the tech guys asked, "If the guy who snatched Bannister's daughter is this Hines character, are we going to try and negotiate with him?"

"No. I have our hostage negotiator on standby because that's required procedure, but I don't think Hines would be susceptible to a deal. We have to consider four scenarios: he releases the hostage and surrenders; he releases the hostage and commits suicide; he kills the hostage and commits suicide," Brennan glanced at Bannister, "or he kills the hostage and then surrenders. We also believe he may be responsible for murdering Assistant US Attorney Kendall Briggs. We don't think he's mentally unbalanced but are assuming he's out for revenge. That's why I instructed the SWAT commander to make a forcible entry and take him out. If we capture him alive it will be a bonus. Time is not on our side, and we don't want the media getting alerted and sending a chopper up over the area."

Bannister considered Leon Brennan the best boss for whom he had worked. He was a man who led from the front. He was respected for his critical thinking and discipline in organizing and delegating tasks. He always had the energy to finish whatever had to be done, and most importantly to Bannister, he demonstrated a capacity to feel what others were feeling. Although he couldn't express it, Bannister felt a bond with Brennan. It was like reliving the esprit de corps Marines felt for one another. The man instilled confidence in his agents and extracted maximum results from them. Bannister trusted Brennan and prayed that his decisions today would save his daughter's life.

CHAPTER 47

H ines walked over to the prostrate Madison and squirted a blast
of cold water into her face. She opened her eyes and jerked her
arms, but the chains restrained her movements.

"Good. You're awake," Hines said staring into Madison's eyes. He
couldn't tell if she was afraid or angry. He knew she was confused.

"I didn't know if you were faking being unconscious or not. This is
a lot better because you'll know what's going to happen."

With that, Hines picked up part of the heavy chain lying on the
garage floor and said to Madison: "I'm going to stand you up."

He pulled on the chain which looped through Madison's handcuffs
and connected to a steel beam. Slowly Madison's body raised into
an upright position. Pulleys squeaked as Hines reeled in the slack.
When Madison's arms were stretched straight above her head, Hines
wrapped the links through the steel handle of a large vise anchored at
the end of the work bench.

"I thought the two of us could have a conversation." He smiled
and rocked his head from side to side. "Oh, stupid me, I almost forgot.
A conversation involves two people talking, and you can't talk if your
mouth is taped shut, can you? Nod your head if you agree."

Hines grinned; Madison nodded.

"I'm going to take the tape off your mouth. Don't scream. I don't
think anyone would hear you and besides, if you do scream, I'll just
knock you out again. Nod your head that you understand."

Another nod.

Hines plunked down on a workbench chair with castors and scooted
over to where Madison was chained. She winced when Hines stood up

and pulled the tape from her mouth along with numerous strands of her hair that had stuck to it. She sucked in a breath but did not scream.

"Why did you kidnap me?" Madison asked in a soft raspy voice.

"First things first," Hines said, wagging his finger at his captive. "You didn't have any identification with you. I'm embarrassed to say, but I don't know your name. And don't lie to me."

"It's Madison Van Otten."

"I intended to grab Bannister's girlfriend. I thought you were the girlfriend."

"I'm not. I'm his daughter."

"You did say that. That's even better. I didn't even know Bannister had a daughter." Hines stood three feet away from Madison and looked directly into her eyes.

"Why did you want to kidnap my father's girlfriend?"

"Bannister fucked up my life and now I'm going to turn it around."

"I don't understand," Madison said.

"If he hadn't arrested me last year I would be living in the Caribbean. He couldn't leave it alone, and now I'm a wanted man."

"I don't even know who you are."

Hines shrugged. "It wouldn't matter if I told you."

—*∞∞*—

One of the technically trained agents (TTAs) assigned to Butch Sutton's entry team radioed Keith Santini, the SWAT team leader, in the Tactical Operation Center's command vehicle.

"I installed a fiber optic camera through an opening by the garage door and the laser microphone is aimed through the window in the back. You should be receiving both audio and visual now," the tech said.

"We've got it," Santini said. "The guy looks like Hines and the girl trussed up appears to be Madison, Bannister's daughter. The subject's facing the camera now and I can't see a gun, but it could be in the coveralls he's wearing."

The TTA replied, "The girl's conscious and looks okay. Sutton's attached det cord charges to the doors. It'll blow the locks and hardware outward. He'll toss in one of our new stun grenades before anyone attempts entry. The one he's using will blind anyone inside for five seconds, cause them to temporarily lose their hearing and disturb their balance for a minute. The entry team's in position and will await your signal."

Santini called Leon Brennan to tell him the girl appeared to be all right. He also confirmed that Butch Sutton would be first through the door.

Brennan informed Santini that he and Bannister were driving to the tactical command post, and he should be prepared to initiate action if necessary. Santini and three team members in the command vehicle listened to the audio and watched the activity inside the garage on their monitor.

—◈—

"Are you going to rape me?" Madison asked, her voice shaking.

"No."

"Are you going to kill me?"

"No. In about two hours I will let you go," Hines said, enjoying the confused look on Madison's face.

"I need to do one more thing and this won't hurt you. I have to put some tape on your face." With that, Hines walked over to the workbench and retrieved a plastic plate which had six strips of pre-cut duct tape on it. He put the plate down on the rolling chair and said to Madison, "I need to tape your eyes open, so just cooperate with me."

Hines placed the strips of tape across Madison's eyelids and eyebrows so that her eyes were wide open.

"Why are you doing this?" Madison asked.

Hines just smiled.

"Our conversation is over." Hines wound two lengths of tape across

Madison's mouth and around her head so she couldn't even move her lips.

"I gave this a lot of thought and I want your father to suffer. If I raped you, the two of you might eventually get over it, you know, through counseling and all that bullshit. Bannister's already gone through the grief of losing someone close to him so I discounted the idea of killing his girlfriend. Or you. What I came up with was an idea that will haunt his very soul every single day you're alive." Hines grinned, enjoying the terror he knew was coursing through her body. He went back to the work bench and picked up what looked like a large gray flashlight.

"This is a very special laser. Physically when I release you in two hours, you'll be fine except for one thing. You'll be blind."

CHAPTER 48

Bannister was driving the SAC's Buick with Brennan riding shotgun. A mile from the tactical command vehicle the secure radio squelched and Brennan picked up, putting it on speaker mode.

"Boss, this is Santini. We have a problem. The subject just threatened to blind the girl."

Bannister clenched the steering wheel until his hands hurt, looking straight down the road, waiting for the boss to say something. He stepped on the accelerator.

"Say that again," Brennan commanded.

"He said he's going to blind her!" Santini repeated.

"What are you seeing on the video feed?" Brennan asked, the tension in his voice belying his calm exterior.

"Something weird. He taped her mouth shut, but taped her eyes open," Santini said.

"Let me know if he does anything else," Brennan said.

When they were three blocks away, Brennan radioed their agents manning the outside perimeter that they were coming through.

He said to Bannister, "Butch Sutton will be going in first. You know he's under orders to report to the Hostage Rescue Team at Quantico, right?"

"I heard that."

"How well do you trust him?"

"I'd trust him with my life," Bannister said. His hands were now sweating and his mouth had gone dry.

"Would you trust him with your daughter's?"

"Yes," he said. Quickly he flashed the blue lights at their perimeter team so they could wave them through. It was well known in the office that Sutton was a sniper in Iraq and had been highly decorated for his bravery. In the Marine Corps, Bannister had relied on his own training to save lives. Now he felt a little helpless that he had to count on the training of someone else—Butch Sutton—to save his daughter. But if he couldn't be the one going through the door, there was no one else he would rather have than Sutton.

Bannister saw the black command motor home and pulled right up to its steps. He and the boss were inside in seconds. As they walked through the doorway, it was quiet and Santini held his palm up towards them to be quiet. All eyes and ears were trained on the large monitor.

They watched as Hines turned away from the work bench with what appeared to be a flashlight in his hand and pressed a switch. A thin blue streak shot out directly towards the ceiling.

"That's a laser," Santini exclaimed.

"You've got a green light. Take him down now!" Brennan shouted.

Inside the cramped command vehicle, the agents watched a flash on the screen and heard the charges blow. As one door flew off its hinges, Special Agent Butch Sutton took a step across the threshold of what used to be the side door to the garage. As Sutton tossed a stun grenade over the front of a parked van, two agents stepped through what used to be the front of the garage. All three yelled in unison, "FBI. Don't move!"

Terry Hines was standing ten feet from Madison, whose trussed body was suspended from a large chain. She was directly in the line of sight and fire of the two entry team agents standing in the garage's main door opening. Sutton had jumped to the side near the front of the parked van and taken up his firing position.

He looked directly at Hines and yelled, "FBI. Put your hands in the air."

Hines dropped the laser and put his right arm up into the air. His left hand glided into the pocket of his white bib overalls.

Three quiet *pfutt pfutt pfutt* sounds announced Sutton's bullets finding their marks. Hines was struck twice in the head and once in the heart with rounds from Sutton's silenced submachine gun. As Hines was propelled backwards, an automatic pistol dropped uselessly from his left hand.

Sutton walked over to Hines's body and checked for a pulse. He shouldered his weapon and took off his ballistic helmet. He keyed the radio. "Subject is dead. Victim is alive." Sutton motioned to one of the other SWAT agents who approached Hines's body and, without moving it, used a special digital fingerprint scanner. Sutton bent down to the concrete floor, turned off the laser, and searched Hines's pockets. In the coveralls was a key ring which included a handcuff key and a key to a Yale padlock. He walked a few steps over to Madison and smiled.

He spoke slowly, "You're safe now. We work with your father. I'm going to take the tape off your face first and then unlock you. Nod your head that you understand what I'm saying."

Madison nodded as Sutton carefully peeled the duct tape from around her mouth and then from above her eyes. One of the other SWAT agents put his arms around her waist to hold her as Sutton opened the padlock and then removed the handcuffs.

As soon as she was freed, Madison bear hugged Sutton. Tears raced down her cheeks as she stammered, "Oh, God, thank you. You saved my life. I thought he was going to kill me and then he said he was going to blind me and I didn't know what was going to happen." She gulped for air.

"It's all right; your father's close by," Sutton said.

Inside the tactical command vehicle, Brennan slapped Bannister on the shoulder and said, "Come on, let's go get your daughter!"

A minute later they were at the garage. Sutton had Madison's hand and was leading her over the debris at the side entrance.

Madison rushed towards her father and wrapped her arms around him. "Oh, Dad, I was so scared, but I just prayed you'd find me and you did!" Her voice quaked and her body shivered.

Tension wracked Bannister's body and he didn't want her to hear his voice cracking, so he just held her for a few more seconds.

When he finally spoke, his words were shaky. "It's okay, honey. Everything's going to be fine."

They stood there with their arms around each other until Brennan said, "An ambulance will be here soon. It'll take Madison to be checked out at the same hospital as her friend Katie."

"Oh, no! Oh my God! What happened to Katie?" Madison cried.

"She's okay. I'll explain on the ride over," Bannister said.

With his arm around Madison's waist, Bannister guided her away from the garage. She started shaking again.

"My knees are wobbly. Can I sit down for a minute?" Madison asked.

"Sure," Bannister said with a catch in his throat as he pointed to a patch of grass.

"What happened to Katie? Tell me," she pleaded.

"That man in the garage fired his gun at Katie and a bullet nicked her in the butt. That's why she's at the hospital. The doctor said she's fine. As soon as we get you checked out you can visit her."

Madison sat on the ground and used her hands to wipe the tears from her face. As she began rubbing her arms and wrist, Bannister could see the red marks and welts where the cuffs had been. He tapped the charm bracelet which she was still wearing.

"Did that help you find me?" she asked.

He nodded his head. "Why don't you give it to me. We're going to take you to the hospital." She handed him the bracelet.

"If you hadn't rescued me, he would have blinded me. I don't know if he was going to kill me. What did he want with me? I've never seen him before."

Bannister saw the fear renewed on Madison's face and squeezed her hand. "It's okay. It's over. He won't ever hurt you or anyone else again."

With a thin smile she said, "My arms hurt a little." One of the SWAT agents walked over and handed her a blue wool blanket to wrap around her.

An ambulance pulled into the driveway and two EMTs exited. The older one talked briefly to SAC Brennan, who pointed in their direction. A female EMT came over and asked her a series of medical questions mixed in with ones such as, "What day of the week is it?" She examined the side of Madison's head and then explained the procedures for transporting her to the hospital.

Turning in Bannister's direction, the EMT said, "Your boss said you intend to ride in the ambulance."

"If that's not a problem," he said.

"You can ride up front with Chuck," she said.

Brennan glanced in his direction. "We're going to be here for a couple hours. Call me from the hospital."

"Will do, boss."

"FYI, the fingerprint results positively identified the kidnapper as Terry Hines," Brennan said.

Bannister gave him a thumbs-up. He was glad he'd never have to look at Hines again.

As the EMTs loaded Madison into the back of the ambulance, Bannister walked back to Butch Sutton. He shook his hand firmly, holding it for a few seconds. "Thank you for what you did. For saving my daughter."

He was sure Sutton noticed his eyes glistening. Sutton stared for a second before saying, "I'm glad it worked out well. I really wish he hadn't gone for the gun."

"I'm happy he did," Bannister said.

"Incidentally, the subject had this on his key chain," Sutton said, holding up a flash drive.

"That could be really important. Make sure you mention that to the boss right away and have Evidence Recovery put a call into Germaine White. We'll need to know ASAP what's on it."

"Copy that. The EMT's waving. Better get going."

CHAPTER 49

Bannister sat in the front of the ambulance taking Madison to the hospital. In back, the female EMT took his daughter's vitals, which were all within normal limits. The EMT continued her examination and asked about allergies, medications, and what and when did Madison last have something to eat or drink. As his daughter described the incident leading up to her injury, Bannister made a couple of calls. He left a voicemail for Detective Miller letting him know they had a fluid situation and that he would call him soon concerning developments in the Middleton murder. Next, he called Inspector Glenn Yates.

"This is Bannister."

"I haven't heard from you in two days. What's happening?"

Bannister filled him in about their subject in the KABMUR case being killed resisting arrest.

"Where are you now?" Yates asked.

"I'm a passenger in an ambulance. It's complicated, Glenn. I'll call you later after the dust has settled."

"Okay, so what you're saying is disregard anything I might hear on the news tonight, right?"

"Correct. I just wanted you to be in the loop."

"I appreciate that."

Bannister ended his call as they pulled into the hospital's emergency bay. Ramirez and Jane Reese, the FBI's victim and witness assistance representative, were waiting inside the entrance.

Reese said, "ASAC Witt ordered me to come here and help out. I was glad to do it. We just left Katie McDonald in recovery. She's still a little woozy from the anesthesia but the staff said they expect her to be released in the morning."

"Reese plans on talking with Madison, if that's all right, and will stay here at the hospital until the two girls have a chance to visit," Ramirez said.

"That's fine," Bannister said.

"I retrieved Madison's and Katie's purses. Their wallets and IDs are here in my Bureau purse," Ramirez added. She tapped a large black leather bag around her left shoulder. "I also asked Reese to give you a ride back to your house when you're ready to leave."

"Thanks. I forgot I didn't have a car."

"That's what I thought. When it's time for Katie to be released tomorrow, I'll pick her up and drive her to your house. I'm assuming Madison is okay and can be discharged in a couple of hours."

"Thanks."

Ramirez continued, "Carrie Howell called me to say she and her team are on their way to search a two-bedroom house off Hunnicutt Street rented to Hines under his alias of Nathan Shane Quinn. I'm going to head over there. One of the SWAT guys is taking Hines's flash drive to Germaine so she can have a crack at the information on it."

Before Bannister could respond, his phone rang. It was the boss.

"You're at the hospital, right?" Brennan asked.

"In the emergency room. Everything is okay at this end," Bannister said.

"Good. I have my hands full here at the garage scene but should be back at the office in two hours. Witt's coordinating everything from the operations center so make sure you keep him up to speed. I called the Marshal's service, our headquarters, and US Attorney Prescott to report Hines's death. Prescott wants to schedule a press conference tomorrow morning, even though it's a Saturday."

"If you want my opinion, we have too many dots left to connect. I wish Prescott could hold off until Monday," Bannister said, pacing outside the ER room where Madison was waiting.

"You and I think the same way," Brennan said. "There's too much we don't know about Hines's activities and contacts. We might unnecessarily alert others who may be co-conspirators."

"Exactly."

"I'll see if he'll postpone it. By the way, another shooting inquiry team is flying in. They'll be here late tonight and will do their investigation and interviews tomorrow. They're a pain in the ass, but it has to be done."

"We're certainly staying in the spotlight," Bannister said.

"You're right. Speaking of spotlights, it's a shame your girls missed their show."

"I'll have to make that up to them."

"You'll think of something. Better get back to your patients. I'll see you at the office."

After the call, Bannister accompanied Madison for her CT scan. The hospital technician said it would be a half hour before the doctor could go over the results.

"Dad, who was that man who shot Katie and kidnapped me? Why did he do it?" Madison asked.

"It's a long story but you deserve to know."

"He's dead, isn't he?"

"Yes, he is."

Bannister filled Madison in on who Hines was and his connection to him. He explained how he threatened to get even with him and others involved in his arrest and prosecution. She asked some logical questions and Bannister didn't hold back. He assured her they believed Hines acted alone and that both of them were out of harm. After answering her questions, he told Madison he was going to the hospital's security office to make some phone calls.

The first call was to Tim McDonald, Katie's father. He'd talked to him briefly earlier in the week to reassure him and his wife that his daughter would be in good hands and there wouldn't be any problems. Bannister had even joked that he worked for the government so

McDonald could trust him. They both laughed at that. This call was different.

McDonald picked up right away. "Tim, this is Ty Bannister in Atlanta."

"Hello. I just got home a few minutes ago. Katie texted me the girls got in okay and were heading to your house. Everything all right?"

"There's been an incident. Bear with me for a couple of minutes while I explain."

"Is Katie all right?" McDonald asked.

"She was injured but she's okay. Let me try and explain. The girls were heading down my driveway in my SUV to go to their concert when they were accosted by a man wanted by the government. He was in a delivery van blocking the end of my driveway and pretended to have a package for me. We believe he thought I was in the SUV. The man forcibly abducted my daughter who yelled for Katie to run because the guy had a gun. When Katie started running back to the house, the guy fired a shot which struck her in the side of the butt."

"Oh, my God. Where is she? Is she all right?"

"She's fine. I'm at the hospital right now and just left Katie's room. She'll give you a call in about thirty minutes. The bullet passed completely through the side of her butt. The doctor said other than some blood loss and deep tissue bruising, it didn't do any damage. She'll be sore for a couple of days, be on antibiotics for a while, but will come out of this okay."

"What happened to Madison?"

"I'm with her now. She'll be fine, too. The guy who was responsible had been a fugitive for over a year. An hour after Madison was abducted our SWAT team located her and the kidnapper. The team rescued my daughter. Unfortunately, the subject refused to surrender and when he drew his gun, our agents had no choice but to shoot him. During the ordeal Madison suffered a minor concussion but otherwise is fine."

"I can't believe this," McDonald said. "I think Katie's mother and I should get to Atlanta as soon as possible."

"I understand your concern. I'd feel the same way. In fact, I do feel the same. I realize how frustrating it has to be for you to get this call out of the blue and for you to be in California with the girls here in Atlanta."

"If you were in my shoes, what would you do?" McDonald asked.

"I don't know. But here's what I propose. Why don't you wait until after you talk with Katie? If you or your wife or both of you want to fly here that's fine. I'll help at this end any way I can." Bannister had no problem with picking up the tab for their flight to and from Atlanta. It would probably help minimize some of the guilt he was feeling. If the girls needed to fly out on Monday or later, he'd arrange for a first-class upgrade for them.

Because it was an ongoing case, certain details could not be discussed with McDonald. He told him Katie was anxious to talk with him and would call him and his wife as soon as their investigators were done interviewing her. They talked about the fear that every parent has when unexpectedly being called by law enforcement. Of course, Bannister's experience at being a parent was less than a month. After giving McDonald additional reassurances about Katie's well-being, he requested he and his wife not discuss this situation with anyone until after their office talked with him. McDonald agreed to call him back with his plans after he had a chance to talk with his daughter.

Next, Bannister called Amy Dixon in Beverly Hills. She was stunned about the developments in Atlanta. After he filled her in and the initial surprise wore off, she resorted to her professional persona, offering to help if needed and expressing her appreciation for his confiding in her.

There was time for his last call.

"Robin, it's me."

"Well, Tyler Bannister, I hope you have a good excuse for ignoring my text and voicemail for the last two hours," Robin said in a haughty tone.

"It's complicated, but I'll do my best to explain what happened." He spent the next five minutes going over the recent events.

"Where are you right now?" Robin asked.

"We're all at the hospital. Katie's in a room waiting for the effects of anesthesia to wear off and Madison's fine except for a bruised head."

He could hear Robin sigh before saying, "This is unreal. I can't believe this has happened."

"Neither can I."

"Do you think Hines was waiting for you?"

"I don't know," he said, not noticing the death grip he had on his cell phone.

"I'll gladly fly there tonight if you want me to come out. I can probably be there within three hours," Robin volunteered.

"Thanks for offering, but I don't want you to have to do that."

"Madison and Katie will need someone to talk to, especially once they're both back at your house. I'm assuming you're going to be tied up at the office or at one or more search scenes for most of the night, correct?"

"I guess you're right about that. I thought Mercedes could pinch hit for me but she just left to search the house Hines rented."

"Case closed. I'll make some notifications at my end and call you back in thirty minutes with details. Okay?"

"Okay. Thanks, Robin."

"I love you, Ty, and although these aren't the circumstances under which I imagined meeting Madison, it might give her and me a chance to get to know each other."

"You're great."

"I know. I'll call you as soon as I can."

CHAPTER 50

Bannister knew that whether you were a patient or a visitor, trips to a hospital's emergency room involved lots of waiting followed by more waiting. Tonight, things were moving rapidly.

Bannister spotted Dr. Shaw, the trauma surgeon who had patched up Katie two hours ago, and stopped to thank him.

"I guess you could say she was a lucky girl. I'm on my way to the doctors' lounge for a quick cup of joe. Want to join me?"

"Sure."

As the doctor pushed a large stainless-steel button, two doors swung open. They took a right turn and walked a few steps to another door where he swiped his card. Bannister followed him into the lounge. Except for them it was empty. Bannister was immediately struck by the subdued lighting, dark paneling, and how quiet it was.

"We have seven minutes," the doctor said.

"Until what?"

"Two ambulances with three auto accident victims will be rolling in. Pick out the flavor of coffee you want."

Bannister stared at a Nespresso coffee machine and saw a variety of single cup containers. He picked up one that said dark roast.

"If you prefer, the stack to the right is decaf."

"I'll stick with high-test. Tonight will be a long one for me."

Dr. Shaw took the liberty of operating the machine so Bannister didn't screw anything up and handed him a cup of coffee. His was ready thirty seconds later and they both sat down in comfortable chairs.

"The last time I was in an emergency room was earlier this year to be treated for a gunshot wound," Bannister said.

"Obviously, it wasn't fatal," Dr. Shaw said with a soft chuckle.

Bannister had to smile, maybe his only one of the night. "One shot below the left shoulder. No bones or major blood vessels hit. Six weeks of rehab and I was cleared for full duty. Do you anticipate any complications for Katie?"

"No. The penetration of the round was straight through and missed everything. There was no bullet fragmentation. Cavitation damage, that is the shock wave to her tissue from the bullet, was marginal. She'll have some bruising and probably be sore for a week. By the time her stitches come out she should be back to almost normal."

They made small talk for a while until Dr. Shaw tapped his watch.

"Two minutes—need to get back," he said.

They drained their cups and returned via the same route. As they entered the ER, two gurneys entered with victims on back boards. Bannister observed the action for a minute and then made his way to the corridor where Katie's room was located. He checked with the duty nurse before entering her room.

"I just saw your doctor. He said you were a great patient and things are going to be fine."

"The nurse also went over the procedures I had and told me I shouldn't expect any problems."

Bannister noted she spoke slower than usual and her voice sounded syrupy. "You know you'll still feel the effects of the anesthesia for a while longer."

"That's what they told me. Whatever they gave me is working because I don't have any pain, but my body feels like it weighs two hundred pounds."

"Well, enjoy the feeling of no pain. I know two people who are anxious to hear from you."

"Mom and Dad?"

"Right. Here's my cell phone to call them. I gave your father the basic details. Your parents love you very much and are worried. I think they might want to fly out here, but I'll let the three of you decide that. Tell your dad to call me after you're finished."

"I will. Would you mind pouring me a glass of water? My mouth's really dry." He handed her a cup of ice water with a straw.

"What if you get a call while I'm talking to them?"

"Just let it go to voicemail. I'll be back in ten minutes." He handed Katie his phone and left to check on Madison.

———❧———

"Hey!" Madison exclaimed. She was propped up in bed wearing a blue and white polka dot gown. "The radiologist just told me everything's normal inside my head. I can be released."

"That's wonderful. We'll get you back to the house as soon as we can."

"I want to stay here with Katie."

"What do you mean?"

"I already talked to the head nurse and she said I can sleep on the sofa bench next to Katie's bed. She'll bring a pillow and some blankets for me."

"Are you sure you want to do that? You won't get much sleep here and there's nothing you can really do for Katie," Bannister said, hoping Madison's remarks were just a show of support.

"I don't really care about the sleep. I just want to be there for her. It's kinda my fault, anyway." She was frowning and sounding stubborn.

"It's not your fault."

"Well, Katie can't go anywhere until tomorrow. She doesn't know a soul in Atlanta and there's nothing I'm going to be doing in the meantime except worrying about her. So, why can't I stay?"

She had a point.

"Okay. Sounds like a plan. I've got to go down the hall and get my phone from Katie. I'll let her know."

When he walked into her room, Katie was all smiles. She handed him his phone. "Mom and Dad are flying here tomorrow. They'll be in at 3:00 p.m. Dad also said they booked two seats on the same return flight as Madison and me on Sunday."

"Were you able to answer their questions?"

"I think so. Parents are such worrywarts and always brace themselves for the worst. I tried to talk them out of coming here but it was useless. So, you'll get to meet my parents tomorrow."

"I look forward to that. You'll be pleased to know Madison insists on spending the night with you here in your room."

"Wow. She doesn't have to do that, but it would be really neat. Oh, Mr. Bannister, I almost forgot. You got one call and one text."

"Thanks. Just to let you know, all your personal belongings are safe at my house. We'll figure out later what you'll need for tomorrow. A friend of mine is also flying in tonight and the two of us will bring you girls something to eat. If you have any special requests, let Madison know."

"Okay, I'll do that. By the way, Miss Reese from your office is very nice. She helped me make some sense about what happened."

"She's assisted a lot of people. We'll talk later," Bannister said as he left her room.

He checked his messages. The first was a call from SAC Brennan to let him know he scheduled a meeting tonight at the office. The second was a text from Robin with her flight info. Bannister texted her.

"It's me. Where are you right now?"

She texted back, "On the plane."

He sent, "When do you land?"

"On time at 9:40 p.m."

He sent, "I appreciate what you're doing. The boss wants us at the office at 10:30."

She replied, "Do you want me to catch a cab to your house or rent a car?"

"Neither. Why don't I pick you up and we can both go to the office?"

"Won't that raise questions?"

"Maybe. But I don't care. Anyway, you're cleared for the investigation and there won't be a problem with you attending the meeting. It shouldn't last more than an hour."

"Sounds fine with me. What about the girls?"

"They're both going to spend the night at the hospital. Katie will be released in the morning and Madison insisted on spending the night in Katie's room."

"I can almost read your mind. I hope you didn't try to argue with her," Robin sent.

"I thought about it for a few seconds but caved. I'm stopping at the house first to pick up some stuff. I thought you and I could grab a bite somewhere later and get some sandwiches to go and bring them to the hospital. There's a 24-hour Kroger grocery a mile from my house."

Bannister smiled as he read Robin's final text. "Gee, you're thinking about food. Glad things are returning to normal. Love you. I'll call as soon as I land."

Jane Reese was sitting at the end of the ER's waiting room. As Bannister waved to her, Tim McDonald called back. He gave Bannister his arrival information and confirmed he and his wife would be returning to LA Sunday afternoon with the girls. He asked if Bannister would mind making hotel reservations for him and his wife at a location suitable for all of them. Bannister told him he'd handle it.

Reese looked up. "I'll bet you're ready to leave this place."

"At least for now. Thanks for talking to both girls and also giving me a ride."

As they left the hospital, Bannister called the operations center and instructed them to let the Rapid Start members still at his house know he'd be returning in fifteen minutes.

CHAPTER 51

At Bannister's home, the Rapid Start Team had logged off their computers and packed up their gear. One of the guys helped him move the tables and extra chairs back to the patio and rearrange his furniture. As they went out the door Bannister looked around his silent great room, which was the same as when he'd left it earlier to go to the airport to pick up the girls. Now, it was back to the airport to pick up Robin. Before leaving, he grabbed a sleeping bag from his storage closet. He put it into a large duffle along with a sweatshirt, set of sweatpants, and an extra pillow from the spare bedroom. He knew from experience that hospital rooms were cold and figured Madison might appreciate the items.

Fortunately, Robin's flight was on time and he met her at the gate. She walked right up to him and gave him a quick kiss. He relieved her of her garment bag, which he draped across a chair and held her for a minute.

"At first I thought there was no way I wanted you flying to Atlanta," he said. "But now that you're here I'm really glad you came."

"So am I. And I thank God both Madison and Katie are safe and that you're okay."

"I guess we must be doing something right."

"Are you going straight to the office?" Robin asked.

"Yes. I'll fill you in on the way over. And before I start rambling, you look smashing as usual." Robin was wearing a black pantsuit set off by a white blouse with a wide pointed collar. Businesslike and functional, even at this late hour. She smiled at the compliment and squeezed his hand.

They got to the office ten minutes early. Barnes spotted them in the hallway and asked them to go with him to White's vault. White was fixated on her monitor as she typed in data. Bannister was surprised to also see Carrie Howell and Ted Mims standing there. Both recognized Robin and shook her hand.

Howell spoke first.

"We searched Hines's rental house. I don't have answers to what we discovered but we have a lot of work to do. A white Ford Taurus which he'd rented under the Quinn alias was in the driveway. We searched it with negative results. The results in the house were different. On his desk was a passport in the name of Nathan Shane Quinn. Inside a desk drawer was a nine-millimeter Kahr automatic whose serial number matches the one owned by Kendall Briggs. The gun was lying on top of this file." Howell handed Bannister a manila folder.

"Go ahead. Take a look at it," she said.

He opened a file labeled Tyler Stetson Bannister. On the left side was a dossier on him prepared by Bunkie Black, a private investigator in Atlanta. Black had an enlarged copy of Bannister's driver's license photo, what appeared to be printouts of vehicle movements from a passive data logger, and a biography of Bannister, which Black obviously had written. The right side of the folder contained several pictures of Dr. Theresa Andrews, a page of handwritten notes supposedly by Hines, two pages of what looked like a surveillance log of Bannister's comings and goings for a one-week period last month, photos of both his 4Runner and FBI car, and a picture of him with a blond in his 4Runner exiting his driveway. Robin stared at the last photo and recognized it was of the two of them the night he gave her a ride back to the Grand Hyatt Hotel.

"You certainly were on Hines's radar," Howell said.

Bannister glanced at Robin, whose face had paled. "What else did you find?" he asked.

"We copied his flash drive, which has a lot of documents and notes. Germaine's trying to sort it out but channeled the financial information to Ted."

Looking at Mims, Bannister asked, "How about a quick summary of what you've found so far?"

"Let's just say Hines had a major league recent investment in commodities futures. He was betting the agricultural sector would skyrocket within the week and the meat industry was going to take an unbelievable hit."

"A bioterrorism attack would accomplish that and more," White said, swiveling her chair. None of them said anything but just looked at her. "I'm going to keep crunching all the data on Hines's flash drive while you're in the meeting, but I have a really, really sick feeling about this. I'll try and prioritize everything and list the emergency leads you'll need to send out. I'll call you if there's something that can't wait until early morning."

CHAPTER 52

Bannister's alarm sounded at 6:00 a.m. He turned it off on the second ring and looked to his left at Robin, who was breathing deeply. After last night's office meeting and visit with the girls at the hospital, they agreed to try and squeeze in some time together tonight if it was possible. Katie and Madison had been in good spirits and devoured the mini-gourmet sandwiches and decadent brownies they brought them. Robin saved a brownie and ate it in the car on the way back to the house. She agreed to pick both girls up when Katie was expected to be discharged around 9:00 a.m.

Bannister had time to run three miles, shower, and get to the office by 7:30 a.m.

His mind was still trying to process the events of yesterday as he finished dressing. Robin's cell phone alarm went off exactly at 7:00 a.m.

"Good morning, beautiful," he said leaning over and kissing her gently.

"Why don't you stay home for a while?" she asked with a mischievous grin.

"Right" is all he got out before his cell phone went off. It was Witt with bad news.

"What's happening?" Robin asked after he ended the call.

"We have a Code 7 Alert."

"Doesn't that involve WMD?"

"Close. Biological terrorist threat."

"What do you want me to do?" Robin asked.

"Let's stick with the plan we discussed last night. You handle getting the girls safe and sound from the hospital and back to the house. I'll call you later from the office as soon as I find out what we're dealing with.

And thanks for everything. It means a lot to me that you made the trip here."

"You know I love you and will help anyway I can."

"You're great. Coffee's in the pot and help yourself to whatever you find in the refrigerator. I know Sophia picked up a bunch of fruit."

———⟋⟍⟋⟍⟋———

The agents on the emergency call list were assembled in SAC Brennan's conference room at 7:30 a.m.

"I always assumed that one day the FBI would have to activate this plan," Brennan said. "I just never anticipated it would be in the Atlanta Division.

"Thirty minutes ago, the Deputy Director called me from the Strategic Intelligence Operations Center advising that headquarters initiated an immediate threat assessment of a possible biological attack involving bovine spongiform encephalitis, also called mad cow disease.

"Both the *New York Times* and *The Washington Post* received identical threat letters along with contact lens cases purporting to contain some of the BSE. Circumstances indicate a high probability the lens cases contain some of the pathogen missing from the CDC. Both newspapers turned the items over to the FBI. The letters said cattle in three US stockyards were infected last week. The writer of the letters indicated receiving the biological agent from Kevin Middleton at the CDC. The letters were sent from a FedEx office in Kansas City.

"Agents in New York and Washington took possession of the letters as well as the samples, which are on a flight to Atlanta where they'll be taken to the CDC. Our Kansas City office has already sent agents to the FedEx office. Two epidemiologists from Fort Detrick, Maryland, are flying to Atlanta and will coordinate the examination of the biological agent.

"Right now, we've been designated the national Joint Operations Center for incident response and criminal investigations. FEMA has activated its national command center for consequence management and has notified the White House as well as placed a National Emergency Response Team on alert. FEMA is contacting the governor of Georgia."

"Why the governor?" the technical supervisor asked.

"He's in the decision-making stovepipe," Brennan responded.

"We don't know if anyone has actually infected cattle, do we?" Witt asked.

"Correct," Brennan replied. "We've been ordered to do a threat assessment and answer three questions. First, did whoever sent the letters have the ability to obtain the biological agent? Second, could they deliver the agent in the manner threatened? And, third, from what we know, was there a likelihood they would carry out the threat?" Brennan paused and then looked at Bannister. "You care to address this, Ty?"

Bannister stood up and looked around the table. "Well, we know BSE prions are unaccounted for at the CDC lab where Kevin Middleton was a key researcher. The letters mention obtaining the agent from Middleton, who was murdered earlier this week. We know Middleton was heavily in debt but had a huge recent deposit in a foreign bank account and had ten grand in his apartment when we searched it. By way of background, the BSE agent is microscopic and can be easily sprinkled on feed to be consumed by cattle or be dissolved in a solution for injection into animals. As for the third part, we don't know who sent the letters but we know there's an operational terrorist cell in Atlanta. We're trying to identify and locate the cell members." Bannister sat back down.

Brennan continued: "Whenever we have a major case, there are always concerns about the media finding out and leaking information." Brennan stood up and put his hands on the glass covered conference table, scanning the faces of the agents assembled in the room. "In this case, the media was the first to know and has a running start. They'll be all over this like white on rice. Some of you have worked bombing cases where everyone knew there was a crime scene and where it was located. In our case we have greater challenges since there may be one or more crime scenes and we don't know where they are.

"Although eventually we might be dealing with a cast of thousands, we have to function on a strict need-to-know basis. With that in mind, in our conference room a floor below are inspectors from DC working the shooting inquiry into Terry Hines's death last night. They have no reason to know anything about this operation, so be careful what you say. In front of you is a packet with the protocols for the units each of you will be responsible for coordinating until the national team arrives. Questions?"

"Not a question—just a concern," Barnes said as the conference door opened and White stepped in. Barnes continued, "We're working backwards from Kevin Middleton to ID all possible cell members. We don't know who they are, how many there are, or where they are. And time is definitely against us."

White held a hand up. "I'm sorry to interrupt your meeting, Mr. Brennan. I found something on the flash drive Terry Hines was carrying. I think it's extremely important."

"Tell us," Brennan said.

"Hines mentions names I believe are part of a three-person terrorist cell here in Atlanta. Bashir Rahman al-Ahmad is the first name. He was the man who left Atlanta the day after Middleton was murdered. He was taken into custody by Egyptian authorities and died under mysterious circumstances in Cairo. The other two names on Hines's drive are Hassan Fadi and Kasim Musa."

Mims raised his hand and Brennan pointed at him. "Musa's the name on a Visa credit card with ties to the Detroit Hezbollah operation. His Visa has been used for gas purchases in Atlanta and Detroit and recent charges in Kansas City and Grand Island, Nebraska."

White raised her hand and Brennan nodded for her to continue. "The credit card charges from Grand Island occurred on the next to last day of the Nebraska State Fair. That was the same day and location the fair sponsored the largest cattle show in the Midwest. The next morning the FedEx envelopes were mailed from Kansas City."

"We've got to find these subjects and fast!" Brennan said. "I want a full court press on both names. We need to know everything possible about them, where they're from, where they've been, and most importantly, where they are right now. They have to be taken alive so we can determine what they did with the BSE agent." He pointed to Ramirez, who had raised her hand.

"Warrants for the arrests of Fadi and Musa should be authorized within the hour," Ramirez said. "The task force will contact every car rental agency in Atlanta to see if we can identify the vehicle they're using."

"Good," Brennan said, nodding. "We don't want to issue an all-points bulletin and have some locals blow them away. We need a plan for taking them alive and forcing them to talk." He looked around at the assembled agents. "Everyone will be back here tomorrow morning at 7:30 a.m. Bannister, see me in my office," Brennan concluded.

It was silent as everyone took their packets of material and instructions with them. Bannister whispered to Robin to wait at his desk until he met with the boss.

Brennan was sitting in one of the side chairs near his desk as he waved Bannister in.

"Close the door." He crossed his legs and interlaced his fingers over his knee. "You know, the two people in this office in whom I have the most confidence are you and Germaine. I hope to God we can solve this and fast."

"I do too," Bannister replied.

"Your daughter was kidnapped, her friend wounded, and Terry Hines killed. Your girlfriend Robin Mikkonen flew in a couple of hours ago and I'm assuming the wounded roommate's parents are coming here also. Right?"

"That's correct."

"Our backs are against the wall and with everything going on in your private life, I've got to ask you straight out. Can I still count on you to give this your best effort?" Brennan leaned back in his chair.

"Absolutely. Katie McDonald's parents are flying here tomorrow afternoon. They and the two girls are booked on a return flight to LA Sunday afternoon. Agent Mikkonen will be flying back to DC right after they leave. They won't cause any diversions for me."

"I know you'll stay focused and not let personal issues interfere with getting the job done."

"Thanks," Bannister said.

"Hold off for a second. I don't want you to hear this from someone else, but you're being reported to the Office of Professional Responsibility for misuse of government property."

Bannister looked at the boss for a few seconds before the words registered. "You mean the bracelet?"

"Yes. The SWAT commander was talking with Witt in the command center and told him about the signals leading us to the garage. When Witt went downstairs for an update from the inspector handling the shooting inquiry, the inspector asked him how our office found the girl. After Witt laid it out, the inspector called me and said he had no choice but to have Witt send a report to headquarters advising them of the alleged misconduct."

"Well, the device worked better than expected and it saved Madison's life. I'll take responsibility for the dereliction and gladly live with the consequences."

"Good. I thought that'd be your response. Everyone in this office is going to be called upon to go above and beyond. I'll be funneling a shitload of requests to Witt. I can say this to you but not to others. Hopefully he'll be so busy he won't have time to screw up anything else. I instructed Barnes to focus on everything that has to do with Terry Hines. I'll personally call Chief Spina in Dahlonega, Inspector Yates at GBI, and US Attorney Prescott.

"I'm letting the head of the National Emergency team know you are Atlanta's point man for the bioterrorism investigation. Everything to do with Middleton, the BSE agent, and the search for this Fadi and Musa will be going through you. I expect you to be in touch with me every hour with developments. Are you okay with that?"

"I'm just one agent, but I promise you I'll do my best."

"That's all I ask." Brennan stood up and shook Bannister's hand.

CHAPTER 53

As he walked back from White's vault, Bannister was reviewing her list of leads when Detective Roy Miller called.

"Agent Bannister. I think we need to meet right away. Where are you now?" he asked.

"We're in a firestorm. I'm in my office. What've you got?"

"I have an address we need to talk about."

"I'm listening. Tell me more."

"Our cases keep intersecting. I'm going downtown to meet with my detectives working the Middleton murder. You remember the two guys you're interested in who are still in the US?"

"Right."

"I was following through on a hunch of my own. I had one of my men checking motels, and around midnight last night he stopped at the Extended Stay Inn on Peachtree Road. You had given me the name of Kasim Musa to check out. My detective discovered a K. Musa was listed as a registered guest. He's paid up through Monday. And to answer your next question, I don't know if he's there now." Miller paused. "You still there?"

"I'm here. What else did your guy say?" Bannister asked.

"Only that this Musa listed a white Nissan as his vehicle. Since it was so late, my detective waited until 7:00 a.m. this morning to call me."

"I agree I need to see you right away. Where can we meet?"

"I'm heading to APD headquarters as we speak but am going to swing by the Starbucks on Peachtree Road about a mile from your office. You want to meet me at my car in their parking lot?"

"I know the Starbucks. I'll be there in ten minutes."

Bannister called SAC Brennan and explained to him why he had to leave the office and might be late returning. Brennan said he'd tell the others Bannister was responding to a high priority lead. Bannister grabbed his coat and gun and saw Ramirez in the hallway.

"I've got to run. We may have caught a huge break from Detective Miller. I've told the boss but nobody else. Trust me on this and stay close to the office. I'll explain when I return."

"Okay. Go for it" is all Ramirez said.

Ten minutes later he spotted Miller's black Dodge Charger and pulled alongside. Bannister opened the passenger door and got in.

"Before I tell you what I've got, fill me in on the status of your investigation," Miller said. He sipped at a large coffee drink with whipped cream and caramel on top.

"A lot of what we're dealing with is classified. It's big—really big. As we're sitting here, about five hundred people with top secret clearances are scrambling to resolve what may be a terrorist action. What I'm going to tell you needs to stay between us girls."

"It'll stay in this car," Miller said.

"We agree there were probably three guys involved with murdering Kevin Middleton. As you know, one of them, Bashir al-Ahmad, made it to Egypt and then dropped off the radar. We believe the Egyptian secret police interrogated him and when they were finished, killed him. We think he and two other men, Kasim Musa and Hassan Fadi, not only were responsible for Middleton's death but also may have dispersed a biological weapon within the last couple of days."

"Son of a bitch!" Miller said, wiping a cream moustache off his lip. "Are you talking about something like smallpox or anthrax?"

"You're not hearing this from me, but the biological pathogen is targeted against livestock. That's why we need to find those guys and get them to tell us what they did."

"I never thought I'd be working on something like this."

"That makes two of us. Here's what we're going to do. I'm going back to our office and notify the command. If we confirm your information, we're going to set up an operation to capture Musa and whoever is with him if they return. We've got agents checking every rental agency in Atlanta to identify a car they may have used to travel to the Midwest. Knowing he may be driving a white Nissan is a big help. At the appropriate time we'll put out an APB on them. We don't know if they still have any of the biotoxin with them, but we have to make the assumption they do."

"You're not going to lose track of the fact I have an open murder case with them as the key players, right?"

"Right. Hopefully, you can finesse your team to back off for a day. I'll call you as soon as we get a positive locate on these guys, okay?"

"I can live with that," Miller said.

On the way back to the office Bannister went past the Extended Stay Inn, which had 115 rooms on three levels. He drove through the parking lots in front and back but did not see a white Nissan.

Agents were filing out of the conference room when he returned. He asked Ramirez if she'd wait at his desk until he briefed the boss. Brennan signaled Bannister to follow him to his office. He shut the door.

"What've you got, Ty?"

He relayed to him what Detective Miller had said. Brennan informed him that while Bannister was out, one of the Special Operations Group agents located a Budget Rental office from which Kasim Musa had rented a white Nissan Sentra last week. It had not yet been returned. The agent got the car's license number. The SOG was watching the rental facility. Brennan told Bannister he had to interrupt his meeting to take a call from the director, who offered whatever resources Atlanta required. The director also ordered the inspector currently heading up the shooting inquiry to report to Brennan and, if necessary, assist in the terrorist investigation. The epidemiologists from Fort Detrick with the biotoxin-laden contact lens cases had just arrived at the CDC.

"How do you want to play this out, Ty?" Brennan asked.

"I'll take Ramirez with me and head back to the Extended Stay Inn and confirm our subjects may have been or are still staying there. She has photos we can show to their manager. We'll wait there until you can get a surveillance team to watch the place. I'd appreciate if you could have the SWAT team draft up a tactical plan for a takedown."

Brennan said, "Sounds good. I'll personally direct from the command post. At the hotel, see if you can rent the rooms on each side as well as above the one rented by Musa. If the registered guests are long term, tell the manager there's a minor gas leak or something that needs to be fixed. He can move the occupants to other hotel rooms at our expense. You can tell him we have a warrant for Musa for murder."

"I better get going," Bannister said.

"Call me immediately if you determine Musa and Fadi are there."

"I will."

Ramirez was standing by his desk. He grabbed two extra magazines for his Sig Sauer in addition to an extra set of handcuffs.

"Let's go. We're driving over to the Extended Stay Inn on Peachtree Road. Take your car and follow me. We may have found the hotel where Musa and Fadi have been living. I'll fill you in as soon as we get there."

CHAPTER 54

annister and Ramirez parked their cars at the south side of the hotel and walked to the office. A desk clerk and manager were on duty. The manager, a white male in his mid-twenties, said he worked Wednesdays through Sundays. After the female desk clerk stepped into the back office, Ramirez showed the manager photos of their subjects. He positively identified Musa as a guest who stayed in room 114 during the last month. He was fairly certain Hassan Fadi was the second man staying in the room. He remembered him because he was tall, but had only observed him twice during the month. The manager had not seen either man for more than a week. Bannister rented room 113 which was vacant and next to the end unit rented by Musa. He and Ramirez returned to their cars.

Ramirez walked over and climbed into Bannister's car. "We have no idea where they are, do we?" she asked.

As they both sat there looking through the windshield, Bannister said, "No. We're in a waiting game."

"We have warrants for their arrest and could put out an all-points bulletin right now, correct?" Ramirez asked.

"Yes, but if we issue an APB it should only be for a person of interest. If we put out a standard APB for an armed and dangerous murder suspect, we might have some trigger-happy local blow both of them away and unintentionally cause an economic meltdown for our country."

"So, what exactly are we doing here?" Ramirez asked with a scowl.

"Sitting tight. I phoned the office. We're going to stay here until relieved by the Special Operations Group, who will set up surveillance. They'll relay necessary information to the SWAT supervisor who's preparing an arrest plan right now. In the meantime, why don't you and I take a casual stroll around the perimeter of this hotel and identify the best vantage points?"

"Sounds good. By the way, don't you have to go to the hospital to get Madison and her friend?"

Bannister glanced at his watch as he stepped out to his car. It was 9:00 a.m. exactly. "Robin agreed to handle that for me. She's probably at the hospital waiting for them to be discharged. I'll call her in a little bit."

Bannister had taken a couple of steps past the front of his car when a white Nissan Sentra zipped by and pulled directly into a parking spot halfway down the first row. It was forty feet away. The license plate instantly registered with both of them. Just then, two men exited. The driver moved towards the trunk of the vehicle while his passenger stood by the right side. They looked directly at Bannister and Ramirez.

"It's them," Ramirez whispered.

"Go!" Bannister yelled, and then shouted, "Fadi and Musa! FBI!" His badge waved in his left hand.

Fadi's hand was a blur as he reached for his waistband.

"Gun!" Ramirez yelled. They both saw the pistol in Fadi's hand and moved instinctively. Ramirez's reaction time was a fraction of a second faster than Bannister's. She got off three rounds in less than a second, all slamming into Fadi's chest. Bannister fired once, hitting Fadi in the right shoulder. The rounds propelled him backwards. The single bullet Fadi discharged ricocheted off the asphalt in front of his feet.

Musa, who was standing next to the open passenger door, raised his hands straight above his head and stood frozen, a petrified look of shock etched on his face.

His ears ringing, Bannister moved quickly toward Fadi's accomplice.

"Kasim Musa. You're under arrest." Bannister holstered his gun while Ramirez covered him. He spun Musa around to face the Nissan, patted him down and then handcuffed him. Bannister glanced to his left and observed Mercedes moving Fadi's gun away from his body, and then checking him for a pulse. She shook her head side to side.

"Do you have any weapons in this car?"

"No. Hassan had the only gun," Musa replied.

Several people on the second and third stories who had heard the gunshots had stepped onto the balcony. "Police," Bannister shouted. "Get back inside!"

"We need to get Musa to our office where we can question him," Bannister said to Ramirez. "Keep an eye on him while I make some calls."

Ramirez said, "I have no idea what protocols the CDC and FEMA people are going to follow once they get here. They may assume both of our subjects have been in contact with BSE prions and might have trace samples on their clothing, vehicle, room, etc. Just giving you a heads up."

"We'll wait only until the locals clear us and then get Musa out of here."

Bannister walked their prisoner back to his Bureau car and strapped him into the backseat. Mercedes stood by the open rear door and watched him while Bannister called the SAC.

"Boss, Ramirez and I are at the Extended Stay Inn on Peachtree Road. Fadi and Musa drove up and made us. I made a command decision to arrest them right here, but Fadi drew a weapon. We had no choice but to shoot back. We're okay, but he's dead. Musa wasn't injured, and I'll transport him to our office for questioning as soon as I talk with the sheriff's deputies."

Brennan said, "I know I'm the Special Agent in Charge and normally would dictate procedure, but this is not a normal situation. You have a handle on the facts and I trust your judgment. What do you need from the office?"

"I'm going to ask Detective Miller to grease the skids with Dekalb County Sheriff's Office since we're in their jurisdiction. We'll have to go through the same drill we did at the warehouse this week. Would you make sure the SOG is on the way here and notify Carrie Howell to send her evidence team? She's going to have to work it out with the CDC people, who may want to do searches a different way."

"Okay, we've got you covered. What else?"

"You may as well notify the inspector he's got another FBI-involved shooting to handle."

"Will do," said Brennan. "I'll give instructions to Witt and then come out to the scene ASAP."

"One last thing, boss. I want to take Musa directly to the processing room inside our caged area. Have Witt try to line up an Arabic-speaking polygraph examiner as quick as possible. If an FBI examiner isn't available, we can tap the Defense Department for their help."

"We'll handle it. I hope I don't have to eat these words, Ty, but good job."

Bannister hung up and called Detective Miller, who said he'd phone Dekalb County while driving to the hotel and get a medical examiner out to the scene. Bannister told him to inform the ME that the deceased subject may have recently handled a biotoxin that could be infectious to animals.

Bannister was a little concerned when he looked at Ramirez, who appeared perfectly normal. "You did great. I'm proud of you."

"Thanks. That's the first time I've ever had to shoot somebody. I'm not shaking or anything. It happened so fast that adrenaline didn't have time to kick in. Do you think I'm all right?"

"You're fine right now. You responded instinctively to your training and haven't had time to think about it. It'll probably hit you later." Bannister knew Ramirez would replay this scene in her head dozen of times and ponder all the what-ifs. That was normal and that was healthy. When he talked to her later he would reinforce that she did everything 100% correctly. The important thing was that neither of them got shot and that there were no innocent civilian casualties.

CHAPTER 55

Two Dekalb County deputies in marked cruisers pulled into the Extended Stay Inn lot at the same time as Detective Miller of the Atlanta PD. While the three law enforcement officers discussed how to handle the scene, Bannister called Barnes.

"Derek, where are you?"

"I just got back to the office after witnessing Hines's autopsy. What's up?"

Bannister told him what had occurred. "I need some favors. I'd like you to assist me in interviewing Musa at our office. Mercedes would be a logical choice, but she's a woman and Arabs dismiss females as inferior."

"Copy that. I'll get ready."

"Make sure the interview room in back is prepared to record both video and audio."

"Anything else?"

"Yes. I'm fairly certain they'll want to expedite an autopsy of Fadi. Do you mind witnessing that one also?"

"No. But it reminds me of that movie quote where the kid says, 'I see dead people.'"

"Hopefully there won't be any more this week," Bannister said.

"You should know our Omaha and Kansas City offices did some great work. Omaha checked surveillance videos in Grand Island from entrances to the Nebraska State Fair as well as its Livestock Exhibition Hall. Our subjects were identified coming and going at both locations on two consecutive days this week. Kansas City obtained surveillance from a FedEx office where our guys are also seen entering and leaving.

A female FedEx clerk positively identified Fadi and Musa as mailing envelopes."

"Great. What about the cattle shown at the Nebraska competitions?"

Barnes let out a loud "Ah ha!"

"What's that for?"

"We hit the jackpot. Every bull or cow entered by a cattle producer or a 4-H Club kid had to have a certificate from a veterinarian showing they had been inoculated for bovine diarrhea virus. We have a complete list of all animals present during the two days Fadi and Musa were at the fair. The certificates have the addresses of the owners and the animals' identification numbers, which should match ear tags."

"We could use more breaks like that," Bannister said.

"The boss mentioned that if you get any confirmation they actually carried out their attack, the president will order FEMA to activate a predetermined national management response."

"Did he translate that?"

"Not exactly. All the boss said is the federal government has highly specialized response teams that will move like World War III is around the corner. Let's wait and see if we can get anything out of Musa."

"I'll be there in twenty minutes."

—◦◦◦—

Barnes met Bannister outside a building in the rear of the FBI complex, which in addition to housing the automotive garage, radio shop, and technical offices, had an interview and booking room for federal prisoners. Barnes took Musa inside and secured him to a chair bolted to the concrete floor. One of the task force agents stood inside the door keeping an eye on him while Barnes and Bannister conferred outside.

Bannister told Barnes, "He had his passport in his bag. His full name is Kasim Abdullah Musa. By the way, Fadi's passport was in a nylon pouch around his neck. Although it had two bullet holes in it, you could still read his full name as Hassan Fadi al-Sidon. I gave both names to Germaine to run. How about taking Musa's photos and prints while I step into the admin office and make some calls?" The task force agent continued standing guard.

Ted Mims had phoned twice, so Bannister returned his calls.

"I have search warrants for Middleton's financial accounts," Mims said. "I also have warrants for records of Terry Hines, a.k.a. Nathan Shane Quinn, and for Bunkie Black if he doesn't cooperate. Unless you object, I'll serve those Monday morning when everyone's at their offices."

"That's fine," Bannister replied.

Mims added, "Germaine wanted me to tell you our New York office dispatched two agents to interview Hines's mother in Long Island. They're going to break the news to her of his death as well as masquerading as Quinn. We believe the mother somehow funneled money to him so we tasked the New York agents with finding out the particulars."

"You're on top of things, Ted. Let me know if you come up with anything unusual."

Bannister speed-dialed Robin. For a second, he wished none of this was taking place and he could just call to hear her voice and talk about nothing in particular. But that wasn't happening. He was worried about Madison and Katie, and concerned about Robin.

"What's the status at the hospital?" he asked Robin before volunteering any information.

"Katie's been discharged. Madison and a nurse went to get a wheelchair to bring her to the front entrance. Right now, I'm walking out to the parking lot to get your car. Everything okay with you?" The concern in her voice was evident.

He spent a few minutes bringing Robin up to date and letting her know it would probably be two hours before he could take a break. While stunned that for the third time in a week Bannister had been involved in a shooting where someone lost their life, she was overjoyed he had not been hurt and that Ramirez was okay. He asked her not to tell the girls about this most recent shooting. He also mentioned the FBI had to coordinate with a Domestic Emergency Support Team, which had flown out from Washington, DC, under orders of the president.

Bannister rubbed his eyes and ran his hand through his hair. "It would be nice to talk to Madison, but that's not going to happen right now. Tell her I love her and explain something extremely important is happening and I absolutely can't get away. Will you do that?"

"I'll tell her. Please be careful. You know the last time I was in a hospital was to visit you after you were shot. I don't want to sound like a broken record, but I'm worrying more and more about you."

"Well, that makes two of us. Everything's going to work out, but it's going to take more time. I'll call when I have a chance."

CHAPTER 56

Barnes had cuffed Musa once again after taking mugshots and his prints with an FBI optical scanner. Another agent was uploading the prints and delivering the photos to White. Barnes joined Bannister in the adjacent soundproofed office where they looked through the bulletproof glass at their subject and the task force agent guarding him.

Barnes leaned with his back against the wall and his arms crossed in front. "The CDC experts should be finished analyzing the contents of the contact lens cases. Do we want to wait for their results before interviewing Musa?"

"No. Mercedes will relay the information as soon as it comes in," Bannister said.

"So, we don't know if they actually carried out their attack. We don't know how many terrorists are involved. We don't know how many state fairs or stockyards they visited. And we don't know how many cattle might have been infected. Have I missed anything?"

"No."

"Besides all of that, we have no idea if Musa will talk to us or anyone in authority. If he does talk, we don't know if he'll talk today or next year, or if he'll tell the truth. So exactly what are your plans to break down a terrorist without using drugs, waterboarding, or some other violence?"

"Most experts agree there is nothing intelligent about torture. If you have to inflict pain on your subject, you've lost control of the situation, the subject, and yourself. The key is just to get him to start talking—about anything."

"I beg to differ," Barnes said. "There's nothing intelligent about terrorists. They don't give a rat's ass about anyone. And we shouldn't be a bunch of dick heads begging them to come clean."

"Two years ago I interrogated several Arabs involved in a kidnapping that happened in Beirut. You might remember that case. All the suspects were linked to Hamas and I learned a great deal from the interviews I did. For Arabs, a person's honor and dignity are of the highest importance. Loyalty to one's family also takes precedence over personal needs. As investigators we need to avoid saying something that offends the person's self-image. Arabs rarely will admit to mistakes openly if it will cause them to lose face. Their perceptions are frequently more important than the facts."

"We know very little about Musa and we killed his brother-in-law right in front of him.

What makes you think he will cooperate with us?" Barnes asked.

"I don't know if he will," said Bannister, "but I read Musa as a follower and not some radicalized zealot. He let himself get pushed into being a participant because of his family ties, not because of some commitment to a cause. I don't think he ever gave a moment's thought to being arrested or possibly killed. He never considered being held accountable for his actions. Right now, his defenses are at their lowest and he has no support structure. I'm going to try and exploit that. Wish me luck."

The two walked back into the booking room, and Bannister told the task force agent to wait outside. Their prisoner was seated in a padded but armless chair inside the ten-by-fourteen-foot concrete room. Across from the prisoner was a small metal table and two folding chairs. Bannister's notebook was on the right side of the table. As he sat down, Bannister noticed Musa's lower lip quivering and his right hand was shaking.

"Take his cuffs off," Bannister ordered.

After Barnes removed the restraints, Musa slowly rubbed his wrists and hands before looking at Bannister.

"Would you like some hot tea?" Bannister asked. Musa just stared.

Smiling, Bannister said, "We're not going to poison you."

His lip stopped quivering. "Yes. That would be nice."

The fact that he said anything was surprising, and Bannister took it as a positive response. If he were going to stonewall them, he would have remained silent.

Bannister called White and asked her to send a cup of tea with extra honey to the interview room.

"Hassan's dead, isn't he?" Musa asked.

"Yes."

"What do you want from me?"

His question surprised Bannister, who knew the US government would extract the information Musa held by one means or another. If Bannister was unsuccessful, Musa would be turned over to another agency. Most likely that agency's special personnel would take him to a black site where he would be severely stressed; the politically favored phrasing for the stress was "enhanced interrogation techniques."

Bannister had to gain Musa's trust and make him believe he could help him with his goals and priorities from this moment forward. When he interviewed even hardened criminals, Bannister treated them with respect. He tried to never do or say anything that insulted their dignity. Even when their crimes were so heinous that experienced police officers would have feelings of utter disgust for them, Bannister suppressed his personal emotions. He didn't view this as a weak approach, but a smart one.

"We just want to talk with you and hear your side of things," Bannister said.

"Where do you want me to start?" Musa responded.

"Anywhere you want."

Bannister had told Barnes not to ask any questions, that he would do all the interviewing. If Barnes wanted Bannister to ask Musa a specific question, he would write it down and hand it to Bannister. He used principles from a class he took a long time ago taught by Avinoam Sapir, a former Israeli polygraph examiner. Sapir's basic premise was that a person's denying guilt was not the same as his denying the act. When a subject said "I am not guilty" or "I am an innocent person," he was not denying the act. He was only denying his guilt. Another lesson Bannister learned from Sapir was to let the person talk and don't interrupt. Get his entire narrative first. Sapir called this technique "obtaining the pure version." It was simplistic, and it worked.

Musa began. "Six months ago, Hassan and I went to London. While there, he was directed to meet with a man wanted by US authorities. Hassan said the man would give us the name of a scientist in Atlanta who would assist us in our assignment."

Bannister wanted to ask him about Bashir al-Ahman and Hassan Fadi as well as Terry Hines and Kevin Middleton, but that would have to wait. They were all dead and Musa was the only one alive.

"Please go on," Bannister said.

"When it was time to leave, Hassan and I flew to Detroit where we stayed a month. Hassan received orders and American dollars from someone in Detroit, but I never met that contact. The man gave him two cell phones, a gun, and a credit card with my name on it. I was only to use the card when ordered to by Hassan. About a month ago the two of us drove to Atlanta where we met up with Bashir. I had met Bashir in London and was told he was part of our team. I don't know where Bashir was living in Atlanta, but Hassan and I rented a room at that motel where you surprised us."

They were interrupted by a knock at the door which Barnes answered. A task force agent handed Bannister a large Styrofoam cup of hot tea.

Handing it to Musa, Bannister noted his eyebrows arched, conveying he was pleased. He said, "Take your time."

Musa took a few long sips of the tea and slowly nodded his head in approval before continuing.

"Hassan made arrangements to meet the CDC scientist named Middleton at a coffee shop near where the man worked. Bashir and I were told not to be observed by Middleton, but to follow him after

Hassan gave him a payment. He did not meet anyone, but drove straight to his job."

There was a pause and Bannister observed Musa's chin suddenly pointing downward, a sign he lacked confidence. Bannister knew he needed a slight prodding. "Please continue," he repeated.

"A week later he delivered to Hassan what he was paid to get. Sometime after that, Hassan got a phone call from Middleton. Hassan was very worried. Middleton said he had been contacted by the FBI, and he wanted to talk with Hassan. Hassan told Bashir and me he had a plan. Bashir arranged for a prostitute to rent a hotel room near the airport for a night. Hassan instructed me to stay outside in the parking lot and watch the room. I was to call him on his phone if I saw anything suspicious when he and Bashir were meeting with Middleton."

Musa took another long sip. "Thank you for this tea. It is very good."

"I'm glad you like it." Bannister smiled and tilted his head to the side, letting Musa know he was listening and interested. "Please tell us more."

"I saw Middleton drive up, park his blue car, and then enter the room where Hassan and Bashir were. After about fifteen minutes, Hassan called me and said to come to the room. He opened the door part way and told me to step inside, but not touch anything. I saw Middleton lying on the bed with a knife sticking out of his chest. I asked Hassan what had happened. He said Middleton was a frightened and weak man who could not be trusted. That he was a loose end that had to be eliminated."

Bannister saw that Musa instinctively moved his chin close to his neck and slightly rubbed the side of his nose with his index finger, signs he was stressed and insecure. Opening his hands, Bannister smiled again and when Musa looked at him, simply said, "And?"

"Oh, you want to know how Middleton was killed. Hassan put a choke hold on him that made him unconscious. He and Bashir then partially undressed Middleton's body on the bed to make it look like he was going to spend time with the prostitute who rented the room. Hassan said Bashir killed him. Bashir only said, 'Problem solved.'"

"The last time I saw Bashir was when we left the hotel. He called us a day later from Cairo as he had been ordered, but he failed to make a pre-arranged call two days after that. We don't know what happened to him."

Bannister did not volunteer any information. "And you and Hassan continued with your plan, right?"

"Yes."

"Tell us what you did," Bannister said.

For the next hour Musa detailed everything he and Fadi did with the BSE prions. He was positive they had injected a total of four animals at the Nebraska State Fair: two bulls at the Red Angus section in the Exhibition Hall and two dairy cows in an adjacent section. Fadi had the idea to say in the letters that they had infected animals at three different stockyards in the United States in order to create greater fear. Musa said there was still some of the BSE biotoxin in a sea salt bottle in their hotel room. Fadi decided to keep it in case they got orders to use it again.

Bannister and Barnes had been questioning Musa for two hours and obtained his personal data as well as names and descriptions of people he knew in Detroit, Atlanta, and overseas.

Bannister whispered to Barnes, "He's cooperating and I believe what he's told us. Babysit him while I go and update Brennan. As soon as one of the task force agents relieves you, join me in the boss's office."

CHAPTER 57

A few minutes later Bannister was outside SAC Brennan's open doorway. As the boss hung up his phone, he waved him in.

"Close the door, Ty. That was the director on a secure line. He's ordered you, Derek, Mercedes, and me to report immediately to the CDC."

"Did he say why?"

"No, only that a special team was there and would explain everything to us. The Attorney General has sent a Deputy AG to our office to coordinate the investigation. I've never heard of anything like this. Supposedly, the Deputy AG was on the same plane as the polygraph examiner coming to our office. Give me your read on Musa. Is he telling the truth?"

"I think he's coming clean and after seeing Fadi killed, he's too scared to lie. He's also adamant that he and Fadi injected a total of four animals with what they believed to be BSE prions."

Brennan's phone rang and he listened for ten seconds before hanging up.

"That was Witt. The polygraph examiner and the Deputy AG just arrived. The examiner has orders to verify if Musa's information is accurate. Gary will run things while we're at the CDC and will call us when the examiner gets confirmation."

"Mercedes is being interviewed right now by the shooting team inspectors," Bannister said.

"I know," Brennan said. "I left instructions for her to give the polygraph examiner whatever background information he needs before she joins us at the CDC. I also told the inspector your shooting interview has to be delayed."

"I appreciate that. Barnes is coming up to your office any minute. Do you want the three of us to go in one car?"

"Makes sense. We'll take mine."

When Barnes arrived, Bannister filled him in. As Brennan grabbed his sport coat, Bannister remarked, "Mercedes is up to speed on everything except for what Musa has been telling us this last hour." The boss nodded.

The three men didn't say a word as they took the elevator to the ground floor and walked to the boss's car parked in the caged area. They each had dozens of thoughts running through their heads. When Brennan clicked the remote to his car, he turned in Bannister's direction.

"Incidentally, how are your daughter and her friend?"

"They've been released from the hospital and should be at my house by now."

"Is someone with them?"

"My friend Robin is at the house and Katie's parents are due to arrive in a few hours from LA."

"If I can cut you loose for a while, I will," Brennan said.

"I'll keep my fingers crossed," Bannister replied with a forced smile.

They got into the boss's car and proceeded to the CDC located five miles away.

Looking straight down the road, Brennan commented, "You know, this case is getting weirder by the hour, sort of like Alice in Wonderland when she said things were 'curiouser and curiouser.'"

"I know what you mean," Bannister said.

A short time later they had visitor badges and were escorted to a secure room off the CDC's Emergency Operations Center. Seated at a conference table were David Ash, Dr. Klaus Wulfsberg, Gloria Sanchez, and two men Bannister didn't know. He guessed the guys sitting next to each other might be the epidemiologists from Fort Detrick, Maryland. Standing at the far end of the table was a solid-looking man about fifty years old. He stood maybe six-two, had a buzz haircut, and was wearing black slacks with a light gray sport coat and white shirt, no tie. David Ash introduced the man as Colonel Scott Ramsey from the Joint Special Operations Center at Fort Bragg, North Carolina, and also introduced the two scientists from Fort Detrick.

Colonel Ramsey didn't waste any time. "I appreciate all of you coming here on such short notice." Just then, Mercedes Ramirez entered the conference room and took a seat next to Bannister. Ramsey continued, "Before we get into things, I want you to look over the document in front of each of you. It's a non-disclosure agreement for the Spartacus Project. After signing it, you will be indoctrinated into the project and your names will be added to the list of cleared personnel. Take a minute to look it over and as soon as you've signed it, we'll begin."

He offered no further explanation, no time for questions, no thought that any of them might not sign the agreement.

After everyone signed their names and looked up, Colonel Ramsey continued. "I'm going to spare you hours of details because we don't have the luxury of time. As you know, Presidential Decision Directive 39 directs that the lead agency for operational response to a biological agent incident that appears to be caused by an act of terrorism is the FBI. That's why you're here. The agency responsible for consequence management for such an incident is the Federal Emergency Management Agency. Spartacus is a compartmentalized program under the umbrella of continuity of government. It concerns biological attacks and special measures that may be taken in response. Last March the president signed an executive order for national defense preparedness. That executive order directs the Secretary of Defense to oversee coordination. What has taken place this week falls squarely under the purview of the Spartacus Program, and I am the on-site coordinator for all efforts pertaining to our current problem. That means I will coordinate actions involving the epidemiological tracing of the agent, identification of all perpetrators, the identification of all animals infected, their euthanization and disposal, equitable indemnification to the animals' owners, overview of FBI criminal and counterterrorist investigations, intelligence gathering and analysis, and all releases to the media of any kind."

Colonel Ramsey stopped talking for a minute and looked at the faces of everyone sitting around the table. He clicked his ballpoint pen a couple of times and then continued. "What I just said is a mouthful, but the incident we're dealing with can cause unbelievable damage to our national economy and foreign trade, not to mention the long-term impact it could have on our agricultural sector due to the public's perception of a disease risk.

"I will be running the National Joint Operations Center here out of the CDC. The FBI Director ordered the full staffing of the Bureau's Strategic Intelligence Operations Center in Washington, DC. The Defense Department this morning airlifted a sixty-foot, 60,000 pound mobile command center vehicle, which is on the ground at Grand Island, Nebraska. Special Deputy Attorney General Frye is at your office right now. You can presume that any order he gives is backed by the authority of the Attorney General and the president. Now, I'll try to answer your questions." Colonel Ramsey put his pen in his suit pocket, then held his hands out with palms up. He looked at SAC Brennan.

"To begin with," Brennan asked, "were the samples in the contact lens cases delivered to the *Washington Post* and *Wall Street Journal* confirmed as bovine spongiform encephalitis?"

Colonel Ramsey's thin lips had a slight smirk. "What will be released to those newspapers and other media is that the substance has been identified as a vaccine resistant, mutated version of infectious bovine rhinotracheitis (IBR), commonly referred to as 'rednose.' Rednose is a highly contagious virus that can cause respiratory disease, abortions, and infertility in infected cattle. It poses no danger to humans." He shot an icy glance at the two Fort Detrick scientists, who sat there expressionless.

"That doesn't answer my question," Brennan said, taking off his gold-framed glasses.

"Bear with me a little longer," Ramsey said. "The Japanese sea salt specimen, recovered this morning from the hotel room rented by Mr. Fadi, is being analyzed. Dr. Wulfsberg will be furnished with the results. Right, Klaus?"

"Correct," Wulfsberg responded curtly.

"We're confident the analysis will be consistent with a finding of IBR," Ramsey said.

Brennan glared at the colonel. "I may have been born at night, but not last night. Don't bullshit us! This sounds like a carefully orchestrated disinformation ploy, which won't work because Kasim Musa, the third member of the terrorist cell, is at our facility right now and he'll confirm they received mad cow prions and injected that biotoxin into cattle in Nebraska."

"He can only confirm what they were told. Allegedly Kevin Middleton said he was providing them with BSE prions. They did not know what they actually received," Ramsey said, again with his annoying smile.

Bannister raised his hand and Ramsey acknowledged him. "And what do you think's going to come out during Musa's eventual trial for Middleton's murder and federal charges under the Patriot Act?"

"Nothing. There won't be a trial," Ramsey said.

"What are you talking about?" Brennan snapped, leaning forward at the table.

"Exactly that. He will not be going to trial. Arrangements have been made to deliver him to officials in another country."

"Under whose authority?" Brennan asked.

"The Attorney General."

At that moment a CDC official knocked, then entered the conference room. "You'll have to excuse me but there's a priority secure telephone call that SAC Brennan needs to take." Nodding towards Brennan, the official said, "Sir, please follow me."

Colonel Ramsey said, "Let's take a five minute break."

A couple of minutes later Brennan returned and walked back to his seat looking at the FBI agents and remarking, "That was the White House. I'll fill you in later."

It was quiet for a few seconds, then Bannister asked, "Do we know to what country Musa is being taken?"

Ramsey said, "We do know and security arrangements are being made, but we are not releasing that information."

Bannister glared at him and then pushed on. "With Musa being taken out of country, what's going to happen to the Atlanta PD's murder investigation?"

Colonel Ramsey ran his hand over his buzz cut. "They can close it administratively after we inform them that Musa fingered Bashir Rahman al-Ahmad and Hussein Fadi as the killers. And they're already dead."

CHAPTER 58

B efore pulling out of the CDC's parking lot, the SAC turned on a jazz station for the short drive to the office.

"I hope you guys don't mind, but I need a few minutes to collect my thoughts," he said, with a quick look at Bannister and Barnes. They gave him a respectful nod and remained silent. Bannister glanced in the side mirror and saw Ramirez following in the car behind.

Ten minutes later they were back at the office. Bannister and Barnes sat down in two of the three chairs in front of SAC Brennan's large executive desk. As soon as Mercedes entered and took the empty seat between them, Brennan got up and closed his door.

"Have you ever experienced anything like this, Boss?" Bannister jumped in.

"No, this is a first for me," he said. "That secure call I took at the CDC was from the National Security Advisor. He informed me that DOD and FEMA are coordinating all consequence management actions and that Deputy Attorney General Frye was placed in charge of the investigation involving the Fadi cell."

"Didn't Colonel Ramsey say he was in charge and running everything," Barnes said.

"He was," Brennan said, "until the National Security Advisor stepped in and reported that Colonel Ramsey's leg of the relay race was over and that the baton was officially passed to Deputy AG Frye, who would finish the race for us.

"While we were driving back to the office, Frye ordered everything in our computers to be uploaded to the Attorney General and deleted from our files. As we're sitting here, all physical evidence and documents are being boxed and will be couriered to DC."

"That doesn't even sound legal. What about Barnes's and my interview of Musa?" Bannister asked.

"It's over for you. It's over for us. Our entire case has already been transmitted. Pending leads will be completed and reported to Mr. Frye; search warrants will be executed and the results also reported to Frye. Any new investigation at our end will be directed and coordinated by the Attorney General's office. I mean everything. They've demanded a complete blackout on this. No interviews, comments, or acknowledgments to anyone except by me, and I'll probably have orders to talk to the director first."

"You may as well know Detective Miller called requesting access to Musa," Bannister added.

"Well, he's not going to get it," Brennan said.

"The Middleton murder is still an open case for them," Bannister advised.

"I'm sure the AG's office will offer them some type of solution."

"They may be forced to accept it, but they're not going to like it," Bannister said.

Ramirez asked, "What about the newspapers and their knowledge of a biotoxin?"

Brennan answered. "The papers turned over the only physical proof they had to our agents in New York and Washington. They haven't released any information publicly and won't, unless they get irrefutable verification. They're not going to cause a national panic. We gave the contact lens cases as well as the Japanese sea salt bottle taken from Fadi and Musa's hotel room to the epidemiologists at the CDC. So far, I'm not missing anything, am I?"

Ramirez frowned in thought. "I don't think so. Except for what was injected into the cattle in Nebraska, one hundred percent of what Middleton supposedly took is accounted for."

Brennan said, "From what Colonel Ramsey implied, reporters will get stonewalled at every turn and come up empty-handed. Ramsey's people will have already identified and rounded up all the livestock from the Nebraska site as well as other cattle that may have been in contact with those at the state fair exhibit. The CDC will have been ordered to slam the lid on their facilities and people."

"What we're being told to believe as fact is what Colonel Ramsey told us, right?" Barnes asked.

"Exactly. You and I may not believe him, but except for Musa, there is no proof to the contrary," Brennan said.

"And even though Musa's physically here at our office, we no longer have any control over him," Bannister said. They heard a tap at the boss's door and everyone turned to look at Witt as he walked in without being invited.

"What's the latest, Gary?" Brennan asked.

Witt sauntered into the middle of the room. "Somebody at the top of the food chain is pulling strings. The Defense Department polygraph examiner just said that whatever Musa told to Bannister and Barnes showed no deception. He wouldn't elaborate. Deputy AG Frye made some secure calls from my office and informed me Musa was being turned over to a special operations team. He said FBI access to Musa is over. Can someone tell me what the hell is going on?"

"Deputy AG Frye asked for a meeting in my office at 5:00 p.m. for those who received the special briefing at the CDC," Brennan said. "Afterward, I will share whatever information can be released, to you, Gary, as well as the Task Force members and anyone else in our office who worked KABMUR and the terrorist cases. I'll talk to you before we meet tomorrow at 8:00 a.m."

"Tomorrow's Sunday," Witt said.

"Correct. Things are moving fast. I'll see you in the morning. Now, you'll have to excuse us."

Brennan pointed to his door. Witt gave them a deer-in-the-headlights stare before taking the cue and walking out, shutting the door behind him.

Brennan spent another fifteen minutes going over the steps he intended to take and outlined tasks for each of them. Obviously, there would be additional work and problems to solve once they met with Deputy AG Frye.

"You're all free to go and do whatever you need to until five o'clock. Ty, see the chief inspector before you leave. Once he gets your statement they'll pack up their stuff and fly back to DC."

CHAPTER 59

Bannister called the general manager at the Ritz Carlton Hotel in Buckhead and reserved two suites on the concierge level. Bannister then sent a text message to Tim McDonald telling him to take a taxi to the Ritz Carlton where he and Robin would check the girls in first and then wait for the McDonalds to arrive. Bannister called Robin.

"Are you still tied up at the office?" she asked.

"I have to talk with the chief inspector and then am free for two hours." After he filled her in on the McDonald accommodations, she agreed to drive the girls to the hotel as soon as they were packed.

As Bannister pulled up later to the hotel's entrance, he saw his SUV there with Robin behind the wheel. One of the hotel's staff, as well as a valet, were assisting the girls with their suitcases. Bannister pulled in behind them, pleased to see Katie walking normally.

"Hi Dad." Madison beamed.

"Hi, Mr. Bannister," Katie said, and without prompting, walked up to him and gave him a big hug. "I just talked to my dad. He and Mom are in a cab and should be here in a few minutes."

"That's great. Let's go inside and get organized," Bannister said.

Robin put her arm lightly around his waist and gave him a quick kiss.

"Wow. I've been here for a minute and received attention from two attractive women," Bannister chirped.

"Well, make it three for three," Madison said, hugging him and planting a loud smooch on his cheek.

Bannister and Robin checked the girls into the guest suites on the twenty-first floor.

Madison said, "I texted a picture of you and me to Katie's dad so he could pick you out if he needed to."

"That's good. You're learning some of my tricks," Bannister said, enjoying the smile on her face. He told the girls he and Robin were going to the lobby to wait for Katie's parents.

Once back at the check-in desk, Robin said, "This sure is a contrast to the hospital. We've all been through a lot these past twenty-four hours. I just hope this evening can be something special."

"I'm sure it will be once everyone is settled. I wouldn't have been able to manage all of this without you." He took Robin's hand and gently squeezed it.

"I think once the McDonalds arrive they'll want to talk to the girls a while. There's a store across the street where I'd like to stop by and pick up a little something I have in mind for Katie." Robin winked and tilted her head mischievously.

"That'd be fine," Bannister said as a smiling couple walked across the lobby toward them. The woman was tall, blond, and thin, and dressed to go out for dinner. The man was stocky, balding, and wearing chinos and a bright blue NASCAR jacket. They looked about forty.

"Hi. I'm Tim and this is my wife Rachel," Tim McDonald said, extending his hand.

"I'm glad both of you made the trip. I know the girls can't wait to see you," Bannister said. After introducing Robin, she said she had an errand to run but would join them shortly. Bannister told the McDonalds they were already checked in, and together they proceeded to the suites.

As soon as the bellhop left, there were hugs, tears, laughter and a few satirical comments about how wonderful it was flying cross country. As they adjourned to the living room of the suite, Madison found a pitcher and filled it from the small icemaker in the room and poured glasses of ice water for everyone. Katie sat between her parents on the sofa.

"So, what's the game plan? We're not prisoners here, are we?" Tim McDonald asked with a grin.

"No. You're free to come and go. You can do anything you want. The important thing is being with your daughter and knowing she is all right. If you have cabin fever, Lenox Square across the street has two hundred and fifty stores and is one of the largest shopping meccas in the southeast. Of course, the girls didn't get much sleep at the hospital last night, and I'm guessing the two of you might be a little exhausted from your trip."

"These rooms look fabulous and we'd be happy to just chill out here for the night," Katie said as Madison nodded in agreement.

"I hope you and Robin can join us this evening," Rachel said.

"Thanks. I'm sure Robin would like that. Unfortunately, I have a meeting this afternoon. I'm hoping to make it back later, maybe for an after-dinner drink."

"That sounds good," Tim McDonald said.

Bannister then reassured the McDonalds that neither the girls nor they were in any kind of danger. He talked in general terms about the various ongoing investigations the FBI had in several states and countries involving Terry Hines and his known associates. Bannister said the cases would take months to sort everything out. Just as he finished, Robin called and said she was on her way up.

When she walked through the door, Robin handed a package to Katie. "It's a little something that might come in handy tomorrow."

"What is it?" Katie asked.

"Go ahead and open it," Robin said.

Katie reached into the bag and took out a self-inflating airline seat cushion. Blushing, Katie said, "Wow. I certainly don't have one of these. Thank you."

Robin smiled. "I was thinking that I'll be flying back to D.C. at the same time as your flight to LA, but mine will be three hours shorter."

CHAPTER 60

SAC Brennan asked Bannister to stop by his office before the meeting with the Deputy AG.

When Bannister walked in, Brennan said, "I've got some good news for you. One of my golf partners is the Director of Operations for the Fox Theater. I told him I couldn't play tomorrow and when I shared the information about your daughter and her friend's situation he reached out to the *Jersey Boys* manager. He just called me to say he's got four tickets for one of their concerts next February at the Pantages Theatre in Los Angeles. So, that's something that should brighten the day for your young ladies."

Bannister couldn't suppress an open-mouthed smile and said, "I don't know what to say. You didn't have to do that, but that news will definitely be a cause for celebration."

"On that positive note, let's go see what surprises Mr. Frye has."

Bannister had not yet met the Deputy Attorney General. Brennan and Bannister took seats at the conference table across from where Barnes and Ramirez were already seated.

The gentleman standing next to a large executive chair at one end of the table introduced himself as Carter Frye. He was African American and short, maybe five foot five, and looked impressive in a dark blue suit with wide banker's pinstripes. He had on a white shirt with a gold colored tie. For this late in the day, he looked remarkably fresh.

Frye spoke in a firm clear voice. "If I were sitting where you are, I would have a mixture of emotions. I would be mad and upset at what I had been told and, at the same time, confused and concerned about what I had not been told. I am going to try and answer your questions so that when I leave here, at least you'll know I am not the enemy and that together we are trying to contain a national emergency the best way we can. So, bear with me a few minutes.

"Kasim Musa just left your office in the custody of a special operations team, which is driving him to Fort McPherson. From there he will be flown to Warner Robins Air Force Base and then be transported to Eglin Air Force Base in Florida. His final destination is classified, but he will be flown to a foreign country. Colonel Ramsey's people are handling all of that."

"I'm sorry I have to interrupt you," Brennan said, "but is this part of some secret prisoner exchange?"

"No, it is not."

"Then why isn't he being sent someplace like Guantanamo Bay while all this is sorted out?" Brennan's eyebrows lowered to a V above his nose as his eyes narrowed.

"You know what he has told your agents. We cannot have him in communication with anyone." The four agents around the table just stared at Frye, who was quiet, like he was waiting for the next question.

"Can I assume that all questioning of Musa is finished?" Bannister asked.

"Yes. Let me recap what's been done today. All livestock in Nebraska exposed to the mutated rednose virus have been located, transported to a secure agricultural site, and euthanized. Biopsies will be conducted on samples taken from each animal. And to answer the question you're wondering about, the animals' owners had no choice but to surrender their livestock. They have all been compensated at a rate of 200% of the current market value paid for a prize-winning animal. The Exhibition Hall at the Nebraska State Fairgrounds where they were shown was totally sanitized and is in a cleaner condition now than when it originally opened. There will be no issue of possible contamination anywhere."

"Who will have access to the biopsy results?" Bannister asked.

"Only Spartacus-cleared personnel with a need to know," Frye answered.

"Correct me if I'm wrong, but are you saying there's no longer a biological threat or a need to pursue logical avenues of investigation?" Barnes asked.

"Not exactly," Frye said. "The FBI and other agencies still have many unanswered questions involving the terrorist investigations. For example, we don't know who gave Fadi his orders. How did Terry Hines get linked up in London with Fadi and his terrorist cell? How did Hines manage to work Middleton into the equation? Did Hines receive assistance in Canada? You'll still be working with all the involved agencies and especially with MI5 to close those loopholes. The big difference is that I'll be the one setting out any necessary leads."

"How do you propose closing the loop with the Atlanta PD on the Middleton murder?" Bannister asked.

"One of our attorneys will accompany your office's general counsel to their department and suggest a way for the Atlanta police to administratively close their case. They won't have the normal satisfaction of an arrest or conviction. However, they'll be able to use Musa's confession as corroboration. We'll sweeten the deal by having our asset forfeiture team transfer $100,000 to their police department with no strings attached. That amount consists of the contents in Middleton's foreign bank account, which we froze earlier today and have already initiated steps to seize."

"Are you aware Hines also had significant assets?" Bannister added.

"Correct. We will be seizing those too, and they will revert to the United States Treasury."

"What about the public's demand for an explanation from the CDC as to how one of their trusted microbiologists could smuggle out a biological agent?" Ramirez asked.

"The CDC will have to handle that. They have been briefed and I'm confident their protocols will withstand any kind of external scrutiny," Frye responded.

"The National Security Advisor called me when we were in

the CDC briefing. Can we assume the president himself is aware of developments?" Brennan asked.

"Remember what they say about the word "assume," Frye said with a slight grin. But you can be assured that the National Security Advisor, who is part of the Spartacus Program, will advise the president appropriately." In Frye's voice was the implication of plausible deniability if anything went wrong.

The Deputy AG continued to answer their questions for another twenty minutes until none of them had anything else to ask. He stood up and thanked Atlanta for its efforts before announcing he had a flight back to Washington in ninety minutes and was going straight to the airport. Barnes and Ramirez left the conference room while the SAC and Bannister remained.

"There's no doubt in your mind that Fadi and Musa infected cattle with mad cow disease?" Bannister asked Brennan.

Brennan took off his gold-rimmed glasses and tapped them in his hand, pausing as if in thought about what he wanted to say. "What you and I believe doesn't really matter at this point. It's speculation. It's possible Middleton double-crossed them and never delivered the real stuff. It's also possible that he substituted something different than what he promised."

"Well, the biopsies should confirm what really happened," Bannister said.

"They probably will, but I'm sure that neither you nor I will ever get the results. I don't think Colonel Ramsey will permit that information to be shared with Dr. Wulfsberg or anyone else at the CDC, regardless of whether they're cleared for Spartacus. For the common good of the nation, we're going to be kept in the dark."

"So, what is FBI Headquarters going to think about all this?" Bannister asked.

"The Attorney General's office will handle the additional information they are furnished, and regarding the FBI Director, you can answer any questions he might have when you see him," Brennan said.

"What do you mean when I see him?"

"He talked with Frye when you were at the hotel," said Brennan. "The director requested that the agent or supervisor most familiar with last week's events and investigations brief him personally in Washington at 1:30 p.m. Tuesday. I volunteered your name." There was just a hint of a smile on his face.

"And I'm supposed to repeat that spiel Frye gave to us?" Bannister said.

"Look, I'm sure the director's already received that information. You'll have to come up with some rationalization you can live with. You just have to let it go. If I didn't have confidence in you, I wouldn't send you. You'll do the right thing. I remember a former US Air Force general, Toohey Spaatz, who gave some advice to his officers who might have to testify before Congress or before a high-ranking government executive. He told them, 'Remember three things: Don't lie, don't try to be funny, and don't accidentally blurt out the truth.'" Brennan chuckled and even Bannister had to laugh.

"I get the message. I'll put together some talking points you can review before I leave. Okay?"

"That'd be fine. It's still early. You may be able to catch dinner with your daughter and her friend's parents."

———෴෴———

When Bannister arrived at the hotel, the girls were watching a chick flick on TV and Robin was visiting with the McDonalds.

"You look like you could use a drink," Tim McDonald said as Bannister walked into the living room.

"You're right about that, but I think I'll wait until I get home."

"Do you have a second?" McDonald said as he nodded in the direction of the dining room. Bannister took the cue.

"I went down to the front desk so they could run my credit card and the clerk informed me all charges for the suites, including food and beverages, were being picked up by you. That's not right," McDonald said.

"All of us have been through a lot. If I hadn't insisted on our daughters making the trip, maybe none of this would have happened. It's the least I could do for you and Rachel."

"I still don't think it's fair to you."

"I think it's fair and besides, it will go a long way to making my guilt trip feel less bumpy."

"If you change your mind, I won't have any heartburn over it," McDonald said.

They shook hands and then rejoined Robin and Rachel.

"We took your suggestion and decided to dine in this evening. I was just about to call in our order. Why don't you look over the menu and I'll add your selection," Rachel said.

Later, as the six of them experienced a four-star meal, Tim McDonald informed Bannister he owned a cardboard box manufacturing company in Los Angeles and that Rachel had her own online franchise selling jewelry and fashion accessories. After a casual hour of conversation, they went over the schedule for Sunday. Bannister and Robin would stop by the hotel after the McDonalds and the girls had brunch. He told the McDonalds he'd arranged for a hotel shuttle to take them and the girls to the airport. They said their goodbyes and Robin followed him back to his house.

"How about we just sit by your fireplace and have some quiet time?" Robin suggested.

"That sounds great," Bannister said, turning on the fire and going to his room to put on some casual clothes. As he put his gun away, his mind flashed back to that morning. He called Ramirez just to make sure she was doing okay.

"You're such a worrywart," Ramirez said. "I'm fine and I'll see you at the office in the morning. But hey, thanks for calling."

Ten minutes later Robin joined him in the great room. He gave her an embrace and a light kiss. As he poured himself a drink of single malt whiskey from a bottle of Talisker, Robin turned off all the lights except for one small lamp near the bookcase. They stretched out on the sofa and put their feet on the ottoman, enjoying the fireplace's warmth and watching the flames casting dancing shadows. Robin nestled in next to his right shoulder. By the time his drink was finished, Robin's eyes were closed and she was breathing softly.

CHAPTER 61

Sunday morning came fast. The Task Force agents were seated in the SAC's conference room when Brennan arrived. After updating everyone about the events of the past twenty-four hours, the SAC made it clear that all comments about their ongoing investigations would go through him. After US Attorney Prescott held his press conference scheduled for Monday morning, Bureau agents would fan out serving search warrants at banks, investment firms, property management companies, vehicle rental agencies, hotels, doctors' offices, and a private investigative firm. Brennan said, "You've done a great job and I'm proud of every one of you. We neutralized a major threat to our country. Before I submit our final report, there's additional investigation that must be wrapped up. ASAC Witt has everyone's assignments."

After looking over his leads, Bannister called Robin and the McDonalds before returning to his residence at 11:00 a.m.

Robin was packed and ready to go, so the two of them headed to the Ritz Carlton.

Madison, Katie, and the McDonalds had finished a quiet breakfast in the hotel's restaurant. After the bellman came and picked up their luggage, Bannister shared the news with the girls about the *Jersey Boy* tickets reserved for them in Los Angeles. For once he enjoyed hearing shrieking teenage girls. When the excitement subsided, their small entourage proceeded to the lobby and the trip to the airport.

They said their goodbyes in the concourse before the travelers had to go through TSA's screening. After more hugs and kisses, the LA contingent proceeded to the gate. Madison promised she would call as soon as she got back to her apartment.

Bannister and Robin waited to make sure they cleared the checkpoint.

"I don't know what to say about this weekend except that I'm glad it's over," Robin said.

"I second that. I can't tell you enough how much I appreciate your having made the trip here," Bannister said. "You were a godsend."

"I miss you all the time and am glad I'll see you again in two days," Robin said. "There shouldn't be any problem with my driving you to the airport Tuesday after work. I have a proposal. How about I buy you a drink at the airport that you can savor while we discuss plans for our Paris trip?"

"I'd like that very much."

He pulled Robin close, gave her a kiss, and watched her until she was past the checkpoint. She turned and, with a quick wave, was gone.

This week had been filled with shootings and meetings. Hopefully next week would be quiet.

Monday was frenetic with warrants served, records obtained, and dozens of interviews reviewed. Good on his word, Carter Frye dispatched a Department of Justice lawyer who, along with the office's legal advisor, was at Atlanta Police Department's headquarters. Hopefully, Atlanta's Chief of Police and Detective Miller could satisfactorily close the Middleton murder case.

By late afternoon Bannister had talked with Inspector Yates at GBI, Chief Spina in Dahlonega, and David Ash at the CDC. Despite the weariness in their voices, they all accepted the results of the joint investigation.

After getting home, Bannister called Robin and went over his schedule for the next day. His last call was to Madison.

"Hi Dad. Thanks for the flowers and box of chocolates." Madison sounded excited and her voice was loud and happy. She continued,

"There was a note from your lawyer, Amy Dixon, which said you thought we deserved something special."

Bannister had to think about that for a minute. He hadn't ordered anything. It was obvious Amy Dixon was earning her retainer by looking out for his best interests. He'd send her an appreciation text message after the call. "Well, she's part of our team" was his somewhat lame response. "How's Katie?"

"A whole lot better. Classes and practices start again next week, and Katie said she's ready for both. So am I. Last weekend seems like it didn't happen, that it must have been some kind of dream or . . . " She paused.

"Nightmare?" Bannister finished the sentence for her.

"Exactly. But like you said yesterday, I shouldn't dwell on it, but stay focused on school and the semester ahead. I like that you reminded me to be strong and stay positive. Aren't you a little bit proud I'm listening to you and remembering your advice?"

"I am, but I also have some additional advice."

"Like what?"

"You remember Jane Reese from our office whom you talked with at the hospital?"

"Yes, she was very nice."

"We talked yesterday and both she and I think it would help if you talked to one of the psychologists our Los Angeles offices uses. The doctor's name is Sarah Orenstein. You don't have to remember that; she's been given your contact information. We use her in cases involving shootings, deaths, and other trauma. You're familiar with the term 'post-traumatic stress,' right?"

"You mean like the military guys who return from combat?"

"Exactly. Sometimes a person who has undergone a high stress event has difficulties afterward. It might not be right away but could develop over a period of time. You haven't shown any indication you're having or even going to have problems, but to be on the safe side, I'd be able to sleep a lot better knowing you at least talked to an expert."

"So, do you want me to call her?"

"No. Our LA people will handle everything. They'll set up an appointment that fits into both yours and the doctor's schedule. Is that okay with you?"

"Sure. What would you have said if I hadn't agreed?"

"I would have ordered you to go."

Madison didn't say anything right away. "You mean you would have demanded I listen to you and demanded that I follow what you ordered?"

Bannister was quiet for a few seconds. "I guess."

"Well, I don't want to be the disobedient daughter, so I guess I'll just have to do what you say!" Madison laughed.

After Bannister quit laughing also, he and his daughter talked for another ten minutes. After they said their goodbyes, Bannister still couldn't believe he had a daughter. She was now part of his life; he just hoped he didn't say or do anything to screw it up.

CHAPTER 62

f Monday was a blur, Tuesday was a flash. During his flight to Washington, DC, Bannister revisited all aspects of the Atlanta investigations and tried to anticipate questions the director might ask. He had met three former directors during his Bureau career, but had never briefed one or visited the director's office at the J. Edgar Hoover Building. Even though his name was on a list of official visitors and he was an active Special Agent, it still took thirty minutes for him to clear the hurdles at the guard desk and reception checkpoint before being escorted to the director's office on the seventh floor. The director's executive secretary showed him into his office promptly at 1:30 p.m.

Bannister quickly scanned the office. There weren't any visible windows, but heavy tapestry-type drapes were closed behind a large mahogany desk. Along one entire side wall was a black, glass-covered credenza. Atop the credenza were display cases containing items that were probably gifts received by the director during his visits to many of the sixty-three foreign cities in which the FBI had legal attachés assigned. Two large, wing-backed leather chairs in red Moroccan leather were in front of the director's desk.

The director walked in, hand extended. "Agent Bannister, it's nice to meet you. I've reviewed your file. It's impressive. You have my gratitude for your recent efforts in Atlanta. Please have a seat." He pointed to the two leather chairs in front of his desk.

"It's a pleasure to meet you," Bannister said.

"How's your daughter doing?" the director asked, easing into the other guest chair.

"She's back at UCLA and ready for the next semester."

"Living through a kidnapping is absolutely traumatic for the victim, the family, and everyone involved. I have kids and worry about them all the time. I hope I never have to face anything like you went through." The director interlaced his hands, leaned forward, and looked directly at his agent.

Bannister shifted and crossed his left leg over his right. He didn't want to say anything that was terse, insensitive, or untruthful. "I agree it's a terrible experience, but it ended well and opened my eyes to what many parents and families are forced to endure every year."

"If there's any help your daughter needs in LA, just let me know."

"I appreciate that. Like I told Madison last night, we need to be grateful for everything we have, lean on our family and friends for support, not dwell on what might have happened, and move forward."

"That sounds like good advice. I just returned from a working luncheon with the Director of National Intelligence at his office at Bolling Air Force Base. He made the observation our jobs are becoming more and more impersonal. We get constant briefings, are forced to make decisions every hour and, as we get involved with more and more crises, we seem to be spending more and more time in meetings."

"I'm only one of your thousands of agents and seem to have plenty on my plate every day, too. I can't imagine what it must be like for you to try and plan your day or week."

"It's definitely a challenge in time management. I've met the directors of the seventeen agencies making up the Intelligence Community. Each of our days starts early and ends late. In between we're constantly re-prioritizing what our organizations need to do. Last year most of the directors participated in a national exercise involving coordinated responses to a hypothetical outbreak of Ebola hemorrhagic fever. While talking with the DNI, we both agreed the lessons learned from that exercise were a good rehearsal for what our country went through when your terrorist cell in Atlanta went operational."

"We were lucky. We know our battle is not over, but at least we thwarted what could have been a catastrophe for our nation," Bannister said.

The director looked him in the eye. "In your opinion, Ty, are there any critical loose ends that I can help tie up?"

"In the US, I think there's a lot that needs to be done in Detroit to identify who gave orders to Hassan Fadi. Outside the US, the bulk of the remaining investigation will be up to the British Security Service."

"I'll have our London legal attaché notified. I understand when you leave my office you'll be meeting with our two section chiefs in charge of Middle East terrorist investigations. They have detailed information they'll share with you. They expect you will relay it to SAC Brennan. By the way, I think Leon is an excellent executive. He knows how to lead and extract the maximum effort out of his supervisors. I told him I might need to promote him back to Washington." The Director paused, then smiled. "He didn't say anything in response to that."

Bannister finished the afternoon being questioned by two senior counter-terrorist executives. They had an extensive give-and-take. Bannister finished the session feeling confident FBI Headquarters had a handle on the big picture and that everyone was doing the right things. It was a refreshing change.

It was a crisp evening. Leaves fluttered between the government buildings and as it was still dusk, DC commuters had their headlights on. He stood in front of the FBI Building on Pennsylvania Avenue looking official in coat and tie with briefcase in hand when Robin approached, flashing her lights.

He opened the passenger door and climbed in. "Believe me when I say I'm really happy to see you." He leaned over and gave her a quick kiss before she eased the car back into traffic.

"How did your meeting with the director go?"

"Great! I think. He was as knowledgeable about our operation as anyone in Atlanta. Impressive! He had excellent questions and filled me in on some aspects about what our sister agencies were doing that I wasn't aware of. He promised that our investigative leads would receive priority attention."

Traffic surrounding Reagan International was always hectic, and inside was just as chaotic, but luck was on their side. Forty minutes later, they secured a secluded table in the back of Sam & Harry's with a view of the concourse and two large televisions tuned to CNN. Bannister ordered a Philly cheesesteak sandwich with a Coke. Robin settled for a Diet Coke.

"I think this is the first time I've dined with you when you didn't have a glass of wine or drink in front of you," Robin said, tapping his hand lightly.

"You're right. I didn't want to be under the influence when we discussed plans for our Paris trip," he said.

Robin leaned into him and, flipping her hair to the side, gave him a quick kiss. "I love it! Actually, I have some suggestions for flights and accommodations. We can go over them if you want." Her face was beaming.

"Absolutely. Why don't you give me your ideas as I enjoy my sandwich and fries." The waitress plopped his order down in front of him and he thanked her with a nod.

"Do you suppose they have anything like this in Paris?" he asked.

"Sure, I believe it's called a French dip sandwich." Robin laughed.

Robin had done her homework and for the next ten minutes went over hotel options and must-see sights and activities for them. They were not the usual ones suggested in travel guides. Her enthusiasm was contagious. After he politely devoured his meal, Bannister wiped his mouth with a napkin.

"So, what do you think?" Robin asked, just as a Late Breaking News banner came across the screen of CNN. They glanced up.

The announcer said, "We're here in Heliopolis at Cairo's International Airport where an unknown gunman earlier this evening shot and killed a man in US custody who allegedly was being turned over to Egyptian authorities. Reliable sources have said the person killed was Kasim Abdullah Musa, a terrorist subject arrested earlier this week in Atlanta, Georgia. If true, it is unclear why he was in Cairo."

"Wow. There's some unexpected news," Robin said.

Bannister put his finger up to his lips for her to be quiet. "Let's see what else they say."

The announcer continued. "One eyewitness was an airport mechanic who said he was refueling a plane when he saw a motorcyclist come out of nowhere and approach a group of men who had gotten off a private jet. As the men walked toward several vehicles parked nearby, the assailant, riding a Suzuki Hayabusa motorcycle, fired two shots from a pistol at the man in handcuffs, hitting him in the head. The motorcyclist sped off across the tarmac toward Ring Road, where there was a small explosion at an unmanned, locked gate. The motorcyclist drove through the hole in the fence and disappeared. The mechanic, who happened to be a motorcycle fanatic, said the Hayabusa is one of the world's fastest bikes.

"Egyptian police would only confirm that a person was shot and killed at their airport and they were investigating. A high-ranking official, who must remain anonymous, suggested this was an assassination and had the earmarks of a Mossad operation. No other details are available at this time."

Their eyes locked. "Isn't that the same Musa you arrested and interviewed Saturday?" Robin asked.

Bannister winced. "That's correct."

"What was he doing in Egypt? Who would want to kill him?"

"There are people who would not want him to tell what he knows."

"Did you know he was being taken to Egypt?" Robin asked.

"No. Even though I was cleared and briefed on a top-secret program involving him, I had no knowledge where he would be taken."

"Well, someone knew he would be there," Robin speculated.

"You're right, and whoever carried this out had detailed information."

"He was in US custody. It would have had to be someone cleared for that information, right?" Robin's eyes were wide and her face etched with concern.

"Right."

"What does it mean for you?" Robin asked.

"I seem to have some kind of Washington airport curse. I was here last year when the major case I was working on was finished. The serial killer's body left the airport tarmac on a flight to a foreign country. Today I'm back at your airport when the subject of the major case I was working on is in a foreign country, dead on an airport tarmac. What it means for me is this case has closure. I don't like it, but it's over." Bannister stared out the window at a plane lifting off.

The two were quiet for a minute until Robin said, "Ty, have you ever experienced such a stressful period in your life?"

"No. The past three weeks take the cake! I discovered I'm the father of a teenage girl. I've had to deal with murders, terrorists, a kidnapping, and a plot to unleash mad cow disease. Normally at the end of each day I like to unwind with a glass of wine, put on some blues music and reflect on things I'm grateful for. Right now, I'm asking myself how did I get so lucky to have two wonderful women in my life—my daughter Madison, and especially you."

"Well, I'm feeling pretty lucky also. We have a lot to look forward to," Robin said, deliberately batting her lashes.

"I almost forgot to mention that while I was standing on the street corner waiting for you to pick me up, I got a text message from my office. Do you want to know what it said?"

"Only if you feel like sharing it."

"The office said I need to schedule an appointment with one of our clinical psychologists to discuss possible post-traumatic stress. Do you care to comment on that?"

"That's one appointment you should definitely make."

Bannister let out a resigned sigh. "I guess you're right. I can't help but wonder what's going to happen the next time I'm at a Washington airport."

Robin was quiet again for a few seconds. Then her eyes lit up and she beamed.

"The next time you're here, you'll be taking me to Paris!"

ABOUT THE AUTHOR

C.W. Saari is a graduate of Whittier College, Willamette University Law School, and the National War College. He served his country in the U.S. Marine Corps, then spent twenty-seven years as an FBI Special Agent where he supervised undercover operations and espionage investigations. He is experienced as a private investigator and currently resides in Lexington, South Carolina with his wife, Carol. In his spare time, he enjoys bicycling, playing golf, and traveling.

IF YOU ENJOYED...

Prime Impact, don't miss
The Mile Marker Murders

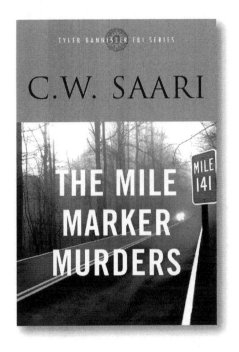

The first book in the Tyler Bannister FBI Series

When Caleb Williamson, a career officer with the CIA, disappears, officials are left wondering whether he is a spy who has defected or the victim of a crime. Meanwhile, Williamson's friend, FBI agent Tyler Bannister, is focused on catching an extortionist who has threatened to unleash a biological poison if a multimillion dollar demand is not met. When Williamson turns up dead alongside the corpses of two women near a northern Virginia highway, Bannister is assigned to a task force to identify what looks to be a cunning serial killer. While Bannister becomes obsessed with finding the murderer before he strikes again, a fourth body is discovered. The stakes become more personal when the killer targets Bannister's new love interest.